THE BOOTMAKER'S WIFE

Janet ~ Enjoy the adventure!

THE BOOTMAKER'S WIFE

a novel

MERSHON NIESNER

The Bootmaker's Wife

Cover and interior designed by Lance Buckley
www.lancebuckley.com

ISBN: 978-0-9743076-2-6

Names: Niesner, Mershon, author
Title: The Bookmaker's Wife
Description: (Marco Island, Florida) : (The Bell Group), (2022)

Identifiers: ISBN 9780974307626 (Paperback) | ISBN 9780974307633 (Ebook)

Subjects: Historical fiction, western, prairie, women

Library of Congress Control Number: 2022923136

To my dear dad, Leon Horn (1917–2008)

The best father and storyteller ever!

When (the West) fully learns that cooperation, not rugged individualism, is the quality that most characterizes and preserves it, then it will have achieved itself and outlived its origins. Then it has a chance to create a society to match its scenery.

Wallace Stegner, The Dean of Western Writers

CONTENTS

CHAPTER ONE

UNREALIZED EXPECTATIONS

It's early afternoon and the white eye of an August sun bears down on the Iowa prairie. Dust devils race tumble weeds across the vast landscape. Heat has diminished the chatter of birds and people. Elizabeth Schultz trudges down the wagon trail, set upon by gnats and thirst. Anxiety about her future swarms about her alongside the tiny insects, as she straddles ruts and sidesteps fresh manure patties.

Sensing movement to her right, Elizabeth turns in time to see the front wheel of a covered wagon hit a rock, causing the wagon to lurch. "Watch out!" She rushes toward her traveling companion, Lucy, and gives her a powerful shove, sending her to the ground, safe from the wayward wagon. After waving the startled driver on, Elizabeth squats next to her friend who sits up and rubs her backside. "Are you alright?"

"What'd you be doin' that for Lizabeth? You tryin' to kill me?"

"See that?" She points toward the rock partially submerged in the hard-packed earth. "It's a miracle Mr. Whimple didn't break an axle or your leg."

Lucy looks from the rock to the wagon rolling down the trail. She smiles up at Elizabeth. "Thanks for watchin' out for me."

"That's what friends are for."

Elizabeth stands, then offers a large, grimy hand to help Lucy to her feet. Normally self-conscious about her broad shoulders, muscular arms, and five-foot-seven height, today she's grateful for the strength to push her friend to safety. *What if Lucy had been run over? It feels like we're just one accident away from a catastrophe.*

While she's dusting off the back of Lucy's dress, boys snicker and girls giggle behind their hands as they walk nearby. At barely four-foot-six, Lucy's roughly the height of the teasing children and a target for their bullying. Her face flushes, her blue eyes look down, and her dirty blonde braids which have escaped from under a sweat-stained sunbonnet, hang limply down her back. Lucy marches forward with arms folded across her chest.

Poor, Lucy. I know how it feels to be judged by your size. Elizabeth adjusts her own blue, calico bonnet that has slipped off the thick black braids coiled on top of her head. She pulls a once-white handkerchief edged with ragged lace from her sleeve and wipes dust from her broad, smooth forehead. Sweat trickles down her back. She resumes walking, her nose filled with the pungent odor of cow, mule, and oxen dung. A sense of resignation fills her chest. She's surrounded by other sun-burned, bedraggled women in sweat-stained, flour-sack dresses. Walking with them are snot-nosed, whining children with dirty faces. The older boys and girls who poked fun at Lucy, run ahead.

The monotony of the landscape has a stupefying effect on Elizabeth as the afternoon drags on. In an effort to regain her focus, she uses her elbow to shield her dry eyes from the relentless sun. She looks beyond the dusty trail and wonders why God used so much brown. Sun-dried, brown buffalo grass waves in the wind next to brown wagons pulled by brown mules and oxen. In the distance, she spots golden brown prairie dogs with stubby tails scampering between their holes. She groans when she sees Lucy's, still-dusty, ugly brown dress gently swaying several yards ahead. *I imagined this trip as an exciting walk through a golden, sun-lit prairie.* Elizabeth shakes her head from side to side. *I was so naive.*

She reaches down to pull up her white wool stocking, hoping a blister isn't forming where her heel rubs against her scuffed, brown, high-top. The soles of her shoes have worn thin and her feet are sore from constantly stepping on stones and dirt clods. "I wonder if we're getting close to stopping for the day." Elizabeth's so hot and tired she no longer knows if she's wishful thinking or speaking out loud. The only woman traveling without a husband, she's accustomed to talking to herself and never expects an answer.

"Yep, somewhere's up ahead we'll be crossin' a creek. I heard somebody say that we'll be makin' camp on the other side."

Elizabeth jumps. "Where did you come from, Lucy? I thought you were a ways ahead."

"I were a ways ahead but while you was a lallygagging, I came back to walk with you."

Elizabeth brushes a bit more dust off the back of Lucy's skirt. "How's your backside? Sore?"

"Nah. I'm tougher than I look." She swats a horse fly about to bite her neck. "Once we cross the creek, we'll be in Nebraska and then before you know it you'll be gittin' married." She grins up at her companion.

Elizabeth feels a mixture of joy, relief, and apprehension as she considers this significant juncture of the trip. Joy at the prospect of reuniting with her fiancé, Charles, after eleven long months of separation; relief that her grueling trip west with a wagon train will soon be over; apprehension and doubt about whether he will be there to meet her and, if he is, fear that she won't have what it takes to succeed as a wife on the prairie. *Before I left home, I was excited and confident about embarking on this romantic adventure. Now, I'm wondering if I made the right decision.*

Calculating just how soon she'll, hopefully, see Charles, Elizabeth makes an effort to remember dates. "We left Illinois on August fifteenth. Right?"

Lucy nods.

Elizabeth counts on her fingers. "And today is September seventh?"

Her friend nods again.

"That means I should be meeting up with Charles in a little less than two weeks—barring storms, illness, bandits, or Indians."

A stern look crosses Lucy's face. "Don't even mention them things."

"Sorry."

Lucy places her hand on Elizabeth's arm to slow her pace. "What date you gettin' married on?"

"Saturday, September twenty-fifth." Elizabeth closes her

eyes for a moment. *Am I really getting married in a couple of weeks? Am I ready?*

Lucy voices her thoughts. "You ready?"

Elizabeth shakes her head. "I don't know. Were you ready for marriage when you and Jake got together?"

Lucy looks down at her dusty shoes. "That's a story for another day."

The comment piques Elizabeth's robust curiosity. "Another day—like tomorrow?"

"Maybe."

They walk in silence for a few minutes until a flicker of movement in a hedgerow twenty yards to the left catches Elizabeth's attention. She tips her bonnet and looks up just as three buzzards ascend into the cloudless sky. Her heart races and she shivers as the big birds, with their blue-black wings and bumpy, red, turkey-necks, circle the wagons. "Look there, Lucy!" She points. "I'll betcha those black-hearted buzzards are surveying our wagons' canvas covers and see them as a bunch of ships destined for disaster."

"Hey, quit bringin' up disasters. Besides, ain't all God's creatures good?"

Elizabeth gazes at the buzzards until she stumbles on a rock and turns back to Lucy. "To me, buzzards are a bad omen and having them nearby makes my skin crawl. Didn't you just about get run over back there?"

Lucy puts her hand on her hip. "Well, I didn't git run over, now did I! Where'd you git the notion that buzzards are bad luck anyways?"

"From my Granddad Schultz saying things like, 'God, here come those black-feathered, bald demons.' He believes they're a sign of death and I suppose he passed his ideas down to me."

Lucy puts her hand on her friend's arm again. Her short legs are no match for Elizabeth's long ones. "Let's talk 'bout somethin' besides buzzards, dyin', flies, how tired we is, and me 'bout gettin' kilt. I'm miserable enough without talkin' 'bout it."

Respecting her friend's wishes, Elizabeth is quiet as she slowly eases ahead. As she walks she allows her mind to wander. She feels a flutter in her stomach when she reflects on the night her life turned in an unexpected direction. She vividly recalls the dilapidated red barn where she first laid eyes on Charles Horn.

CHAPTER TWO

MEETING CHARLES

On an unseasonably warm, late October night in Illinois, we were packed into old Doc McKenzie's barn for the annual Fall Festival Dance. The air smelled of moldy hay, manure, unwashed bodies, and dust. I occasionally put my lavender-scented handkerchief to my nose to stifle the unpleasant odors.

My favorite tunes, "Jennie, the Flower of Kildare" and "Silver Threads Among the Gold," had just been played on two, out of tune fiddles and a harmonica. I sat alone on a hay bale covered with an oil cloth, positioned against a rough wall near the open barn door where I could catch an occasional breeze that carried the welcome scent of fresh earth from harvested fields. My girlfriends had long-since abandoned me for dance partners. They paraded around with one boy after another, occasionally returning to gossip about their partners.

"Did you see the older man with the beard?" my best friend, Jenny, asked in a voice loud enough for me to hear above the noise reverberating around the crowded barn. "Can you believe he had the nerve to ask me to dance? He's here visiting from Nebraska. He's a bootmaker of all things."

"That sounds like a solid trade. I think he looks," I paused to come up with the right word, "rather distinguished."

Jenny scrunched up her nose as if she'd bitten into a rotten walnut. "What girl in her right mind would want to marry a man his age and move to Nebraska? Not me, that's for sure!"

"I think living in the wild west would be a great adventure. Don't you read *The New York Ledger*?"

"No, what's that?"

"It's a weekly story paper published in New York City. My father subscribes and I whisk it away before it hits the trash barrel. It's full of stories about the waving, golden grasses of the plains, the herds of magnificent buffalo, a world where women are strong and respected as equals. I wouldn't mind living that life."

Jenny shook her head and gave me a look like I'd lost my mind.

Several of my friends danced with the older man from Nebraska, but none danced more than once. I wondered if that was their choice or his.

An hour into the party, my heart did a little jig when I noticed him striding across the dusty floor in my direction. I smoothed invisible wrinkles from my muslin dress with the matching green silk-taffeta belt, grateful my mother had insisted I wear it. I patted my braids to be sure they were in place. Even my mother, who I knew considered me unattractive, recognized my hair to be my best feature.

Most girls, especially Jenny, wouldn't consider Charles handsome but I liked the looks of the genuine smile that reached his small, close-set, dark eyes, his thick black hair, and neatly trimmed black beard and mustache. He walked with the confidence of a man, not the slouchy shuffle of a self-conscious boy. He carried himself like someone who might have been in the military. I hoped I wouldn't tower over him like I did most boys my age.

Suddenly, there he was, standing in front of me. "Good evening, Miss Schultz. Your friend, Jenny, suggested that you might like to dance. I'm Charles Horn and it would be my pleasure to escort you to the floor if you're so inclined."

"I'd be delighted." I looked him in the eye and smiled. "Please call me Elizabeth."

I stood to take his offered hand and was relieved to see that I was only an inch or two taller. He didn't seem to mind the difference. In fact, after the first dance, he asked if he might be my partner for the rest of the evening.

When the musicians took a break, we returned to my hay bale with cups of pink punch ladled from bowls laid out on trestle tables at each end of the room. I was curious and wanted to learn more about him. "Jenny says you're a bootmaker from Nebraska."

"Yes. I could tell your friend didn't think much of my trade or my home."

I liked that he was direct. "Jenny has her sights set on Amos, the tall blonde boy in the corner." I pointed toward a handsome boy lounging against the wall surrounded by adoring fans. "She thinks he'll be successful like his father and take care of her in the style she's used to. I think she'll be disappointed, assuming he ever gives her the time of day."

"And you, Elizabeth? What are your sights set on?"

I took my time to decide whether I should be honest or coy. "To be perfectly honest, Charles, I'm not looking for a man to take care of me. I'm looking for a partnership in which I can be an equal and, unlike Jenny, I'd like to have an adventure. In other words, I don't want the same life my friends desire nor the life my mother and her friends are living."

My face grew warm after saying these brazen words and I quickly changed the subject. "I hear you're only in the area for a short time?"

"Yes, I'm visiting my uncle for the next three weeks, then I'll return to my shop in Grand Island. Next year, however, I'll move north to a region of Nebraska referred to as the Sand Hills."

"Oh? What will you do there?"

"I've recently accepted the position of bootmaker for Fort Hartsuff. My shop will be in the nearby town of Calamus."

I took a sip from my punch. "Where did you live before moving to Nebraska? I believe I detect an accent." Strangely, I didn't feel the need to reign in my curiosity as I usually did.

"You're very astute, Elizabeth. After arriving from my homeland of Germany, I enlisted in the Civil War, fought for three years, and learned my trade. I've moved around a bit since, but I now consider Nebraska home."

When the music started, we resumed our dancing. During the rest of the evening, I felt like the heroine in one of my romance novels. Just before father came to fetch me home, Charles kissed my hand and asked if he might call on me the next evening. I enthusiastically said yes. I wasn't about to act demure and pretend I wasn't interested because I was interested … very interested.

CHAPTER THREE

A DIP IN THE CREEK

The screech of a blue jay brings Elizabeth back to the present. She slows her walking when she sees wagons stopping up ahead. She spots her wagon midway down the line. Prior to starting this journey, Elizabeth's father made arrangements with James and Gretchen to store her trunk and give her space in their wagon during a storm. In exchange, she helps Gretchen with the chores and shares in the cost of food.

When she gets closer, she sees wagons lining up on the bank of a narrow, sandy beach leading to a creek of slow-moving, brown water. A tall cottonwood and a few scrub sage bushes cling to the shore.

She spots Mr. Nichols, the wagon master, riding in her direction. He reigns in his handsome black stallion, then hollers to those assembled. "This here Salt Creek ain't deep and, as you can see, it's got a gentle flow." Nichols rides farther up the line of wagons. "Men, guide your animals and wagons across. Women with small children and those who want to stay dry, form a line and, when it's your turn, take off your shoes and git into one of them bull boats." He points toward four, oval boats covered in skins resting on the shore attached to ropes held by Indians.

Elizabeth sharply draws in a breath when she sees the strange boats and their paddlers. *Why boats and why now?* She recalls that prior to this crossing they forded rivers on rafts either built on-site or left by earlier travelers. She remembers them taking a whole day to cross the Mississippi on a ferry.

She watches closely as Nichols leads the way, his horse splashing as he prances into the water. Men shake their reins to encourage mules and oxen to follow. Older boys and some girls prod livestock into the cloudy water. *Are the boats safe? Will my paddler be reliable? I hope I don't drown just as I'm about to enter Nebraska!*

Her thoughts are interrupted when she sees Lucy rushing up behind her. She calls to her friend. "Over here." Elizabeth takes off her shoes and carefully steps into the tippy boat. It's a big step for Lucy's short legs so she gives her a hand up. The boatman then helps a woman holding a baby and two wide-eyed children climb aboard. After everyone's seated, the muscular, young Indian, dressed in leather pants rolled to the knees and a short leather vest over his bare chest, uses an ore to push the boat away from the sandy bank. Animals thrashing in the water buffet the lightweight boat but he manages to move it forward at a steady pace.

Midway across, the water becomes rough with the addition of more wagons and livestock. Elizabeth struggles to hang on. Just as she leans into the side to get a better grip, a horse rears up, making a wave.

"Dear God!" Lucy shouts when Elizabeth tumbles overboard. She flails her arms, bobs up, then finds her footing on the muddy bottom. Lucy leans over and grabs her arm.

"I gotcha, Lizabeth." Lucy pulls and Elizabeth flops into the boat.

Breathless from the shock of the cold water, she presses her hand to her wildly beating heart. "Thanks, Lucy. You're stronger than you look." When the boat stabilizes and the thrashing animals move ahead, Elizabeth kneels, then bends over the side to wring out her skirt. The breeze carries droplets to the boy and his mother sitting nearby. "Sorry."

The boy smiles. "It's alright, lady. Feels right refreshin'."

Lucy grabs Elizabeth's arm and pulls her to the bottom of the boat. "You're holdin' us up."

Dropping down, Elizabeth tries to deflect her embarrassment. "I see why this is called Salt Creek. Did you get a taste of the water?"

The young mother smiles at the remark but Lucy's face remains grim. "Nope and I don't want to neither." She laces her arm through her friend's elbow. "For Heaven's sake, Lizabeth! Sit still, keep your mouth shut, and your eyes peeled for waves. You makin' me wonder how you gonna survive alone all day in a sod house in the middle of nowhere."

Elizabeth sits back down, intimidated by Lucy's fierce side. *Does Lucy really doubt my ability to survive out here? What if she's right?*

When they reach the opposite shore, Elizabeth holds her shoes and lifts her sodden skirts with one hand then takes the boatman's offered hand with the other. She steps out of the boat and moves a few feet to the left so others can disembark. Then, putting aside the fact that she knows she looks like a drowned rat, she embraces the moment. "So, this is Nebraska!"

The boatman turns to help the mother and her children then looks toward Elizabeth. "Yes, ma'am. You'll soon be walking on the Nebraska City-Fort Kearny Cutoff Trail." He then picks up his oar and pushes off. "Safe travels."

Elizabeth stares at him with an open mouth, surprised that he speaks perfect English. Remembering her manners, she hollers, "Th-thank you, sir." Then she leans over, buttons her shoes, and rushes toward the wagon she shares with James, Gretchen, and their baby daughter, Louise.

After crossing the creek, the wagons begin forming their customary circle and prepare camp for the night. James has already positioned their wagon and is busy watering the mules when Elizabeth approaches. She grimaces when she sees the slight upward curl of his lips. "You okay, Elizabeth? Looks like you decided to take a dip."

She raises her chin. "I'm just fine, thank you, James. Now, if you don't mind, I'm going to duck into the wagon and change before I set out to gather fuel."

James adds more water to the bucket. "No rush. I'm off to get supplies at the outpost. We should have meat, potatoes, and fruit for supper." He turns his back to his wife, who sits in the shade of the wagon nursing their baby and lowers his voice. "Keep an eye on Gretchen and the baby will ya? I'm worried about em."

"Of course."

Elizabeth struggles to climb into the wagon with her sodden skirts weighing her down. As quickly as possible, she removes her wet clothing in a wagon smelling of rancid cooking grease, dirty diapers, and gun powder, then washes herself as best she can with a wet rag. She pulls a clean, wrinkled, yellow calico dress over her, damp, dingy-gray camisole, petticoat, and corset. She'd washed her extra stockings earlier and, thankfully, they'd dried in the heat of the wagon. She pulls them on before replacing her soggy shoes. She joins Gretchen who's sitting on the wagon's tongue sadly gazing down at her sleeping baby. Gretchen's normally rosy complexion is pale, her blue eyes sunken. "How's baby Louise?"

"I'm real worried 'bout her." Gretchen's voice is flat.

Louise's tiny face is the color of a bruise, her breath is coming in shallow bursts. Elizabeth sees a look of resignation cross Gretchen's sweet face. "She's been sleepin' restless-like most of the day and not nursin' much."

With an ache in her chest and tears in her eyes, Elizabeth fingers the gold locket hanging from a thin chain around her neck. Gretchen looks at her with a question in her eyes. Wishing she hadn't drawn attention to her locket, Elizabeth ignores the look and grabs two wicker baskets from inside the wagon. "I'll go gather fuel."

She strides through knee-high grass with long, tired legs. Elizabeth barely notices the prairie's golden light spreading across the western skies. Her mind is occupied with dead and dying babies. As she gathers buffalo chips, or nik nik as James calls them, sticks, and dried grass, Elizabeth recalls the year she was eight years old and her beloved baby sister died.

My heart still aches after all these years when I think of Anna. Unlike Louise, she was a strong baby who thrived the first three months of her life...until she was struck down with pneumonia. Then, she was like Louise, weak and struggling to breathe properly. I just couldn't bare to tell Gretchen that a lock of her hair is in my locket. She probably thinks I'm rude for walking away but better that than adding to her miseries.

With baskets full of fuel, Elizabeth returns to the wagon where Gretchen is still resting with Louise in her arms. Without a word, Elizabeth lugs the black spider, an iron skillet with legs, out of the wagon. She's arranging kindling for the fire when James appears with a string of fresh fish, iridescent in the late sunlight. He dumps out a bucket of dark-purple prairie plums on the ground near Elizabeth, then hands her a small bag tied with string. She looks inside and sees five, round, red potatoes. "Looks like you found us a good supper."

With a barely perceptible nod, James ambles toward the side of the wagon to clean the fish. Elizabeth uses a small knife to peel the potatoes. The chore takes her mind off the heavy feeling of sadness that encircles her.

James returns and hands her the cleaned fish. "I'll check on Gretchen."

When the black spider is hot, Elizabeth adds yesterday's grease, carefully saved in a jar, to the skillet. She fries the potatoes, then adds the floured fish. When the food is cooked, she sticks her head into the wagon. "Supper's ready. Come eat while it's hot." After Gretchen and James join her by the fire with their plates and utensils in hand, Elizabeth takes a bite of the crisp, succulent fish. "Did you catch the fish, James? They're delicious."

He forks slices of fried potato into his mouth. "Nah. I traded tobacco for 'em with one of the boat-paddlin' Injuns."

Elizabeth looks up from her plate. "Did he speak perfect English?"

"Don't know. He held up the fish and I gave him tobacco. No words were exchanged."

The couple are quiet for the rest of the meal and Elizabeth misses their usual friendly banter. After supper, she washes the dishes and Gretchen dries while James banks the fire and makes sure the mules are secure for the night.

With the supper chores done, Elizabeth ducks into the wagon, removes her dress and corset, leaving on her shift. She wraps her shawl about her shoulders, gathers up her bedroll, and lays it on the ground near the wagon. Whole families are sleeping outside on this warm evening, and she feels secure in their company.

Even though she's exhausted, Elizabeth lays awake watching the silver moon rise as stars come out in clusters looking like points of fire in the vast sky. She rolls one way, then another on her thin, straw mattress while the pungent odor of campfires settles over her like a warm blanket. She misses her feather bed in Illinois and wonders what kind of bed she and Charles will have.

Tears roll down her cheeks as she considers the possibility of another baby dying. *Dear God, please take care of Louise and spare her parents the grief of losing a child.*

To take her mind off of Louise, Elizabeth returns to memories of her whirlwind romance with Charles.

CHAPTER FOUR

THE COURTSHIP

After the night of the dance, Charles came to court me nearly every evening when my schoolwork was done. At first, we had to overcome my parent's objections. They said fourteen was too young to consider a serious relationship, especially one with an older man. Charles was nearly thirty-four. However, as they got to know him, they came around to accepting our courtship.

The last week of Charle's visit, I overheard my mother trying to convince my father that Charles might be my best hope of marrying a respectable man with an established trade. Because I was the eldest of five children, she also had to reassure my father that my brother and sister were old enough to help care for the two younger ones. She had yet to tell him she was going to have another baby and had sworn me to secrecy about the matter.

Even though I had come to love Charles with his kind and considerate ways, I too wondered if I was ready for marriage. I tried to separate marriage from the fact that I was drawn to the prospect of living on the prairie and being my own person.

Charles told me of his plans to build a sod house on property leased to him by the army. I couldn't imagine living in a sod house, but I could see myself as mistress of my own domain and living in a world where I would be valued for who I was.

My banker-father provided me with a comfortable, secure life, but I was willing to give it up if Charles offered me a chance to be a wife plus an opportunity to prove myself as a woman capable of thriving in the west. The prospect of adventure seemed very romantic at the time. I was tired of helping out with my younger siblings and, now that Mother was about to have another baby, I decided that I'd rather be caring for my own.

Also I was sick of my looks being constantly scrutinizing and my mother's friends referring to me as "handsome." Even as a child, I knew I wasn't pretty and I wanted more than the superficial life of a Victorian woman whose worth was determined by her looks and social graces. If given the chance, I was willing to be tested by the elements and a way of life completely foreign to me. I wanted to prove that looks can be deceiving and, despite my parents' lack of confidence in me, I could be a successful prairie wife, mother, and, perhaps, teacher.

Two days before returning to Nebraska, Charles came to the house early in the evening to speak with my father. I hid behind the table in the hall to listen in on their conversation. My father was in his study, sitting behind his desk. Charles knocked on the door. "Sir, I'm wondering if I might speak with you?"

"Of course, Charles. Come in and take a seat."

"I'll get right to the point, sir. I'd like to ask for your daughter's hand in marriage before I leave to return to Nebraska."

I knew my father paused to take a puff on his cigar, I could smell the smoke wafting through the crack in the door. "I must say, this doesn't come as a complete surprise. In fact, her mother and I have discussed the possibility. She's very young, you know, and I'm hesitate about her moving so far away from the family."

Thankfully, Charles didn't argue. My father can become bull-headed in an argument.

"Yes, sir. I understand your concerns."

"However, I believe you're a solid man with a good career. If you and Elizabeth will agree to wait a year before marrying, I'll give my permission."

I put my hand over my mouth to stifle my excitement. *He said yes!*

The next day, while on a picnic, Charles got down on one knee. I remember every word as if it was yesterday. "I know we've only known each other a short time, Elizabeth, but it would be my honor if you'd consent to be my wife."

Of course, I said yes. He told me about my father's terms of waiting a year and I agreed. I was glad I'd overheard the conversation and had time to consider both the proposal and the request to wait. It would give me time to get used to the idea of being a wife in the Sand Hills of Nebraska.

Charles wrote to me regularly and through our letters, our love grew stronger. He promised to meet me on the trail just west of Grand Island around the middle of September the following year and we'd be married right away before going to our new home near Fort Hartsuff.

Elizabeth rolls over and returns to the questions currently on her mind. *What if Charles has changed his mind and isn't there to meet me? What if I don't measure up as his wife? What if I can't bear the loneliness and I'm desperately homesick for my family?*

She looks up at the full moon and imagines it shining over her intended. With a fluttering heart and warmth growing in her private parts, she imagines sleeping with Charles. *I hope we have a bed for our first night and we aren't wrapped up in a blanket on the hard ground.*

Thinking of making love with her husband brings up yet another worry. *What will it be like to have a baby on the prairie? Will there be a mid-wife or a doctor to attend me? What if Charles or I become ill, or our baby gets sick?*

As the coyotes begin their evening song and a cool breeze replaces the hot wind, Elizabeth finally gets clear of her worries and feels her body relax.

CHAPTER FIVE

BABY LOUISE

A mournful howl awakens Elizabeth. With eyes still closed, she breathes in the cool, morning air, the lingering smell of smoke from last night's fires, bad breath, and body odor.

Still half asleep, she wonders why James is looking down at her. His hair stands up at the crown, his tanned face is flushed, his blue eyes are bloodshot, and his rough hand is shaking her shoulder. "Wake up, Elizabeth. Louise died in the night and Gretchen needs comfortin'. She's crying dreadful like and I ain't been able to calm her."

Elizabeth quickly reacts to the sight of James and his words. She abandons her warm, cozy blanket and wraps her old, gray shawl around her shoulders. She shuffles to the wagon entrance in unbuttoned shoes. When she looks in, she sees her friend wrapped in a well-worn, patchwork quilt, sitting up in the bed of the wagon with her back against the flour barrel. Her long, blond braids are askew. Elizabeth's heart breaks when she sees her puffy, red eyes and the look of despair on her face. Cradling her lifeless baby in her arms, Gretchen looks up when Elizabeth climbs into the wagon.

"Our precious baby is gone, Elizabeth. We never should have come on this God-forsaken trip. Our baby, our beautiful baby! What am I going to do?" Tears stream down Gretchen's cheeks as she reaches out with her free hand. Elizabeth crouches down and encircles mother and child with her long, strong arms. Gretchen rests her forehead on Elizabeth's bony chest.

"Shhh ... it'll be alright," Elizabeth whispers, gently rocking Gretchen from side to side.

After a bit, she hums a favorite childhood lullaby into Gretchen's ear. The tune floods Elizabeth's heart with sweet and painful memories—her mother's comforting arms when her baby sister died, the scent of vanilla on her mother's neck, and the soft tickle of tendrils escaped from her mother's bun. After several minutes, the soft hum of the lullaby work their magic and Gretchen's sobs turn to hiccups.

Elizabeth takes advantage of this quiet moment to throw on yesterday's, now dried, dress and undergarments. She smooths her tangled hair with her hand. She's buttoning her high top shoes near the opening at the back of the wagon when she sees Mr. Whimple walking slowly in her direction. She watches as he places a wrinkled, blue-veined hand on James' broad shoulder. "I'm sorry about your baby."

"Thanks, Whimple."

Elizabeth continues to watch Whimple as he follows James to the side of the wagon. "I found a couple of flat sticks down the way a bit. I'll fashion them into a cross if you'd like."

James barely looks up from his task of pulling tools from storage. "I'd be much obliged."

Elizabeth ducks her head back into the wagon and offers to hold Louise while Gretchen slips into her clothes. Then, the women quietly sit side by side on the wagon seat where they can watch James digging a grave several yards from the wagon. Elizabeth senses his anger as he swings his pick into the hard-packed earth. After loosening the thick prairie grass roots, he uses his shovel to dig a small, rectangular hole.

Still silent, the ladies continue to watch as James replaces his tools. He goes to the water barrel at the side of the wagon, washes up, and slicks back his unruly hair. He approaches the women and reaches up to retrieve Louise from his wife's reluctant arms. "You need to give me the baby, Sweetheart." His voice is soft. "It's time to lay her to rest."

Elizabeth sees Gretchen looking into her husband's eyes. Silent tears flow down her cheeks. As if trying to delay the inevitable, she reaches behind her into the wagon and retrieves a beautifully crocheted, white blanket that she uses to replace the soiled one currently swaddling the baby. She turns to Elizabeth. "This blanket was a sending-off gift," she chokes out, "from Louise's grandmother."

After securely re-wrapping the baby, Gretchen hands her to James then quickly ducks into the wagon. When he frowns, Elizabeth touches his arm. She feels her face redden and she stutters with embarrassment. "G-gretchen will need to bind her b-breasts before the service. Best to give her some privacy."

There's a low buzz around the circle of wagons as word of Louise's death spreads from family to family. Everyone, even the usually loud and rambunctious children, are respectfully quiet as they eat their meager breakfast rations and delay their morning start in order to attend the simple burial ceremony and offer their condolences.

Elizabeth considers that, although the Schmidt children were recently sick and everyone feared for the life of the youngest, this is the first death the group has experienced.

James, standing next to the grave, signals Elizabeth to bring Gretchen toward him. When she stumbles, Elizabeth tightens her grip on her arm and helps her over the tuffs of thick prairie grass and rocks as they walk the short distance to the grave.

Standing a bit apart from the couple, Elizabeth takes a deep, calming breath. She gazes across the now sunny prairie as she considers the many lives lost crossing this desolate stretch of land. Recalling Mr. Whimple saying he counted ten graves for every mile, Elizabeth imagines Louise's grave reclaimed by grass and weeds with broken wheels and abandoned barrels lying nearby. She chokes back a sob.

During the short service, Gretchen remains quiet while the group sings "To God Be the Glory." Mr. Whimple reads a short passage from his worn, thumbed-through Bible. Then James, who placed Louise in her grave before the service began, quickly fills the hole with black, heavy soil and, with the help of others, covers the small mound with rocks to protect it from wild animals.

Mr. Whimple hands James the cross with *Baby Louise—September 8, 1875* scratched onto the surface. The group disperses except for Gretchen and Elizabeth who stand next to one another as they watch James pound the cross into the ground with a heavy stone.

Elizabeth remains alone near the fresh grave while James

and Gretchen slowly walk back to the wagon hand in hand. Noticing wild flowers growing nearby, she reaches down and plucks two small, purple, ironweed flowers from the patch. She straightens then tucks them into her pocket.

Halfway back to the wagon, a shadow moves across the ground prompting her to look up. Four, red-headed buzzards are circling high above the grave. With a shiver, she rushes forward, rolls up her sleeping pallet, and stores it in the wagon. She opens her trunk and pulls out her favorite book, *Alice's Adventures in Wonderland,* then presses the flowers between its pages. She tries to ignore the anxiety she feels from, once again, seeing buzzards and welcomes the familiar command to begin the day's journey.

On another day Elizabeth might appreciate the vast beauty of the whipped-cream clouds in the azure sky as it meets the golden river of grass. But today, she only sees the hard-packed, rutted trail as she walks with downcast eyes and a heavy heart. After about an hour, she senses Lucy walking behind her and motions for her friend to come forward.

Lucy speaks softly. "How are Gretchen and James?"

"Gretchen looks to be in a daze. She seems to not notice the milk stains down the front of her dress and there are dark circles under her eyes. James isn't much better. I feel so bad for them." Without giving Lucy a chance to respond, Elizabeth continues. "I've heard stories about women who simply give up as the journey west becomes more and more demanding. I hope Gretchen has the strength to recover."

Elizabeth sees a look of disbelief in her friend's eyes. "Ain't you ever know'd nobody who lost a baby before? Seems to me 'bout every woman loses at least one."

As tears fill her eyes, Elizabeth acknowledges Lucy's question and recounts her baby sister's death. "Louise's burial reminded me of my sister's. Anna wasn't wrapped in a blanket and laid in the bare ground. She had a tiny white casket with a pink rose on top. But however nice the burial, it makes no difference in the feelings of loss. Sorrow took over my family for months."

Lucy looks at her friend with sad, blue eyes. "You wonderin' how you'd be doin' if you lost a baby?"

Elizabeth silently lowers her head not wanting to voice her fears.

"You're a strong girl, Lizabeth. I think you'll be able to handle whatever comes your way." Lucy pats her arm. "I jus' hope you ain't never tested." When she gets no response, Lucy remains quiet for several minutes. "Why don't you tell me somethin' about that town where you're getting married at."

Smiling faintly, Elizabeth appreciates her friend's attempt to distract her. "Charles wrote that Grand Island was settled almost thirty years ago. It was known then as La Grande Isle by French traders."

Lucy looks from horizon to horizon. "An island on this here prairie? What you talkin' about?"

"Apparently the town was built on an island formed by the Wood and Platte Rivers."

Snickering, Lucy asks, "Does that mean more river crossings? You didn't do so well on the last one."

Elizabeth ignores the jibe. "Charles said the Platte near Grand Island should be about an inch deep this time of year. If that's the case, we'll be able to walk across."

"You gettin' married in a church?"

"Yes. If I have a chance, I'll show you the lavender voile dress I'm planning on wearing." When she sees a look of envy cross Lucy's face, she can't help adding. "And my white kid gloves with tiny pearl buttons."

The day turns cool and cloudy and there's the sweet scent of rain in the air. Elizabeth notices that her fellow creatures are delighted to have relief from the heat. Crickets are chirping and bees are buzzing as they dip into the abundant stalks of goldenrod growing nearby. Walkers are chatting with one another; children are racing between the wagons.

Lucy shoos away a horsefly about to bite her neck. "I'm shore tired of this here walkin' and these damn flies—ain't you?"

Elizabeth rolls her eyes as if it goes without saying how sick and tired she is of it all.

The wind shifts and Lucy protects her face from a swirl of dust. While she's wiping her eyes with a dirty hankie pulled from inside her sleeve, she's bumped by three, skinny children playing a game of tag. "Hey, watch out! You 'bout knocked me over!"

Elizabeth can't help but smile at the children. Young as she is, she longs to be a mother. She imagines kissing tiny perfect toes and caressing downy soft curls.

Lucy interrupts her thoughts. "You said you was goin' to Fort Hartsuff after the weddin.' I've heard 'bout Fort Kearny but I ain't never hear nothin' about a Fort Hartsuff. What do you know about it?"

Elizabeth recalls Charle's letters. "It's an infantry outpost in Nebraska's North Loup River Valley. Charles wrote that it's a buffer between the settlers and Indians. I think that means it's there to keep them from killing each other." She looks over and sees Lucy's grimace. "Besides protecting the settlers, the fort also protects the Pawnee Indians from what Charles called 'the war-like Sioux'."

Lucy adjusts her bonnet then turns to look at Elizabeth. "I hope you're safe there. At least you'll have protection from the army."

The girls walk in silence until Lucy abruptly stops. "Hold up a minute." She rushes over, picks a handful of white flowers growing near the trail, then returns to her friend's side. "This here's yarrow. Smell it."

"It smells like pine. Why'd you pick it?"

Lucy crumbles a bit between two fingers. "It's good for all kinds of things like colds, diarrhea, scrapes. Just dry it, then put a good pinch into hot water and drink it like tea." She hands the flowers to Elizabeth who tucks them into the waistband of her dress.

"Thanks, Lucy. Speaking of medicine, I'm sure grateful we've stayed heathy. Aren't you?"

No response.

"Did you know that thousands died during the cholera epidemic in '50 while on the trail?"

No response.

"Mrs. Schmidt's kids had fevers a while back and they feared it was cholera but at least no one's died." She lowers her voice. "Not until today."

Still no response.

Elizabeth gently pokes her friend's arm. "You sleep-walkin' over there? Do you hear what I'm saying?"

"I heard you, Lizabeth." She kicks a clod of dirt. "I just don't want to think about it. I got 'nough problems on my mind as it is. Baby Louise dyin' last night, me 'bout gettin' kilt by a wagon, you falling in the creek, trouble with Jake. I want to keep the thought of fevers and such out of my head. We need to quit postulating 'bout trouble that ain't happened and likely won't."

The girls return to their wagons for the noontime break, then Elizabeth walks alone the rest of the afternoon. Even with the burial causing the train to start late, she's feeling the weight of the morning's drama followed by a long, eight-hour-day on the trail.

When the train begins to circle, Elizabeth approaches her wagon. James is unhitching the mules but Gretchen is still on the wagon seat staring ahead. "You okay?" Gretchen nods and Elizabeth reaches into the wagon for the fuel-gathering baskets. She notices that her friend's cheeks have pinked up a bit. "I'm off to gather fuel. I'll get dinner started when I return."

While searching for fuel, she sees Lucy and calls her over. "Can you spare a bit of jerky for Gretchen?"

No response.

"It might give her a bit more strength. All we have left is beans."

Lucy looks around, making sure no one is listening. "I'll see if I can sneak a stick into my pocket without Jake knowin'. He'd be mighty sore if he found out. He don't take much fancy to no charity. Just know that it be your fault if I shows up with a black eye tomorrow." Lucy stomps away.

Elizabeth is concerned about Gretchen, but she also fears for Lucy who seems genuinely afraid of Jake. She wonders how far he'd go if he felt provoked.

Sitting around the low-burning fire with James and Gretchen after supper, Elizabeth feels comforted by their proximity while listening to the far-off sounds of a harmonica and banjo playing. Although they've only been together for a month, she feels like they've become part of her family.

The moon is high in the sky when Elizabeth finally settles into her blanket and allows herself to have a good cry. After she's cried out, she looks into the vast, black-velvet sky. *I hope I don't have to bury a baby in this wilderness. I also hope my decision to come west wasn't just the pipe dream of a headstrong girl in love.*

CHAPTER SIX

LUCY'S STORY

The next morning Elizabeth makes corn cakes smothered in sorghum, and a pot of strong, black coffee. Gretchen is listless as she helps Elizabeth wash up. They're putting away the dishes when the familiar "Move out!" echoes around the circle and the wagons and walkers resume their trek.

Elizabeth walks alone for a few hours, glad to have time to think. The wind has died down, causing gnats and mosquitoes to flourish. Elizabeth mindlessly swats and tugs her sleeves down over her arms.

"Mornin' Lizabeth. Mind if I join you?"

She smiles and slows her pace to match Lucy's.

"Looks like we're headin' straight west on this here cut-off. Jake says it'll save a day or so of travelin' on the old trail."

Elizabeth looks at the rolling grassland then up to the cloudy sky. "Truth be told, Lucy, I've got no sense of direction. If I'd grown up on a farm like you did, maybe I'd know about stuff like that. My mother's instructions on how to knit proper stitches and make butterscotch pie aren't doing me much good. At least Gretchen taught me how to cook over a fire and you've been pointing out plants that are remedies for ailments."

"Well, ain't that somethin'! You ain't perfect after all." Because Lucy says it with a grin, Elizabeth takes no offense. She studies her companion out of the corner of her eye thinking that the brown homespun with the white, bone buttons marching down the front is the ugliest dress she's ever seen. *Lucy says she's nineteen but she dresses like an old woman.* She sighs. *Goodness, I'm starting to think like my mother's friends. Judging Lucy by how she looks. Shame on me.*

Lucy tugs at her dress bodice. "Hey, what you lookin' at? I know I's a shrimp wearin' my ma's old dress. Mrs. Whimple and some other ladies thought I were one of them ragamuffin kids 'fore they found out I was Jake's woman. So embarrassin'. Have a little sympathy, will ya?"

Dropping her eyes, Elizabeth feels warmth coming to her cheeks. "I'm sorry for the look, Lucy. I know what it's like to be judged on appearances and I don't want to be like that. It's one reason I'm here—to get away from people judging me. No disrespect intended."

"None taken."

Elizabeth is also sympathetic to Lucy struggling to keep up with the pace of the wagon train. "How come you don't ride with Jake? Doesn't look like there's much in your wagon causing the oxen to strain."

Pulling her faded sunbonnet tight over dishwater blonde, greasy hair, Lucy's pale blue eyes look down at the ruts. "I knowed I should insist on ridin' with Jake on that there wagon seat but when I asked him 'bout it, he cuffed my ears. I figure my good health is more 'portant than my pride, so I walks while Jake rides. Sometimes I think I deserves how he treats me, but mostly, I jus' try to stay outta his way."

Elizabeth makes an effort to hide her dismay. "How did you meet Jake anyway? You promised to tell me."

Lucy slowly tilts her head to one side and is silent for a long moment. "Well, I was just mindin' my own business at Webber's General Store and in walked this handsome stranger lookin' for supplies. Found out he was goin' ta be in Nauroo for a few weeks 'fore headin' west."

When she pauses in her story, Elizabeth looks around for some variety in the waving sea of grass. Finding none, she returns her attention to Lucy, delaying the inevitable need to relieve herself. She hopes she can hold it until they stop for the night. "And?"

"Whenever I brung eggs and butter to town for sellin', I made a point of showin' up where he might be 'til he finally noticed me and ask'd my name. Jake seemed mighty appealin' with that there curly brown hair and strong muscles. At the time, my fate was to marry Wendell and I was feelin' pretty dern sorry for myself."

"What's this Wendell like?" Elizabeth wonders if Wendell might have been a better choice.

Lucy frowns and pinches her lips together. "Scrawny, like me. Borin'. Only talked bout plantin', harvestin', or the weather. No sense of adventure at all. I'd a died of boredom if I'd a married Wendell."

"So, you traded a life with Boring Wendell for adventure with Mysterious Jake. Is that it?"

"Yep. But now I'm thinkin' I might have gottin' me the short end of that stick." Lucy groans with a sense of resignation. "Wendell was boring as hell—sorry, I mean, heck—but at least he were a gentleman."

"And, Jake wanted to marry you?"

"Well, not exactly." Lucy fidgets with her bonnet strings. "He was headed to Wyoming where he planned to make his fame and fortune and he needed somebody to help him. Problem is, he weren't planning on that somebody bein' a puny girl the likes of me."

Elizabeth looks to her left and right for any sign of shrubs. She hates to interrupt Lucy's story but she's growing desperate. "Do you mind if we stop to relieve ourselves? I can't wait until we circle up."

"Shore, but you need to be quick about it. Takes me a bit to catch up."

The girls veer off the trail and find a screen of brush. Elizabeth watches Lucy pick up a stick and prod around in the nearby grass. "What are you doing?"

Lucy looks up. "We don't want to get bit by no snake, Lizabeth. I'm just makin' sure none's here." She pokes some more, then throws the stick aside. "You go first. I'll hold my skirt out for you. That bush ain't goin' to hide much."

"Thanks." Elizabeth squats close to the ground taking care to keep her shoes and bloomers dry. When she's finished, she returns the favor and holds out her skirt for Lucy. *I never dreamed I'd be squatting out in the open. It's bad enough during the midday break to go off with the other women. It's just one of the many things I didn't consider before starting this trip.*

When Lucy's done, the girls hustle back to the trail and their conversation. "But, eventually, Jake did propose. Right?"

"He didn't exactly ask me." A blush creeps up Lucy's neck to her cheeks and she clears her throat. "Pa found us, ahh, you know, compromised, in the barn and demanded, right then and there, that Jake marry me."

Elizabeth looks straight ahead and makes an effort to contain any look of surprise or judgment. She keeps her voice matter of fact. "And that was that?"

Slapping a blood-bloated mosquito for emphasis, Lucy replies. "Yep. That was that. Two weeks later we was married by the Justice of the Peace at the Town Hall. I never even got to have me a pretty dress or nothin'. Ma was beside herself, me bein' her only girl and all, but Pa wouldn't budge. He can be a force of nature when he puts his mind to it. 'Sides, he's real friendly with the sheriff."

Elizabeth sees a look of defeat cross Lucy's face. "I thought I'd have me a great adventure with Jake, but instead, I'm findin' myself stuck with a mean, self-centered, smelly old man. I'm hopin' and prayin' ever'thing will git better once we're in Wyomin'."

When she drops her head, Elizabeth takes the hint and resumes walking in silence for the next few miles. Thinking back to Lucy's plight, Elizabeth remembers that, before she met Charles, a girlfriend warned her about men like Jake—scoundrels heading west who were looking for a partner to cook their meals, wash their clothes, maintain the gear, and keep them company in their blanket at night. *Guess I didn't consider these miserable creatures might also be abusive. I hope Lucy will be alright.*

Lucy breaks the silence. "Did you see Mrs. Whimple in that there ridiculous black dress? Who does she think she is anyways, the Queen of England? She sits on her throne of a wagon seat all day lookin' down her nose at the rest of us."

"I guess her husband doesn't want her to tire out." Elizabeth knows there's sarcasm in her voice but can't help herself. "She's probably at least sixty, old enough to be our grandmother. Wish I knew what in the world they're doing on this trip." She ticks the possibilities off on her fingers. "Maybe her husband is running from the sheriff or a bill collector. Maybe he's a murderer and heading west where lawmen are few and far between!"

"Good grief, Lizabeth, you're lettin' your 'magination git away from you. Mr. Whimple seems like a nice 'nough man. He even read from his Bible at the baby's service. I think they jus' got bored bein' rich in Saint Louie and decided to have themselves an adventure."

Elizabeth's eyes flash as she feels her pent-up anger about the difficulties of the journey getting the best of her. "I also thought this would be an adventure. But I was wrong. This ... this is like going through purgatory!" She looks down at her sunbonnet hanging by its ribbons around her neck. In an effort to calm herself, she slowly and deliberately secures her braids, which have escaped from their pins on top of her head, and replaces her bonnet.

Tears well up in her eyes and slide down her cheeks. She's embarrassed by the unaccustomed display of emotion. "Sorry, Lucy. I didn't mean to snap at you like that. I just didn't think this trip was going to be so hard. I'm sick of being dirty and eaten up by bugs. I want to wash my hair, eat decent food, and sleep in a proper bed. That's all."

"I don't reckon I thought it'd be so hard neither."

Later, when the gentle hills flatten out to plains, Elizabeth spots a small herd of buffalo about a quarter of a mile in the distance. Their big heads nod; their tails swish away the flies. She watches their mouths rhythmically chewing the tough prairie grass. "Look!" She points to the herd. "Aren't they enormous? I heard the men around the campfire saying that, only a few years ago, buffalo roamed these plains in the hundreds of thousands. One said he saw black shaggy humps as far as the horizon. I hope we'll see bigger herds farther west."

Lucy follows Elizabeth's pointed finger but doesn't comment.

The late afternoon sun peeks out from behind the clouds and Elizabeth's glad another day on the trail is finally drawing to a close. She sees women with slumped shoulders, children dragging their feet, and hears a baby crying. Her feet are hurting and her legs are heavy. She can't imagine what it would be like to have children along.

Looking to her left, she spies the rotten remains of a raccoon carcass, shimmering with black flies, resting on the side of the trail. Just then, a wake of buzzards swoops down for a feast. Her stomach lurches and bile comes up to her throat. She staggers forward. Determined to overcome her fright, she peels her eyes away from the spectacle, jams her hands into her armpits, and marches straight ahead, leaving Lucy in her wake. After recovering from the grisly scene of buzzards, she looks back at her companion who shows no sign of being ruffled by buffalo, buzzards, or Elizabeth's sudden departure. In fact, Lucy's eyes are fastened on the ground.

Just then, Nichals hollers and the wagons slowly begin to form the familiar circle that becomes their stockade for the night. Elizabeth waits for Lucy to catch up. "I'm sorry I took off."

"It's alright. After you left, I spied two perfect arrow heads carved from stone." She pats her skirt. "Got them right here in my pocket. My very own secret treasure."

Elizabeth hears a man's deep voice. "Lucy, stop yur lolly-gagging with that moose of a girlfriend and git yurself over here! I'm hungry!"

Cringing at Jake's description of her, Elizabeth rushes past him towards James' and Gretchen's wagon.

CHAPTER SEVEN

WIND, EGGS, AND INDIANS

The next three days drag by for Elizabeth. Monotonous and endless flat plains have replaced the gentle hills. Louise's death continues to sadden her, and the dull look in Gretchen's eyes causes Elizabeth to worry about her friend's future.

On the fourth day, Elizabeth awakens to wind. Not the usual wind blowing grasses to and fro, but a wild wind that causes dust to spin and wagon covers to sway. She covers her head with her shawl, relieves herself a few yards from the wagon, then returns to retrieve her pallet and climb into the wagon to get dressed. She sees that Gretchen is already dressed and huddled in a corner of the wagon, an arm across her face for protection from the dust blowing through every crack and crevasse.

After dressing, Elizabeth climbs out of the wagon and experiences a wind so strong it causes her to stagger. It sands her exposed skin and requires her to keep her eyes closed to bare slits. She finds James tending the mules. "Do you think we'll travel today? Will the mules find their way in this blizzard of dust?"

James squints up at her. "Don't worry. Like you, they put one foot in front of the other and follow the wagon ahead, but you need to ride inside today. I know it ain't comfortable but at least you'll be out of the worst of it."

Elizabeth can't smell smoke and hears no breakfast preparations. "What about breakfast? Doesn't seem like anyone's cooking."

"There's no fire building for fear of it spreading to the dry grass. We'll get by on whatever you and Gretchen rustle up. Just bring me a bit of leftover biscuit and a cup of water."

After their meager breakfast, the women settle into the back of the wagon as the train slowly gets underway. They pile their bedrolls around them for protection from bruising as the wagon lurches along. They can barely hear each other speak over the crunch of the wagon's wheels and the howling of the wind. Panicked birds hit the canvas sides. Imagining that they're buzzards, Elizabeth's heart skips a beat when she hears them.

Gretchen covers her hair with a shawl and shouts at her companion. "I wonder if this will last all day."

"I certainly hope not. The wagon's taking on dust like a boat taking on water."

By noon, the women are ready to leave the wagon and brave the wind. Every part of Elizabeth's body aches from the buffeting and she's covered from head to toe with dust as James helps the women from the wagon.

Gretchen smiles at James. It's the first smile Elizabeth's seen on her face since Louise's death. "You look like a bandit with that bandana covering your face." James pulls his scarf down and returns his wife's smile. "Elizabeth and I need a break from riding in the back. Do you think we can fit on the seat beside you?"

James shakes his head from side to side as he looks around at the dust-covered animals and travelers. "I don't think we'll be pushing on. Too hard on the animals. We need to find water. I'm going to talk with the men and find out what's happening. You ladies stay inside. I'll be back soon."

James quickly disappears into a cloud of dust. The women climb back into the wagon bed and, though the day is hot, burrow into blankets so they can breathe easier. After more than an hour, Gretchen leans over and speaks into Elizabeth's ear. "I wonder what's taking James so long. Don't you think he should be back by now?"

Elizabeth pats Gretchen's arm reassuringly. "He probably went with the men to find water for the animals. Try to get some sleep."

Waking with a jerk, Elizabeth looks to Gretchen, wondering how long they've been sleeping. She hears James hollering into the wagon. "Anybody in there?"

"We're here." Elizabeth climbs out, her body stiff.

Still in the wagon, Gretchen asks, "What took you so long?"

"We found water, but it was full of silt from this damn storm. Had to let it settle before we could water the stock. Not much extra. I drank from the crick. You ladies get the water you need from the barrel."

Unable to light a fire, the women put together a supper of cold beans and dried out corn bread spread with leftover bacon grease. They drink sparingly from the water barrel.

Elizabeth feels anxiety about the lack of water and the length of the storm but she's careful to keep her feelings to herself.

When they retire for the night inside the wagon, Elizabeth feels guilty that she's crowding the couple but she's grateful for shelter from the continuing storm. She peeks out the back of the wagon, hoping that no one is having to sleep outside. She sees only two or three blankets spread under nearby wagons. Once again she thinks how difficult this trip must be for families.

Elizabeth feels her body relax as it's lulled by a wind powerful enough to rock the wagon. When she wakes during the night, she notices that James is gone. She assumes he's checking the stock.

In the morning, Gretchen, with a shawl over her shift and her hair flying, sticks her head into the wagon. "Come quick, Elizabeth. James is sick!"

Elizabeth throws her blanket around her shoulders and joins Gretchen on the wagon seat. She sees James, pale and droopy-eyed, sitting in the dirt at the side of the wagon. He lifts his head and offers his wife a small smile. "I'll be okay, Sweetheart. I was up all night with the runs, that's all. I'm thinkin' that crick water weren't no good. At least not for humans. Glad you didn't drink any."

James struggles to stand. Elizabeth sees the fear in Gretchen's eyes and speaks forcefully. "You're as weak as a kitten, James. Sit down and let me get you water from the barrel." Elizabeth returns with a ladle and asks James if he has a fever.

"No fever. Ain't got the cholera if that's what's worrin' you." He takes a long draw from the ladle. "The storm blew itself out just before daylight and I gave the mules hay and the last of the water. I hope I can hang onto the reins today."

Hearing this, Elizabeth gathers up her courage and speaks with more confidence than she feels. "I can drive the team, James. You rest in the back. It's not comfortable but it will give you time to get your strength back. Gretchen can sit up front with me. We'll call if we need help."

James frowns. "But you're a city girl."

"But I'm good with animals and I learned to drive a horse and buggy while visiting my uncle George's farm last summer."

James looks doubtful.

"Don't worry. I can do this. Let me help."

James nods and the women climb into the wagon to dress then scurry off to gather fuel for breakfast before he changes his mind. When they return, Elizabeth starts the fire while Gretchen whips up batter for corn cakes. When the fire is hot, she pours the mixture into grease. The coffee perks and the aroma makes Elizabeth's stomach growl in anticipation of the first hot meal in a while.

The women are chatting at the back of the wagon while they wash, dry, and store the breakfast dishes in readiness for an early start to the day. When Elizabeth reaches down to pick up the black spider, she sees Mrs. Whimple slowly walking over. Her stiff, black dress makes a swishing sound as she approaches. Her steel gray hair is neatly tucked up into a white, lace bonnet. Elizabeth wonders how she manages to look so dignified after the storm. *She reminds me of my mother's friends.*

Mrs. Whimple looks Elizabeth over then addresses Gretchen. "How are you, Dear?"

Gretchen dries the last dish. "I'm getting by. Thanks for asking." She smiles over at her friend. "Elizabeth's a great help. A godsend really."

Mrs. Whimple pulls her eyebrows together but before she can respond, the familiar, "Move out!" rings through the camp.

"Best be on my way. Good day, ladies."

Gretchen gives a little wave. "Good day, Mrs. Whimple. Thanks for stopping by."

Feeling judged but appreciative of Gretchen's comment, Elizabeth returns to putting the last utensils away. Then she climbs onto the wagon seat next to Gretchen and takes the reins. She's grateful James had the energy to harness the animals. The effort seemed to sap the last of his strength, and Elizabeth notices that he's already laying down in the wagon bed.

Elizabeth shakes the reins and the wagon lurches forward. After traveling steadily for about four miles, the mules suddenly stop in the middle of the trail. Elizabeth shakes the reins. "Giddy up! Get going!" No response. The mules look around as if they sense danger. Elizabeth wants to be patient but the man behind her, who's walking alongside his team of oxen, yells at her. "Hey, girlie! Git them damn mules movin'! We ain't got all day."

Gretchen looks at Elizabeth and raises her shoulders. "Sorry, I don't know the magic words James uses to get them going. This happens all the time. They're stubborn, that's for sure."

Just as Elizabeth's about to appeal to James, the mules begin walking again, picking up their pace to position themselves just behind the wagon in front. She sighs with relief and wipes the perspiration off of her forehead with her sleeve.

Just before the midday break, the mules stop again as something unusual catches their attention causing Elizabeth to reconsider the wisdom of her offer to drive. Sweat is running down her face. She turns to Gretchen. "A horse and buggy is so much easier to control. I certainly have respect for James' ability to keep these beasts moving."

The sun, now directly overhead, is beating down on the travelers. When the train stops, James comes out of the wagon bed and the women ease themselves down from the seat. James comes to stand near them, giving Elizabeth a chance to ask a question she'd been considering all morning. "Mind if I ask why you have a mule team instead of oxen or horses?"

James rubs one of the mules between his ears. "Even though mules are more expensive than oxen, they can travel more miles in a day without tirin' and they're better in the heat. I figured August to be a scorcher." James gets water from the bucket he'd carefully set aside from the barrel of good water. "They'll be more surefooted when we git to crossin' the mountains because, unlike a horse, they can see where they're puttin' their hind feet. Also, they eat hay grass. Gotta carry feed for horses. Speakin' of feed, what we got for food? I could eat a horse."

After the mules are watered, the trio share a handful of hardtack biscuits, a moldy hunk of cheese, and the last of the warm water from the barrel. Elizabeth hears the crunch of sand between her teeth as she bites into the bit of cheese.

James prepares to take back the reins when the train is ready to roll out. "Thanks. Appreciate your help, Elizabeth. I'll take it from here."

Elizabeth doesn't mind walking now that she's experienced the difficulty of handling the mules. During the next a few miles, her pace quickens as she enjoys the melodic calls of red-winged blackbirds and the beauty of golden meadowlarks diving into the tall grasses then soaring into the dazzling sky. The trail is bordered by goldenrod. Blue skies with whipped cream clouds have returned. As she walks, she can taste the residue of dust and feel the grit that has burrowed its way into every nook and cranny of her body.

Just before the sun begins to slide downward, Elizabeth sees a handwritten sign for fresh eggs in the distance. Thinking anything fresh for supper would be a treat, she runs to the wagon.

"Gretchen!"

Gretchen looks in Elizabeth's direction. "Get me a pail and the dishtowels." Gretchen reaches into the back of the wagon, retrieves a bucket and towels, then hands them down. Without a word of explanation, Elizabeth races away from the wagon, being careful not to trip on the thick buffalo grass, hidden rocks, or step in fresh manure. When she gets closer to the sign, she sees a big man with hairy arms and shoulders and a stomach stretching his overalls to the limit. His full, gray beard is waving in the wind as he lumbers over from his seat on an overturned, wooden crate.

"You here for my eggs, Missy? They's laid fresh this mornin'. Sell 'em to ya fur five cents a dozen." He looks down at the two pails of eggs sitting near his feet.

Panting from her run, Elizabeth pulls a soft brown leather pouch from around her neck, takes out a coin, then quickly tucks the pouch back inside her dress. She has no time to barter.

The farmer pockets the coin then holds out his bear-like hand. "Give me yur pail, Missy, and I'll wrap 'em up nice and snug." The farmer continues to speak while he carefully places eggs between towels. "Once was, I'd be sold out by now. Before the railroad come, I seen as many as a thousand or more wagons pass by here in a single day. My eggs was sold before I could set 'em down."

Elizabeth turns away from the farmer to watch the wagon train crawl forward. Her stomach clenches as she feels the familiar anxiety about her lack of direction and fear of becoming lost. "Sir, I appreciate hearing all this, I really do, but I've got to get back to the wagons quick like. Don't want to get left behind."

The man pauses and follows her gaze. "Don't you worry none. You'd be seeing dust fur a long ways after they leave here." He resumes packing. "Jus' nice to talk to somebody. My wife died a while back and it shore gits lonely out here by myself. Gotta git as much talkin' in as I can 'afore winter sets in. This here's probably the last train comin' through 'til spring." He hands Elizabeth her pail of eggs.

She smiles at the farmer as she turns to leave. "Sorry about your wife. Hope you stay well this winter. Thanks for packin' up my eggs." She waves. "Bye, Mister." Then, she briskly walks back to her wagon, being careful not to jar the eggs. She hands the pail up to Gretchen. When she sees others making their way to the farmer, she hopes he gets plenty of talking stored up today.

Elizabeth considers the farmer's plight as she resumes walking. *I think I'd die of loneliness if I was left out here alone all winter. Poor man.* She straightens her back and moves her head from side to side. Young as she is, the daily walking is taking a toll.

As the late afternoon wears on and the breeze becomes a wind, she can't get the farmer's plight out of her mind which causes her to consider what winter will be like in a soddie.

She knows, or hopes, she'll have Charles as company but wonders if he'll be enough.

After another two hours, the train stops for the night and the ladies again gather fuel, start a fire, and cook the fresh eggs along with fried bread. James shovels scrambled eggs into his mouth. "Thanks for rustlin' up these here eggs, Elizabeth. Best thing I've eaten since the fresh fish."

The next day, Elizabeth is back on the trail with Lucy walking nearby. She looks across the flat prairie to where the sky meets the waving grass. To her shock, she sees men on ponies lined up across a low ridge about a quarter mile off the trail. "Lucy, look over there!"

Lucy continues walking with her head down. "I ain't in no mood for buzzard or buffalo viewin'."

With her heart pounding and her breath coming in quick gasps, Elizabeth grabs Lucy's arm and points. "Look! Indians!" Six men with heads shaved except for a knot of hair on top and feathers, sit ramrod straight atop small, muscular horses. One is light tan with white patches, one is brown with white stockings, the others are spotted like leopards. "It's like we conjured them up by talking about them. Let's get to our wagons!"

Lucy stares slack-jawed and slows her pace.

"Lucy! Snap out of it and get to your wagon." Elizabeth pushes Lucy on the back. "Git!"

Waking up to Elizabeth demands, Lucy hightails it to her wagon with Elizabeth close behind.

"Did … you … see … the … Indians?" Elizabeth gasps when she reaches her wagon and directs Gretchen's and James' gaze toward the ridge. James slowly looks in the direction she's indicating. "What should we do? Will they attack? You got your gun handy?"

James remains steady. "Yep, I see 'em. Best thing is to stay calm and keep movin'. I'll hold the mules if you want to climb up but you gotta make it quick." When Elizabeth nods, he pulls back on the reins and Gretchen squeezes over to make room. It's a tight fit. Elizabeth crosses her arms over her bosom for space and the feeling of reassurance. In a few minutes, she catches her breath and feels her racing heart slow to its normal beat.

"Do you think they mean trouble?"

"They might be considerin' their options. We're a small wagon train with not much livestock, but they also know we're probably the last train this year." James shakes the reins. "On the other hand, those scouts may be working for the army. They look to be Pawnee. See their heads?"

Elizabeth squints to get a better look. "What about them?"

"Only the Pawnee shave their heads like that with a scalp lock that stands erect and curves backward like a horn. I've been told they dress the lock with buffalo fat to make it stand up like that." James looks over at the frightened women. "It'll be alright. No need to worry none. They look fierce but Pawnee are considered friendly. After all, they crossed you in the bull boat and traded with me for the fish."

Not comforted by James' assessment, Elizabeth sits up straight, watching as the Indians disappear behind the ridge. Even though they're out of sight, she's watchful every minute of the last three hours on the trail.

"Circle the wagons nice and tight," the wagon master hollers when they stop for the night.

Nerves tingling, Elizabeth is reluctant to go off by herself in search of fuel. "See those folks over there?" James points to a group of women and children. "Go with them to gather firewood. There's safety in numbers. I need to take care of the animals."

"I'll come with you." Gretchen takes Elizabeth's arm, a basket in her other hand.

"It's alright. I'll join the group. You get the corn bread stirred up. Gimme your basket. I'll be quick about it." Women and children stay within sight of the wagons while they look for fuel. Elizabeth feels tension in the group but no one speaks of the Indians until Lucy comes close and whispers in Elizabeth's ear.

"What did James say about the Indians? Jake said I was stupid for bein' scared."

Elizabeth leans over, picks up a stick, and puts it in her basket. "James said not to worry. He thinks they're friendly Pawnee, but I think they might be sizing us up since we're the last train out. Keep your eyes peeled, Lucy."

"Yep. I be doin' that."

After supper, Elizabeth lays out her pallet under the wagon where she feels most secure. She rejects James' offer to sleep inside, knowing how cramped they would be. The sound of distant drums keeps Elizabeth awake. To calm her fears and stop considering the what-ifs, she takes deep breaths and pictures herself in Charles' arms. She can't help wondering if Indians will be a threat to them in their new home.

She awakes just before sunrise and, instead of the usual clanging of pots and whining children, she hears birds chattering as they pluck seeds from the nearby grass. Then she remembers that this is a rare day of rest. Time to do laundry, mend wagons, harnesses, clothing, tired legs, and sore backsides. It's quiet because most people are taking advantage of the extra hour of sleep. Refreshed by a restful night, Elizabeth basks in the luxury of a cool morning without the usual rush.

When she sees James leave the wagon, she wraps her blanket around her shoulders, picks up her pallet and sticks her head inside the wagon. "Alright if I come in?"

Gretchen is dressed but sitting motionless on her mattress with her hands folded in her lap. Her eyes are blank.

"Gretchen?"

She glances up. "Oh, Elizabeth. I didn't hear you. Come on in."

Elizabeth notices that Gretchen frequently seems in a daze. After dressing, Elizabeth finds fuel to add to what's left from the night before, then prepares breakfast.

James stands after eating his cornmeal mush. "I'm taking the wagon down to the Big Blue River to fill the water barrel. After you get what water you need for the laundry, I'll top it off. The river's not far. I should be back by the time you have the fire built up."

Elizabeth starts and stokes the fire while Gretchen takes the washtub from the side of the wagon. Women and older children throughout the camp are also washing clothes and doing other chores. The sun comes up hot and bright. There's a breeze but not the usual wind; a perfect day for drying laundry. While the women are scrubbing, rinsing, wringing, and laying out clean clothes to dry, James is mending a harness, checking wheels, and greasing axles.

At noon, Elizabeth stirs up the fire, still smoldering after heating water for washing. She and Gretchen cook beans and bacon with extra to share. The Young family, consisting of Winnifred, Thomas, and their two daughters, ages nine and eleven, and Mr. Stephens, a scruffy bachelor in his fifties, join them for the noonday meal; each contributing what they have.

Elizabeth looks around the circle of fellow travelers companionably swapping stories. She stares into the glowing fire as the edges of driftwood turn white; hoping she makes friends where she's going.

CHAPTER EIGHT

ENDINGS AND BEGINNINGS

The next few days are uneventful with Elizabeth having no more buzzard or Indian sightings. By midafternoon, eleven days after entering Nebraska, she is, once again, walking along the trail with a heart full of joy, anticipation, and anxiety. After nearly eleven months of separation, the question haunting her is, "Will Charles be there to meet me?"

She turns to Lucy who's walking by her side. "The last of my river crossings is just ahead. I hope the Platte's as dry as Charles predicted. Should be, it's been hot enough."

Lucy nods and Elizabeth decides to share her concerns. "I sure hope Charles found me a place to stay in Grand Island and had time to finish our house."

"I'm sure he did."

"But what if he sent me a letter saying that he's changed his mind and I left before it arrived?"

"It's all goin' to be fine. Look, the wagons are rollin' into the river. It's shallow just like Charles said it would be." The girls come to the river's edge. "Looky there," Lucy points. "It barely covers my toes."

Elizabeth takes off her shoes and steps into the warm, shallow river. "Charles was right about the Platte. Just hope everything else he wrote about is true."

Lucy pats her arm. "Don't you worry none. It'll all work out, Lizabeth. He'll be there. I just knows it."

Grateful for the reassurance, Elizabeth grabs Lucy's hand. "Come on. Let's run across." Holding their skirts up, the girls splash water in all directions as they run across the shallow river. After crossing, they sit on the grassy bank to put on their shoes and socks. Elizabeth sees Gretchen waving at them up ahead. She'd gotten out of the wagon at the crossing for fear the mules might get stuck in the sandy bottom with any extra weight.

When the girls reach her, Gretchen gives them news. "Mr. Nichals says it's just a few more miles before we meet up with the Oregon Trail. He says there'll be a big encampment with other trains and we're stopping early for the night." Although Elizabeth sees the sadness in Gretchen's eyes, her words are comforting. "After we circle, we'll have time to give you a proper send-off."

Elizabeth moves to stand close to Gretchen and pulls Lucy to her side. "I'm sure going to miss you two. James also. You've been good friends and have taught me so much. I was such a greenhorn. I still am, but at least I know a thing or two about living on the prairie. I don't know what I would have done without you." Elizabeth holds back tears and the women have a group hug before walking together in silence until the wagons begin to slow. A few puffy clouds are scuttling across the sky, but the sun is still warm and the air is dry. Up ahead is a large, open space worn bare with the circling of thousands of wagons and the building of many fires. An unfamiliar train has already formed a circle as Elizabeth watches James ease his wagon into position. Elizabeth hopes she has time to freshen up a bit before Charles arrives. *IF he arrives.*

After the wagon is in position, Elizabeth gathers with James, Gretchen, and Lucy. There's a heavy sadness in her breast. "You all mean so much to me," she says with a catch in her voice and tears in her eyes. "I feel like I'm once again leaving family behind."

Gretchen moves closer, reaches into her pocket, and holds out a snippet of baby Louise's hair in the palm of her hand. When she sees it, tears roll down Elizabeth's cheeks. Not trusting her voice, she silently takes the gift and places the blond curl in the gold locket next to her sister's black lock. "Thank you."

Elizabeth walks a few paces away, opens, and reaches into her trunk, which James has taken from the wagon. She takes out her book and removes the tiny, pressed flowers from the pages. She returns to the group and carefully places them in Gretchen's hand. "I picked these flowers from the ground next to Louise's grave. I hope they'll be a remembrance for you."

Tears fill Gretchen's eyes. James looks at the ground. "I'll keep these pressed in our Bible until I can put them in a proper frame. Thank you," Gretchen chokes out.

Seeing Lucy's flushed face, Elizabeth wonders why she's embarrassed. "This here's all I got, Lizabeth." Lucy hands Elizabeth one of the arrowheads she picked up along the trail. "I hope it brings you good luck, not buzzard luck."

Elizabeth gives Lucy a hug. "Thank you. It's a perfect reminder of the time we spent walking together." She pulls out the leather pouch from under her dress and tucks the arrowhead securely inside as she takes out a small, hammered copper brooch in the shape of a maple leaf. She hands the pin to her friend. "I know how much you like pretty things, Lucy. I hope you'll enjoy wearing this. Thank you for being my faithful companion for many miles."

When Lucy embraces her, Elizabeth whispers in her ear, "Don't let Jake harm you. If he does, get away. You hear?"

Lucy replies in a serious voice. "Yes, ma'am." She puts the gift in her pocket then pats it. "And I'll treasure this here broach forever."

When she pulls away from Lucy, Elizabeth spies Charles coming up the trail in a buckboard wagon. Like the covered wagons, it has larger wheels in the back, a high seat, and sides. It's uncovered and pulled by two handsome horses. She waves her arms and calls out. "Charles, over here." Charles looks as she remembers him. Short of stature, black hair and beard. When he returns Elizabeth's wave, her heart races and she feels breathless as she runs to meet him. The underlying fear that he might not show up quickly dissolves and she can finally relax knowing that their plans haven't changed.

Charles jumps down from the wagon and, with a grin on his face, rushes toward Elizabeth and wraps his arms around her. "I'm sure glad to see you."

Elizabeth returns his smile. "I'm glad to see you too." *You have no idea how glad.*

Charles whispers in her ear as they embrace. "I'll give you a proper kiss later." He gives her a light kiss on the lips and she feels heat spread across her cheeks.

As they slowly walk hand in hand toward the group, Elizabeth tells Charles about her friends. "If Gretchen and James seem subdued it's because they recently buried their baby girl."

Charles nods his understanding. "I remember you writing about your father's arrangement with them. I hope they were good traveling companions."

"They were like family."

When the couple arrive at the waiting circle, Charles shakes James' hand and nods toward the ladies. "Thanks for watching out for my girl, James." Then he looks from James to Gretchen. "Elizabeth just told me about your daughter. I'm so sorry."

James looks away for a moment then addresses Charles. "Elizabeth was a great help to my wife and me these past weeks. You can be right proud to take her as your wife."

After Gretchen and Lucy tell Charles how happy they are to finally meet Elizabeth's fiancé, Lucy takes her leave. She turns and waves a final good bye to Elizabeth as she reluctantly shuffles toward her wagon.

"Good luck on your trip to Wyoming. Stay safe. I'll miss you," Elizabeth tells Gretchen while James helps Charles load her trunk and pallet into the buckboard.

She wishes she had time to wash up but Charles is in a hurry to get her to the boarding house. He helps her onto the wagon seat. "Mrs. Seifert likes to serve supper promptly at half past five. I'll tell you more about her on the way into town."

She gives a final wave to her friends. Charles shakes the reigns and urges the horses forward. Alone as last, Elizabeth turns to her sweetheart and gives him her brightest smile. "I missed you."

"I missed you too. You're as lovely as I remember."

Charles' words warm Elizabeth's heart. *I've never been called lovely before. He makes me feel like a real woman.* She smooths Charles' cowlick, then takes his rough, work-worn hand in hers as they bump along the dusty, tumbleweed strewn road to Grand Island.

Charles' muscular arms and the thick, black hair and beard that first attracted her, are on full display as she looks at him out of the corner of her eye. A little laugh escapes when she thinks that soon she'll get a good look at all of him.

"What you gigglin' about?"

Waving off gnats, she feels her face grow warm. "Nothing. Just glad to be sitting next to you."

Charles urges the horses to pick up the pace. "The boarding house where you'll be staying is run by Mrs. Seifert, a widow."

"What's she like?"

Charles shields his eyes from the lowering sun and looks at Elizabeth. "Hard to get to know, that's for sure. She's a short, wiry, crabby woman of about sixty." Elizabeth's eyebrows go up at the picture.

Charles shakes his head. "Don't worry. She'll be nice enough to someone as sweet as you. And, even if she isn't, her palm-sized cinnamon rolls and orange-flavored bread will make up for it. You'll see."

"If she's so unfriendly, how did you get to know her?"

Charles eases the horses to the side of the road to let a farm wagon loaded with hay pass. "I noticed her sitting alone in church, so I went to call on her. Seeing that her garden needed weeding, I put my back to the job. When she found me there on my hands and knees she protested loudly. I told her I used to weed my mutter's garden back in Germany and I missed it. After that she let me weed her garden any time I wanted and we became friends, or, at least, acquaintances."

When she hears Charles refer to his mother as "mutter," Elizabeth realizes how well Charles speaks English considering he had come from Germany just fifteen years earlier. Since her parents were also from Germany, his slight accent is so familiar she barely notices it.

Although she has many stories from the trail to share with Charles, Elizabeth sits quietly as they enter the town. After slowly moving past several blocks of houses, she spies a sign that reads, "Rooms for Ladies". Charles pulls the wagon up in front of a diminutive white cottage.

Elizabeth unclasps her hands and relaxes her shoulders. "What a charming walkway." Gardens, overflowing with mums in fall colors and late-blooming white and pink roses, run up both sides of the long walk from the street to the house.

Charles secures the horses while Elizabeth slowly walks toward the cottage. She notices that the ceiling of the wide front porch is painted blue. When he approaches, she takes Charles' hand. "Look! There's a white wicker, double swing like the one we sat in on my parent's porch."

Charles knocks on the door and Elizabeth hears a bolt scraping, then a key turning. "Double locked?"

"Mrs. Seifert says," Charles mimics a woman's voice as he whispers in Elizabeth's ear. "You can't be too careful where young ladies are concerned." He then raises his shoulders as if to add, that's what she's like.

Mrs. Seifert opens the door. "Come in, come in." She steps aside for the couple to enter.

"This is my fiancé, Elizabeth Schultz."

"Nice to meet you, Dear." Elizabeth sees Mrs. Seifert's frown as she gives her the once-over.

Charles appears oblivious to the scrutiny. "And this is Mrs. Seifert."

"Lovely to meet you, Mrs. Seifert." Embarrassed by her dirty, unkept hair and clothes, she makes an effort to explain. "Please excuse my appearance, ma'am. I've been on the trail with a wagon train for quite some time and didn't have an opportunity to make myself presentable since we just arrived late this afternoon." When Mrs. Seifert doesn't respond, Elizabeth adds, "We didn't want to be late for supper."

Mrs. Seifert continues to give Elizabeth a stern look. "We'll get you a bath after supper. There are clean sheets on your bed, you know."

Elizabeth's glad Charles forewarned her about the woman and doesn't take offense. Mrs. Seifert is just as she imagined her. Short and thin with gray hair pulled into a tight bun with no loose strands. She's wearing practical brown oxfords and a simple gray dress covered with a blindingly white apron. Her small, black eyes dart around, and Elizabeth has the uneasy feeling she can see straight through to her heart—assessing whether or not it's pure.

"What are you waiting for, Charles? Fetch Elizabeth's trunk, and whatever else she has, out of the wagon so you can wash up for supper. The horses should be fine out front for a while."

With heels clacking, Mrs. Seifert briskly walks across the gleaming oak floors of the sparsely furnished parlor to the adjoining dining room where she offers a brisk introduction to two ladies already seated at the table. Elizabeth continues to follow closely behind. "These are my long-term guests, Lydia and her younger sister, Lena." Nodding at the girls, she motions Elizabeth to come forward. "This is Elizabeth who is about to marry Charles. Because of their upcoming nuptials, I've made the exception of inviting him to supper, which will be slightly delayed due to their arrival. We will eat in ten minutes." That settled, Mrs. Seifert shows her new guest the outhouse and the pump for washing up. When Elizabeth reappears with scrubbed face and hands, Mrs. Seifert points to a chair.

Charles walks into the dining room. "I put your trunk inside the front door, Elizabeth. We can haul it upstairs after supper." Charles quickly makes his way to the back porch to wash then takes his place at the table.

When everyone is seated, Mrs. Siefert looks around her table. "Well, now that we're finally all here, we can say grace."

Elizabeth squeezes her eyes tight in case Mrs. Seifert is checking on her.

After saying grace, Mrs. Seifert begins passing the serving dishes. "Charles, do you remember Lydia and Lena?"

Charles looks across the table. "Good evening ladies. It's good to see you again."

Lydia, a blue-eyed blonde with apple cheeks, a turned up nose, and ears that protrude slightly, speaks first. "My sister and I are looking forward to getting to know you, Elizabeth."

She hands a platter to Charles. "We teach in a two-room school house, just outside of town. I teach seventh through twelfth in one room and Lena teaches first through sixth in the other."

Elizabeth looks over at Lena. "How long have you two been living here?"

Lena holds her hand in front of her mouth as she answers the question. "We've lived here six months." Elizabeth thinks Lena looks to be the studious type with wire-rimmed glasses, dark blonde hair bundled into a net at the back of her head, and the same protruding ears as her sister.

Elizabeth does her best to follow the conversation as the girls continue to talk about their school and pupils, but her attention is on the thick beef stew she's ladling onto her plate. It's been a long time since she's eaten a real dinner, sitting at a table. She impatiently waits to spear the potatoes, carrots, onions, and beef cooked in a rich brown gravy. Mrs. Seifert passes her a plate of still-warm, sliced bread, smelling of oranges, accompanied by a dish of golden butter. Elizabeth's mouth waters. As she waits to start eating, she practically swoons when she spies peach cobbler cooling on a nearby windowsill. After all the food is passed, Mrs. Seifert gives the signal to begin. Elizabeth can see that Charles is also pacing himself, trying not to stuff food into his mouth as fast as possible. Conversation halts as everyone eats. Elizabeth is careful to not talk with food in her mouth.

"May I have seconds?" Charles asks politely after wiping his plate clean with a slice of soft, fragrant bread.

"May I too?" Elizabeth knows it's not ladylike to eat so much but she can't resist.

"Of course. I'm pleased you're both enjoying this simple supper." Mrs. Seifert shifts her beady eyes in Elizabeth's direction, leans over, and whispers in her ear. "Don't forget, Elizabeth, you'll be wearing your corset tomorrow."

Mortified, Elizabeth turns red but says nothing as she focuses her attention on ladling a second helping of stew onto her plate.

The three girls take the dirty dishes to the kitchen. Returning to her seat, Elizabeth watches intently as Mrs. Seifert scoops the peach cobbler into dessert dishes and places a small pitcher of heavy cream on the table. Elizabeth savors every spoonful of peaches, which explode with the flavor of late summer in her mouth. "This is the best meal I've had since leaving Illinois, and your peach cobbler is the most delicious that I've had in my whole life! Thank you."

Mrs. Seifert lowers her eyes and Elizabeth can see a tight smile spreading across her face, "You're quite welcome."

Lydia and Lena begin clearing the dessert dishes. When Elizabeth rises to help, Lena intervenes. "Lydia and I will do the clean up tonight, Elizabeth. You and Charles get your trunk upstairs."

Lydia adds, "Then go out and sit on the porch. It's a lovely evening."

Elizabeth looks to Mrs. Seifert. "Do as the girls say. Help Charles get your things upstairs. I don't want anyone tripping over that trunk."

She turns and looks at Charles who is dutifully refolding his napkin. "It's the second room on the right, Charles. I'll expect you to return presently."

The couple quickly do as they're told then escape to the front porch swing. Sitting close together with their hands entwined, they make plans for the next few days. "We'll go to the church in the morning so you can meet the pastor and discuss wedding details. I think you'll like Reverend Shell," Charles says reassuringly. "He's a tall Texan with a bit of an accent."

"I'm sure he will do just fine. Have you invited friends?"

Charles takes his time to respond as he gazes into a sky that's still pink from the setting sun. An older couple nod as they walk by with a small dog on a leash. The evening is cool with the scent of wood smoke in the air. Wind chimes tinkle softly in the distance. "Well, yes. Tomorrow, after our visit to the church, you'll meet my best man, Ron Pollock. I met Ron soon after I settled here."

This is the first time Elizabeth has heard about a best man. She leans forward and looks at Charles. "Tell me about him."

"Ron owns a large cattle ranch north of the fort. I met him when he came to town for supplies that included boots." Elizabeth remains quiet, encouraging Charles to say more. There are crinkles at the edges of his eyes as he remembers the occasion. "Not only did he buy a pair of boots for himself, he also bought them for several of his ranch hands. It was a real good day for me. We only see each other occasionally, but Ron and I have become close friends. I was delighted when he agreed to make the more than eighty mile trip from north of Burwell to witness our wedding and give me a bit of moral support."

Elizabeth gives Charles a gentle elbow to the ribs. "So, you need moral support, do you?" She lightheartedly jokes with Charles but feels a spark of anxiety as she considers the possibility of him getting cold feet. She wonders about what life would be like if she was stranded in Grand Island and had to live with Mrs. Seifert and the girls. She gives herself a little shake. *Stop it! You're being ridiculous! He's contacted a pastor for heaven's sake!*

"Is everything alright, Elizabeth? Are you chilled?"

"I'm fine. It's a lovely evening, but I do need to get in to take my bath. I don't want to keep Mrs. Seifert waiting."

Charles puts his arm around her shoulders. "I love you, Elizabeth. I've been looking forward to this day and our wedding for a long time." He pulls her to him and gives her a gentle kiss.

Breathless, Elizabeth whispers, "Me too."

After they leave the swing, Charles pulls her into his arms and gives her a full-body embrace. "I'll pick you up at ten. We can walk to the church from here."

Elizabeth feels giddy with relief as she returns Charles' seductive hug. "I'll be ready." A giggle escapes as she opens the door, looks back at Charles and smiles. "Good night, I love you too."

The next morning, Elizabeth feels like a new woman with clean hair, a scrubbed body, and wearing a freshly pressed dress over a corset, camisole, shift, and petticoats. She even sees respect in Mrs. Seifert's critical eyes when she greets her in a kitchen filled with the tantalizing scent of fresh-baked cinnamon rolls.

Elizabeth and the sisters set the table and fill coffee cups for an early breakfast. While Mrs. Seifert finishes scrambling eggs, Lydia looks across the table at her new housemate. "If you don't mind my asking, how old are you, Elizabeth?"

"I'm turning fifteen in a few days." She sees a shocked look on the sisters' faces and tries to deflect the issue of her age with a question. "And you two?"

"I'm nineteen and Lena's seventeen."

Elizabeth's glad to have girls close to her age to talk to. "What brought you out West, besides the teaching?"

Lydia looks to her sister who nods for her to answer. "We came out here thinking life was going to be exciting but, here we are, stuck in a small farming community just like the one we left back in Ohio."

Lena chimes in. "We're making the best of it, but respectable men are scarce. You're lucky you got yourself a good one."

Mrs. Seifert arrives with a plate stacked with frosted cinnamon rolls and another filled with scrambled eggs. After grace is said, Elizabeth picks up the conversation. "I'm sure the right man will come along. At least you're doing what you love."

"I hope you're right." Lena looks skeptical.

"A year ago, I was like you two—wondering if I would ever find a good man." Elizabeth looks down at her hands. "To be honest, today is the first day I truly feel confident that I have a future with Charles. I'm still uncertain about life on the prairie but I do know I'll have someone to share it with.

CHAPTER NINE

A WEDDING AND A SEND OFF

The next two days go by in a blur of activity. Elizabeth and Charles meet with the pastor, choose music for their wedding, invite Mrs. Seifert to play the organ, and spend evenings on the porch renewing their relationship.

While Charles packs up his tools, clothing, and closes his shop, Elizabeth is busy washing and ironing her meager wardrobe and reorganizing her trunk. Still exhausted from her trip, she allows herself short afternoon naps to renew her energy. She wants to be at her best when she starts her new life.

On Thursday evening, when Elizabeth comes inside after spending an hour on the porch with Charles, she finds Lena and Lydia having tea in the parlor. "May I join you?"

They respond as one. "Of course." Lydia retrieves a cup from the sideboard and pours tea. "Here you are. It's still hot."

Elizabeth feels the warmth of the tea through the cup along with tender feelings toward the two sisters. The parlor is quiet with one lamp burning on a nearby table. The breeze has picked up and Elizabeth again hears wind chimes in the distance. She closes her eyes and sits back in her chair, luxuriating in the comfort of the moment as the sisters quietly sip their tea. When she open her eyes, she looks from one sister to the other. "I have a question for you ladies. I'm wondering if you would like to be my bridesmaids?"

The sisters smile at one another. Lydia replies. "Us? Bridesmaids?"

"I realize we've known each other for less than a week, but I'd like to think we've become friends and I'd love to have you stand beside me at our wedding." Elizabeth feels a lump in her throat and tears gathering at the corners of her eyes.

"Of course! Thanks for asking us," the sisters chorus.

Elizabeth looks at her lap and hastily wipes away her tears with her thumbs. "You're quite welcome. Thanks for saying yes." She clears her throat. "Mrs. Seifert has agreed to play the church organ so our whole little house will be there." Her eyes well up again and she tucks her trembling lower lip between her teeth. She takes a sip of tea in an effort to control her sad feelings. "Having you all there will make up a bit for not having my family with me."

Lena smiles at Elizabeth. "How'd you meet Charles anyways?" She reddens when Elizabeth doesn't answer right away. She looks at the clock on the mantle then back at Elizabeth. "Since we're going to be a part of your wedding, I figured you wouldn't mind my asking."

Elizabeth gives Lena a reassuring smile. "Of course I don't mind. I'd love to share our story with you." She takes her handkerchief from her pocket and blows her nose. "Last summer Charles visited his uncle Max in Galesburg, Illinois, my hometown. We met at a barn dance. The next day, he came to meet my parents and we started seeing each other."

Lena leans in. "Your folks liked him right off?"

Her intensity amuses Elizabeth. "They weren't pleased about me seeing an older man but Father was impressed with Charles' record of serving with the New York Infantry in the Civil War and the fact he's a bootmaker." She takes a breath as she considers the rest of her story, deciding that there's no point in talking about her lack of prospects. "My mother was comforted by the fact that he's from the Bavarian region of Germany since she's from Munich. Just before Charles returned to Nebraska, he asked my father for permission to marry me. Now..."

Laura interrupts. "Weren't you wanting to finish school?"

Elizabeth looks down as guilty feelings surface. "I was a grade ahead and I knew that if I worked hard, I could complete the tenth grade in the spring, which I did. My parents wanted me to be a teacher." The sisters nod but remain quiet. "Even though I didn't graduate, I hope I can teach in the future. Probably not this year, since school has already started, but perhaps next year unless I have a baby by then."

"Goodness, a baby," Laura whispers to no one in particular.

Lydia looks down at her scuffed, brown shoes. "Isn't your mother sad that she won't see you getting married?"

Elizabeth takes a sip of tea before answering. "My mother was disappointed that we'd be married in Nebraska, but Charles said he couldn't take time away from his business now that he has a wife to think of. Mother still isn't happy about the circumstances, but I'm not going to let it take away from the joy of our wedding day. She'll come around eventually."

Seeing another question in Lena's eyes, she reassures her. "It's okay to ask me anything, Lena. What's on your mind?"

"If Charles is from Germany, why doesn't he have a German name? Horn is definitely not German."

"I don't know." Elizabeth wonders why she never considered this. "I'll ask him. There's so much to learn about each other. I can't wait!"

The sisters roll their eyes, bid their friend good night, then climb the stairs to bed. Sitting alone, Elizabeth contemplates her future.

When Saturday morning finally arrives, Elizabeth has butterflies in her stomach as she dresses for her wedding. Her hands are cold and clammy making it difficult to fasten the tiny buttons on her dress. Despite her nerves, she feels content that the bridal party is a respectable size with three attendants, organ music, an ordained minister, his wife and two daughters, plus a few of Charles' friends in attendance. But a tear splashes onto her dress as she thinks of her family.

She dabs at her eyes, then squints into the tiny mirror above the dresser and purses her lips. Her once porcelain complexion is a shade darker and her nose is still peeling from multiple sunburns. Dismissing the negatives, she gives the girl in the mirror a pep talk. "By the standards of the people back home, you might be considered handsome at best, manly and unattractive at worst. But don't forget, out here your strength and height are an asset." Looking more closely at her image, she continues. "You look rested, your hair is thick and shiny, your cheeks are pink. And besides, Charles says you're lovely—that's all that matters." Even with the pep talk, her nerves ensue. She wonders if all brides are this nervous and what it will be like to sleep with Charles.

Elizabeth smooths her voile dress, tugs on her cream-colored carriage boots, then slips on her long, white, kid gloves. She takes a last look in the little mirror and smiles at her reflection, thinking that even her mother would approve. On the way downstairs, she spots Lena waiting for her in the parlor, holding a white rose.

Lena intercepts her at the bottom of the stairs. "Do you mind if I pin this rose in your hair? I snipped it fresh this morning from Mrs. Seifert's garden."

"Please do. Thank you." With the rose in her hair, Elizabeth steps back. "How do I look?"

Lena looks Elizabeth over. "Lovely. The violet dress brings out the blue in your eyes."

Her friend's gaze and words give Elizabeth confidence that her ensemble is complete. Just as she thinks she's ready to leave for church, Lydia bounds down the stairs with another rose entwined with a white satin ribbon. She presents the rose to Elizabeth. "Would you like to carry this?"

"How thoughtful. What would I do without my bridesmaids?"

When they scurry out the door ahead of her, Elizabeth notices that the sisters' dresses are identical in style. They're made of simple cotton with scooped necklines, ruffles around the bottom and, slightly outdated, mutton sleeves. Lena's is pink, Lydia's is yellow. They're wearing their practical, low heeled, teacher shoes.

Mrs. Seifert left earlier to practice the organ, and Elizabeth's glad that the sisters are accompanying her to the church. When they arrive, she sits in the vestibule and watches the sisters proceed to the front near the altar just as Charles and Ron enter from a side door. She peeks around the corner to get a better look at Charles who's wearing a dark, western-style suit, white shirt, bolo tie, and black, hand-tooled boots.

Elizabeth sits quietly, wishing her father was there to walk her down the aisle. While nervously awaiting her entrance, she notices her friends giggling together, which brings a smile to her lips. In addition to eyeing Charles, she can tell they're both smitten with the best man. She also thinks that Ron, with his broad shoulders, sandy hair, blue eyes, and high cheekbones, looks handsome in a dove gray suit and matching high-heeled boots, but she only has eyes for Charles.

Mrs. Seifert plays the "Bridal Chorus" from Wagner's Lohengrin, often called, "Here Comes the Bride", and Elizabeth begins to walk slowly down the aisle, holding both hands around the rose to keep them from shaking. When she nears the altar, she notices her groom shifting from foot to foot beside his best man. She gives him her brightest smile then joins him in front of Reverend Shell. He takes her hand and holds it throughout the service. Charles' hand feels warm and solid, giving her comfort and reassurance.

Mercifully, the sisters refrain from giggling during the ceremony, at least until Reverend Shell concludes. "I'm pleased to introduce y'all to Mr. and Mrs. Charles Horn." He then turns to Charles. "You may kiss the bride." Elizabeth doesn't mind the giggling that follows the kiss. She feels radiant and full of joy as Mrs. Seifert ushers them all down the aisle with "Mendelssohn's Wedding March" from *A Midsummer Night's Dream.*

Immediately following the wedding, the bridal party and guests make their way to Mrs. Seifert's cottage. As the guests settle into the parlor, Mrs. Seifert beckons to the sisters. Elizabeth watches while she lays out a white lace tablecloth on the trestle table. The sisters bring in glasses of pink lemonade and plates of angel food cake. Whipped cream and preserved strawberries sit in cut glass bowls ready to crown the cake.

The pastor's wife sits next to Elizabeth on the sofa. She's a wide woman and Elizabeth moves over to make room for her. She smells of violets and looks like Mrs. Claus with white hair gathered into a messy bun, spectacles, rosy cheeks, and a double chin. "What a lovely wedding and reception, Mrs. Horn."

Startled upon hearing her new name for the first time, Elizabeth acknowledges the compliment then glances around the room. "Seems the men are having a bit of a struggle balancing plates on their knees."

Mrs. Shell leans closer to Elizabeth. "Indeed they are, but not for long. They'll soon make their way to the porch. They always do."

"Really? And why would that be?"

"To smoke their cigars and nip from their flasks of whiskey, of course. You'll soon learn the ways of the West, my dear."

Elizabeth looks across at the pastor. "Will the reverend be joining them?"

"He would if he could but, as you can see, Mrs. Seifert has him pinned down with questions about church doings."

Elizabeth frowns. "I don't recall my father ever leaving a gathering like this. Don't you think leaving is a bit rude?"

Mrs Shell presses her hanky to her lips. "It's not what I think that matters. It's the reality of men. When they get together, they tend to descend to the lowest common denominator—if you know what I mean."

Elizabeth speculates on who the "lowest common denominator" might be. As she looks from one man to another, she sees them politely placing their dirty plates on the reception table, then walk out the front door, just as the pastor's wife predicted.

Mrs. Shell looks closely at Elizabeth "I imagine you haven't had much experience with men. How old are you anyway?"

Shyly, Elizabeth twists her shiny, gold wedding band. "I'll be fifteen in a few days. I know I have a lot to learn about men and…" Elizabeth's clears her throat. "…other things."

Mrs. Shells pats Elizabeth's hand. "Your new husband seems like a nice fella. Don't judge these men too harshly. We do things a bit differently out here. Besides, this might be the last time Charles sees his friends for a long time."

When Charles returns from the porch, he puts his arm around Elizabeth's waist. "I think everyone's having a nice time, don't you, my dear?"

Not meeting his eyes, Elizabeth mumbles her reply. "I guess so."

Charles' friends are the first to leave. Ron nods toward Elizabeth and shakes Charles' hand as he wishes them good luck. Just before he steps out the door, the sisters rush up. Lena attempts to flutter her eyelashes as she tilts her head to the side. "We do hope you'll look us up the next time you're in town, Mr. Pollock."

"I'll be back for supplies right after Thanksgiving. I'll come by and say a howdy-do."

Lydia steps up. "We'd like that. Until then…" She holds out her hand and Ron gives it a gentle shake.

"Good day, ladies." Elizabeth catches Charles winking in Ron's direction as the sisters run up the stairs.

A few minutes later, Elizabeth hears Mrs. Seifert suggesting it's time for the stragglers to take their leave. "Church will come early tomorrow, Reverend Shell. You wouldn't want to be late."

Although they're officially man and wife, Elizabeth is reconciled to their sleeping arrangements. She stands close to Charles on the porch as they wistfully say their good-byes. "I'm sorry your room is out of bounds and my quarters are too small and uncomfortable for a proper first night. We'll be together soon enough." Charles puts his arms around Elizabeth and draws her to him. He gives her a deep, lingering kiss; the likes of which she's never experienced. The heat generated by the kiss melts away all of Elizabeth's foreboding about Charles' love for her.

CHAPTER TEN

ON BECOMING A REAL WOMAN

After enjoying the best night's sleep she's had in a long time, Elizabeth uses the chamber pot, pours water into the basin, and washes up. Still in her shift, she lays out her clothes for church. When she shakes out her below-the-ankle, navy blue skirt, a black and white cameo pin drops to the floor. *My mother's precious cameo! What a wonderful surprise. I do miss her so. I hope she and the new baby are doing well.*

Elizabeth shrugs off thoughts of home as she puts on her chemise, pantalets, corset, and two petticoats. She tucks her stockings into her pantalets and puts on a snuggly fitted, white, high-necked blouse with long full sleeves. She pins the cameo at the neck then brushes and braids her hair, making a neat nest on top of her head.

She pulls back the lace curtains and greets a new day. Finally, the anxiety about her wedding is behind her and she's ready for the next chapter of her life.

Mrs. Seifert is at church practicing the organ so Elizabeth and the sisters help themselves to cinnamon rolls and coffee left for them in the kitchen. She's putting her dishes in the sink when she hears a knock on the front door and rushes to open it.

"Good morning, Mrs. Horn."

Elizabeth gives a little curtsy. "Good morning, Mr. Horn."

As they walk to church, followed by the sisters, Elizabeth notices that Charles is dressed for travel. He's wearing brown cotton work pants held up by suspenders, a checkered, long-sleeved shirt, and a brown felt hat. "I'm sorry we're not getting the early start you'd hoped for, Charles. I just couldn't say no to the pastor when he asked us to attend church."

Charles nods. "It's alright. We'll make up the time." Elizabeth can see that he's looking at her clothing. "Are you ready for the trip?"

"I am. I'll change clothes when we return from church. How about you?"

"All my worldly possessions are in the buckboard along with a surprise."

"A surprise? For me? For our new home? Oh, I do love surprises!" *For heaven's sake. You're a married woman. Stop gushing like a schoolgirl!*

When they arrive at the church, they slide into the back pew, anxious to get away immediately after the service. Elizabeth sits between Charles and Lydia. During the offering, Lydia whispers in Elizabeth's ear. "Excited about tonight?" Elizabeth can feel her cheeks grow hot and doesn't answer thinking that, this time, Lydia has stepped over the line with asking personal questions.

The service seems to last forever. When it's finally over and they leave the church, Elizabeth watches Charles striding purposefully in the direction of the livery stable. She hurries to catch up with Mrs. Seifert and the girls.

After changing into travel clothes, Elizabeth is busy making cheese sandwiches when Lena runs into the kitchen to announce Charles' arrival. Elizabeth quickly finishes preparing their picnic lunch and rushes to the street.

Charles bows. "Your carriage awaits, ma'am."

Mrs. Seifert bustles forward and, while she and Charles chat, Elizabeth takes time to study the horses. She hadn't particularly noticed them on her ride into town when her eyes were fully on Charles. But now, she's admiring their long manes and tails, their compact, sturdy-looking bodies. She sees that they're nearly a matched pair with shiny brown coats. She strokes the white star markings between their eyes.

Charles moves to stand next to her. "I bought these western mustangs because their breed is known to intensely bond with their owners and they're nearly as strong as mules. Like them?"

"They're beautiful."

Elizabeth shifts her gaze to the back of the buckboard where she sees a large object covered with a tarp. "What's that?"

"That's a combination wedding and birthday gift. Come close and I'll show you." With a flourish, Charles whisks off the canvas to reveal a beautifully crafted, walnut, cane-backed rocking chair with curved arms and a rounded top. "With help from Miss Ruth, a veteran chair caner, I made this rocker for you, Elizabeth. May it give you many hours of comfort and relaxation."

Elizabeth imagines rocking a baby to sleep. "It's beautiful! Thank you, Darling. I'll treasure it forever."

"When's your birthday?" Mrs. Seifert asks as she admires the rocker.

"I'll turn fifteen on September thirtieth. Just four days from now." The sisters, who've been quietly observing, wish Elizabeth a happy birthday.

Charles loads Elizabeth's belongings into the wagon then helps her onto the seat. "It was so nice meeting you all." Elizabeth chokes out with tears in her eyes as she considers how these three were stand-ins for her absent family. "You made our wedding special. We'll never forget your kindness." Even Mrs. Seifert dabs at her eyes with a hanky as the couple wave their good-byes.

Finally on the way to their new home, Charles and Elizabeth travel in companionable silence until they reach the edge of town and Charles asks about her family. "I remember your oldest brother being three years younger than you but I've forgotten the ages of the others."

"Yes, Ernest is eleven, Mary is nine, Reda and August are eight and six."

Elizabeth looks to see if Charles is still paying attention. "And, as I wrote to you, Mother was to have another baby in early August. I'm looking forward to getting mail when we reach the fort. I'm sure there will be news of the new baby." She continues. "I feel bad about leaving Mother but, after helping out with the others, I'd like the next baby I'm caring for to be ours."

Charles smiles at Elizabeth. "Remember that it was your mother who encouraged your father to agree to our marriage and you leaving home. I'm sure she'll have the help she needs."

Elizabeth feels her heart speed up and heat in her cheeks. *Perhaps I've been too bold in saying this. Will Charles think less of me for leaving home at this time? Strange that he didn't respond to what I said about having a baby.* Thinking that she's revealed enough for now, Elizabeth abruptly changes the subject. "Where did you get the horses?"

"Shiriki, a Pawnee friend of mine, traded me the horses for boots."

Elizabeth's curiosity is piqued. "How did you meet him?"

"He's a scout and hunter for the army and I met him at the fort. He and his mother stayed behind when much of their tribe were driven out to a reservation in Oklahoma. He also helped me build our home and—"

Elizabeth grabs Charles' sleeve and points to a kettle of buzzards flying out of a nearby osage hedge row. "Look!"

"Ahh, that's just a bunch of buzzards. You act as if you've never seen one before."

"Oh, I've seen them before," Elizabeth says, sounding harsher than she intends. "I saw them on the trail just after we entered Nebraska and then again the day we buried Baby Louise. I'm not normally superstitious but they feel like bad luck to me."

Charles turns and looks at Elizabeth. The look makes her feel foolish. She knows her fear of buzzards is irrational but she doesn't want judgment from Charles. She wants him to accept her as she is; buzzard-fear and all. She explains her reasons as she did to Lucy, then adds, "My grandpa used to say things like, 'Damned if it weren't for buzzard luck, I'd have no luck at all'."

She juts her chin out a bit. "He thought they were bad luck and so do I."

Even though Charles doesn't seem to be buying her explanation, she appreciates his reassuring words. "Don't worry, it's just an ugly bird. They like to perch in those osage hedges. You made it safe and sound this far, didn't you?"

"Well, yes, but look at those beady, black eyes. . . ." Elizabeth can tell Charles thinks she's being dramatic so she says no more as they continue their journey down the dusty, rutted road.

Their once companionable silence nows seems awkward. Elizabeth feels tension between wanting to prove herself as a capable adult and the need to be authentically herself. She asks a question to move away from the moment. "Tell me more about where we're going today."

"We're heading to St. Paul, a small town about twenty-five miles north."

Charles flicks the reins when the horses slow as they approach a small hill. He looks over at Elizabeth. She sees smile lines around his eyes. "We're staying the night at the home of Mayor and Mrs. E.F. Clapp."

Excited about this revelation, Elizabeth bounces a little on the buckboard seat. "What a wonderful surprise! How do you know the Clapps well enough to get us invited to stay overnight in their home?"

Charles swats at a horsefly as he seems to consider his answer. Elizabeth realizes she's going to have to learn to be patient with Charles' slow, thoughtful manner. "I met the mayor when I returned from Fort Hartsuff after firming up my position there. We were in Stillman Hazeltine's General Store when Clapp noticed my boots and asked about them. We struck up a conversation and he invited me to supper." Charles stops talking to focus on the uneven road, then continues. "The mayor's wife, Mary as I recall, is real nice. They said if I ever came through St. Paul again, they'd like to have me stay the night. I told them about our upcoming marriage, and they offered to have us stay with them when we traveled through." Charles pauses. "It's a lovely house." He winks. "We'll even have our own big bed in a room by ourselves."

The news and seductive wink make Elizabeth's heart thump faster. "I thought when you talked about plans, you meant you knew of a good place to camp. I never dreamed of having a roof over our heads and a bed!"

Charles removes his hat and waves away a swarm of gnats. "The look on your face when I told you was priceless. I'm glad you like the arrangements I made for our first night."

Other than a break for lunch and two more to water and rest the horses, the remainder of the day is uneventful. It's after five and Elizabeth's stomach growls when they finally approach St. Paul. She's looking forward to supper with the Clapps and, although she feels butterflies when she thinks of it, what will follow. "Oh, Charles," Elizabeth exclaims when he pulls up to the Clapp's house. "What a beautiful house!"

Charles reigns in the horses. "Wait until you see the inside."

Elizabeth takes a small satchel of overnight necessities from the wagon then pauses to admire the yard while Charles secures the horses.

Like Mrs. Seifert's, the house is set back from the street with a narrow cobblestone walk leading to a white curved arbor covered in dazzling orange trumpet vines. The two-story house is clad with white wooden shingles. Pink, fuchsia, red, orange, and yellow zinnias are across the front. Butterflies and hummingbirds are bobbing in and out of the colorful blooms. Before Charles can knock, Mr. Clapp opens the door and greets them with his wife just behind.

"May I present my wife, Elizabeth." Charles indicates his friends. "These are our generous hosts, Mr. and Mrs. Clapp."

After the brief introductions, Clapp whisks Charles off to the livery stable, assuring him that their horses and belongings will be safe there.

Mrs. Clapp invites Elizabeth inside. "So nice to meet you, Dear."

"May I leave my bag by the door?"

"Of course. You can take it up later." A short, plump woman in her early seventies, Mrs. Clapp exudes warmth and kindness. She has steel gray hair parted down the middle with braided bundles over each ear. Her smooth, rosy cheeks and spectacles remind Elizabeth of the grandmother she's unlikely to see again.

Before offering her a seat, she looks deep into Elizabeth's eyes. "Do you mind if I give you a hug?" Elizabeth leans down to receive and return Mrs. Clapp's firm embrace. Her hostess draws back from the hug with a sad expression on her face. "Excuse me for staring, but you remind me of my youngest daughter, Gwen."

"Does she live nearby?"

Mrs. Clapp is quiet for a moment. Her shoulders sag and she takes a breath. As with Charles, Elizabeth exercises patience while she waits for the answer to, what she thinks, is a simple question.

She looks down at her hands, then up at Elizabeth. "She died in May giving birth to our last grandchild."

Somewhat flummoxed by such an unexpected and personal revelation, Elizabeth leans over and hugs her new friend again. "I'm so sorry for your loss. I can't even imagine what it must be like to lose a child."

Mrs. Clapp straightens, clears her throat, and smooths her dark maroon dress that features a crocheted, white color. Elizabeth can tell she's embarrassed and wants to return to the joy of the moment. She indicates a comfortable-looking settee covered in a smooth, beige fabric. "You've barely arrived and I'm already wishing you and Charles could stay longer. I do believe time spent with you might help mend my broken heart."

Elizabeth pats her arm. "We're tonic for each other. I'm missing my mother and that hug did me a world of good. I'm glad we can enjoy each other's company." She looks around the room. "Your home is beautiful. I have to admit, I'm a little apprehensive about living in a sod house."

"Your time will come, Dear. Enjoy this stage of your life. Don't be wishing it away."

After Mrs. Clapp asks about Elizabeth's family, she suggests they move to the kitchen so she can finish preparing supper. In less than an hour, Elizabeth hears men's voices in the parlor.

By the time the men take their seats after washing up outside, the women are seated at the long dining room table. The white, linen tablecloth, napkins, china, and silver gleam alongside an array of steaming plates and bowls.

Mr. Clapp, a bear of a man with thick white hair combed straight back, clean shaven except for a robust mustache, and sparkling brown eyes, bows his head, and the others follow.

"Thank you, Lord, for our abundance in friends and food. Bless this new marriage and this couple as they begin their life together. Amen."

Mrs. Clapp passes Elizabeth a large platter. "I hope you like pheasant baked with brown sugar. Ernest was out early this morning and came home with these fat beauties."

"When it's a good year for corn, it's a good year for pheasants," Ernest says with a throaty chuckle, his mustache twitching.

Not familiar with pheasant, Elizabeth tentatively takes a bite. Thinking the taste is a cross between the dark meat of chicken and duck, with the added sweetness of the brown sugar, she continues to eat with exuberance.

Mr. Clapp gives her a word of caution. "Be a bit careful, Elizabeth. There could be buckshot."

When the conversation turns to farming and the weather, Elizabeth tunes out as she admires her surroundings including comfortable, sturdy furniture, a fireplace with a clock on the mantle, braided rugs in browns and oranges. She appreciates the simple room that's devoid of the knickknacks, doilies, and other ostentatious decor of the Victorian homes to which she's accustomed. She hopes to have a similar home someday—large enough for a family yet small enough to feel warm and cozy. She can even imagine children crawling across the polished, wide-plank wooden floors. As she thinks about future babies, she feels a glow spread across her cheeks. When she notices Mrs. Clapp looking at her, she redirects her attention. "Please tell me about the wine, it's lovely."

"It's my own elderberry brew," Mr. Clapp says with pride in his voice. "The missus picks the berries and I make the wine. I'm glad you're enjoying it, my dear."

Elizabeth smiles to herself. *Little do they know this is my first glass of wine on a night of firsts.*

When the men retire to the front porch for a nip of brandy, Elizabeth helps her hostess with the dishes. As soon as they're dried and put away, Elizabeth asks, "Do you mind if I retire a bit early?" She sees a knowing-smile spread across Mrs. Clapp's face.

"Of course not, Dear. Your room is the first one on the right. There's a pitcher with water and a basin; the outhouse is just beyond the back porch."

Elizabeth places the dishtowel on the sink. "Thanks again for the lovely dinner."

"Before you go up, do you mind if I give you a bit of advice?"

Elizabeth feels her heart jump as she wonders if she's going to speak to her about sex. She nervously sits on a bench near the back door. "Of course not."

"I can see that you're a woman who speaks her mind. Take that woman with you into your marriage. I know it's not what proper Victorian women are taught but, believe me, telling your husband what's on your mind will get you started on the right foot."

Elizabeth clears her throat. "I appreciate your advice, Mrs. Clapp. Frankly, being able to be myself is one reason I was drawn to coming out here."

"Well, I know it's not my place to say anything but I want you and Charles to have the kind of marriage Ernest and I have had all these years."

When Elizabeth rises from the bench, Mary smiles up at her. "Now, go make yourself beautiful for your husband."

Elizabeth uses the outhouse, retrieves her satchel from

inside the front door, hurries up the stairs, then enters the bedroom Mrs. Clapp indicated. She sighs with pleasure as she takes in it's lovely charm. The room is tucked up under the eaves and has sloping, pale blue walls accented with white crown molding. The walnut bed is covered with a beautiful medallion quilt made with a blue and white chintz fabric with borders of patterned blocks that build out to the edges. Elizabeth appreciates the workmanship because her mother taught her to quilt as soon as she learned to stitch a straight line. A chair, matching dresser, and washstand complete the room.

After washing up, Elizabeth takes a clean shift out of the travel bag. She takes her hair down and brushes the prerequisite one hundred strokes until it shines. Then she turns down the quilt and climbs into the big, four poster bed. Nervous, excited, and a little scared, Elizabeth tries to relax into the soft feather mattress. She closes her eyes and takes a deep breath. Just as she's slowly exhaling, she hears the doorknob turn. She opens her eyes and her heart skips a beat.

Charles beams when he enters the room. "You look like a queen on her throne in that beautiful bed and I'm going to treat you like one." He leans down, lightly kisses Elizabeth, and whispers in her ear. "Don't worry, I'll be gentle." Charles unbuttons his shirt and throws it across the back of a nearby chair. When he sits on the bed to take off his britches, Elizabeth reaches out and gently moves her fingers down a raised, uneven scar that zig zags across Charles' right shoulder.

"That's a mighty long scar you have. What happened?"

He deflects his wife's question. "Got one on my thigh too but don't worry, I'm as fit as a fiddle. You'll see." He then climbs into bed and takes his wife into his arms. His kisses are soft and gentle. Surprised by her body's response, she's emboldened to run her hands over Charles' chest. When he can tell she's ready, he gently enters her. She feels a moment of pain but as they slowly move together she abandons herself to the intense delight. When they are both satisfied, Elizabeth snuggles close to her husband. Her hair is fanned out over the pillow.

With moonlight streaming through the window, Charles gets up on one elbow and looks at Elizabeth. "Your hair is beautiful. This is the first time I've seen it down." When she doesn't respond, Charles lays back and asks, "Are you okay, Darling?"

She looks up from his shoulder where her head is resting. "I had no idea it would be like that." She can feel her cheeks grow hot as she takes Mrs. Clapp's advice. "I'm much better than okay, Charles. I'm wonderful."

The next morning, Elizabeth tries to act matter of fact and hides her broad smile when Mrs. Clapp greets her in the kitchen. "You look well rested," she says with a grin. "How about a hearty breakfast of pancakes with molasses, thick sliced bacon, and fresh raspberries?"

When Charles appears in the doorway, Elizabeth can see that he too has a sheepish grin on his face. "That's sounds wonderful," they say in unison.

Elizabeth flips pancakes while Mrs. Clapp fries the bacon. After another great meal with friendly conversation, Charles and Elizabeth eventually climb onto the seat of their buckboard and wave good-bye to the Clapps who are standing by the street with clasped hands.

On the road again, the couple are quiet as they bounce along. Finally feeling like a grown woman, Elizabeth thinks about her first glass of wine and her first night with her husband. She's relieved to finally know what being with a man is like. Their physical bonding gave her a sense of closeness she'd never felt before and she's eager to explore this new dimension of her life.

Shy about expressing these intimate feelings, she comments about the Clapps instead. "The Clapp's beautiful home and their loving relationship gave me a glimpse of what I hope our future will be."

Charles looks over with a serious expression on his face. "Barring what fate has in store for us, our future will be what we make it, Elizabeth." Charles then lightens the mood by giving her another wink. "And I believe we're off to a very good start."

CHAPTER ELEVEN

WIND, RAIN, AND FIRE

The morning is overcast and pleasant when Charles and Elizabeth resume their journey. By mid-morning, however, the sun returns and the day turns unseasonably hot. As they bump along over imbedded rocks and potholes, Elizabeth appreciates the spring seat of the buckboard where she rides in relative comfort. They cover their faces with cotton scarves to avoid breathing in the dust kicked up by the wind and horses. She's enjoying sightings of red-winged blackbirds, gold finches, and swallows. On both sides of the road, the friendly faces of sunflowers nod their greeting.

Elizabeth places her hand on her husband's thigh and rests her head against his shoulder. When the wind dies down a bit, she straightens, and asks a question that's been on her mind. "I'm a bit bewildered about my new name. Since you're from Bavaria, I'm wondering why you don't have a German name."

When Charles turns to look at her, she sees his expression change from carefree to serious. "You're right. Horn isn't a German name nor is it my birth name. When I was discharged from the war in sixty-four, I was tired of having to spell out my complicated German name for the record keepers, so I told them my name was Charles Horn. That's my name now. It's official."

Still curious, Elizabeth asks, "What was your name before it was Horn?"

"I'm afraid that's a secret I'll take to my grave, my dear. I'm Charles Horn and there's no looking back. And, I'm pleased to say that you are Elizabeth Schultz Horn. We are the Horn family in America and, God willing, we'll remain so for generations to come."

Charles returns his eyes to the road and pulls his scarf over his mouth and nose. Although she's still curious about the name, Elizabeth remains quiet on the subject, respecting her husband's desire to keep his given name a secret. For now at least.

When the sun is high in the sky, Charles pulls the wagon to the side of the road. "Let's stop and eat the lunch Mary packed for us." He jumps down from the wagon. "I'll peg and water the horses while you lay out the cloth in that bit of shade over there."

Elizabeth retrieves a red and white checkered cloth Mary thoughtfully included in the basket and spreads it out in a secluded spot behind a large rock formation that promises respite from the hot wind. While laying out pickled eggs and thick slices of buttered bread, she thinks about the Clapps' generosity.

After feeding and watering the horses, Charles joins her. "One thing I've learned in the last week is we have the love of good food in common."

His remark causes Elizabeth to feel some trepidation as she considers Mrs. Clapp's and Mrs. Seifert's expert cooking.

"I'm just a beginner but I'm eager to learn. I hope to keep you well fed."

Her husband pats her knee. "I'm sure you'll do fine."

I hope he's right.

Charles puts the basket away, then helps Elizabeth up to her seat."We're about four hours from North Loup; another two from Ord. We'll be spending the night under a tarp somewhere between the two towns."

Elizabeth tries to hide her disappointment. "Is there no place to stay in either town?"

"I'm afraid not. There's Holliday's store, a post office, and a school in North Loop. They'd just started the county building last time I went through Ord. With the Union Pacific coming through, I'm sure both towns will quickly grow." Charles pulls the kerchief from his pant's pocket and wipes his face. "However, there's one interesting thing about the area; the Happy Jack Chalk Mine is nearby."

"What's interesting about that?"

"It's one of only two underground diatomic mines in this country. The chalk deposit was discovered by an army explorer. I've heard that local residents are starting to mine the unusual deposit. Perhaps we can return at another time and do some exploring."

Elizabeth straightens her bonnet as the wind picks up. "I've never heard of a chalk mine. What's the chalk used for?"

"It's used to make structural stone for buildings."

The horses strain to pull the wagon up a high hill forcing Elizabeth to grip the side of her seat. "Will our home be built with chalk someday?"

Charles slaps the reins. "No. Someday soon, I hope to build you a wood-frame house. Perhaps not as grand as the

Clapps' but similarly constructed. Don't worry, Darling, you'll not live in a sod house for long."

Crossing with the wagon train, Elizabeth saw the prairie grass as brown and boring, but today, as they ride over ever-increasing hills, she notices the variety of color in the vegetation. Christmas greens, chartreuse, sage, and lime come together like a patchwork quilt. She wonders if the landscape is so different in the Sand Hills, or if her attitude has improved now that she's married and headed to her new home.

By late afternoon, the air feels heavy with humidity. Elizabeth looks left to right at a sky that's quickly gone from bright blue to gun metal gray. She nudges Charles then points. "Over there! Did you see that bolt of lightening?"

Before he can look in the direction of Elizabeth's finger, another jagged, white flash slices across the horizon. The horses rear their heads. Charles holds the reigns steady. "Easy there." He continues to focus on keeping the horses in check. "A storm's definitely brewing. I'm not afraid of a little rain—actually it would feel refreshing—but the lightning's dangerous. Keep your eyes peeled for an abandoned building or some other shelter for us and the horses. I seem to recall a farm being nearby."

Elizabeth's stomach tightens and her mouth suddenly feels dry. She intensifies her gaze, leans forward, and scans the horizon. "There's a barn!"

"Yes, that's the one!" Charles clucks and shakes the reins. The horses pick up speed, turn, then briskly trot up a narrow lane that crosses a shallow creek. At the top of a slight incline, a sod house and barn come into view.

A tall, thin woman in a faded blue dress is standing in front of the house taking wrinkled, child-sized dresses and britches from a makeshift line strung between two posts. She throws them into a wicker basket. Three small, barefoot children are squatting in the dirt at her feet, intent on a game. Elizabeth smiles when she notices the turf roof of the house thick with yellow wildflowers. A tall chimney pipe dwarfs the house. She guesses it's to keep sparks from dropping onto the thatch-like roof. The white-washed barn she spotted from the road, stands some distance to the left. As they draw closer, she notices a pen of muddy, squealing piglets and a sow. A rooster and several hens are busy pecking at the dirt.

Charles reins in the horses and jumps down from the buckboard. "Howdy, ma'am. I'm Charles Horn and this is my," he stumbles over the unaccustomed word, "my wife, Elizabeth."

The woman holds out her thin, chapped, calloused hand and greets Charles with a small, tired smile. She speaks with a familiar German accent. "Froh...ah, glad to meet you. I'm Mrs. Heidemann. Call me Dorothy. My husband, Keith, is to Grand Island for few days if that is who you look for. He is buying supplies and glass windows for mein haus." She gestures toward the fabric-covered windows and the lopsided front door in need of repair.

Charles looks at the distant horizon. "I'm not looking for your husband, ma'am. I'm wondering if we might shelter in your barn for a spell. We don't like the looks of that lightning." He points over his shoulder.

A look of surprise crosses Dorothy's face. "Guess I did not see." She gestures toward her children who have now gathered around her skirts. "Keeping mein eyes on diese kinder hier." Thunder booms in the distance and she motions Charles to follow her. "Come. Much room in barn for wagon and horses. My husband took hay wagon and two draft horses. Only pony and couple of cows."

Elizabeth gets down from the buckboard as Charles tips his hat to the woman. "Thank you, ma'am, ah, Dorothy. Elizabeth here will be glad to keep an eye on your youngsters."

Dorothy squats and quietly speaks to her children. They nod, then she walks briskly toward the barn. Charles follows with the wagon and horses.

Elizabeth bends down to the children. "Hello. I'm Mrs. Horn. What are your names?"

The little boy and smaller girl look at their older sister. "I'm Pat. I'm eight." She points. "That's Pansy, she's six, and that's Danny, he's only three."

Elizabeth smiles at the children. "Nice to meet you."

Pansy puts her hand on her hip. "What we gonna do?"

Elizabeth thinks for a moment. "After your ma and Mr. Horn get the horses settled, we're going to join them in the barn in case there's a storm."

Pat looks up. "But what are we goin' do now?"

Elizabeth pictures playing with her younger brothers and sisters in the lush grass of their front yard. "Do you know how to play Ring-Around-the-Rosy?"

They answer by grabbing her hand and forming a circle. The redheaded girls' dimples appear as wide smiles reach their big blue eyes. Danny is the spitting image of his mother with thick, tousled, dark brown hair. He gazes up at Elizabeth with sleepy, brown eyes.

Out of the corner of her eye, she sees Dorothy opening the barn door for Charles who guides the buckboard and team inside. After a few moments, a cow bawls in the barn. Elizabeth wonders about the fuss.

After five "and we all fall downs," Elizabeth suddenly smells smoke. Searching around for signs of fire, she sees a dark cloud billowing in the distance just beyond the main road. She's about to take the children to the barn, when she sees Dorothy and Charles running toward her.

"Fire! Save children!" screams Dorothy, her arms churning like a windmill.

"Elizabeth, run! Take the children to the creek! We crossed it on the way in," hollers Charles.

Alarmed that the increasing smoke indicates a bigger event than she'd imagined, Elizabeth scoops Danny into her arms. With supreme effort, she keeps her voice low and calm. "Pat, grab Pansy's hand, hold it tight, and don't let go. Now, take my hand. We're running to the creek as fast as we can to get away from that smoke." She points to the sky.

Although their eyes are full of questions, the girls follow her instructions without a word. Elizabeth scrambles over the rough ground, trips over her skirts, but manages to stay upright. She keeps Danny securely on her hip with one arm and holds Pat's skinny hand with the other. "Faster, faster. You can do it! Come on, we're almost there." In the distance she sees rabbits, prairie chickens, mice, and other critters also running to escape the smoke and flames.

When they reach the shallow, sandy-bottom creek, Elizabeth says, "And...we all fall down." The children respond and sit in the cool water of the creek bed, safe from the oncoming flames. At least, for now.

The children's bodies are motionless, but their eyes dart between Elizabeth and the fire that's now gaining speed, crossing the road, and moving toward the trail to the house. She closes her eyes in an effort to quiet her racing heart and keep her composure as her fear ramps up. *This is no time for girlish hysteria. These children need a reassuring adult right now.* "Don't worry, your ma and Mr. Horn will be fine. They're making sure the fire doesn't get to your house and barn. We're going to sit right here and stay safe. Okay?" Three heads nod simultaneously. The sisters hold hands. Danny sits motionless in Elizabeth's lap. Even though there's a crisis unfolding before her eyes, she can't help thinking that her sister, Anna, would be Pat's age had she lived. She bows her head and prays under her breath. "Oh, dear God, don't let anything happen to these precious children, their dear ma, or my Charles."

Daniel's lower lip protrudes as if he's about to cry. Pat gives him a stern look and he holds back the tears. The girls' faces are white despite their run to the creek, their mouths are clinched tight, but, they too remain tearless. Pat looks up at Elizabeth. "What's Mommy and Mr. Horn doing?"

"They're working to keep the fire away from your house." Elizabeth knows her responsibility is to stay with the children, but she feels helpless as she watches Dorothy and Charles work feverishly to keep the fire contained. She strains to hear their words over of the crackle of burning prairie grass and the gurgling creek. She hears Charles yell. "Dorothy, get something we can soak with water!"

Dorothy runs into the house and returns with gunny sacks and towels, which she throws on the ground near the door. Elizabeth sees that Charles has located a stump and Dorothy is filling two buckets from the pump.

Pansy's eyes are glued to Elizabeth's. "What's happening now?"

"Your mommy is handing up buckets of water to Mr. Horn who's standing on a stump so he can reach your roof and make it wet to keep it from burning."

With eyes big as saucers, the children quietly watch the scene. "Is the roof wet yet?" Pat asks a moment later.

"Yes, I think so. Now your mommy is getting her potato sacks and kitchen towels real wet. I think Mr. Horn is going to make a small fire to keep the big fire away. After the fire burns a black line, your mommy will put it out with the wet sacks."

Elizabeth sees water dripping down the front of Dorothy's dress as she runs to Charles with the wet material. He lights a stick and touches the grass. After a few minutes, he signals Dorothy to extinguish the flames by beating them with the wet sacks and towels. He stomps on any remaining sparks.

"Will Mr. Horn's fire make a big fire too? Will it come for us?" Pat whispers, her voice trembling with fear.

Elizabeth tries to reassure her with an honest explanation as she gently tucks wayward strands of hair behind the little girl's ears. She knows the child may not totally understand what's happening, but, because details help to hold her anxiety in check, she feels it could be true for Pat also. "See how the ground slants this way?" Elizabeth points to the land near the house. "Your house is on a little hill, which will keep the winds from blowing the fire in our direction. Don't worry, we'll be safe here. See where they're making a big black line in the grass?"

Both girls stand and crane their necks to see through the heavy smoke. Although the air is still warm, Pansy shivers. "Mr. Horn is stomping on the flames and Ma is beating them up."

"Yes, and do you see where your daddy left dirt around the house? I think he did that so there would be nothing to burn. He thought ahead and was prepared." With serious faces, both girls nod then sit back down in the creek bed.

After a few minutes, the children become restless. Elizabeth gathers the girls closer to give them comfort and reassurance. Danny's face is turned into Elizabeth's shoulder. He's still dry-eyed but she can feel him shaking with fear. Pat turns her big blue eyes on Elizabeth. "Do you know any songs, Mrs. Horn?"

Wondering why she didn't think of music, she asks, "How about this one?" Taking a deep, calming breath then choking as smoke enters her lungs, she sings just loud enough for the children to hear. "Hush little baby don't say a word, papa's gonna buy you a mockingbird. And if that mockingbird won't sing, papa's gonna buy you a diamond ring. And if that diamond ring turns to brass, papa's gonna buy you a looking glass. And if that looking glass gets broke, papa's gonna buy you a billy goat—"

"A billy goat! That's too funny." Pat laughs and the other two join in.

"Again!" All three demand.

Relieved to have found a way to momentarily distract the children from their fear, Elizabeth sings the song again from the beginning and realizes it's the same tune she recently hummed in Gretchen's ear the morning her baby died. She tries to concentrate on the children, but can't keep her eyes off the fire that's steadily growing out of control. Smoke now engulfs the prairie in all directions with flames blowing toward the farmstead. Her heart is racing, her stomach churning. *My life has just begun. Will this be the end? And these dear children...what of them?* Choking on her fear and sadness, tears gather in her eyes. She hastily wipes them away with the back of her hand so the children won't notice.

Elizabeth begins the song again, all the while considering what to do if the fire turns toward the creek. She searches through the smoke and sees Charles and Dorothy frantically slapping towels and sacks against the burning grass. She knows they must be feeling intense heat. The expressions on their soot smudged faces causes bile to rise in Elizabeth's throat. The wind begins to dissipate, the smoke rises upward, but the flames continue to grow, along with Elizabeth's feelings of panic.

Pansy pulls on Elizabeth's sleeve and she returns her attention to the children. "What did Mr. Horn just say?" She and Pat are standing again.

"I think he told your mommy that they need to get the animals to safety." She points. "See? They're running toward the barn."

Just as Charles and Dorothy reach the barn, thunder booms followed by a blinding streak of lightning. The children shriek. Elizabeth lurches forward and gasps. There's another roll of thunder, then rain—merciful rain. It starts slowly and Elizabeth wonders if it's enough to put out the fire, but it quickly turns into a downpour. The smoke grows thicker and billows upward. A sob escapes her lips as gratitude fills her heart.

Charles and Dorothy stand together in silence for a moment. Elizabeth waves to them. Standing, the children cry out, "Ma! Ma!" The pair look at each other, break into a run, then join the group in the creek. The children pull themselves from Elizabeth's embrace and clamor toward their mother.

Elizabeth hugs Charles and allows her tears to flow. They mingle with the rain on his sweat-stained shirt. After a few minutes, Elizabeth wipes away her tears and Dorothy disentangles herself from her children. She looks down at their angelic faces. When she looks up, her face is wreathed in smiles.

Elizabeth can only whisper, "Thank goodness we're all safe."

Without a word, Charles takes David's tiny hand into his big one, Dorothy's workworn fingers spontaneously surround Elizabeth's as the little girls join in to form a circle. Charles bows his head and the others follow. His voice is faint and hoarse from the smoke. "Thank you, God, for saving our lives and the Heidemann's farmstead. We're grateful for the rain you sent and for these good and brave children."

Dorothy continues in a voice that's just above a whisper. "And thank you, God, for these nett, er kind, folks. Amen."

When rain becomes a drizzle and the air cools, Elizabeth points to two men on horseback galloping down the lane. "Look!" The men wave their hats as they ride the short distance to the group huddled in the creek. A tall man with a black mustache, a mane of gray hair, and a brown, weather-beaten face dismounts, removes his sweat-stained, black Stetson hat, then hands his reins up to his nearby companion, who remains on his horse. He takes stock of Dorothy and her children and glances at Charles and Elizabeth. "I'm Sheriff Johnson, Mrs. Heidemann. I believe we met a while back." He points up to his companion. "And this here's Deputy Weber."

Weber acknowledges the introduction. "Ma'am."

Dorothy disentangles herself from her children and awkwardly shuffles to the creek bank before responding. "We met at the Sutton's picnic, ja?"

Charles helps Elizabeth and the children from the water. The sheriff waves his arm toward his companion. "We were on our way to North Loup and saw the smoke." He looks towards the soddie and the burned swath around it. "Glad to see you were able to contain the fire." The drizzle continues, causing steam to rise from the ashes. A sliver of late afternoon sun is pushing its way through the clouds. A muted rainbow arches across the sky to the west. Johnson continues. "I crossed paths with Keith on his way to Grand Island earlier in the week. He said he'd be gone a few days."

Weber dismounts and stands next to the sheriff before speaking. "When we saw the smoke, we were worried about you and the children being out here alone, but I see you had help." He nods toward Charles.

Dorothy smiles at her new friends. "These kind menschen are Elizabeth and Charles Horn."

The sheriff looks over at Charles. "Nice to meet you."

Charles shakes his hand. "Likewise."

Then he shakes hands with Weber who asks, "Don't recognize you from bein' from around here. How did you happened upon this family?"

Elizabeth comes to stand next to Charles. "My wife and I are on our way to Fort Hartsuff. We saw lightening and sought shelter from this kind lady." Charles tousles Danny's hair. "We're sure glad we came along when we did."

Johnson nods. "Providential to be sure. Now, I can imagine you're anxious to replace those wet clothes, so we'll be on our way."

Dorothy makes an effort to smile at the sheriff. "Thank sie for coming, Mr. Sheriff."

As the men leave, Dorothy and the children turn to walk

back to the house. Charles calls after them. "I'll milk the cow, Dorothy." She nods.

The couple are too tired to speak as they change in the barn. Elizabeth dazedly watches Charles locate a bucket, then milk the undoubtedly grateful cow. Shaking off her exhaustion, she turns her attention back to the task at hand and spreads their wet clothing across the wagon tongue in hopes they'll be dry by morning. Not long after the milking is done, Dorothy comes to the barn door and hands Elizabeth a pail of something that smells delicious. "Had this simmerin' when you rode up. Is not much but you hungrig. Nein?'"

Elizabeth gives Dorothy a warm smile and takes the pail. "Yes, we're very hungry and this stew smells wonderful, thanks."

Charles gives Dorothy the pail of milk. "We'll be enjoying this meal, settle in early, then return to the road at first light. In case we don't see you, thank you for your hospitality. It's been a pleasure to make your acquaintance."

Dorothy puts her hand over her heart. "Gute nacht, friends."

Elizabeth and Charles eat the stew then pull their pallets from the wagon. Before she takes off her dress, she hears Charles softly snoring. She snuggles in beside her husband and watches him sleep for a moment before whispering, "You're a good and kind man, Charles Horn. I'm proud to call you my husband." She softly kisses him on the cheek, nestles into the crinkly straw, then quickly falls asleep.

CHAPTER TWELVE

AN UNEXPECTED PASSENGER

It's still dark when Elizabeth awakens to sounds of Charles dressing in yesterday's clothes. She gets up and checks her dress to see if it's dry. She frowns. Still damp. Charles gives her a peck on the cheek. "Don't bother with heating anything for breakfast. We can eat the leftover biscuits on the road. I'd like to get started by first light. We've got a mighty long day ahead of us."

"How long?"

Charles pulls on his boots. "About thirty minutes to North Loop, then a couple of hours to Ord, and another three hours to the fort. About six hours on the road but that doesn't account for resting and watering the horses, bad roads, or the unfavorable weather we might encounter. I hope to be at our house before nightfall."

Elizabeth removes her only other workdress from the trunk, pulls it on over her corset and petticoat, then quickly buttons up the front. She folds the damp dress from yesterday and locates the hard, stale biscuits. She comes behind Charles, who's feeding and watering the horses, and hugs him around the waist. "I'm ready to head home."

Charles turns and kisses his wife. "Me too."

The sky is just turning pink, the doves are cooing, and the larks are singing their morning songs when Charles pulls the wagon from the barn, hitches up the horses, swings onto the seat, then offers a hand to Elizabeth. When the wagon crosses the short distance from the barn, Elizabeth sees Dorothy standing barefoot in the gray shadow of her house. Her hair is down, her shawl is wrapped around her thin shoulders and tattered shift. Elizabeth thinks she looks fragile, still a bit frightened, and very tired with dark shadows under her eyes. The couple wave, then Charles shakes the reins and the horses pick up speed trotting down the lane toward the road.

Elizabeth takes a bite of stale biscuit then looks over at Charles. His eyes are bloodshot, his hands are marked with small, red, burns from the fire. Black ash darkens his fingernails.

"How are you this morning? Sleep well?"

Charles looks ahead then eases the horses onto the main road. "I slept fine but, I'll admit, I'm a bit spent after yesterday's ordeal."

Elizabeth looks back at Dorothy's barn receding in the distance and pictures her standing by the door. "Dorothy sure has her hands full. I hope her husband returns soon."

Charles pats his wife's thigh. "Don't worry about her, Darling. Dorothy's a hardy and capable woman. At least she was yesterday. She came very close to losing everything but she didn't panic. She fought hard and kept her head." He looks over at his wife. "You're a mighty strong woman too. I was drawn to you from the moment we met because I recognized your strength. Not only your physical strength but a strength of character; a natural reserve. I'm confident you too will be able to handle whatever comes your way. Yesterday, you stayed calm and kept the children safe. I was proud of you."

Elizabeth smiles at her husband's compliment. *I hope I can measure up to be the strong woman he thinks me to be.*

Indian summer has finally given way to fall and the morning is cool and comfortable. The air, however, smells like burnt porridge. The patchwork quilt of greens Elizabeth admired earlier, is now a landscape of black and brown parched earth. A raccoon with two little ones scuttle across the road in front of the wagon causing the horses to snort and shy. "Whoa," Charles calls. "Whoa there. It's just a raccoon family." He urges the team forward and returns to the conversation. "Life is hard on the prairie, especially with three, young children, but I believe Dorothy has what it takes to make a go of it."

Elizabeth sighs. "I certainly hope so." She looks up at the gathering clouds and pulls her shawl closer. "I'm glad yesterday's rain dampened the road enough to keep down the dust."

The couple ride in silence for about a mile until Elizabeth points. "Look! Smoke!" A tendril of smoke rising in the distance brings yesterday's drama to mind. Her heart races. She sits up straight and strains to keep the smoke in view as the wagon draws closer. She sees from Charles' posture that he too is concerned. When the wagon is even with the smoke, Elizabeth relaxes her shoulders, touches Charles' arm, and points. "It's only smoke from the chimney of that farmhouse." She sighs. "Thank goodness."

The corners of Charles' mouth go up slightly. "I think we're both still on high alert for fire. It's only natural."

Elizabeth adjusts her bonnet that has slipped back on her head. "Can you tell me what causes fires like the one we experienced yesterday? Are they common out here? Are we likely to have one on our property?" When she sees Charles furrowing his brow, she adds, "I think talking about it will help me feel better."

Charles speaks slowly as if he's considering the full picture. "First and foremost, it's been an extremely hot and dry summer. The worst in recent memory. That, combined with the constant wind, is a recipe for disaster." The horses slow and Charles prods them to a faster pace before continuing. "Like Dorothy, we have a creek nearby and, like Dorothy's husband, I've cleared the grass from around our house. Soldiers survey the perimeter of the fort twenty-four hours a day. They're on the lookout for Indians, of course, but they're also looking for smoke. They'd send word if there was a prairie fire heading our way."

Elizabeth looks down at her folded hands. "It gives me some peace of mind to know we'll have protection from the army but I'm still wondering about what causes the fires."

Orioles and sparrows peck seeds from the tall grass. The trail has dried and the horses are again kicking up dust. Charles responds. "As you know, lightening probably caused yesterday's fire but they can also be the result of settlers felling trees for buildings, firewood, and opening land for cultivation. When men leave stumps, piles of dead branches, and bark behind, there's opportunity for fire."

Elizabeth bites her lip. She's about to comment on her thoughts of how disappointed she feels that the settlers aren't better stewards, when a farmer approaches from the opposite direction with a wagonload of hay. Charles tips his hat in acknowledgement then continues his explanation. "In the area around Grand Island, the railroad workers are compounding the fire problem by clearing the right-of-ways and leaving piles of brush that can be ignited by sparks from passing locomotives."

Elizabeth rides in silence for several minutes pondering Charles' words. "Have you been in a prairie fire before?"

"No. I did, however, have to put out small fires during the war, and I heard stories of prairie fires devouring great swaths of land." Charles chuckles when Elizabeth opens her mouth to ask another question. "So many questions so early in the morning. You're one curious lady."

When Elizabeth pouts, he gives her a reassuring smile. "I don't mind your questions, my dear. In fact, I find your curiosity quite charming."

Elizabeth sighs with relief. "My mother used to say she wished I was less curious and more content to stay nearby instead of wondering what was around the next bend. I'm glad you don't feel the same since you're stuck with this curious girl."

Charles leans over and kisses her on the cheek. "I'm happy to be stuck with you. I want us to be stuck together for the rest of our lives."

After traveling for several miles, Elizabeth sees a small building in the distance with "Holliday's Store" hand-painted on a board placed near the road. She points. "Is that North Loup?"

Charles' gaze follows her finger. "Almost. Holliday built the store on his homestead just outside of town."

Elizabeth spots buzzards flying overhead. Uneasy, she sits up to focus more carefully on the terrain. She hears hooves thudding along the road as a horse gallops toward them and races past followed close behind by another man riding at breakneck speed. Charles struggles to control his skittish team. He turns and cocks his head in the direction of the last horse. "Wasn't that Weber's dapple gray?"

Elizabeth turns but can no longer see the rider. "The sheriff's deputy?"

"Yes. Let's find out what's going on." Charles pulls alongside a portly, older man dressed in bib overalls, a straw hat, and a dirty, blue shirt. He's standing several steps from the store staring down the road where the riders just passed. "Excuse me, sir."

The man removes his hat and looks up at Charles. His unshaven face has a sheen of perspiration even though the day is still cool. "Mornin' Mister. What can old Amos here do fur ya?"

Charles tips his hat. "What's going on here?"

Amos moves a wad of tobacco from one cheek to the other. "Somebody's been shot. Might be the sheriff."

Charles' forehead furrows. "That wouldn't happen to be Sheriff Johnson would it?"

The man nods. "Don't know for sure but I heard a gunshot, then I saw Deputy Weber hightailing it outta here." He points in the direction from which Charles and Elizabeth just came. "Reckon he's after the shooter. You folks know the sheriff?"

"We met him yesterday at the Heindemann farm. Nice man. Hope it's just a flesh wound." Amos tilts his hat forward in acknowledgement then ambles into the store.

Charles hitches the horses to a post then helps Elizabeth down from the wagon. They enter the small, dark building that smells of tobacco, rotting potatoes, and cabbage. When her eyes adjust, Elizabeth sees Amos standing near a gentleman with long, white whiskers. Both are leaning over a man who she recognizes as the sheriff.

"How is he?" Charles asks.

The whiskered man looks over at Charles and introduces himself as Holliday, the store owner. "Not good, I'm afraid. Gunshot to the thigh. Bullet in deep. You a doctor?"

Sheriff Johnson's eyes flutter open. Blood is soaking through his pants and pooling on the rough, dirty floorboards. A woman in a grease-stained, flour-sack dress and apron rushes over with a handful of clean rags. Johnson acknowledges her in a whisper. "Thanks Annie."

Charles, with Elizabeth close behind, squats to look more closely at the wound. He pulls his pocket knife from his pant's pocket, opens it, then cuts away the sheriff's pant leg. "I'm not a doctor but I had a similar wound during the war." Annie hands him the rags and he uses them to apply pressure to the injury in an effort to staunch the bleeding. "Is there a doctor nearby?"

Amos spits his tobacco into a nearby spittoon. "No sir. You'd find the nearest doc at Fort Hartsuff's infirmary — almost a day's wagon ride from here."

Charles lifts the rags, sees blood still flowing, and replaces them. "He needs to get the bullet out right away. Don't want gangrene to set in." He looks around the room. "Got any whiskey in this place?"

Holliday moves away and reaches up to a shelf behind the counter. He hands a bottle of whiskey to Charles. "Here you go. What else you be needin'?" Charles takes the bottle and pulls the cork out with his teeth.

"Water. The sheriff's lost a lot of blood."

Annie, her face lined, her voice low and rough, turns to Amos. "Go get a ladle of water and an old sheet from the cupboard, will ya?"

Charles holds the whiskey bottle out to Elizabeth. "Here. Give the sheriff a swig. Not too much." She holds Johnson's head and helps him drink from the bottle. When Charles removes the rags, the bleeding has slowed. He takes the bottle from Elizabeth. "I'm going to dribble whiskey into the bullet hole. It'll cut down on infection. Trick I learned in the war. Brace yourself, Johnson. It's goin' to hurt like hell." Johnson clenches his teeth but doesn't call out. Charles turns his head from side to side. "You're a better man then me, Sheriff. I screamed like a banshee." He places a clean rag over the wound then speaks to Elizabeth. "Tear that sheet in strips and bandage the wound."

While wrapping the strips around his leg, Elizabeth asks the group, "Does the sheriff have any kin nearby? Is he married?"

Annie responds. "He's a bachelor. He lives over by Ord."

Amos, who's been standing with the ladle of water, hands it to Annie. She helps Johnson raise his head, guides the water into his mouth, and helps him lay back down all while describing the shooting. "I was in the back of the store and seen it happen. When the sheriff walked in, some stranger was robbin' the register." She nods toward the man with the beard. "Holliday had gone out to his root cellar for turnips. I saw the man walk in but I didn't see him go behind the counter."

In a low, halting voice, the sheriff adds to Annie's story. "When I saw him with his fist in the till," Johnson coughs and takes a breath, "I told him he was under arrest for stealing."

The sheriff coughs again then motions for another sip of water. "That's when he pulled his gun and shot me. I was just inside the door. Had I been closer, I might've been a goner. The robber ran out the back. Weber was just behind me and I hollered at him to give chase."

Charles checks the bandage, which shows no sign of blood. "We saw both riders. They were coming toward us. Weber wasn't far behind the shooter." He stands. "Right now the main thing is to get you to a doctor."

Elizabeth speaks softly near Johnson's ear. "We're on our way to the fort and we can get you to the doctor today."

Johnson nods.

Elizabeth continues. "Our wagon's out front. Will you come with us?"

Johnson closes his eyes for a moment. When he opens them, he seems to gather his strength and looks intently at Elizabeth. "I'd be much obliged."

When she looks at Charles, he responds. "I'll bring the wagon around." Before he leaves the store, Charles calls back."Will someone get us more water and a couple sticks of jerky?"

The sheriff slowly sits up, takes a ragged breath then says to no one in particular. "When my deputy returns, ask him to bring my horse to the fort."

Amos puts a hand on Johnson's shoulder. "I'll take care of it, Sheriff. You see to recoverin'."

"Thanks, Amos."

When she sees the wagon out front, Elizabeth leaves the store, climbs into the back, rearranges the trunks, rocker, windows, and other supplies then spreads out her sleeping pallet in the narrow stretch of space that's left. With Charles under one arm and Amos under the other, they manage to get Johnson into the wagon. Elizabeth gently pulls him onto the pallet and arranges a blanket over him. She hands him a canteen. "Take another long swig, Sheriff. You've lost a lot of blood."

"Yes, ma'am."

Elizabeth holds Johnson's head while he drinks. "We'll get you to the fort as quick as possible. You're going to be alright."

Johnson closes his eyes. "Thank you... " He pauses. "What's your name again?"

"Elizabeth. Now, you get some rest." She leans over the wagon side and speaks softly to Charles. "Should I stay back here with him?"

He looks at the patient who seems to be resting quietly. "The bleeding's stopped for now. You ride up front. We'll stop in about an hour to see how he's doing unless he calls us sooner."

The couple return to the wagon seats and wave to the onlookers. Heading out of town, Elizabeth is quiet, contemplating what just happened. She looks at Charles who's concentrating on the road and keeping the horses at a steady pace. He speaks without looking away from the road. "You okay, Elizabeth?"

She takes a deep, ragged breath then lets it out slowly. "I'm fine. Just a bit overwhelmed by the events of the last two days and wondering if our life will always be this..." She searches for the right word, "exciting."

"I certainly hope not."

"I've never seen a gunshot wound before. Besides in the war, have you seen anyone shot?"

Charles looks to the sky as if remembering something from a long time ago. "I was in the Ford Theater ten years ago when President Lincoln was shot."

Elizabeth takes a sharp intake of breath and opens her mouth. Without looking at her, Charles adds. "Can't say more, gotta concentrate on keeping these horses moving."

About an hour after leaving the store, they stop to check on their patient and water the horses who are lathered from their faster than usual pace and heavy load. While they're pulled over, a farmer comes toward them with three crates of squawking chickens and two small children in the back of his wagon. The children wave and call out, "Hello!"

Charles hollers, "How much longer to Ord?"

The farmer slows his team. "Not far. Just a couple of miles."

"Thanks. Have a good day."

Back on the road, Elizabeth offers the canteen to Charles who takes a drink then wipes his mouth on his sleeve. "I'm looking forward to seeing the fort and our house." She sighs thinking that this last leg of the trip is taking a very long time.

Charles clicks his tongue to spur on the horses. "The fort is another eleven miles or so past Ord, but it's located in this valley." He shakes the reins. "This was, and sometimes still is, a route for the Sioux to carry out raids on the Pawnee."

Elizabeth looks at him sharply. "Are we in danger?"

He shakes his head. "Not likely. Most of the attacks happened a few years ago; one in October of '73 at Sioux Creek and again at Pebble Creek in January of '74. The skirmishes frightened the white settlers and they requested military action, which led to the building of the fort." Charles glances toward his wife. "If you're worried about our safety, be assured that there's not much danger in the area now that the fort's been built."

The couple are quiet for about forty-five minutes until Charles spots a creek and pulls to the side of the road. "You check on the sheriff while I water the horses."

When Elizabeth jumps down and looks in the back of the wagon, she sees the patient has kicked off the blanket. She joins Charles and offers him a bit of jerky. "I think he's sleeping but I won't feel at ease until we get him to the doctor. He looks flushed. Sure hope infection hasn't set in." With the horses watered, Charles pulls back onto the road and they begin the final leg of their trip.

Thankfully, the day continues to be mild with clouds frequently crisscrossing the sun. Charles keeps the horses at a steady walk. "I'm glad the robber was headed in the opposite direction from the fort. Wouldn't want him thinking he needed to finish what he started with the sheriff."

Elizabeth squints, focusing on the distant hills. She's impatient to get to the fort and home. "Why have we slowed down?"

Charles stretches his neck from side to side. "The horses are tired. It's a heavy load and I've pushed them all day. We should be at the fort in less than an hour."

Relieved to be riding the last few miles of a nearly two month journey, Elizabeth wants to get her mind off of the fire and the recent shooting. She looks around. "What are the buildings at the fort made of? I don't see many trees around here."

"All the fort's buildings were made from poured lime, cement, and gravel aggregate. I heard it took about a hundred men two years to build it. They were paid a dollar a day. The fort was a big boast to the local economy. The buildings aren't grand but they are sturdy and will last a long time."

Making an effort to keep the whine out of her voice, Elizabeth asks, "So why are we living in a sod house?"

Charles removes his hat and wipes his temple with his sleeve. He replaces the hat before answering. "As you know, I have a contract with the army to supply boots to the soldiers. I'm paid in cash and supplies. We're regular civilians living on the prairie in our own home built on land leased to us by the government. A sod house was the best I could do given our current circumstances."

Elizabeth tries to imagine what life will be like. "How far is our house from the fort?"

Before he answers, Charles points to two white-tailed deer in the distance. "If I had my rifle handy, I'd get us some supper." He watches the deer disappear over a small rise. "We're living near Bean Creek, less than two miles from the fort. It's a beautiful spot. We have neighbors and a small town nearby."

Elizabeth sits up straighter. "A town? I didn't know about a town." She squirms in her seat; tired after a long day of riding. "Tell me about it."

"Calamus is a town that's grown to serve the fort and the settlers in the region. We'll quickly pass through on our way to the fort. Tomorrow we'll explore it properly when we return the wagon and settle the horses at the livery stable."

Charles flexes one tired hand and then the other. "I have the impression you're worried about living in a soddie."

Elizabeth again straightens to look more confident than she feels. "Not worried exactly, just wondering what it'll be like. That's all. I know something about sod houses, of course. Besides seeing a few along the trail, I saw Dorothy's up close. Still, I can't quite imagine living in one."

"What are your concerns?"

"I'm worried that it will be dark and damp with dust flying every time we walk across the room." She hopes her husband understands her need for details about their future home. She wants to be prepared for what's to come. "How big is it?" Charles is quiet and Elizabeth hopes he's contemplating the specifics.

"Our house is sixteen feet wide by twenty feet long and eight feet high. The walls are about twenty inches thick, which will keep some of the cold out in winter and the heat in summer. It took an acre of sod to build it. The roof is wood covered with sod. The wood will keep the water out when there's a heavy rain. You can judge for yourself about the dark and dust."

"How long did it take to build?"

"With help from our neighbor Richard, my friend Shiriki, and, occasionally, a few off-duty soldiers from the fort, it took about a month. Richard lent me his sod cutting plow, which made a world of difference. The goal was to finish in time for me to return to Grand Island, close up my shop, and fetch you. It was an ambitious schedule, but we made it."

Elizabeth hears moaning coming from the back and interrupts the conversation to check on their patient. "You doing alright, Sheriff?"

Johnson gets up on one elbow. "How much further?"

Charles answers. "Less than an hour. How's the leg?"

"To be honest, it's hurtin' like hell but I'm a tough old bird. This ain't my first bullet." He clears his throat, his voice is rough. "Can't thank you folks enough for gettin' me to the doc."

Elizabeth hands him a stick of jerky. "Eat this then rest easy. We're almost there."

Johnson lays back down. "Thank you, ma'am."

CHAPTER THIRTEEN

FORT HARTSUFF AND HOME

Shortly after traveling down the main street of Calamus, a large grassy space surrounded by a white, picket fence comes into view. The tallest flagpole Elizabeth has ever seen sits in the middle of the expanse with an enormous American flag whipping in the wind. She glimpses a row of beige buildings along the far side of the field. With meadowlarks singing in the tall grass growing along the road and the blue sky as a backdrop, the buildings look inviting. She points. "Is that the fort?"

Charles nods. "That's it. The grassy area is the parade ground."

"Where are the walls? Aren't forts supposed to be surrounded by walls with parapets for guns? This looks like a small village plopped down in the middle of the prairie." She looks at Charles when she hears him chuckle.

"It looks like a village on the prairie because, basically, that's what it is. Like I told you, there's not much action here. In fact, the men say they're bored. Sorry, no parapets, Darling. Do you like what you see?"

"Yes, but it's not at all as I imagined."

The wagon enters the gravel drive leading to the first building, which is just east of the parade ground. Elizabeth swivels her head from side to side. "What's here besides an infirmary?"

Charles slows the horses. "The building on our right is Headquarters for Company A of the 23rd Regiment of Infantry." He points around the semicircle. "The duplex with the pines in front and the pickets formed into x's are where the two lieutenants, Capron and Stivers and their families, live. Captain Munson, the base commander, lives in the house next door."

Elizabeth notices dark green shutters alongside tall windows on the duplex and a boardwalk running the length of the properties. Wooden rocking chairs are in front of the lieutenants' quarters. Cottonwood trees shade some of the buildings but most of the grounds are bathed in the late afternoon sun. Charles points out other buildings as they ride along. "There's the enlisted men's barracks, the bakery, laundry, carriage house, stables, blacksmith and carpenter's shops, quartermaster's storehouse, guardhouse, and wagon scale."

"Why a scale?" Elizabeth asks as Charles takes a breath.

"When the settlers bring in supplies like hay, grain, or firewood, the government pays them according to weight."

Elizabeth secures her sunbonnet and smooths her dress as she anticipates seeing people on the grounds. As she does so, she notices her once clean dress is splattered with blood along the hemline reminding her of how much blood Johnson lost. She asks Charles another question to distract her from thinking the worst. "How many soldiers are stationed here?"

"At the most, there's about fifty soldiers at any one time. There are a fair amount of desertions though. Especially since the Black Hills gold rush started last year." She appreciates that fact that Charles is trying to be as exact as possible.

Charles slows the horses. "Now let me concentrate on getting our patient to the infirmary."

Elizabeth observes a few men dressed in identical dark blue shirts and trousers lingering in front of the barracks. A large, black dog dozes on the dirt walkway between two buildings and a rider in a dark blue jacket with gold braids approaches on horseback from the far end of the parade ground. "The bakery must be nearby. The smell of baking bread is reminding me that we've only had dry biscuits and jerky today."

Without taking his eyes from the driveway, Charles comments. "The baker bakes each soldier a loaf of bread everyday. Sometimes, he gives extras to civilians passing through."

"Too bad we don't have time to find out if today is one of those days."

Charles halts the horses in front of a building with an "Infirmary" sign above the door. "You stay here, Elizabeth. I'll find someone to help me with Johnson and alert the doctor." Charles jumps down from the wagon and quickly disappears into the small, low building.

Elizabeth gets down from the seat then climbs into the back of the wagon to see how Johnson's doing. The bandage wrapped around his leg is soaked with blood and his lips are nearly white. Worried that he might pass out, she tries to reassure him. "We're at the fort and help is on the way, Sheriff. Just a few more minutes now and you'll be taken care of."

With closed eyes, Johnson nods.

Charles quickly returns with two orderlies and a stretcher. When Elizabeth gets out of the wagon, one man climbs in, lowers Johnson onto the stretcher, then they rush him into the infirmary. Elizabeth follows them into a small room with a single bed and cabinets along the walls. After meeting Doctor Towar, Elizabeth returns to the wagon to give Johnson privacy knowing the doctor will remove his pants to inspect the wound. Elizabeth considers the infirmary. *That was hardly what I'd consider a hospital! Barely the size of my bedroom in Illinois.*

Several minutes pass. *I hope we're not too late!* Elizabeth fidgets with her bonnet strings. *What's keeping Charles?* Finally, he exits the building. "Johnson's in good hands and the doc says he thinks he'll make it. The orderly just sedated him and Towar is preparing to remove the bullet."

Elizabeth lets out a breath she didn't know she was holding. "That sounds like good news. Is there anything else we can do?"

Charles gets into his seat and takes the reins in hand. "Pray. Aside from that, we'll check on him tomorrow when we return the buckboard to town."

Elizabeth looks around. "Can we pick up our mail before heading home?"

"We'll stop at Headquarters on our way out." In a few minutes, Charles quickly enters the building, returns, and hands Elizabeth a letter.

She tears it open. "It's from Mother. She had a girl! I have another sister."

Charles takes his seat, calls out, "Giddiup," and the horses slowly leave the fort. "That's wonderful news. What's her name?"

She scans the page. "Her name is Pauline and she was born August sixth." With a strong sense of relief flooding her heart, she sets the letter aside to concentrate on the final mile to her new home.

The wagon approaches a low rise and Charles points. "Look straight ahead. You'll see our property in a minute."

At the crest of the hill, Elizabeth spots the house. "What a beautiful location!" She stands to get a better view. "The rolling hills, the creek—why, there are even yellow and pink wildflowers growing on our roof! Just like at Dorothy's."

Charles pulls on her arm. "I'm glad you approve, Darling. Now, please sit down before you fall."

"Oh, Charles…it is truly lovely!"

"It's a gorgeous spot, alright."

She notes the pride in Charles' voice. He pulls alongside the path to the house, steps down from the wagon, then pegs the horses. Elizabeth jumps down and they walk up the path to the door. Taking in the square building made of blocks of sod, Elizabeth looks around the corner. "I'm happy to see we have an outhouse. I'd like to use it before we go inside."

"Of course, Dear."

The necessary is built of wood and set several yards from the house. Elizabeth opens the door, which is secured with leather hinges, and sees that it's an over-large, one holer. She sits leaning forward with her palms braced against the plank seat. Strips of newspaper on bent sixpenny nails are arranged along the wall. When she's finished, she closes and latches the door then walks back to where Charles is waiting by the door.

For once, the sparkly feeling in her chest isn't from anxiety. It's from a sense of pure delight.

Charles opens the plain, unvarnished, wooden door, stands aside, then makes a slight bow. "Your new home awaits, Mrs. Horn."

When she steps inside and scans the room, she notes spider webs in the corners and mouse droppings on the floor but says nothing, thinking instead of the pleasure she'll have making this their home. She walks across the single room, then turns back to Charles. "The floor is hard and smooth. How's that possible?"

He squats and runs his hand across the surface. "Shiriki showed me how to take care of dirt floors. While I was finishing the interior, I sprinkled the floor daily with water and swept it with a grass broom until the surface was nearly like concrete."

Stepping to the far wall, Elizabeth runs her hand over the surface.. "And the walls… they feel like plaster!"

Charles comes to stand next to her. "There's plenty of limestone around here so I burned the stone and mixed it with sand to make the plaster coating. I thought it made the walls look more like what you're used to. Plus, when we brush against them, we won't send dust flying."

Elizabeth embraces her beaming husband. "Thank you for the special care you've taken in building our house. It's so much better than I ever imagined. We'll certainly make it into our home." She examines every nook and cranny of the room. A rope bed faces a raised, stone hearth and fireplace, a rectangular table with two chairs takes center place, and various cooking utensils hang on hooks. A water barrel is within easy reach of the fire. Openings in two walls are secured with scraps of wood awaiting the installation of the glass windows in the wagon.

While she's looking around, Charles moves to the open doorway. "I'll see to the unloading." He returns with his arms full. "Where do you want your rocker?"

She points. "In front of the fireplace where I can be warm and cozy as the days grow shorter."

After the couple unload the wagon, Charles lights the lantern and a fire in the fireplace. Elizabeth notices that the kerosene lamp is spilling circles of light onto the unfinished, wooden table. She turns away and locates a black spider similar to Gretchen's, sets it in the coals, then fries potatoes and salt pork from the last of their supplies. She covers the table with Mary Clapp's red and white checkered cloth. After they've eaten, Charles takes two buckets from just inside the door. "I'll get more water."

Elizabeth heats the last of the water in the barrel, washes the dishes, then opens her trunk, which is sitting at the foot of the bed. After removing some clothing and laying it aside, she unpacks the quilt her mother lovingly made them for a wedding gift. Taking it from the old sheet in which it's wrapped, she runs her fingers over the stitches, admiring the double wedding ring design in three shades of blue. When she examines the back, she's surprised to see *Charles and Elizabeth, 1875* embroidered in the corner.

After Charles returns with full buckets and pours water into the barrel, Elizabeth calls him to come near. "Look!" She points to the made-up bed. "My mother made this quilt for us. Isn't it beautiful?" Before Charles can answer, she puts her face into his shoulder then wraps her arms around his neck. "I declare, I'm the luckiest girl alive. The rocker, this beautiful quilt, a cozy home." Feeling emboldened as a woman with her very own home, she says, "Let's finish our unpacking tomorrow and try out our new bed."

With a twinkle in his eye and a smile on his face, Charles takes his wife into his arms. He releases her, then removes his blood-stained shirt while Elizabeth steps out of her dress.

CHAPTER FOURTEEN

CALAMUS AND BUFFALO STORY

Early the next morning, hammering wakes Elizabeth. She gets out of bed, throws a shawl over her shift, and smooths the hair that has escaped the long braid down her back. She wiggles her toes on the smooth dirt floor. Not caring that she looks like a school girl, she whispers to herself, "I'm the lady of this house, these are my dirt floors, and I'm calling out to my husband."

She sticks her head out the door. "What's going on out there?" She steps outside just in time to see the horizon come to life with the orange glow of sunrise. The smell of fresh saw dust brings to mind her Grandpa Schultz who was a woodworker. The chill in the air reminds her that she's ill-prepared to survive the dark, cold winter.

Charles comes to the door and kisses her. "I'm sorry to wake you. In my haste to get these windows in, I didn't take into consideration that there's two of us now."

Elizabeth draws her shawl closer and shakes off her gloomy thoughts of winter. "I'll make breakfast then come out and help you." After using the privy, washing up, and quickly dressing, Elizabeth stokes the fire and makes corn cakes and coffee. Her thoughts of winter return during breakfast. She also thinks of the sheriff and wonders how he's doing. "After we finish installing the windows, we're checking on the sheriff and returning the buckboard. Right?"

With a mouth full of corn cake, Charles nods to the affirmative.

"Then, can we saddle up the horses and take a ride?"

Helping himself to another corn cake, Charles responds, "Of course."

"I'd like to scout out herbs and berries before the frost takes them. Do you think it might freeze in the next few weeks?"

"I would't be surprised."

Elizabeth takes a sip of coffee. "I'm worried that we're getting a late start on preparations for winter."

Charles responds with his fork in mid-air. "We'll have to buy more supplies than usual this year but, don't worry, I've accounted for that. Next year we'll have a big garden."

Remembering her day dreams of the prairie, she asks, "Will we see huge herds of buffalo on our ride?"

"No."

When Elizabeth opens her mouth to ask another question, Charles holds up his hand to stop her. "I'll tell you the sad story later." He gets up from the table. "Now, I need to get back to work."

With a team effort, both windows are installed by early afternoon. Then, after a quick lunch, Charles hitches up the buckboard and the couple climb aboard. During their two mile trip to town, recent events return to Elizabeth's mind. "What do you think about naming the horses after the Heidemann girls?"

"Remind me what they are."

Elizabeth recalls their frightened faces. "Pat and Pansy. They were so sweet and brave."

"Pat and Pansy it is then."

As they approach the livery stable, Elizabeth swivels her head from side to side taking in the boardwalks on each side of the main street. She'd barely noticed a thing while driving through Calamus yesterday in her haste to see the fort and her new home. Today, she spots a general store, a post office, and a saloon with swinging doors. Modest, wood-frame houses run down adjacent streets.

"There's more in Calamus than I thought there'd be."

Charles gives her a wink. "See? Not so bad living in the wild west after all."

They return the wagon to the livery stable. A handprinted sign, "Webber's Wagons", hangs above the door. George, Mr. Webber's son, welcomes them. "Howdy, hope you were able to make good use of my wagon."

Charles hands the man his reigns. "Absolutely." He turns to Elizabeth. "I was able to bring my wife out here to our new home."

"Howdy, ma'am. Welcome to Calamus. I'm George. I'll take good care of your horses and saddles."

"Thank you, George." Elizabeth gets out of the wagon and stands near Charles who is taking their saddles out of the back. "Right now we're going to saddle up and take a ride around the area."

Elizabeth notices that George is about her age; tall, thin, and dressed in chaps and the kind of work boots Charles frequently makes. He seems eager to please the Horns who plan to board their horses long-term. Elizabeth walks inside the stable to see where the horses will be kept. It smells of leather and manure. Dust dances in the sunbeams coming through the windows. While Charles is saddling one horse, Elizabeth places a blanket over the other, picks up the saddle, throws it over Pansy's back, and tightens the cinch under her belly.

Charles looks over. "You seem to know a thing or two about horses. I'm glad I bought these secondhand saddles."

"I learned while visiting my uncle's farm."

Charles settles up with George for the wagon rental, then they lead their horses from the stable out into the sunshine. A passing gentleman tips his hat. He has a full head of white hair, which curls around his large ears, a florid complexion, and a clean shave. A pair of wire-rimmed glasses perch midway down his bulbous nose. He's dressed in a black suit with a crisp, white shirt and vest under his jacket.

"Good afternoon. You folks passing through or new to our town?"

Charles reaches out to shake the man's hand. "We're Charles and Elizabeth Horn. We just moved into the soddie on Bean Creek. I'm the new boot maker for the fort and surrounding area. My shop will be in the store front next to the saloon."

"Welcome to the area. I'm Mr. Mitchell, the town lawyer. My office is right above The Mercantile."

Elizabeth seizes the opportunity to ask questions about the town. "If you have a moment, Mr. Mitchell, I'd appreciate it if you'd tell us about Calamus."

Mitchell looks up the street then returns his gaze to Elizabeth. "Of course, Mrs. Horn." He puffs up with pride. "I'll start by promoting our weekly newspaper, *The Valley County Herald.* It's the first paper in Valley County, and I'm the publisher." He extends his arm, gesturing along the street. "We also have a brickyard, a post office, a saloon, a freight station, two stores, some houses, and a school… and now, a boot maker."

"How many people live here? Where does this main street go? Where does the name Calamus come from?"

Although Elizabeth is genuinely curious about these things, other, unasked, questions are bubbling up in her mind. *How many people have died from gunshot wounds, fires, or illness? Are there any women near my age?*

Charles shrugs his shoulders when the gentleman looks in his direction. Mitchell directs his attention back to Elizabeth. "To answer your questions, Mrs. Horn, about fifty or so people live here, but the town also serves the surrounding area. This main street goes all the way to Deadwood, Dakota Territory."

Mitchell pauses to wipe his forehead with a clean, white handkerchief that he takes from his breast pocket. "The town was named after the Calamus River, which joins the North Loup River ten miles to the northwest. The name Calamus is derived from the Indian name of a plant. It means food of the muskrat."

"Just two more questions, please, Mr. Mitchell. Is there a doctor in town, and who hires the school teacher?"

Mr. Mitchell stares at Elizabeth a moment. His lips tighten. Pulling out his pocket watch, he flips open the lid, then closes it. "The only doctor is at the fort. In the instance of civilians, he mostly treats only serious cases but this spring he did deliver the first white baby in the county."

Elizabeth is glad to know the doctor is available if they need him. She remains quiet, however, awaiting the answer to her last question.

"Oscar Babcock is Superintendent of Schools; however, I oversee our local teacher, Miss Harvey. If you have any interest in being a substitute teacher, please come see me. Now, I must open my office. Good day, folks."

Charles salutes the gentleman then gives his wife a hand up into the saddle. Although she's wearing a dress, Elizabeth mounts her horse western style then takes up the reins. Their first stop will be the fort to check on the sheriff. It's a short ride, less than a mile from town.

Elizabeth smiles to herself as she moves in sync with her horse. Strands of hair escape her sunbonnet and fly about her face but she doesn't care. She feels free and alive. "This is so much better than jolting along in a wagon."

Charles looks over and smiles at his wife.

When they dismount and tie up their horses in front of the infirmary, they find the sheriff strong enough to be sitting up in bed. They have a few words with the patient then leave him to rest. The doctor walks outside with them, then speaks quietly. "It' a good thing you got Johnson here when you did. Don't think he'd of lasted another day."

Relieved to find the patient recovering, the couple bid the doctor good-day, mount their horses, and ride in the opposite direction of town following Bean Creek. On the way, Elizabeth spots a clump of a yarrow plant growing near the side of the trail. When she reins in and dismounts, her husband raises his eyebrows. She stoops down to pick as much as she can carry. "Lucy told me this plant can be used to heal all sort of ailments. I'm gathering this now in case I forget where it is later." Back on her horse, Elizabeth soon points toward another treasure. "Mint! It will make lovely tea." Just then, a red squirrel scurries up a small, bent tree and directs her attention to a thicket of plums growing nearby. Elizabeth makes a mental note of the location so she can return the next day with her gathering basket.

They continue riding only a short distance before Charles reins in his horse and pulls up next to a man walking along the dusty road with a scythe slung over his shoulder. He's tall and rangy with straight, slicked-back hair, a scraggily straw-colored mustache and heavy beard. Elizabeth estimates the man to be about her husband's age. "Good to see you, Richard." He turns to his wife. "This is the friend I told you about who loaned me his sod cutter and taught me how to build a proper sod house." After introductions are made, Charles continues. "The Voogds are our closest neighbors and have a homestead a ways back from the road, about a half mile from here."

Richard shoves back his hat and leans on his scythe. "Sure glad to have you and Charlie for neighbors. My missus will be over soon to give you a proper welcome. She's been lookin' forward to your arrival. She tells me that lady friends are hard to come by around here."

Elizabeth can't help but grin as she thinks about the possibility of having a friend. "I'll look forward to her visit."

The couple ride back to town where they stable their horses then walk home in the twilight. Elizabeth feels much better about her new life now that she's experienced a full day. She grabs Charles' hand. "I like it here more than I thought

I would. I'm really excited about meeting Richard's wife. I'm also glad we have a town nearby and a doctor available should we ever need him."

After a supper of beans and corn bread, Charles and Elizabeth relax in front of a glowing fire. Elizabeth wraps her shawl around her shoulders then turns to her husband. "Feel like telling me the sad tale about the buffalo?"

Charles slowly nods, moves his chair closer to Elizabeth's rocker, tips back, and momentarily closes his eyes. She watches as he opens his eyes and looks into the fire. He sighs. "My story comes from what I've read, been told, and seen for myself. A short four years ago, the southern herd of buffalo was about three million strong." Elizabeth looks over and sees Charles' eyes narrow before he continues. "Sadly, in the last few years that giant herd was decimated when three to four thousand buffalo were killed every day." He seems to spit out the last few words in disgust.

"Everyday! How can that be?" She sees that Charles' straight back is slumped, his arms are hanging limp at his sides, and his left eye has a slight twitch. Even though more questions hammer in her head, she waits patiently for him to continue a story that seems to be causing him anguish.

"It is a staggering figure and, worst yet, it happened so quickly. From about '72 to just last year, close to two million buffalos were killed and wasted by sport hunters."

When Charles pauses, Elizabeth asks, "Was it all for sport?"

"No. White men who were looking to make a profit, killed another million and shipped the hides east over the Atkinson, Topeka and Santa Fe Railroad."

Charles gets up, opens his trunk, and rummages around. He returns with a yellowed, crumpled sheet of paper. "One day, as I was walking close to the tracks near Grand Island, I found this leaflet. It's advertising excursions to …" Charles reads from the advertisement, "shoot buffalo from the train!" He passes the paper to Elizabeth so she can see the drawing of a man and woman leaning out of the window of a railcar, both smiling gaily behind their shotguns.

She hands the paper back. "This is outrageous. And the numbers! I can't even imagine. Are there any buffalo left? I saw a few on the trail but are there any great herds?"

Charles slowly shakes his head. "You were lucky to see that small group. Both the northern herds and the southern are nearly gone. I've been part of one or two hunting parties and have helped kill a few buffalo myself. But, like the Indians, my friends and I used every bit of meat and hide. We didn't slaughter them for sport." Elizabeth watches as her husband seems to be reaching deep into his thoughts.

"I believe killing the buffalo was partially about something else. With the buffalo gone, the Indians have nothing—no food, no clothing, no tepees. The lives of many tribes in this area revolved around the great beasts. Many rich folks, like those pictured on that leaflet, may not have realized that they were paying to play a part in a bigger plan."

"A plan to rid the plains of the Indians?"

"Yes, I believe so. I also believe that someday history, and God for that matter, will not look kindly towards the people who did this."

Elizabeth feels a sense of dread. "Do these barbarians live in our midst?"

"No, Dear. For the most part, the settlers love this land and respect its resources. They hunt for food, not sport. Most of the mass killings were done by outsiders who had no regard for the prairie."

Elizabeth sits quietly, trying to digest what she has just heard. Finally, she says, "Let's put this behind us for now and go to bed."

The next morning, just as she awakens, Elizabeth recalls dreams filled with enormous rotting buffalo carcasses being ravaged by red-necked buzzards and cackling, blood stained men with blackened, jagged teeth mounting their horses and riding away.

She opens her eyes to Charles smiling over her. "Happy Birthday!"

Glad to be out of her terrible dreams, she flings her arms around his neck. "You remembered!"

He kisses his wife. "Of course."

Left alone after breakfast, Elizabeth thinks of her family and wonders if there will be mail for her in the coming days. *Surely they won't forget my birthday. Will they?*

Elizabeth does her chores then takes her gathering baskets off the hooks, puts her shawl around her shoulders, and walks along the creek edge where she and Charles rode their horses earlier. Fall is in the air but the sun warms her back as her eyes scour the ground looking for herbs and fruit she can store for winter. Soon, in a shady spot near the water's edge, she finds mint, walks several yards to find rose hips for tea, then more medicinal yarrow. When she gets thirsty, she leans over and gathers creek water in her cupped hands. It's icy cold. She wipes her hands on her skirt.

Further up the creek she discovers pokeberries, chokecherries, and prickly pears. Happy to return home with two full baskets of winter supplies, Elizabeth treats herself to a cup of soothing, aromatic mint tea before tying the mint and yarrow into bundles to hang from the ceiling to dry.

That evening after supper, Elizabeth looks out the window. Charles steps behind her and puts his arms around her waist. "Good thing we got the windows in yesterday. October will bring much colder temperatures. Perhaps snow."

Elizabeth gives an involuntary shudder at the thought of endless, dark, and lonely winter days. Although they'll soon be stocked with food for the near future, she wonders where supplies will come from when the snow is deep and the temperatures are below zero.

CHAPTER FIFTEEN

FOREVER FRIENDS

On an overcast, chilly mid-October morning, Elizabeth looks up from her bread-making, hoping to see someone coming up her path. It's been at least ten days since she met their neighbor, Richard, and she's disappointed that she's not yet had a visit from his wife. She tries to keep her mind on her bread-making but can't help feeling sorry for herself. She's beginning to wonder what she was thinking when she agreed to live in such a desolate place. *I've always had school chums or family around. Even on the trail, I had Lucy and Gretchen. I can't imagine what winter will be like isolated and alone in this cold room all day.*

By midafternoon the smell of freshly baked bread fills the house. Elizabeth has swept the dirt from the floors and the spider webs from the corners, put the makings for dinner in a pot to simmer, and hauled water from the creek. She sits in her rocker reading and sipping rose hip tea to take her mind off her loneliness. Bored with reading *The Cousins* for, what seems like, the hundredth time, she lays it facedown in her lap. This time, however, when she looks out her window, she spies a woman and two girls turning from the road onto the path to her house. She puts her book aside, jumps up from her rocker, and twirls around. "Visitors! I finally have visitors!"

Smoothing her skirt and wishing she'd put her corset on, she hurries to the window and sees that the wind is whipping her guests' dresses around their ankles. The girls are clutching homespun, grey, woolen capes to keep them closed. They have blue, knitted caps with matching scarves swirled around their necks. The woman wears a beige, knit shawl and a felted gray hat pulled over her ears. She has broad shoulders, a straight back, and is nearly as tall as Elizabeth.

As they come closer, she notices that the older girl has neatly braided, dark-red hair peeking out from under her cap and is walking sedately beside the woman, matching her stride for long stride. The younger girl is small with short, stout legs. Her dark blonde, curly hair whips across her face as she runs ahead in, what seems to Elizabeth, a great hurry. She opens her door. "Hello neighbors, welcome!"

The woman, who has a woven wicker basket over one arm, waves back and smiles. The older girl, whose hands are occupied with a bundle wrapped in a white cloth and keeping her cape closed, mouths a greeting. The younger girl, no bigger than a minute, greets Elizabeth with a bright, missing-two-front-teeth smile. "Hello, Mrs. Horn. My name is Jan and I'm six."

Elizabeth smiles down at the little girl. "Nice to meet you, Jan. Do you have a last name?"

Jan rolls her big, blue eyes. "Of course I do. It's Voogd. You know my daddy."

"I sure do. He helped build this house. Please come in." Showing no sign of shyness, Jan rushes through the door and swivels her head from side to side as she surveys the interior of the house.

"Jan, mind your manners," her mother calls out.

When the girl and woman approach, Elizabeth steps from the doorway. "I assume you're the Voogd ladies. I'm Elizabeth and I'm delighted that you've come."

Mrs. Voogd extends a large, work-worn hand. Her forehead is lined and her serious, deep blue eyes have the starting of crows' feet at the corners. Her smile is warm, her voice is low. "I'm Violet. My friends call me Vi."

Elizabeth stands aside and holds the door open. "Please come inside." After she closes the door, she takes the bundle the older daughter hands her. "And what's your name?"

"I'm Sharlene but you can call me Shar. Pleased to meet you, Mrs. Horn." Elizabeth eyes the bundle with curiosity. "My mom baked this here Sally Lunn Hot Bread for you this mornin'."

Jan pipes up. "And I helped her make it."

Elizabeth opens the edge of the towel and peers in at the shiny, brown dome of bread inside. "It looks delicious." She turns to Jan. "I'm sure you were a great help to your mother. Will you give me the recipe sometime?"

"Yes, ma'am," Jan says with a serious face.

Elizabeth smiles at Vi. "Charles and I will have this with our supper. Thank you very much."

Vi sets her basket on the table and removes her cape. "I'm sorry it took me so long to come for a visit. Jan's twin brother, Gary, has been sick with the croup and I couldn't get away."

The thought of a sick child sets off alarm bells for Elizabeth. "I do hope he's better."

"He is, but I thought he shouldn't be out in this wind. I left him with my friend, Harriet Mitchell. Her husband's away for a few days meeting with clients up near Burwell so she had time on her hands and offered to come by our house and entertain Gary so we could come for a visit. Richard is busy with the harvest."

Shar continues to stand quietly next to her mother.

"I've already learned that Jan is six, how old are you, Shar?"

"I'm thirteen, ma'am."

Nearly as tall as Elizabeth, Shar reminds her of a colt—all arms and legs. Besides the dark-red braids, Shar has serious brown eyes, a gap between her front teeth, and a small, red birthmark on her throat. She senses that Shar is making an effort to act like the grown-ups.

If only she knew I'm just two years her senior.

Elizabeth surveys the room trying to determine where to seat her first guests. After a moment, she directs Vi to the rocker, Shar to a chair, and Jan to the rug by the hearth. With logs glowing in the fireplace and the afternoon sun finally showing itself through the spotless windows, it's a cozy setting. After everyone is settled, Elizabeth puts the tea kettle on, then sits in the chair opposite Shar. "Do you girls go to school?"

Shar answers for them both. "I went as far as the sixth grade, but Pa can't afford to send me on. I want to be a teacher, so I do lessons with Jan and Gary every day after I help Pa in the barn or fields." With pride in her voice, Shar adds, "Jan can read the primer and they both know their numbers."

Elizabeth feels the twinge of guilt she always experiences when she thinks about teaching. "I also had a dream of becoming a teacher. Perhaps I can help you teach the twins."

Shar nods, fidgets with her knit cap, then remains quiet as her mother pulls two skeins of off-white yarn from her basket and hands them to Elizabeth. "I thought you might like a bit of my home spun. We know a fella up north who has sheep. He brings me wool every spring. I have a small spinning wheel."

"What a thoughtful gift." Elizabeth fingers the soft yarn. "I love to knit. I'll make good use of this beautiful wool." Hearing the kettle boiling, she rises and makes a pot of rose hip tea. She slices some of her just-baked bread and slathers it with butter and chokecherry jam, then sets the refreshments on the table after handing a slice to Jan. "A few hours ago I was feeling lonely and wondering how I'd get through the next few months. Now I have three lovely ladies sitting by my fire." Feeling her face grow warm, she adds, "I'm so glad you've come."

Vi pats her arm. "I understand, Elizabeth. Women friends are hard to come by out here. I have my children, of course, but there's nothing like sharing a cup of tea with a friend."

While the ladies share stories about their past, Elizabeth notices that the girls are quiet as they seem to be taking in every nook and cranny of her house.

Elizabeth shares how much she misses her family in Illinois and the challenges of traveling west by wagon train. Vi responds. "I also traveled west by wagon train after leaving my family in Ohio. I'll be honest, Elizabeth, it's not an easy life living out here in a soddie, but I wouldn't trade it for anything. You'll see." Although Elizabeth guesses that Vi's more than twice her age, it seems to make no difference as their friendship quickly blossoms.

"Who's that lady on the mantle?" Jan asks when there's a pause in the conversation.

Elizabeth get up, walks to the fireplace, and takes down the china figurine. "This lady is an angel. My Auntie Hazel put her on top of my first birthday cake as a decoration. I brought her all the way from Illinois because she's so special to me. Want to hold her?"

Jan vigorously nods her head and comes to stand nearby. Elizabeth carefully hands her the angel that's about six inches tall with blond hair and a white robe. Jan carefully looks her over then exclaims, "She's bee-u-ti-ful! I especially love her golden wings."

Elizabeth sees Shar admiring books on a nearby shelf and guesses they are more interesting to her than the angel. She makes a mental note to bring one with her when she pays a visit to the Voogds.

After an hour of good conversation, the Voogd ladies bid Elizabeth good-bye. Just before Vi passes through the front door, she gives her hostesses a quick hug. "Please feel free to drop by anytime, Elizabeth. We'd love to have you."

Elizabeth watches her new friends hurry down the path with Jan running ahead. She places her hand on her heart feeling relieved and delighted that she's finally made some friends. She senses that she and Vi have already formed a bond and she's looking forward to visiting their home in the near future.

When Charles returns from work, Elizabeth's bursting with news of her afternoon visitors. While she's chattering away, Charles pours himself two-fingers of whiskey then settles down in front of the fire to listen. After she's talked out, Elizabeth goes to stir the stew and take plates from the shelf.

Charles sets his glass on the table. Elizabeth can feel him studying her. "I've been worried about you, Darling. In the short while we've lived here, you seemed to have changed. Tonight, I see the girl I married."

Elizabeth takes a seat at the table across from him. Remembering the advice Mary gave her, she gathers her courage to speak about her feelings. "With you at work all day, I've been lonely, Charles. I've never experienced life alone. I've always had people about." She shows Charles what she hopes is a confident smile. "I think I'm going to be just fine now."

She sees a look of concern cross her husband's face. "You weren't thinking of giving up were you?"

"Oh no, Charles! Of course not."

I wasn't—was I?

The smell of wood smoke and dampness fill the room. The silence is only interrupted by the hiss of moisture escaping from the logs. Elizabeth feels her heart beating in her ears. She fears that she's disappointed her new husband by saying too much about feeling lonely. She watches his frown lines soften. "Life out here is going to take a bit of getting used to. I'm happy you've found friends, Darling. I'm confident that you'll make others." Charles reaches down with a smile playing on his lips. "Now, do you want to know what's in my bag?"

Elizabeth's curiosity returns along with her joy and relief. "Of course! And I didn't even ask about your day. How was it?"

"My day was very productive but not nearly as exciting as yours." Charles puts the bag on the table and opens it. "You mentioned you wanted to make leather moccasins for your parents for Christmas. I thought we'd better get started. Here are leather scraps big enough for at least two pair."

Elizabeth sets the leather aside when she spies another package in the bag. Charles reaches in and pulls out a small rawhide sack. "Shiriki gave me this in exchange for a jar of your jam. I hope you don't mind that I took some from the shelf."

"Of course not. I'm happy to share." Elizabeth opens the bag and peers inside. "Glass beads! They're beautiful! They'll be perfect for decorating the moccasins and perhaps an amulet bag if there's enough leather. Why does Shiriki have beads?"

Charles grins. "I'm happy to see that the questions have returned. Shiriki's mother makes and sells beaded jewelry. She's a lovely lady whose had a very difficult life."

Without asking more questions, Elizabeth sets the bag aside and serves a supper of salt pork and beans soaked up by Vi's Sally Lunn Bread. While Elizabeth is putting away the dishes, Charles lays out the leather. Elizabeth comes to the table and he shows her how to cut patterns for the moccasins out of old newspaper using his boot templates as a guide. After the leather is cut, Charles uses a punch to make holes for the rawhide laces while Elizabeth sketches decorative designs on scraps of paper. "I'm thinking of using this simple four-point star for my father's moccasins and a sun design for my mother's. What do you think?"

Charles surveys the designs. "You're quite the artist."

"I dabble. Mostly, I like to paint but I didn't have room for supplies in my trunk. Maybe my parents will send me some for Christmas." Elizabeth chooses blue and white beads for the star; red, orange, and yellow for the sun. Not wanting to lose a single bead, she sorts them according to color in her muffin tin for safe keeping. By the end of the evening, two pairs of moccasins lay in pieces on the table ready to be assembled when the bead work is complete. Delighted to see that enough leather remains to make an amulet for her mother and small medicine bags for the younger Voogd children, Elizabeth moves closer to her husband. "We're a good team, aren't we, Mr. Horn?"

Putting his arm around his wife's waist, he replies, "We sure are, Mrs. Horn. Now, let's get cozy in our bed."

The next morning, just as the horizon begins to color, the crunch of the straw mattress wakens Elizabeth. She sees Charles creeping away from the bed. After pulling on his britches, he slowly and carefully takes his gun from the pegs above the mantle. As he moves toward the door, Elizabeth clutches the quilt to her chest and stares into the darkness. Then she props herself up on one elbow and shout-whispers. "What in the world are you doing?"

"Stay in bed and be quiet, Elizabeth. I heard something or someone near the house. It's too early for friendly visitors." Charles opens the door a crack and peers out.

"What is it?" Elizabeth asks, ignoring his request for quiet.

Pushing the door wide, but still holding his gun, Charles shouts. "Hello, there."

Elizabeth climbs out of bed, throws on her shawl and rushes to the window. She sees Shar eyeing Charles' gun. She's holding her hands in front of her to show she's friendly. "Hello, Mr. Horn. I'm Shar, Richard's daughter. I'm here to see your wife. It's important."

Charles puts the gun down. "It must be important for you to be out so early." He stands aside to allow the girl inside then speaks to Elizabeth. "You have a visitor."

Elizabeth rushes toward Shar. She fears the worst but keeps her voice low and calm. "What brings you here so early?"

Panting, Shar leans forward and places her hands on her knees to catch her breath. When she looks up, Elizabeth notices her running nose, red face, wrinkled dress, and loosely laced boots. There's a hint of fear in her eyes. Elizabeth hands her a hankie. "My mom sent me. I'm sorry to bother you so early but my little brother was sick all night with the croup again. He's worse than before. Yesterday, my mom noticed yarrow hanging from your ceiling. She used hers up and, in the past, it helped ease Gary's cough and the wheezing in his chest. She sent me to see if you'd share yours."

Bad as this news is, Elizabeth feels a sense of relief. "Of course!" She pats her rocker. "Sit here for a minute and catch your breath while I get you the yarrow and some honey."

She reaches for her dried yarrow and its leaves that she'd hung from the ceiling. While she's doing this, Charles introduces himself to the young girl. "Pleased to meet you, Mr. Horn. Thanks for not shooting me. I must have given you a fright coming to your house so early."

Charles pulls up a chair and sits next to Shar. "You did raise the alarm a bit but I'm glad you came. We're always here for our neighbors, no matter the time of day or night. I'm sorry to hear your little brother is under the weather. Is your pa home?"

"No sir, he already left for the fields. It's harvest time and every minute counts. I'll be helping him as soon as I get this here medicine home to Ma. None of us got much sleep last night—what with Gary coughing and all."

Elizabeth quickly puts the yarrow in a bit of cloth, secures it with string, and hands the package to Shar along with a small jar of honey. "Tell your ma to add a little honey to the yarrow and hot water. I'll be over this afternoon to see how Gary's doing and bring supper."

"Thank you, Mrs. Horn. Ma said she knew you'd be able to help. See you later. Nice to meet you, Mr. Horn."

Charles and Elizabeth stand in the open door as Shar runs back down the path toward home. Charles closes the door. "My goodness. That was a fast and early visit."

Elizabeth tightens the shawl around her shoulders. "That girl is all business. You should be one to appreciate that."

While his wife straightens the quilt and sorts out her clothes, Charles pulls on his boots, shoulders his gun, and heads for the door. "Guess I better bag some game before I leave for work if you're gonna be fixin' supper for a family of five plus us." He opens the door. "I'll have my breakfast when I get back."

After breakfast and seeing Charles off to work, Elizabeth cuts up the rabbits he'd killed and dressed then puts them in a big, black pot along with carrots, potatoes, and onions. She hangs the heavy pot on the hook over the fire to simmer. Before she starts on the biscuits, she makes up a packet of chamomile buds so Vi can enjoy a relaxing cup of tea before bed.

Midafternoon is gray and chilly when Elizabeth sets out for the Voogds with a pot of rabbit stew hanging from the crook of her elbow and a basket of biscuits and chamomile buds in her other hand. She shivers when the cold wind blows through her cape. As she hustles along the trail she notices large, black birds soaring on the updrafts. Their fully extended wings are motionless as they drift in the sunless sky. She tells herself they aren't buzzards, but her stomach churns as she thinks of the possibility. This isn't the joyful first visit she'd imagined, but she's glad to help the family who's been so welcoming to her and Charles.

When the Voogd's homestead comes into view, Elizabeth notices that the house looks much like her own—only double the length from front to back. There's a lean-to on the north side of the house and a large, red barn. To her left is a vegetable garden topped with straw and bedded down for winter. Only crumbling vines and a few gourds and pumpkins remain visible. She also notices a small, man-made cave dug into the side of the hill behind the house. She surmises that Vi keeps root vegetables and other supplies in the cool, dark space.

The property reminds Elizabeth of the Heidemann's homestead. As she considers this, she remembers that, as homesteading families, both the Voogds and Heidemanns own one hundred and sixty acres each and must live on the land for at least five years. She doesn't know when the Voogd's first arrived but she hopes they will remain.

Elizabeth softly knocks on the door, being careful not to disturb a sleeping child. Vi opens the door and greets her with a hug. She looks haggard with her hair escaping its braid and the buttons of her dress askew. Elizabeth sets the pot on the black cooking stove and her basket on a trestle table big enough to seat six. She notices a churn and a small spinning wheel to the side. Pegs with sparse, worn clothes line the walls next to shelves full of crockery, canned vegetables, meat, and other supplies. A braided, rag rug in brown tones covers the middle of the floor. This living space is the size of Elizabeth's house.

Vi motions for her to walk through to a wide, curtained opening into the next room. There's a dresser along one wall, bunk beds, and a low, single bed. Vi pulls aside the curtain that surrounds the big bed. Elizabeth peers down at a small boy sleeping. Vi whispers, "His breathing is still labored but he's stopped coughing for now and his fever's down."

The ladies return to the main living area. "I hope you can stay for a cup of tea. I'd like to explain something to you." Elizabeth, wondering what Vi's thinking, remains quiet as she watches her build up the fire and put the kettle on.

Vi turns from the fire. "The yarrow and honey helped ease Gary's cough so he could finally get to sleep. The supper smells delightful. I must admit, I'm pretty tuckered out after being up all night with Gary. Thanks for your kindness."

With steaming cups of rosehip tea in front of them, Elizabeth notices that Vi's forehead is laced with lines as she pulls her chair close to Elizabeth. "I think you should know the reason I panic when one of my children is sick." She takes a sip of tea. "We lost a son a few years back. Richard, we called him Junior, was only four when he passed. I've also lost two babies. One was stillborn, the other died within her first month. That's why I'm particularly fearful when one of my children becomes ill."

Although her heart breaks for Vi, Elizabeth's glad she's willing to share these sad stories. She takes Vi's hand. "I'm so sorry for your losses." Vi nods. "I also feared the worst this morning because I have a bit of a history too. My sister, Anna, died from pneumonia when she was just a baby. And, more recently, the family I traveled with coming west had to bury their baby girl along the trail." The two women are silent for a moment and Elizabeth feels the bond of friendship cementing between them. Then, not knowing what else to say, she looks around the room. "Where are the girls?"

"I sent them to gather eggs so Gary could get to sleep. It's not easy bein' five people in two rooms. The curtain helps but it doesn't keep out girls' giggles."

Elizabeth finds it hard to imagine five people living in this cramped space. She wonders what it must be like for this family to be cooped up here during the long, dark, winter months.

Not wanting to further contemplate winter, Elizabeth reaches into her basket. "I brought a book with me. I'd be glad to read to the girls while you get some rest or finish up your work."

Vi rises from her seat, her face wan. "They'll love that."

Just then, the girls rush through the door. Their cheeks are rosy from the cold and they smell of fresh air when they greet Elizabeth with hugs. Shar hands the basket of eggs to her mother and they take off their heavy sweaters and muddy boots. Their eyes sparkle when they see a book sitting near Elizabeth's chair. When she beckons them over, Shar quietly goes to the back and returns with the quilt from her bed. After she's made a nest, she sits down and motions for Jan to settle onto her lap. Elizabeth stays in her chair so both girls can see the pictures in the book. "If you girls are real quiet so your brother can sleep, I'll read to you from *Alice's Adventures in Wonderland*." She picks up the book. "Have you read it, Shar?"

Shar's eyes shine, her answer comes out in a squeak. "No ma'am, I haven't read it. I haven't even heard of it, but I really love books. Thank you so much for bringing one and reading to us."

Warmth spreads through Elizabeth's chest. "Well, it's my pleasure because I love books too. Books have helped me feel beautiful and capable even when I wasn't. They've taken me places I'll never go and introduced me to people I'll never meet." She pauses as she watches the girls take in her words. After a minute, she catches Vi's eye and looks at her conspiratorially. "Just one thing. Before I leave, Jan needs to give me that recipe for Sally Lunn Hot Bread."

Jan squirms in Shar's lap, then looks at Elizabeth who can see that she's taking the request very seriously. "Yes, ma'am, don't you worry none. Me and Ma will get you that recipe. Now, p-l-e-a-s-e start reading."

Vi spins wool and Jan snuggles close to Shar while Gary sleeps. Elizabeth's heart is warm with friendship and mutual understanding. She holds out the book so the girls can see the cover. "*Alice's Adventures in Wonderland* was written by Lewis Carroll but his real name is Charles Lutwidge Dodgson."

"Charles, like your Charles?"

"Yes, Jan. He lives in England, far across the sea …."

CHAPTER SIXTEEN

WISHFUL THINKING

Before cooking breakfast the following morning, Elizabeth dresses in her navy blue skirt and crisp, white blouse. She pins her cameo at her neck then carefully braids her hair. Charles looks up from his seat at the table where he's sharpening a knife. "And where might you be going so dressed up?"

Elizabeth feels a little trepidation as she answers. "I thought I'd walk with you to town this morning and visit Mr. Mitchell. I'd like to speak with him about being a substitute teacher." She sees Charles' eyes widen with surprise.

"Why haven't you spoken of this before?"

With the sunrise, the room brightens along with Elizabeth's confidence. She looks over at her books on the shelf. "Reading to the Voogd girls yesterday, reminded me of how much I enjoy being with children. I taught my younger siblings to read and helped them with their lessons. I miss teaching." She walks to the fireplace to start breakfast. "Of course this all depends on if Mr. Mitchell finds me suitable. What do you think?"

"Why now?"

"I thought taking care of a house and cooking meals would take up all my time but I'm finding that, after developing a routine, I have time on my hands and I'd like the opportunity to occasionally teach."

Charles wipes the knife. "I think substitute teaching is an excellent idea and I'm sure Mitchell will find you suitable. You certainly look the part."

Relieved, Elizabeth whips eggs with a splash of milk and pours them into the spider. After breakfast, she quickly clears the dishes then puts on her winter cloak. Charles tucks her hand into the crook of his arm and they briskly walk to town. When they arrive at Mr. Mitchell's office, Elizabeth's confidence begins to falter. Charles gives her a peck on the cheek. "Good luck, my dear. See you at supper."

With a nervous flutter in her stomach, Elizabeth climbs the stairs and knocks on Mr. Mitchell's door.

A low voice responds. "It's open."

When Elizabeth enters the room, Mitchell rises from a substantial desk strewn with papers.

"Good morning, Mr. Mitchell. I was wondering if I might speak with you for a moment." Elizabeth looks at the clutter. "If you're not too busy."

Mitchell walks around his desk and pulls a chair from the corner. "Have a seat, Mrs. Horn." He returns to his chair behind the desk. "What's on your mind?"

Elizabeth tentatively sits on the edge of her chair. "I'd like to apply for the job of substitute teacher. You mentioned something about the position when we met?"

Oddly, the school bell rings before he has a chance to respond. "Well now, I can't say that we have an application process exactly but I'm interested in what you have to say.

Our teacher, Miss Harvey, is quite reliable but even she can catch a fever from time to time."

Seeing that her idea isn't rejected out of hand, Elizabeth sits back and thinks carefully before she answers. "I'm the oldest of six children, Sir, and, now that I've left home, I miss helping them with their lessons. They progressed quite well under my instruction and I believe I can handle a classroom even though I've not had previous experience." Elizabeth holds her breath, hoping Mr. Mitchell won't ask her age.

He pushes his glasses up from the tip of his nose. "What grade did you complete?"

"Tenth, sir. But I keep up my learning by reading books and *The New York Ledger* and..." Elizabeth quickly remembers Mitchell's pride in the local newspaper. "...*The Valley County Herald,* of course."

Mitchell strokes his chin. Elizabeth feels as though he's using his lawyer's brain to scrutinize her intensions. "Normally, I wouldn't consider a married woman for a teaching position. We like to hire women who don't have husbands to support them, plus, most qualified, married women have children to care for."

Elizabeth can feel her cheeks redden. She wants to tell him just how much she wants children, thinks better of it, and remains silent.

Without another word, Mitchell reaches inside his desk drawer, pulls out a piece of paper, dips his pen in the inkwell, and writes a few lines. "Since you're our only applicant and seem qualified, I'd like you to consider this offer." He blots the ink and turns the paper toward Elizabeth. She moves closer to the edge of the desk and quickly reads the short document. Mitchell summarizes. "We'll pay you fifty cents a day, about the same as Miss Harvey. You'll have to teach on very short notice. I'll send my messenger, Peter, to your house when you're needed." Elizabeth remains quiet, and Mitchell concludes. "I expect you to observe the class for one day without pay so the students can get to know you and you can see how Miss Harvey conducts the class." He reaches across the desk and thumps the paper. "It's all right here. Is this agreeable, Mrs. Horn?"

"Yes sir."

He clears his throat. "After your observation, I will ask Miss Harvey her opinion and take what she says into consideration. Understood?"

"Yes, sir."

Mitchell hands the pen to Elizabeth. "Then sign here under my name. Being a lawyer, I like to keep things official."

Elizabeth signs her name then rises. "Thank you Mr. Mitchell. You'll not regret your decision."

"I trust not. Good day and give my greetings to your husband. I assume he's on board with this decision?"

"Yes sir. He is. Good day, Mr. Mitchell." Elizabeth quickly turns to leave before he can change his mind. Before returning home, she decides to stop by the boot shop to give Charles the good news. On the way, she passes the open door of the saloon. Smelling rancid grease and old beer, she peers inside and sees chairs upended on tables and a young man sweeping the floor. Before she can duck away, he tips his cap. Elizabeth guesses that he's about her age with black, unruly hair hanging lank around his ears. He's wearing brown pants that reach just above his ankles, and a red flannel shirt with rolled-up sleeves. Elizabeth gives a little nod then hustles next door to Charles' shop.

Two shelves of boots fill the plate glass window. A sign reading "Boots For Sale" hangs above the door. A bell tinkles when Elizabeth enters. The small room, with a counter across the front, smells of leather and glue. Charles looks up from his workbench behind the counter. "Elizabeth! What a nice surprise."

Elizabeth puts her elbows on the pockmarked, wooden counter. "I thought I'd stop by and give you the good news. I have the job of substitute teacher...that is, if Miss Harvey, the teacher, approves when I make a visit."

Her husband gets up from his bench and walks to the counter. "That's wonderful!"

Elizabeth feels relieved that Charles is still onboard now that she's spoken to the lawyer. "Mr. Mitchell even drew up a contract for me to sign. It's all very official. When I'm needed, he'll send his messenger, Peter, to the house."

Charles nods toward the saloon. "Peter works next door. You might have seen him when you walked by."

"I saw a man sweeping the floor."

Charles gazes out the window at a passerby. "That's Peter. Very reliable. I can understand why Mitchell uses him as a messenger."

Elizabeth gathers her cloak around her as the couple say their good-byes. The walk home is cold but Elizabeth barely notices. She feels warm on the inside as she sends a thank-you heavenward. *This is a wish come true! I can't wait to write my parents.* A horse gallops by distracting Elizabeth from her thoughts. As she approaches the path to her house, she returns to her rumination. *I won't write to them until after my visit to the classroom. I wouldn't want to disappoint them all over again.*

Charles returns from work that evening with mail in his pouch. He hands Elizabeth a letter from her mother and a two-month old copy of *The New York Ledger.* Elizabeth slips the letter into her apron pocket to read later by the fire. She wants to savor the news about her family.

After eating supper and settling into her rocker, Elizabeth pulls out the letter and opens it. Her mother's sing-song voice hums in her ears and the black ink becomes blurred, diluted by Elizabeth's tears. She sniffs loudly, wipes her eyes on her sleeve, then tucks the letter into her trunk. Without a word, she goes to the privy, returns, undresses, and gives Charles a kiss on the cheek. "Good night, Darling."

Two days later, on a Sunday morning after breakfast, Charles and Elizabeth are sitting around the table taking turns reading a Bible passage. They make an effort to observe the Sabbath without a church building or a congregation. Elizabeth notices Charles looking toward the window. He gets up then calls Elizabeth. "It's Peter. He probably has a message from Mr. Mitchell." He opens the door and greets the young man.

"Hey, Charlie, good to see you. I have a message for your wife from Miss Harvey." Charles takes the message and gives it to Elizabeth. Introductions are made and tea is offered.

Peter turns from the door. "Thanks but I gotta be on my way. I need to deliver a message to Dr. Towar."

Charles and Elizabeth return to the table. Elizabeth unfolds the sheet of paper and reads aloud. "Please come to observe my class on Monday. I will be there by eight to light the stove. Bring your lunch. Miss Harvey."

Charles opens the Bible. "Looks like Mitchell didn't waste any time in contacting the teacher. That's a good sign."

Elizabeth covers Charles' hand with her own. "I can't believe this is really happening, Charles. I'm a lucky girl to have a wonderful husband, a home, and, I hope, a part-time job. I never could have had all of this if I'd stayed in Illinois."

The couple resume their Sunday devotions. By afternoon, the day turns warm for late October and Charles suggests they exercise the horses and enjoy a ride. They walk to the livery and saddle up. Elizabeth has her hands full keeping control of Pansy who is particularly frisky. She reigns her in to marvel at the bright red sumac growing near the creek. Many fields are harvested. However, as they ride by the Voogd homestead, they wave at Richard who's picking the last of his field corn.

After an invigorating ride, stabling the horses, and walking home, Elizabeth pulls together a meager supper of leftovers from their Sunday dinner of fried prairie chicken and dumplings. She washes the dishes and makes porridge for the next morning. Then she heats her iron and carefully presses, what Charles refers to as her "teacher outfit"—the skirt and blouse she wore to her interview. "Be sure I'm up early. I want to leave the house by seven fifteen to be at the school when Miss Harvey arrives."

The next morning, Charles gently kisses Elizabeth on the forehead to wake her. She smiles when she sees a fire already heating the room and kettle. She dresses by lantern light, heats the porridge she prepared the night before, makes a jam sandwich, and places it in a metal bucket along with a jar of tea. After breakfast, Charles banks the fire, extinguishes the lantern, then holds the door for his wife. Even in her excitement for a day at school, as she steps out the door, Elizabeth takes time to admire the beautiful golden sunrise coming up over the distant hills. She sighs. "Breathtaking isn't it?"

Charles puts his arm around his wife's shoulders. "It never gets old."

Elizabeth slips her hand through the crook in Charles' arm. She feels a mixture of excitement and gratitude all stirred up with a pinch of anxiety. "Do you really think I can do this, Darling? What if there are older children in the class? They could be close to my age. What if Miss Harvey doesn't have the same confidence in me you and Mr. Mitchell have?"

Charles pats Elizabeth's hand. "One step at a time, my dear. Just one step at a time."

When they arrive at the schoolhouse, Charles gives Elizabeth a kiss on the cheek. "Good luck. You're going to do just fine. I'll leave the shop early and pick you up after school." Elizabeth gives him a weak smile before he turns and walks toward his shop.

The schoolhouse door is ajar, seemingly in need of repair. With some effort, Elizabeth swings it open. Then, she pulls back her shoulders and walks into the room. She sees Miss Harvey turn from the stove and walk toward her.

Although she is at least four or five years older, Elizabeth thinks that her diminutive size makes them seem nearly the same age. Her dark brown hair is pulled back into a tight bun and she's wearing a blue, calico dress with mutton sleeves—much like what Elizabeth's bride's maids wore. She's also wearing brown, practical, low-heeled shoes which makes Elizabeth somewhat self-conscious in her cream-colored, heeled boots she wore to her wedding.

Elizabeth sees a look of surprise cross Miss Harvey's face when she comes within a few feet. *She undoubtedly realizes how young I am, despite my size.*

"I presume you are Mrs. Horn," Miss Harvey says without so much as a smile.

"Yes, but please call me Elizabeth."

"Of course. However, you are Mrs. Horn when the children are present." Without offering her first name, Miss Harvey motions to Elizabeth. "Please follow me."

The classroom, not much bigger than Elizabeth's house, is smaller than she'd imagined it. The teacher's desk is at the front of the room, opposite the door. The black, wood stove is positioned in the left-front corner. Two rows of three small desks each face the front. Next to the desks, two tables with two chairs each, are set one behind the other. Pegs for coats line the back wall near the entrance and bookshelves are attached to the wall on either side of an unadorned window. A chair sits beside the teacher's desk and another faces the front corner of the wall opposite the stove.

Miss Harvey indicates the chair beside her desk. "You may observe from this chair." She picks up a book from her desk. "Are you familiar with this?"

Elizabeth takes the book and looks at the cover. "Yes, of course. This is an edition of the *Eclectic First Readers*. We called them *McGuffey Readers*."

The teacher retrieves the book from Elizabeth and marks a page with a scrap of paper. "I'd like you to read today's lesson to the children and then ask them questions about the reading. You may also circulate when the children are doing their seatwork and offer help when it's needed. Do you understand?" Elizabeth nods and Miss Harvey continues. "I will ring the bell in five minutes at precisely eight thirty. We start early here so the children can return home in time for afternoon chores. Some have a long walk. We dismiss at two thirty and take thirty minutes for lunch at twelve o'clock." Before Elizabeth can respond, Miss Harvey takes the bell from her desk, her shawl from the back of her chair, then marches out the front door. Elizabeth follows close at her heels.

The children come into the classroom and quietly remove their coats, placing their lunch pails beneath. As they do this, Miss Harvey points out the two Henderson children, ages six and eight, and four other children ranging in age from seven to nine. Each child promptly sits at their assigned desk. Only one older boy sits on a chair behind the front table. Miss Harvey nods in his direction. "That's Eli Holt. He's thirteen. He's the son of The Mercantile's owner. The other three older children will be here in late November when the harvest is complete."

Elizabeth is quickly introduced as the prospective substitute teacher then Miss Harvey begins arithmetic lessons, working first with the younger children. Elizabeth notices Eli watching her over his slate. He's almost Elizabeth's height, with skinny arms and legs, and a smirk on his face. At the noon break, he approaches Elizabeth. "Ain't you a bit young to be callin' yerself a teacher?"

Before Elizabeth can respond, Miss Harvey takes control of the situation. "Mr. Holt, march yourself right over to that corner." She points to the chair facing the wall. Eli walks slowly in the direction indicated but not before giving Elizabeth a withering look.

After lunch, Elizabeth feels that her brief time in front of the class reading and asking questions goes well but, by the end of the day, she's still uncertain whether or not Miss Harvey will recommend her to Mr. Mitchell.

After the children leave at two thirty, Elizabeth helps tidy up the room. Just as the women come out the door, Charles arrives. Introductions are made, then Miss Harvey addresses Elizabeth. "I will speak with Mr. Mitchell this afternoon. Good day."

Elizabeth takes Charles' arm. "Let's go home. I need a cup of tea."

The following morning, after Charles has left for work, there's a knock on the door. Elizabeth wipes flour from her hands then peers out the window. Peter is there with his cap in his hands.

Elizabeth opens the door and greets him. "I hope you have good news for me."

Peter hands Elizabeth a large envelope. "I have no idea, Mrs. Horn. I just deliver messages for Mr. Mitchell; I don't read 'em." He then turns and replaces his cap. "Good day."

Before opening the envelope, Elizabeth sits in her rocker. She opens the flap and pulls out a heavy sheet of ivory paper. "It's a copy of the contract!" Elizabeth gives a sigh of relief then gets up and twirls around before returning to her bread-making.

CHAPTER SEVENTEEN

A KNIGHT TO REMEMBER

At twilight on a Wednesday in early November, Charles uncharacteristically rushes through the door. His nose is pink from the cold. When Elizabeth comes to greet him, he gives her a warm smile and peck on the cheek before he quickly hangs up his coat and hat. He beams. "Guess who's coming to the fort?"

Elizabeth puts her hand on her hip. "So, now it's your turn for questions?"

Charles sets his satchel by the door and Elizabeth returns to the fire and her pot of soup.

"That's not a real question, my dear. It's a rhetorical question. I know the answer and you don't." Charles grins. "I spoke with Little Buckshot this afternoon and..."

Elizabeth turns from the fire. "Hold on. Who in the world is Little Buckshot?"

"I've spoken of him before. His real name is Conrad Wentworth, the post's guide and hunter."

Elizabeth nods.

"May I go on?"

Elizabeth returns to the fire and her pot. "Why don't you sit down first?"

Charles sits on the edge of his chair. "When I saw him…"

"Little Buckshot?"

"Yes. When I saw him at the fort today, he said that Sir Rose Lambert Price is coming to the fort."

"And he is?"

Charles sighs. "He's a very famous sport hunter and a world-class adventurer. He's an English knight and baronet. He's been to South America and began his trip across the country earlier this year." Having made his important announcement, Charles moves his chair closer to the fire and holds his hands toward its warmth.

Elizabeth's interest is now piqued. She leaves her pot and pulls a chair near Charles. "Will we have a chance to meet this famous person?"

Charles rubs his hands together then places them in his lap. "I certainly hope so. They're organizing a hunt for him, and I've been invited to be part of the hunting party. I'm sure there will be some sort of reception when he arrives. If there is, you'll get a chance to meet him too." Charles leaves the comfort of the fire and returns to the well-worn leather bag he takes to and from work each day. From it he pulls a package and hands it to Elizabeth. "When I spoke with Little Buckshot today, he gave me these elk steaks."

Elizabeth carefully unties the string and peers inside the wrappings. "They'll be a nice change from our usual rabbit, pheasant, and prairie chicken. I've prepared our supper for tonight, but we'll enjoy them tomorrow. Why did he give them to you?"

Charles returns to his seat. "They're partial payment for

boots I made for him a while back." Elizabeth scrutinizes the dark meat and detects a gamey smell. Charles frowns slightly then continues to speak with unaccustomed enthusiasm. "I hope you like elk. If possible, I plan to bag one on the hunt with the knight."

Increasingly worried about adequate food supplies for the winter, Elizabeth sighs with relief when she hears her husband talk about the hunt. Still, she wonders about having enough to eat if or when they're snowed in.

The next morning, cold drafts creep around the window frames, the dirt floor feels like ice. Elizabeth tightly wraps her shawl around her shoulders and drinks a second cup of hot, rose-hip tea. Charles brings in an armload of wood before leaving for work. "The house should warm up soon. Until it does, stay close to the fire so you don't catch a chill. I hope to be home early tonight."

Elizabeth moves the table closer to the fire where she kneads her bread and dices root vegetables to accompany the elk steaks. Gradually feeling more comfortable as the house warms up, she wonders what it will be like when the weather really turns cold. Distracted by her thoughts, she doesn't notice someone approaching the house until she hears a knock on the door. She jumps and looks out the window to see who's come to visit on this cold, dreary, Friday morning. A young woman stands on her stoop dressed in a threadbare, brown, wool, hooded cape with no gloves or scarf. She flings open the door. "If you're looking for Elizabeth Horn, you've found her."

The woman nods and speaks softly. "Good morning, Mrs. Horn. I'm Tina, Mrs. Capron's maid. You might have met her husband, Lieutenant Thaddeus Capron?"

"I don't believe I've had the pleasure. Do come in and sit down. I'll get you a cup of tea. You must be chilled to the bone."

Standing just inside the door, Tina responds, "Thank you, ma'am, but I can't stay. I'm here to deliver an invitation to tea. Mrs. Capron would like to have you come at two tomorrow if that's convenient. She'll send a wagon to fetch you."

Tina looks close to her own age, and Elizabeth's hoping to get to know the girl. She reminds Elizabeth of a small, timid rabbit with alert brown eyes, washed-out brown hair, and larger-than-usual ears on either side of a small, oval face. Her childlike hands constantly fidget at her sides, giving Elizabeth the impression that she's very anxious.

Tina turns to leave. "I'm sorry I can't stay, Mrs. Horn. I need to git back to my chores. Mrs. Capron will be sore if I dawdle. Should I let the missus know you'll be comin' tomorrow?"

"Of course. Tell her I'm looking forward to it. Thank you for coming, Tina. Are you sure you can't stay and warm up?"

With sad, downcast eyes, Tina looks at Elizabeth. "Thank you, maybe 'nother time."

Elizabeth spends the afternoon mending socks and stewing apples. While she works, she wonders about Tina and the unexpected invitation to tea. She thinks that perhaps this will be an opportunity to meet more ladies and become a part of the community. *Or, maybe they'll think I'm just a girl who's too young to join their circle.*

When Charles returns from work, Elizabeth tries to contain her news until he takes off his coat, pours himself a small glass of whiskey, and warms himself by the fire. She feels him watching her while she's stirring the vegetables.

She continues to hold in her excitement until he speaks. "How was your day? Did anything unusual happen?"

Elizabeth turns from the steaming kettle and sees a little smirk on Charles' face. The comforting smell of ginger bread fills the air. "Yes! Mrs. Capron invited me to tea tomorrow. Her girl, Tina, brought me the invitation."

Taking a sip from his glass, Charles smiles. "That's lovely, Dear. I know you like having friends."

"I do. Now, tell me all you know about the Caprons." Swinging the pot to the side so the vegetables won't burn, Elizabeth pulls her rocker next to her husband's chair. "I'm wondering what to wear and if I should bring a gift and if tea will be very formal and—"

He puts a hand on his wife's arm. "I'll tell you what I know of the Caprons at supper. Now, how about searing one of those elk steaks you promised me."

Elizabeth fries the steaks in aromatic garlic butter, finishes cooking the vegetables, and boils potatoes while Charles finishes his whiskey. She tries to wait patiently remembering a saying of her mother's. *Patience is not simply the ability to wait. It's how we behave while we're waiting.* She knows Charles doesn't purposely try her patience. He's just a slow and thoughtful man.

At last, while they're drinking hot tea with warm gingerbread, Charles addresses her questions. "Lieutenant Capron, his wife Cynthia, and their three children live in the Infantry Officer's Quarters, one-half of the duplex you saw coming in. The family came here from Camp Ruggles, which is across the river." He takes a sip of tea. "While Lieutenant Capron presided over the building of the fort, Mrs. Capron and her children remained at Ruggles. You wouldn't know from speaking with him, but as Post Quartermaster of a $110,000 fort, the lieutenant was in a position of power and influence."

Elizabeth passes Charles another square of gingerbread. "What do you know of his family?"

Charles pours heavy cream over his dessert. "Sure glad Vi is willing to sell us her extra cream and butter."

Elizabeth impatiently clears her throat.

Charles furrows his brow. "I believe they have a daughter and two sons. I've heard that the youngest child and Mrs. Capron are not in good health."

Elizabeth leans towards Charles. "Is that all you know about them?"

"I'm afraid so. But I'm sure tomorrow night you'll have many more details to share."

Having finished his dessert, Charles gets up, retrieves his satchel from beside the door, and returns to the table. "I need to start work on a new boot order."

After she washes the dishes, Elizabeth looks over Charles' shoulder. "What exactly are you working on?"

He holds up a piece of brown leather. "These are the preliminaries of a custom order. Boots for the soldiers are without decoration but some local men like something a bit fancier. This is an order from a rancher up north a ways." Elizabeth pulls her rocker up to the table and waits for Charles to continue. "This cowhide is the shaft." He points to the items on the table. "When the boot is finished, it will have a one inch stacked heel and a squared toe." Charles turns the leather over in his hands. "After I finish the tooling on this shaft, I'll sew the boot together. The process is similar to how you made your moccasins. You created the beaded design then assembled the parts." Charles runs his fingers across the smooth leather then hands it to Elizabeth. "That's the beginning of my design."

Elizabeth holds the leather to the lantern to examine it closely. "I see an arrowhead. Will you add other elements?"

Charles indicates a scrap of paper with a pencil design showing an arrowhead with a starburst behind. Elizabeth sits across from Charles to watch him work on the hand-tooled motif. He squints his eyes when he uses an awl and small hammer to transfer the star design from the paper pattern to the leather. He picks up another tool then explains his process. "I use this leather maul to bruise the leather and perfect the design."

Elizabeth moves in closer as Charles taps the small knife-like tool along the design one dot at a time. She thinks that it's no wonder her husband is a slow, patient man. His work requires him to be. After observing for several minutes, Elizabeth leaves her husband to his work, crosses the room, opens her trunk, and surveys her spare wardrobe. She wants to save wearing her lavender wedding dress for a possible Christmas celebration. *I can't imagine a Christmas without my family!* Shaking off the grim thought, Elizabeth considers her next-best: "the teacher outfit." Her only other choices are her two calico work dresses, which, although carefully mended, are faded and worn.

Charles looks up from his work. "How are you coming with your Christmas gifts?"

With her mind taken up with preparations for the tea, Elizabeth is taken aback by the change of subject. "I've finished the moccasins and I'm nearly finished with the beadwork on the amulet bag. I wrote a poem to my mother, which I'll put inside as a surprise."

Charles stands to stretch. "Don't forget we need to get everything on the next supply wagon to Grand Island if it's going to arrive in Illinois in time for Christmas. If you finish up tonight, you can take your gifts with you to the fort tomorrow. Lieutenant Capron will see that they get on the wagon." Taking Charles' advice, Elizabeth stays up past her usual bedtime in order to finish her gifts.

The next morning, after cooking breakfast and seeing Charles off to work, she heats her flat iron and presses her modest ensemble. She has the feeling of being an imposter as she steps into her skirt, pins her cameo at the neck of her blouse, and slips on her short tea gloves.

When the carriage arrives shortly before two, Elizabeth dashes out the door with her Christmas packages in hand. She's pleased to see another woman sitting in the buckboard. A young man in a pressed, dark blue uniform holds his hand out for Elizabeth. "I'm Private Symmons, ma'am. May I help you into the wagon?"

After settling into her seat, Elizabeth is delighted to learn that her traveling companion is Mrs. Mitchell. She smells of lilac water, has rosy, wrinkled cheeks, sun-freckled skin, and a warm smile. Her bell-shaped felt hat covers much of her salt and pepper hair. After introductions are made, Elizabeth looks over at her companion. "Tell me about your family, Mrs. Mitchell. I've already met your husband, of course."

With blue eyes sparkling, Mrs. Mitchell turns to look at Elizabeth. "I know there is a great difference in our ages, Dear, but please call me Harriett." The corners of her mouth turn up. "We have six grown children and twelve grandchildren." She pauses and looks down at her gloved hands. "Unfortunately, they have all moved farther west and we rarely see them. Four families live in California and two in Wyoming. We planted the pioneer spirit in them, and it grew like topsy. I sure do miss seeing the little ones grow up."

After asking Elizabeth about her family, the ladies are quiet as Private Symmons pulls the horses to the side of the road to let a wide wagon pass. Elizabeth picks up on the thread of the conversation. "I hope to have a little one someday soon. You'd make a wonderful stand-in grandma."

Harriet pats Elizabeth's hand and gives her a sweet smile. "I'd like that Elizabeth, but all in good time."

When the ladies arrive at the Caprons, Elizabeth asks Private Symmons to deliver her Christmas package to the lieutenant for safe passage to the Grand Island railway station. Symmons secures the packages under his arm. "My pleasure, Mrs. Horn. You ladies have a nice afternoon. I'll be by later to drive you home."

Tina answers the door looking thin and frail in a gray, wool, homespun ankle-length dress covered by a white, starched apron. She ushers Harriett and Elizabeth through a cold room with a spinet piano sitting in one corner and a hair wreath in a gilt frame on the far wall.

She then indicates for them to proceed to the next room, which Elizabeth assumes to be the parlor. Mrs. Capron greets them. Elizabeth observes two, black leather rockers with white doilies across the back and three dining room chairs forming a half circle in front of the fireplace. Family portraits adorn the walls. The warm room smells faintly of camphor.

Elizabeth sits in the chair next to Harriett and takes in the details of her surroundings. Unlike the simplicity of the Clapps' home, Mrs. Capron's parlor is stuffed with knick-knacks and heavy furniture including a walnut bureau against the wall. The maroon flowered wallpaper features a gold, vertical stripe. Heavy maroon drapes hang at the windows barely allowing the tepid sun to peek through. Thinking this dark house isn't her idea of what she wants for her future home, Elizabeth remembers all she loved about the Clapp's. Her attention is recalled when Mrs. Capron introduces her to Mrs. Coppinger, the commandant's wife, and Ada Hutchens, a young woman whose husband is a civilian employee of the fort. Elizabeth nods her greetings then asks about the baby peacefully sleeping in a basket next to Ada.

Mrs. Hutchens looks down. "That's Maude." She gives Elizabeth a prideful look before adding. "She was the first white baby born in Valley County. She's five months old."

Elizabeth wants to know more about this young mother and her baby but senses Mrs. Hutchen's reluctance to speak. Her curiosity, however, gets the best of her and she asks one more question. "Do you live near the fort?"

Mrs. Hutchen shifts in her seat. "We live in a sod house behind the officer's quarters. Maude was born there. Living so close, Doctor Towar was present at the delivery."

Elizabeth has many other questions but Mrs. Capron quickly moves the conversation on to events that transpired before Elizabeth's arrival. While the ladies chat, Elizabeth has an opportunity to observe Cynthia Capron more closely. She's fashionably dressed in a dark blue, two-piece ensemble with several petticoats and a small bustle. The bodice of the jacket hugs Mrs. Capron's ample bosom. Her dark brown hair is meticulously styled with long, single curls in front of her ears and a neat bun in the back. Despite her sophisticated look, her face is drawn and pale and she has dark circles under her chocolate brown eyes.

When the conversation wanes, Mrs. Capron calls for her children. "I'd like you to meet my children, Mrs. Horn." She looks in the direction of her son who has just entered the room holding the hand of a little girl. He takes the cue from his mother and bows slightly toward Elizabeth.

"I'm Hazen. I'm seven and this is my little sister, Louise but we all call her Elo. She's five. We're pleased to meet you, Mrs. Horn."

Elizabeth feels her stomach tense. *What a coincidence. Another little girl named Louise!*

Elo gives a polite curtsy. Hazen then looks over at Tina, who stands in the corner with the tea tray. "And that's Tina. She makes our supper and gives us our baths."

Mrs. Capron cuts in. "Our son, Henry, is sleeping. He's two and has a bit of the croup I'm afraid. I'm sure you'll meet him another time."

Elizabeth smiles at the two children, then nods toward Tina. "I do hope your son's health improves, Mrs. Capron."

After Tina serves tea and cakes, the hostess announces the main reason for the gathering. "If you ladies are agreeable, I'd like you to help me plan a reception for Sir Rose Lambert Price. As you've probably heard, he'll be arriving next week for a hunt." Elizabeth nods the affirmative along with the others. "I'd like to give him a proper welcome the night of his arrival. After the hunt, I'm sure the men will have an eating-drinking-smoking party to which we will not be invited."

While the ladies talk of fancy decorations and food, Elizabeth thinks about the knight and why he's visiting from England. She finally gathers the courage to address the others. "May I offer a suggestion, Mrs. Capron?"

Mrs Capron looks toward Elizabeth, brows raised. "Yes?"

Elizabeth takes a breath and moves to the edge of her chair. "I believe Mr. Price has come all this way to have an authentic prairie experience. If he wanted all the finery and fancy foods of England, he would have stayed home. I propose we have a simple potluck supper featuring our best home cooking and a barn-style dance with fall decorations." When she sees that her idea garners nods of approval from most of the ladies, she elaborates. "On a recent horseback ride, my husband and I spotted a good deal of bittersweet. Our neighbor, Vi Voogd, has gourds and a few pumpkins left in her garden and I'm sure we can locate plenty of Indian corn. The colorful fall decorations will fit nicely with our casual theme. I'd be glad to ask Vi about the gourds and gather the bittersweet if you're open to the idea."

Being the newest and youngest member of the group, Elizabeth cringes at the thought that she's overstepped her place. She feels heat spreading across her cheeks as she sits back in her chair. Although Mrs. Hutchens remains quiet and unsmiling, the other three ladies express their enthusiasm for Elizabeth's plan and immediately begin sketching out the details.

After the tea, Symmons returns with the wagon and Elizabeth and Harriett settle themselves for the short ride home. As the carriage bumps along the road, Harriett reaches over and, as she did on the ride to the fort, pats Elizabeth's hand. "For one so young, it was quite brave of you to speak up at the tea. I believe you garnered the respect of the officer's wives."

Elizabeth acknowledges Harriett's compliment. "Still, I'm wondering about Mrs. Hutchen's reaction."

Harriet shakes her head. "Don't fret about her, Dear. She may be feeling a bit jealous of a newcomer. As for me, I'd like to get to know you better. I hope you'll come to visit soon. Just ask anyone in town and they'll direct you to our house."

The following week, Elizabeth gathers the decorations she'd promised for the party and, on Friday, she makes pies as her contribution to the potluck.

On Saturday morning, she and Charles deliver the decorations to the fort. He gives her a strange look when she leads the way to the enlisted men's quarters. "Most of the soldiers are away on patrol and we're using this space for the party." Inside the building, beds and footlockers are stacked at one end of the room and make-shift tables, made from long boards set between saw horses and covered with gingham fabric, contributed by Mrs. Coppinger, are taking up the center. Elizabeth points to a table perpendicular to the others. "That's the head table where the officers and Price will be sitting. Put your bundle there. I'll start decorating the food tables."

Charles looks around the room. "Where do the rest of us eat?"

Busy with arranging bittersweet, Elizabeth doesn't turn as she answers. "The other guests will eat standing unless they're lucky enough to snag a table not covered with food."

When she's finished, Elizabeth stands back to admire her work, then Charles steers her toward the door. "It's lovely, Dear. Now, let's return home. I have work to attend to before we leave for the reception."

By five o'clock, the sun is close to setting and the air is crisp when Vi and Richard stop for the Horns. Elizabeth carefully places her butterscotch pies in the back of the wagon.

The couples chat companionably during the short ride to the fort. When they arrive, the ladies of the organizing committee sweep Elizabeth up as they work together to take care of the last-minute preparations.

About a dozen couples are in attendance including people from town, a few homesteaders, the officers and their wives along with some other personnel from the fort. Elizabeth quickly spots the guest of honor surrounded by a circle of admiring men. Charles is off with Richard so Elizabeth, pretending to arrange bittersweet, stands near enough to overhear Sir Price speaking in a slow baritone. He looks exactly like the knight in Elizabeth's imagination. He's a tall, robust gentleman with thick gray hair covering his ears, piercing black eyes, a broad big-tooth smile, and large hands and feet. Elizabeth doesn't expect, however, to see the knight wearing Western dinner attire including a long, black leather coat, gleaming black boots, and a stiff white shirt with a bolo tie.

The knight looks from man to man as he confidently speaks. Elizabeth picks up the thread of the story midway through his monologue. "While I was hunting antelope with officers from Fort Sanders near Laramie City in Wyoming, I killed one by a chance shot with an American Springfield rifled musket, 45 caliber. The ball went in at the eye and passed through the neck."

Charles, who has quietly come up behind Elizabeth, whispers in her ear. "The rifle he's describing is the standard infantry rifle of the type commonly used by the military. I have the same gun. A Springfield model of '73, breech-loading with the 'trapdoor' mechanism, caliber .45-70 often referred to as the needle gun." When she looks at him expectantly, Charles continues. "Among the officers witnessing the remarkable rifle shot Sir Price speaks of, was one under orders to proceed to Fort Hartsuff on court martial duty. He invited Sir Price to join him here for a hunt and that's how all of this got started."

Elizabeth is dying to meet this man-of-the-hour and hopes her husband will find a way to introduce her. In a few minutes, when the men start to wander off, Charles takes his wife's elbow and guides her toward Price. He holds out his hand and Price gives it a hearty shake. "So, the bootmaker. What's your name again, Son?"

"Charles Horn, sir, and this is my wife."

Elizabeth gives a slight curtsy. "Pleasure to meet you, Sir Price."

Price nods. "I'm sure the pleasure's all mine, Mrs. Horn."

She smiles sweetly then launches into her customary questions. "If you don't mind my asking, Sir, how did you happen to accept an invitation to our lovely valley?"

Price takes a puff from his cigar and slowly blows out the smoke. "To tell you the truth, I heard that prairie chicken shooting in Nebraska was celebrated and there was also a chance of bagging an elk. So, naturally, I willingly accepted the invitation to make the trip."

"Did you come by rail?" Elizabeth asks after taking a half-step closer to Price.

"Yes, we arrived in Grand Island three days ago on the Union Pacific Railroad. When we left the train, I was glad to break the spell of monotony of traveling through flat land in a railway carriage."

Other guests begin to gather nearby. Someone calls out. "I heard you and your party overnighted at Beebee's. How was your stay?"

Price turns to look at the speaker. "You are correct in your assumption. Half-way between here and Grand Island, I had the opportunity to experience a dugout at Beebee's. I must say, a queerer-looking crib I have seldom put up at." Price pauses while his audience chuckles. "After a fine meal, our party of seven was glad enough to settle down for a night in a room of some twelve by fourteen feet, with but three beds between us. We chatted and smoked well past midnight." He smiles at the enraptured audience now surrounding him. "Our next day's drive was more interesting. Settlements were more scattered, hills began to crop up, we constantly passed close to the banks of the river. Prairie chickens were sufficiently numerous to keep us in active employment until we reached the fort just in time for this lovely reception and dinner."

Price looks over Elizabeth's head toward the other end of the room. "I see my host requesting that I come to his table." He bows toward Elizabeth who is the only woman standing in the circle. "Now if you'll please excuse me."

When Elizabeth and Charles move toward the food-laden tables, she sees Mrs. Hudgens scowling in her direction. Ignoring the look, she takes in the abundance before her. The smell of potato chowder, fried chicken, sauerkraut, and apple pie make her mouth water. The food her neighbors have provided reminds Elizabeth of her mother's home cooking. Some of the special German dishes that her mother made, and Elizabeth has not mastered, like sauerbraten and sausage, are a special treat. She and Charles load their plates and join Richard and Vi who are standing at the back of the room near the stacked beds and trunks.

Candles burn low in saucers on windowsills, giving the room a soft glow. Elizabeth gazes around at couples with jovial faces holding full plates of food. She feels proud to have brought to fruition this genuine, rural Nebraska party. After the food is eaten, the make-shift tables are dismantled and someone strikes up a fiddle. Elizabeth grabs Charles' hand. "Doesn't this remind you of the night we met?"

Charles takes her into his arms and they twirl into the crowded circle of dancers. "It certainly does."

Shortly before the festivities end, Vi approaches Elizabeth. "I hate for us to leave early, Elizabeth, but Shar is watching the twins and we don't want to stay out too late."

"Of course. Let's gather up our dishes and our husbands."

Richard brings up the buckboard and they climb in. It's a quiet ride home while each person stows away their memories of the special evening. Elizabeth breaks the silence. "When I came to Nebraska, I never dreamed I'd be meeting a knight and enjoying a party such as the one we just attended."

Vi looks back at her friend. "What did I tell you, Elizabeth? Life can be hard out here but it's also full of wonderful surprises."

Although it's not late when Charles and Elizabeth return home, they're tired and quickly make their way to bed. Too excited to sleep, Elizabeth looks over at her husband. His breathing is slow and he looks peaceful, but Elizabeth can't help herself. "Now, that was a knight and a night to remember, wasn't it?"

His eyes remain closed, his voice is soft. "Ahh, I get your pun. Yes, it was quite a night. Now please let me sleep. I must get up before sunrise to prepare for the hunt. Good night, my love."

The next day dawns with only a slight wind coming out of the west. Charles is up and out of the house before the sun rises. With no one needing her attention, Elizabeth lingers in bed a bit longer. She isn't looking forward to being alone all day but she plans to use her time well by finishing Charles' Christmas sweater. She hurries through her chores then retires to her rocker in front of the fire. With knitting needles clacking, Elizabeth works on the half-finished, blue sweater sitting in her lap. As she knits, she recalls how she dyed the yarn from the skin of elderberries too ripe for jam. Using a fisherman's rib stitch pattern, she completes the sleeves and assembles the sweater. She blocks it with her heated flat iron, then tucks it into the bottom of her trunk.

When the sky turns a deep purple, Elizabeth eats a meager supper of biscuits and gravy. It's dark and the coyotes have begun to howl when Charles finally stumbles through the door. Elizabeth goes to greet him. "Glad you're finally home. How are you?"

Charles leans against the wall. "I'm dirty, dog tired, and hungry." He pushes himself off the wall and grins. "But I had a fantastic day."

Elizabeth opens her mouth to begin her usual line of questions. Charles holds up his blood and dirt-stained hand then takes off his coat. "After I eat my supper, I'll tell you all about it."

Besides the dirty hands, Elizabeth notices black gunpowder smudges on his face. "Before you eat, please put your coat back on and fetch extra water while I bring in the tub. You're way beyond a washup."

As Charles slowly retrieves his coat from the hook, Elizabeth puts on her shawl. She hauls the tub from the side of the house and puts it in front of the fire to warm. Then she stokes up the fire, and puts meat pies on to heat. When

Charles returns, Elizabeth begins heating bath water while her tired husband hunches over his supper. Turning from the fire, she points to the coat hook. "Is that blood on your jacket?"

Charles ignores her question for the moment as he pops the last of the pheasant pie into his mouth. Then he leans back in his chair and nods in the direction of his coat. "Thaddeus Capron and I teamed up and bagged ourselves two antelope. We field dressed and quartered our kill, put them on a travois, then hauled them out with our horses. And, yes, that's antelope blood on my jacket. It's messy work."

Assuming there's more to this brief account, Elizabeth wonders what happened next. "Where's the meat? You didn't bring anything in except your dirty self."

Charles takes his plate to the dishpan. "I left the meat at the fort in the cooling house. I'll go back in the morning and get it. If you'll come with me, we can pack it back to the house in one trip." When Elizabeth nods her agreement to help, Charles adds. "You'll need to brine the meat right away."

Elizabeth tries to look confident but she sees Charles looking at her with one eyebrow raised. "You do know how to brine meat, right?"

Elizabeth reaches for the bar of soap. "Ah, not exactly." She gives Charles a small grimace. "But, I'm a fast learner."

He purses his lips and nods as if he's considering options. "We can smoke some of the meat in Richard's smoker, but you'll need to brine the rest." Elizabeth directs all of her attention toward Charles as he explains. "Brine is simply saltwater strong enough to float an egg. Brined meats will keep for months but it will take a bit to rinse and soak the meat before it's edible." He points to a jar on the shelf. "Add some of your tomato juice to the top of the jars. The acid will protect the meat from bacteria."

Elizabeth stores away the information about brining and goes about the business of the evening. She pours hot water mixed with cold into the tub and indicates that the bath is ready. She turns her back while Charles takes off his clothes and slips into the hot water, she then sits on the edge of the bed. "I'm glad you were invited to the hunt with the knight and got the antelope you wanted. Did he bag one also?"

"He did. I believe he gave the meat to the cook for the soldiers to enjoy."

After his bath, Charles immediately retires to bed while Elizabeth puts his dirty, blood-stained clothes into the tub for soaking. Relived that there will be meat on the shelf as winter fast approaches, Elizabeth feels a sense of peace that she hasn't felt in recent weeks. She quickly undresses, climbs into bed, and spoons with her warm, sleeping husband.

CHAPTER EIGHTEEN

THANKSGIVING GUESTS

As the days grow shorter and darkness prevails over the valley, Elizabeth notices that Charles is restless in his sleep. At times, when she awakens in the night, she sees him sitting in the rocker staring at the embers in the fireplace.

On a Thursday night, a week before Thanksgiving, Elizabeth again observes Charles sitting before the fire. When she awakens later, he's still there and her concern grows. She wonders if he's worried about something, is unhappy, or having nightmares. *Maybe it's something I've done, or not done.* At breakfast, Elizabeth gathers her courage to ask Charles about this late night habit. "When I woke up in the night, I noticed you by the fire, Darling. Is everything alright?"

Charles dips a corner of his toast in egg yolk before he replies. "I'm fine. I just have trouble sleeping from time to time that's all. It's nothing to worry about." Finishing his egg and toast, he sits back in the chair, picks up his coffee cup, and looks at his wife. "There's something I've been considering."

Elizabeth feels her stomach clench. *Here it comes!*

"I was wondering if you'd be open to inviting Ron for Thanksgiving?"

Elizabeth sighs with relief. "Ahh, Thanksgiving!"

"Yes. What did you think?" When she doesn't respond, he pours himself another cup of coffee then continues. "Just before Thanksgiving, Ron's going to be traveling through on his way to Grand Island for supplies before drifts close the road." Charles blows across his hot coffee. "He'd be staying overnight."

Elizabeth looks around the small room that is her entire house. "Overnight? Where would he sleep?"

"Men like Ron always travel with a bed roll. I'll install a curtain around our bed to give us privacy. Even if we don't have company, a curtain is a good idea. It'll help keep us warm as winter comes on."

Elizabeth is caught off guard by the request and doesn't respond. Charles continues in a soft voice. "And, perhaps Peter too?" When Elizabeth still has no response, Charles rushes on. "Even though I've heard there's going to be Thanksgiving festivities at the fort, I know Peter isn't fond of crowds. But I believe he'd be delighted with an invitation to have dinner at our house."

Finally finding her voice, Elizabeth asks, "Why Peter?"

Charles looks into the fire then back at his wife. "You know he lives in the back of the saloon. His parents died from cholera on the trail and he somehow made his way to Calamus. He's fifteen and on his own, considers himself lucky to have gainful employment. He stops by the shop to talk when business is slow. I suppose I've become a father figure of sorts."

Elizabeth pulls herself together. "I was thinking of the details. Of course, you can invite them. They're our friends and they'll help make our first Thanksgiving special." To stir up enthusiasm for the enterprise, she summons up memories of Thanksgiving at her grandparents' house. "We'll honor our guests with the traditional five kernels of corn."

Charles looks up from his now-empty cup. "What do you mean, 'five kernels of corn'? I've never heard of this."

While she speaks, Elizabeth smears pokecherry jam on her bread. "It's a story my uncle tells. Two years after the first Thanksgiving, I believe the year was 1623, the colonists experienced a terrible drought, which resulted in a near famine." Seeing that she's captured Charles' interest, she continues. "William Bradford, the leader of the colony, compared their situation with that of the Romans who reported they had survived on a ration of five kernels of corn." Elizabeth pauses to take a bite of bread. "So, in the best tradition of our American forefathers, my family showed gratitude for their abundance by offering their guests five kernels of corn on Thanksgiving." She smiles at Charles. "Now, we can pass the tradition on." When she's finished with her story, she notices Charles' mouth is slightly agape.

"You constantly amaze me with your storehouse of lore, my dear. Five kernels it will be." He gets up from the table. "Would you like a goose to cook for our feast?"

Pausing with dirty dishes in both hands, Elizabeth asks, "You've seen geese nearby?"

"Not recently, but Ron sent a message offering to bring a snow goose with him when he comes for the boots he ordered a while back. The note also said he's bringing a sack of wool for you." He walks to the door. "I'll send a message back inviting him to stay for Thanksgiving." Charles puts on his coat, crosses the room, and kisses his wife as she washes the dishes. "I'm fortunate to have friends and, I'm the luckiest man alive to have you as my wife." He walks briskly to the door and retrieves his satchel. "Have a good day, Dear."

Elizabeth feels warmth for her husband mixed with anxiety about her commitment to Thanksgiving festivities and Charles' sleepless nights. So, later that morning, while mixing a batch of muffins, she decides to seek advice from Vi.

After a midday meal of antelope jerky and bread, Elizabeth goes to the shelf and pulls down a book. With *Alice in Wonderland* under one arm and a package of mint tea and muffins in a basket on the other, she sets off for her friend's house. The sky is overcast, there's a light dusting of snow on the trail, and the prairie grass glistens with frozen droplets of dew. Dressed in a faded blue housedress, shawl, cape, a red hat, scarf, and mittens, her heart feels light as she approaches the familiar homestead. She hears Jan call out her name even before she has a chance to knock.

"Mrs. Horn!" Jan beams as she opens the door. "Mama, it's Mrs. Horn."

"I heard you, Jan. For heaven's sake, let the lady in."

Upon entering the snug house, Elizabeth feels the usual warmth as Jan skips excitedly around her. "Gary and I are shellin' peas and my sister and pa are milkin' and feedin' the cows in the barn." Jan looks at Elizabeth's arm. "What's in the basket?"

Vi rises from her spinning wheel and walks toward Elizabeth. "Jan, it's not polite to ask."

Elizabeth holds out her basket. "Here, look for yourself."

Jan peers in. "May I have a muffin?"

"If your mother approves."

Vi nods.

"Here's a muffin for you and one for your brother." She watches as Jan skips to the corner then looks back.

Pointing to the book under Elizabeth's arm, Jan asks, "Will you be readin' to us, Mrs. Horn?"

Elizabeth sets the basket and book on the table. "I'll read when Shar returns. Now give your mama and me a few minutes to talk." Vi takes Elizabeth's cape and hangs it on a hook. "I know you're busy, Vi. I promise to make this visit short but I need some advice about some things."

Vi walks back from the coat hooks and pulls out a chair at the table. "I'm never too busy to spend time with you." Elizabeth sits down and tells her about the Thanksgiving plans she and Charles have made asking her advice about cooking dinner and serving guests in a small space.

Then, satisfied with the menu advice and, seeing that the children are occupied, Elizabeth draws her chair closer to her friend's and speaks in a low voice. "There's something else on my mind, Vi."

"Yes..."

"I'm worried about Charles. He's not sleeping well and sometimes I find him up at night. He won't talk about it, but I know something troubles him."

Vi takes a sip of her tea. "He was in the war, right?"

"Yes, he fought with the Sixty-eighth New York Infantry for three years. He was wounded twice. The scars are pretty bad."

Vi's brows come together and she stares into the fire for a long moment. "He might be worried about supplies for winter." She takes another sip of tea. "Or, perhaps how business will be once the snow flies and people don't get out much." Elizabeth waits patiently, sensing that Vi isn't finished. "But, my best guess is he's thinking about his time in the war. My Richard fought and won't talk about it either. It was a terrible time. Rivers of blood. Fields of dead bodies."

Scrunching up her forehead, Elizabeth asks, "But why now? He seemed fine earlier."

"It's the dark. I think the dark, cold days bring out dark feelings. You have yet to experience winter on the prairie in a soddie, Elizabeth. It's not an easy time. My advice is to leave it be for now. Whatever it is that's bothering him, he'll talk about it if and when he's ready." Vi pauses and Elizabeth wonders if there's more. "Your Charles is different than most men out here. Frankly, I've never met a husband so loving and attentive to his wife. I believe he's a sensitive soul. You are blessed to have him, my friend."

Elizabeth is pleased and surprised by Vi's view of her husband but chooses not to comment. She takes a last sip of tea then squeezes Vi's hand. "Thanks for all the advice, Vi. I'm lucky to have a friend like you." She gets up, takes the book from the table, and moves her chair to the corner near the twins. Just as she sits down, she sees Shar rush through the door carrying a pail of milk. She sets it down near the churn then takes off her heavy sweater and throws it over the back of the chair.

Elizabeth sees her eyes lighting up. "Thank you for bringing your book again, Mrs. Horn. I love hearing the stories as much as the twins do."

After reading to the children and making arrangements with Vi to spin the wool Ron is bringing her, Elizabeth heads home to fix supper. The wind has picked up and she can smell wood smoke from Vi's fire.

On Wednesday, Elizabeth makes pumpkin pies, cleans out the hearth, carefully saving the ashes for future soap making, strings corn to use as napkin rings, and hems scraps of fabric for napkins. After placing bittersweet on the mantle, she steps back to admire the effect. She eats her noonday meal, then stirs up a rabbit stew and places it over a low fire.

She hears a knock on the door, looks out the window, and sees Ron's wagon. She opens the door. "Ron, welcome! It's so good to see you."

Ron takes off his Stetson. "Thanks for havin' me, Elizabeth. Thought I'd unload the wagon before I head over to the livery."

Elizabeth takes her cape from the peg. "I'll help you."

Besides his bedroll and a satchel, Ron unloads two burlap bags and hands one to Elizabeth. "Shot this beauty on my way so it'd be nice and fresh."

Elizabeth opens the bag and sees a fat, headless goose.

Ron takes the bag back. "I'll go out back and pluck him."

"Thanks. Be sure to save the feathers."

"Don't worry, I will. If you'll get a pot of water boiling, I'll get those blasted pin feathers out when I come back in." Ron hands Elizabeth the other bag.

"Another gift?"

Ron explains. "That's un-carded wool. Charles said you know someone with a spinning wheel."

"I do. Thank you."

When Ron returns to the house with the plucked and cleaned goose, Elizabeth watches as he surveys the hard dirt floor, plastered walls, shelves filled with jarred food, and the natural stone fireplace glowing with embers. "Do you know that Charlie built you a soddie that's much improved from the usual?"

Elizabeth feels her face grow warm as pride and gratitude fill her heart. "I do."

"And you've done a wonderful job of turning it into a home, Elizabeth. Now, tell me what smells so good?"

"Rabbit stew for supper. It's not much, but tomorrow we'll feast on goose."

Ron turns to leave. "Charlie and I will be here in time for that stew."

A few hours later, Charles walks in with Ron, hangs up his coat, and greets his wife. He pours Ron and himself two fingers of whiskey and they sit down at the table giving Elizabeth time to make biscuits to accompany the stew. After supper and a nice chat by the fire, Ron settles down on his bedroll at the far end of the room.

Before dawn the next morning, Elizabeth hears Ron and Charles talking softly. She peers around the curtain of their bed. "Where are you two going so early in the morning?"

Charles looks sheepish for waking her. "We're going to the livery, saddling up Pat and Pansy, then see if we can rustle up some game."

Ron nods. "The muskrats, beavers, and mink have abundant coats this time of year. If we can trap a few, I'll sell the pelts in Grand Island and split the profits with Charlie."

Satisfied they woke her for a good reason, Elizabeth is also happy that the men won't be underfoot while she prepares dinner and sets the table for her guests.

The men have a sparse breakfast, then Elizabeth lays out

enough jerky, cheese, bread, and water to sustain them until they return for an early supper. Just before Elizabeth puts the goose on the spit, she hears a wagon pulling up. She looks out and sees Richard walking up the path with two chairs. "Vi thought you might need these for your guests. We won't be wantin' them back until tomorrow."

Elizabeth waves at Vi and the children. "Thanks, Richard. Happy Thanksgiving!"

By mid-afternoon the aroma of roasting goose permeates the small house and Elizabeth feels confident that the feast will be a success. She arranges leftover sprigs of bittersweet around the candle on the table covered with her red and white checkered cloth and napkins ringed with corn at each place.

Soon after the men return with their pelts and skins, there's a knock at the door. Charles answers and Peter sticks his head inside and asks, "Now?"

Charles nods. "Yes, now."

Elizabeth thinks it's strange that Charles didn't invite Peter in. "What is it, Charles?"

"Be patient, my dear. Peter brought you an early Christmas present that I asked him to procure."

"Christmas present? On Thanksgiving?"

Charles opens the door and Peter enters with a black, curly haired, wiggly puppy yipping in a wooden crate. Elizabeth squeals with delight. "A puppy? For me?" She looks at Charles, surprised by his sober expression. She raises her eyebrows, prompting him to explain.

"I recently observed wolves in the area. In fact, while Ron and I were out trapping this morning, we saw an alpha wolf with his pack. Even from where we were standing, we could see that he stood about three feet at the shoulder. Now that it's dark early, I want you to have protection when I'm away. I thought a pup was just the ticket."

Elizabeth can't contain her excitement as she takes the puppy out of his crate. "Being a city girl, I never had a dog, but I always wanted one." The pup licks Elizabeth's face. "What should we call him? Or does he already have a name? How old is he? Where did he come from?"

Peter answers. "He's four months old, housebroken, and has no name. I call him Pup. He's part of a late litter from my friend's dog."

Elizabeth is quiet for a moment. "Let's call him Laddie. What do you think, Charles?"

"Why Laddie?"

"My uncle had a dog that I loved and his name was Laddie."

"Laddie it is. Now, are you ready to serve us that succulent goose we smell cooking on the spit?"

Elizabeth sets the puppy down and rushes to the fire. "Of course." She turns, "Peter and Ron, please have a seat. Welcome to our home and happy Thanksgiving." Elizabeth carries the beautifully roasted and browned goose to the table along with a large knife. "While Charles carves the goose, I'd like to tell you the story about the corn encircling your napkins."

After enjoying the main course followed by dessert and coffee, the men walk Peter to the road while Elizabeth finishes tidying up. When the men return, they join Elizabeth in front of the fire. Ron pats his stomach. "That was a wonderful dinner, Elizabeth. You did a beautiful job cooking the goose. Thanks for havin' me."

Elizabeth smiles as Charles responds. "It was our pleasure, Ron. You helped to make our first Thanksgiving special."

Elizabeth watches with a thankful heart as Laddie, tired from all the excitement and, presumably, grateful to have a forever home, retires to his crate for a nap as his new people continue to chat quietly by the fire.

CHAPTER NINETEEN

A BUNDLE OF BLANKETS

Before first light the following morning, Elizabeth is awakened by a howl. She sits straight up in bed and shakes Charles by the shoulder. "What was that?"

Charles replies with his eyes closed. "I believe it's Laddie giving us notice that he wants to go out. Have you forgotten you have a pup?"

"I'll take him," Ron offers from the other side of the room. "You two will have plenty of opportunities later." It's not yet sunrise when Ron returns with Laddie. Before he leaves to retrieve his wagon, Elizabeth insists on cooking him a hot breakfast of flapjacks, salt pork, and strong coffee topped with a bit of leftover cream. She packs him leftover goose and buttered bread for the road.

The evening before, Charles and Elizabeth made plans to visit Ron in the spring as soon as the roads were passable. Elizabeth is excited about the prospect of a trip but she's particularly happy that Charles will have something to look forward to during the winter.

After Ron's departure, the couple feel an additional sense of urgency with winter nipping at their heels. Charles spends time away from work, cutting as much wood as he can find. Elizabeth pushes away her ongoing sense of foreboding as she preserves the last of the fall produce. She has no root cellar so she stores vegetables in a barrel Charles brought from the fort.

On November twenty-ninth, they quietly celebrate Charles' thirty-fifth birthday. Since his birthday falls between Thanksgiving and Christmas, he requests they celebrate alone with a nice dinner and one of Elizabeth's butterscotch pies.

After their meal, Elizabeth retrieves a package from her trunk. "Happy birthday, Darling. Before you open your gift, I'd like to read a poem I wrote for you."

Charles leans toward her as she begins.

"I walked a mile with pleasure,
She chattered all the way,
But left me none the wiser,
For all she had to say.
I walked a mile with sorrow,
And ne'er a word said she;
But oh the things I learned from her,
When sorrow walked with me."

Charles gets up and gives Elizabeth a hug. "Your poem is beautiful, my love. Thank you. I had no idea you could write so well."

A sense of pride radiates around Elizabeth. "Now, open your other gift."

The gray scarf and matching mittens Elizabeth knit delight Charles. "What a perfect birthday. Thanks for honoring my wishes for a quiet day."

The beginning of the following week is cold and dreary but there's still no snow. On December third, right after a quick lunch of buttered bread, pokecherry jam, and a handful of walnuts Charles had discovered while looking for wood, Elizabeth stirs a pot of beans. The night before, she had ladled a half dozen scoops of dried beans into her cooking pot, topped them with water, and set them on the hearth to soak. She looks at Laddie who is watching her closely. "They need a bit more soaking time. Don't worry, we'll get the soup started soon."

Laddie wags his tail as if he understands every word. He follows Elizabeth as she retrieves her mending bag and sits in her rocker with her darning egg, needle, cotton thread, and socks in need of repair. She pricks her finger when Laddie suddenly barks and paces in front of the door. Putting her finger in her mouth, Elizabeth cautiously walks across the room and peers out the window before opening the door. A wagon full of supplies is parked just beyond the path. A small person wrapped in blankets is sitting next to the driver who waves and shouts over Laddie's yipping.

"It's Ron, Elizabeth."

Elizabeth opens the door and watches with impatient curiosity as Ron slowly and deliberately helps the bundle of blankets out of his wagon and up the path. "Ron! What in the world are you doing here? Shouldn't you have returned to your ranch by now?"

Not answering, Ron and the mysterious person walk through Elizabeth's open front door.

"I brought someone who wants to see you."

As soon as Elizabeth sees the blonde braids and tiny hands, she knows it's her friend Lucy from the wagon train. "Lucy, is that you?"

Hearing her name seems to pull Lucy from her stupor. She runs into Elizabeth's embrace, dropping blankets along the way. Lucy throws her arms around her friend, buries her face in her bosom, and sobs.

Ron turns to leave. "I'm taking the wagon and horses to the livery. You girls get caught up. I'll walk back with Charlie."

Elizabeth can't believe her eyes. Her friend from the trail stands in her house. Lucy's hair is even dirtier than it was on the trail. She looks as though she has two dresses on, her face is smudged, her lips are cracked, her neck has the green shadow of an old bruise, and there are dark circles under her dull, lifeless eyes. After Lucy has a good cry, Elizabeth disentangles herself from her friend and offers her the rocker. Without saying a word, she wraps her gray shawl around Lucy's skeletal shoulders, stokes the fire, and puts on the kettle for tea.

Lucy's sad, tired eyes follow Elizabeth around the room. Laddie breaks the silence by whining at Lucy's feet. Smiling, she picks up the pup, places him in her lap, and absently strokes his soft coat. He gives her face a friendly lick. "What's his name?"

"Laddie. He was an early Christmas gift from Charles on Thanksgiving."

Elizabeth moves the table next to Lucy, so she has a place to set her teacup and muffin, then pulls a chair up across from her and patiently watches Lucy sip her tea. Finally, unable to wait any longer, she speaks in a voice just above a whisper. "What happened, Lucy?" Tears begin to fall, and Elizabeth gives her a hanky. "It's okay, take your time."

Lucy takes another sip of tea. "The last words you said to me was 'If he hurts you, just get away.' You 'member?"

"Yes, I remember."

Lucy takes a bite of muffin and slowly chews. "It took me a bit, but I finally did what you told me. I got me away from Jake and here I is, sittin' by your fire with your pup in my lap."

Elizabeth wonders about all that must have taken place for Lucy to be here but, for once, she holds her tongue and lets her friend slowly unspool her story. To help herself stay quiet, she gazes out the window wondering when the men will return. The wind has whipped up and the windowpanes are rattling. She takes a sip of hot, comforting tea, then sets her cup back in its saucer.

"After you left the train, things got worse. Jake figured nobody cared 'bout me no more so nobody'd notice the bruises. My life was barely tolerable, but I kept gittin' on. The really bad stuff started happenin' when the weather got stormy. That's when Jake got sick of travelin' and decided to stop at North Platte for the winter rather than push on to Wyomin'."

Elizabeth feels a pang of sadness as she considers how Gretchen and James might be doing. "Did others stop there too?"

"Yep. The Youngs, Mr. Spence, Gretchen and James."

Elizabeth sees the expression on Lucy's face change and tears return to her eyes. "Gretchen didn't git better. It was so sad to see her. I afeared for her life. I really did. I guess James did too 'cause they stopped and stayed in a hotel for a while tryin' to decide what's next. I seen them when I went to town for supplies."

Her eyes swimming with tears, Elizabeth takes another sip of tea. "I'm so sorry to hear that. Now go on with your story."

Lucy nods then strokes Laddie's head. He opens his eyes a slit before resuming his nap.

"After Jake sold the rig he made us a dugout to live in. We weren't far from town. I think we was a squattin' on somebody's property. Anyways, we lived in this damp hole. It weren't nothin' nice like you got here. It really were just a hole in the side of a hill. Livin' in the wagon on the trail was better."

Elizabeth pours more tea. "How did you have money for food? Are you hungry? I have some leftover stew."

"This here muffin is fine for now, Lizabeth." Seemingly to prove her point, Lucy puts the last of the muffin in her mouth, wipes away the crumbs, then clears her throat. "Jake worked parttime at the livery stable just to make 'nough money so's we could eat. Most of what he earned went for whiskey. He give me just 'nough to git by. After he bin drinkin' he come home mean, real mean. He yelled and hit and I had me no place to hide."

Blowing on her second cup of tea, Lucy takes a sip then sets her cup down. Elizabeth notices her lower lip quiver as she struggles to regain her composure. "I'm so sorry. It must have been terrible."

Lucy slowly nods and looks up. "It were terrible. One night, I thought he was gonna kill me. That was when he nearly broke my wrist." Lucy holds out her arm, displaying a dirty bandage wrapped around her right wrist. Elizabeth examines it and wishes that, somehow, she could have gotten her away from Jake sooner.

Cradling her arm, Lucy sighs. "Not long after, I seen James in the general store. I musta looked pretty bad 'cause he asked how I was doin.' I told him I wasn't doin' so good. He said he was takin' Gretchen back to where they come from and they was leavin' in the mornin.' He told me I could come with them as far as Grand Island if I needed to git away. They was selling their gear there and takin' the train back east. He said they'd be by the river crossing just after dawn and would look for me in case I decided to come."

Although she's thinking about what might have happened if Charles hadn't be there to meet her and how brokenhearted James must be to give up on his dream, she keeps her focus on Lucy. "And you did. You got away."

A smile creeps across Lucy's face. "Yes, thank God, I got away. That night I put on my two dresses and my one extra pair of bloomers. I ain't own nothing else except ..." Lucy reaches into her dress and pulls out the broach. "I ain't never lost this here beautiful pin you give me. I hid it in my bloomers so's nothin' would happen to it."

Elizabeth smiles and touches Lucy's hand.

"That night Jake got good and drunk. I was real nice to him anyways so'd he'd git right to sleep. Then, with Jake snorin' away, I grabbed my blankets and walked out the door." Lucy tilts her head to the side. "Well, there weren't no door exactly but I walked out. Believe me, I was mighty scared. It were dern cold waitin' by the bridge but, eventually, James picked me up just like he'd promised. They's good folk. I hope Gretchen will be alright once they git back East."

Laddie jumps from Lucy's lap and trots to the door. He looks back at Elizabeth and whines. Elizabeth takes her extra shawl from the peg and wraps it snuggly around her shoulders. "I need to take Laddie out. I'll be right back. Help yourself to more tea."

The wind whips across the prairie and right through Elizabeth's tattered shawl. She shivers while Laddie finds just the right mound of dry grass. When he dashes across the path to run off a bit of puppy energy, Elizabeth considers all that she's heard. Her mind is flooded with questions. *What's going to happen to Lucy? Where will she go? Will Gretchen get better when she returns home? How will they start over? How will Lucy start over?*

"Laddie, come!" When Elizabeth calls, the pup runs back to her side and they rush through the door trying not to let in the cold air. Before returning to her chair, Elizabeth stokes up the fire, still shivering from her time outside. "Do you mind if I start supper while you finish your story?"

"Course not. Sorry to be so long winded."

Elizabeth rinses the beans, returns them to the pot with fresh water, then adds a jar of chicken stock and some ham from the larder. She hangs the pot on the hook over the fire and brings a cutting board to the table. She chops carrots, onion, and a droopy stock of celery, then adds it, along with a big pinch of pepper, to the stock pot. She returns to her chair. "How did it go with James and Gretchen?"

Lucy crosses and uncrosses her legs. "James pushed hard to git to Grand Island as soon as possible. He wanted to git Gretchen on that there train." Lucy fidgets with her hands and looks down. "Also, he feared Jake might come lookin' for me." She looks up and gives Elizabeth a wan smile. "But we never seen Jake and we made it to Grand Island in jus' two days. Since he was sellin' his rig, he drove us right into town."

"They left right away?"

"Yep. I was mighty sad to see them go but I had no money to travel with them. 'Sides, Pa would throw me out if I went home. I knowed my only hope was to find you." Lucy walks the few steps to the fire, holds out her hands, sniffs at the soup, then turns and looks back at Elizabeth. "Gretchen give me a bundle of food and cried when I left. James give me a bit of money." She turns her backside to the fire. "I was goin' ta use that money to git me a bath. I was askin' the owner of the general store if there were a bath house in town when I seen this here big, handsome man walk in. I was tryin' to mind my business, but I overheard him tellin' the clerk that he'd just come from Fort Hartsuff."

Elizabeth sits back in her chair and stares up at Lucy standing by the fire. "Really? The big man was Ron? That's unbelievable."

Lucy puts her hand on her chest. "Cross my heart, 'n hope to die. 'Tis the God's honest truth, Lizabeth. 'Course I didn't know he were your friend. I just knowed that even though I looked a fright, I had to be brave. You would have said so, right?"

Elizabeth gives Lucy a tiny smile and nods, not trusting her voice.

"So I walked right up to him, introduced myself as your friend from the wagon train, and asked if he knowed you. When he said he'd just come from your place a few days before, I asked if he was goin' back the direction he come from anytime soon. Said he'd been in town for supplies and would be headin' back to his ranch as soon as he got loaded up. Said he was goin' right by your place and I could come along."

When Lucy returns to her chair, Elizabeth stares at her, barely able to believe her amazing story. "But with a loaded wagon and two people, it's a two or three day trip. Where'd you stay?"

"Ron paid for us to stay at Beebee's. You heard of it?"

"Yes, I've heard of it."

"Ron's a true gentleman. He sure 'nough is. I look and smell like a hobo but he treat me like a princess. I told him my story. I thought I owed him that much. He asked me what I was goin' ta do next. I told him I didn't know. My mind only went as far as findin' you. He said he knowed a lady where he come from that would take me in. He said she lives alone and been askin' around for someone to help her with the place. He told me to think on it quick-like 'cause he was leavin' in the mornin.'" Lucy closes her eyes for a moment and Elizabeth senses her exhaustion.

"That's some story. I'm so proud of you, Lucy. I know it took a lot of courage to leave Jake and head out into the unknown. For heaven's sake, you might have gotten stranded in Grand Island and spent the winter there. So many bad things could have happened."

Lucy looks over at Elizabeth. "I guess God was lookin' out for me. That's all I can say. Sometimes you gotta start the ball a'rollin' and He takes it from there."

Elizabeth, for once, is at a loss for words so she sits quietly and looks down at her hands folded in her lap. They're her father's hands, broad with square nails. Lucy seems spent but content with Laddie snoring quietly at her feet. When the room grows dark, Elizabeth lights a lantern and places it on the table. She lights the candles in their saucers on the mantle. The room is quiet except for the bubbling soup that's filling the air with the delicious scent of food from the earth.

Ron and Charles have buckets of water in their hands when they walk through the door a short time later. Pleased that they thought of a bath for Lucy, Elizabeth begins heating the water while everyone sits down to the simple supper of ham and bean soup along with corn bread and honey. Elizabeth's glad that Charles asks no questions during supper. She surmises that Ron filled him in on their walk to the house. After supper, the men go to stretch their legs, taking Laddie with them. When they leave, Charles quietly turns to Elizabeth. "Ron and I will sleep on the floor. You ladies take the bed."

Elizabeth is grateful for his understanding and generosity. While the men are gone, she helps Lucy into the tub of hot water. She washes her friend's hair then gives her Charles' soft, worn shirt to sleep in. Before sending her to bed, Elizabeth hands Lucy a steaming mug of strong tea with a shot of whiskey and a big dollop of honey. Lucy's sound asleep and Elizabeth has washed out her friend's two dresses and underwear when the men return with Laddie leading the way. After laying the laundry by the fire to dry, Elizabeth joins Lucy in the big bed. She can hear the men whispering quietly by the fire. From the gap in the curtain, she sees Laddie trying to stay awake but he soon abandons the men for his blanket at the bottom of the crate.

Elizabeth sleeps for a few hours then awakes from a frightening dream where a faceless man is twisting her arm, then drags her down a dirt road. When the remembrance of her dream evaporates, she hears a noise. *What's that tapping sound?*

Is that Jake trying to break in? She sits up, opens the curtain, and looks around the black, cold room, holding her breath as she listens with every fiber in her body. She hears men lightly snoring but no tapping sounds. Elizabeth sighs with relief thinking that it must have been the wind.

The next morning, Lucy looks like a new woman. The sparkle has returned to her blue eyes and her hair is a shiny gold. She puts on her clean, brown dress that Elizabeth woke up early to press, and pins her broach at the neck. The women giggle together as they prepare breakfast.

When the table is set, Elizabeth and Ron sit in the chairs, Charles perches on the water barrel. From her seat in the rocker, Lucy looks around the table and smiles. "Now, ain't this nice?" Then she turns her attention to her plate of scrambled eggs and toast.

Elizabeth's shoulders tense with anticipation. She swings her crossed leg back and forth as she slowly forks eggs into her mouth. *Will Lucy go with Ron or stay? Where will Lucy live if she stays? Can she find work? Will Jake track her to our home? Are Charles and I in danger?*

Charles reaches over and steadies Elizabeth's swinging leg. Ron laps up his breakfast like he didn't have a care in the world. Lucy looks cleaner and happier than Elizabeth has ever seen her. Finally, Lucy's fork clatters onto her wiped clean plate. She clears her throat. "I just wanna thank Elizabeth and Charles here for takin' me in yesterday and makin' me feel welcome by givin' me your bed and all." Lucy colors as three pair of eyes look at her. "Most of all, thanks to Ron for showin' up at the right time, believin' my story, and bringin' me to this here house."

Elizabeth notices that even Laddie watches Lucy closely, as if he knows an important decision is about to be announced.

Lucy pauses and takes a deep breath. "Now, if that offer still stands, Ron, I'd like to head to Burwell with you when you leave this mornin'. I've trusted you this far, I might as well trust you for the rest."

It seems to Elizabeth that everyone, including Laddie, lets out a breath at the same time.

After breakfast, Charles and Ron walk to town for the wagon while Elizabeth helps Lucy bundle up her few belongings. When Ron pulls up in the wagon, Elizabeth winds her red wool scarf around Lucy's neck, places the matching knitted cap on her head, and hands her the mittens. After wrapping her back up in the blankets, Elizabeth puts on her shawl and walks out with her friend. Laddie trails behind. Snugly perched sidebyside on the wagon seat, Lucy and Ron holler in unison. "See you in the spring."

Elizabeth waves. "You two take care of yourselves." She then turns back inside before her friends see her tears. Lucy's decision to go with Ron relieves her but she still can't shake the fear that Jake might show up at her door.

CHAPTER TWENTY

LOCUSTS AND TARGETS

A few days after Lucy and Ron leave for Burwell, Charles makes an announcement at supper.

"I'm going to Grand Island next week. I need to get winter supplies and retrieve the Christmas box your parents sent. I hate leaving you alone but—"

Elizabeth interrupts. She can feel heat coming to her cheeks, she looks hard at Charles. "It's about time you told me. Last week, Vi informed me that you and Richard were going. I'm not a child, you know. You can tell me your plans."

Charles looks down at his hands then at his wife. "I'm sorry. I held off telling you because I didn't want you to worry about being alone."

Elizabeth can feel her heart racing. Being raised to act like a proper Victorian lady, she's not good with confrontation but knows how important it is to be honest about what's on her mind. She wonders why she didn't talk to Charles about this trip when she first heard about it from Vi. "That's not the point here but, since you mentioned it, why can't I go with you?"

Charles clears his throat. "First of all, the weather will be very cold. Second, it's going to be a fast trip with long hours in the wagon. Third, someone needs to keep this place warm, so the jars don't freeze. Fourth, what about Laddie?"

Still angry, Elizabeth considers Charles' response. She knows her answer will sound sarcastic, but she doesn't care. "Anything else?" She sees a startled expression cross Charles' face and thinks how unaccustomed he is to her sassy side.

Her looks her in the eye. "As a matter of fact, yes. Someone needs to be here so some drifter, or worse, doesn't rob us blind. Are those enough reasons?"

Elizabeth's anger starts to recede. She's glad Charles feels contrite but she's also pleased he didn't back down. "So, I need to stay with Laddie, keep the home fires burning, and bar the door. Right?"

Charles rubs his chin. "That's about it. I'm sorry I didn't tell you sooner and you had to hear about it from Vi. Forgive me?"

Elizabeth sees concern in Charles' eyes. "Yes, I forgive you, but next time, please tell me what's going on sooner rather than later. We're a team, remember?"

Since she's so much younger than her husband, Elizabeth is particularly sensitive to being treated as a frightened, weak girl. One of the main reasons she married Charles and made the trip West was so she'd have the opportunity to earn the right to be regarded as a brave, capable woman and an equal partner. Glad to have this situation out in the open and resolved, she turns to the fireplace and the task of preparing supper. "Go wash up."

The couple eat their supper in companionable silence. After the dishes are cleared, Charles comes to stand next to her as she heats water for washing up. "Tomorrow morning before I go to work, I'm going to teach you how to shoot the Colt."

Elizabeth turns and gives Charles a look that says "Who me?"

"When you're alone in the house, you need to know how to protect yourself if necessary. I'll be taking the rifle but the Colt pistol will serve you well."

Elizabeth starts to put the dishes in the dishpan. "If you say so, Charles, but I don't relish the possibility of pointing a gun at a person—or an animal, for that matter."

Charles gets up to go to the privy. He turns back to Elizabeth. "Sometimes we have to do things we'd rather not do."

While Charles is out, Elizabeth places a soapstone near the fire to heat up before bed. After he returns, the couple read quietly for an hour then Elizabeth retrieves the stone, which has heated to the point that she can pick it up but is too hot to hold for any length of time, and rubs it over the sheet. Then she wraps it in a cloth and places it at the foot of the bed where it can slowly release heat throughout the night. "Charles, come to bed before the mattress cools." He dutifully sets his book aside and walks toward Elizabeth. He gives her a long, loving kiss and embrace. They quickly undress and snuggle down in their deliciously warm bed for surprisingly passionate lovemaking.

At breakfast the next morning, the fat in the pan sizzles merrily as Elizabeth fries salt pork then cracks in eggs. Charles has yet to mention the shooting practice and Elizabeth thinks he might have forgotten. Before he sits down to eat, however, he pulls the Colt from its wrapping in his trunk and lays it on top of the oak water barrel. "Let's go out back after breakfast.

The sun should be up by then and I'll set up a target. You might not be a crack shot after only one lesson but you'll have the confidence to handle a gun."

Elizabeth's not sure how to respond. She appreciates her husband teaching her how to shoot but frightened by the thought of having to actually use a gun.

The cold wind swirls around her as she waits for Charles to nail a paper bull's-eye to the stack of cordwood behind the house. The sun is peaking over the hills behind the creek and the resident pair of cardinals are singing in the bushes. Elizabeth wears Charles' hunting jacket so her arms will be free to shoot.

Charles walks back to Elizabeth with his head down.

"What are you looking at?"

He stops and crouches to get a better look. "There are wolf tracks back here, Elizabeth. Mind that you don't go to the necessary or take Laddie out after dark."

Elizabeth feels a flutter of fear in her stomach. "We'll be careful."

Moving on to the task at hand, Charles holds the gun out to Elizabeth. "This is a Colt Single Action Army handgun. Don't know why, but it's called the Peacemaker."

Elizabeth takes the gun and examines it. It's heavier than she expected and smells of oil. "Did you have it in the war?"

"I had my rifle. The Colt .45 didn't become the standard service revolver until a couple of years ago. I traded boots for this one."

Elizabeth stands straight and points toward the target. Charles comes up behind her. "Hold the gun with two hands." She complies. "That's right. Keep your arms straight and slowly pull the trigger. There'll be a slight retort."

When she fires, she feels the reverberation up her arms and into her chest. It's louder than she'd expected but the power she feels is invigorating. Charles reloads and she fires again. He walks over and examines the target. "You hit it with both shots! The second one was near the bull's-eye."

Elizabeth beams with pride. "I can do this!"

"Of course you can. You're a natural."

When they return to the house, Charles shows Elizabeth how to load and unload the gun.

Satisfied that she's learned another survival skill, Elizabeth turns toward her chores after Charles leaves for work. First, she heats water for scrubbing laundry. She's strung a line from the bed to the window and another between the two chairs where she pegs sheets, clothing, and underwear. While the laundry is drying, she mixes up bread dough, kneads it, and sets the bowl close to the fire to rise.

By late afternoon, just as she's taking down the laundry, Charles and Richard rush through the door giving Elizabeth a little fright. She's not yet lit the lantern which means it's early for Charles to be returning for supper. She regains her composure and quickly removes the laundry lines. "Good to see you, Richard. What brings you two here this time of day?"

Richard stands just inside the door as Charles kisses Elizabeth on the cheek. "We wanted to discuss the details of our trip and it was, ahh, busy at Richard's house." Charles takes Richard's coat and hangs it over his on the peg.

Elizabeth stirs up the coals in the fireplace and puts the kettle on the hook. "Come and settle yourselves by the fire while I'll mix up my special not-just-for-ladies tea." When their eyebrows shoot up, Elizabeth grins. Soon, the men are enjoying her hot tea, whiskey, and honey concoction as they talk about their upcoming trip.

Later, when Elizabeth senses that their conversation is wrapping up, she pulls her rocker over and joins them. "I heard you helped build the fort, Richard. If you don't mind my asking, how did that come about?"

Richard looks from Elizabeth to Charles. "I'm an open book to you and Charlie, but," Richard pauses, "I'm afraid it's a sad story."

Charles subtly winks at Elizabeth. "Don't hold back on account of Elizabeth. Believe me, if you do, you'll get yourself in a heap of trouble."

Richard looks at Elizabeth. "In that case, I'll tell you the whole, unvarnished tale." He settles back in his chair and strokes his mustache. "When the Great Depression of 1873 hit, we'd been homesteadin' for about a year. I was finally gettin' the barn built and findin' buyers for my crops, but cash money was hard to come by."

Elizabeth nods her understanding. "My father is a banker and was hit hard as well. After that what happened?"

Richard drains the dregs from his mug. "The following summer, we had the most serious locust year the old timers around here can remember." He pauses, tilts his chair back, and laces his hands behind his head. "It was July. My corn was in tassel and my small grain was headin' nicely. Our land was full of promise. Then dawned the fatal day." Richard tips his chair back up and puts his elbows on his knees. "It was July twenty-second or twenty-third, I don't rightly remember. The sun was bright in the morning but by noon a strange haziness spread over the clear, blue sky and the sun took on a greenish tint. I wasn't expecting anything, so I didn't take particular notice."

Elizabeth leans forward, not wanting to miss a word. She can see Richard's jaw muscles tense as if he's reliving the moments.

"Then, all of a sudden, clouds of locusts began to settle over everything. Their wings had a strange whistling sound. Their bodies clung to whatever they struck, devouring every planted thing."

Richard shakes his head and Elizabeth can see his distress as he recalls what happened. She quietly asks, "Did you try to scare them away?"

"When Vi tried to shoo the pests out of her garden, they started eating the clothes right off her back."

Elizabeth feels her chin drop and her mouth gape open in disbelief.

"Truly they did. Lawyer Mitchell's wife, Harriett, told Vi that, in an attempt to save her precious flower bed, she spread it over with a quilt only to see the blanket devoured. Some said they saw branches of trees bent right to the ground with the weight of them. They stripped my cornfield with only the toughest part of the stock left." Richard slowly shakes his head and closes his eyes. "Ah, those were sad days around here. We spent our last dollar on seeds for our crops, anticipating a good return. Then, suddenly, all was lost."

Elizabeth feels dismay in hearing Richard's story but heartened by the fact he's sitting by her fire. She thinks there must be a happy ending somewhere in the story.

Richard, still lost in thought, remains quiet. Charles breaks the silence. "Tell Elizabeth how this relates to building the fort."

Again, Richard looks from Charles to Elizabeth. "Vi and me, we were mighty worried to be sure. Winter was coming on and we had nothing put away. Had it not been for the abundance of game in the area we would have been hard-pressed." His lips briefly turn up as if he's confirming his gratitude for nature. "But mainly, it was the construction of the fort that saved us. In September, just as we were wondering how we were going to survive, they commenced hiring at good wages. My working at the fort got us through to spring and we saved up enough to buy seed. That's how I happen to be sitting here today and that's how I happened to help build the fort."

Apparently finished with his story, Richard stands to leave. Charles also rises and thumps him on the back. "We're sure glad you made it through."

Elizabeth takes Richard's coat from the peg and hands it to him. "Your family is surely a role model of courage for Charles and me." She pats Richard's arm. "Give Vi and the kids our love. "

CHAPTER TWENTY-ONE

WOLVES AND ICE

Like most days in mid-December, the next morning dawns cold and windy. Charles lays his canvas coat, scarf, and gloves near the fire to warm. He pulls an old army blanket from his trunk. Elizabeth puts the kettle on then comes to stand beside Charles. "Be sure to get sticks of candy for the Voogd children. Oh, and an orange and a lemon, if you can find them, for the Christmas puddings I plan to make." Elizabeth reaches into her apron pocket. "Here's a letter. Post it to my parents please."

Charles adds the letter to his leather pouch. "I won't forget."

Elizabeth returns to the stove, makes a pot of strong tea, adds a good amount of sugar, then carefully pours the hot mixture into a jar. She wraps several biscuits in a napkin, then hands them to her husband who stuffs them into his coat pocket. "I've left plenty of wood near the door but, if you need it, the split wood is at the front of the pile out back."

Elizabeth puts on her shawl as Charles continues. "Richard and I are stopping at the livery to harness up the mustangs in addition to his team so we'll have the horsepower to pull the heavy load home." Seeing Richard approach, Elizabeth and Charles say their good-byes.

After waving the men off from the stoop, Elizabeth returns inside, lays aside her shawl, and goes about her chores. Per her promise to Charles, before the sun goes down, she takes Laddie for a run, uses the outhouse, and brings in firewood and water for the night and morning.

Then she fixes herself a supper of beans and biscuits. After washing the few dishes, she settles into her rocker, feeling the weight of nightfall coming on. Not only does she miss Charles, she misses her family more than ever. Day to day she tries to keep her sad feelings of separation at bay, but tonight the weight of them is overwhelming. While she stares into the fire, unbidden tears roll down her cheeks. After a good cry, her feelings of sadness and loneliness are pushed aside. Having never spent a night alone in her life, she's overwhelmed by an oncoming tide of apprehension and anxiety.

She knits. She reads. She writes a letter to her mother. She doublechecks the latch on the door. Finally, when she can barely keep her eyes open, she crawls under the cold quilt and closes her eyes. Sleep eludes her. She gives herself a pep talk. "I'm brave, I'm safe, I can do this."

The wind sweeps around the soddie as usual, but tonight, the sound it makes is more ominous. Then, just before she drifts off to sleep, she hears a low howl. Then another. Then a chorus of howls. Laddie soon joins in. Elizabeth gets out of bed, gathers her shawl around her shoulders, lights a lantern, then pulls back the window curtain. She peers out into the cold, black night. Glowing green eyes stare back at her. Wolves. Lots of them. They've formed a half circle from the outhouse to the front walk. She remembers Charles seeing wolf tracks the day before but he said nothing about so many being in the area. She looks down at Laddie who is no longer howling and standing close. "Do they know we're alone?" He jumps up on his hind legs and licks her shaking hand.

She tells herself she's secure in the soddie but, her pounding heart doesn't believe her. She's wide awake, twitching with the sound of every creak and shudder. She paces until her teeth begin to chatter, then she returns to bed. Finally, she calls for her pup. "Laddie! Come!" Patting the bed, she calls him again. "You're the man of the house this week, Little Buddy." She lifts him up to the bed and cuddles him close. With Laddie's warmth and steady breathing giving her comfort and the howls growing fainter, Elizabeth finally falls into a restless asleep.

When she looks out the window the next morning, she sees a steel gray sky filled with, yet darker gray, clouds. Tired and still anxious, she examines the yard from the window before going to the outhouse and letting Laddie out to do his business. She sees tracks and scat but no other signs of her nighttime visitors.

After a soothing cup of camomile tea and a meager breakfast, she makes an effort to turn her thoughts toward Christmas. She slowly rocks and allows her mind to drift back to what it was like back in Illinois with her family. She closes her eyes and takes a deep breath as she brings a childhood Christmas to her mind's eye.

A knock on the door abruptly returns Elizabeth to her cold, lonely, sod house. She jumps from her chair and runs to the window with Laddie close on her heels. Seeing Mrs.

Capron's maid, she quickly opens the door. "Tina, so nice to see you again. Do come in and get out of this terrible weather."

Tina stands just inside the closed door. "Thank you, Mrs. Horn. I have another invitation from Mrs. Capron."

Elizabeth gestures toward the fireplace. "Please, call me Elizabeth. Come, have a seat."

Tina looks at the two envelopes in her hand. "I will have time for tea if you'd be so kind as to deliver this here envelope to Mrs. Voogd."

"Of course. Now, settle yourself by the fire while I put the kettle on."

Keeping her cape on, Tina sits near the fire and holds her hands to it's warmth. When Elizabeth takes a seat, she hands her both envelopes.

"Do you mind if I open mine now?"

Tina nods and Elizabeth carefully opens the square, off-white envelope with *Mr. and Mrs. Charles Horn* beautifully lettered across the front. "An invitation to Christmas dinner. How nice. Please tell Mrs. Capron we accept." Elizabeth returns to the stove, adds hot water to her teapot and brings it to the table along with sugar, cups, and saucers. "Can you give me an idea of what this dinner will be like?"

Tina self-consciously smooths back her hair. "I heard Mrs. Capron say that she's determined to pull out all the stops for what she called 'a Christmas my friends and family won't forget.' She already has me polishing silver and such."

Elizabeth notices Laddie warming up to Tina, resting his head on her boot. "Do you mind my asking how you happen to be way out here working at Fort Hartsuff?"

Tina leans in and speaks softly as if someone else might hear. "To be honest, Mrs. Horn, I ran away from home." Tina looks into her cup.

"Oh dear. Things must have been bad."

Tina looks up. It seems to Elizabeth that's she's weighing whether or not to share her story. She remembers seeing the same look in Lucy's eyes when she told her story on the trail. "Pa beat us kids when he got drunk and took every penny of the money I made working as a maid." Elizabeth shakes her head in sympathy but says nothing, waiting patiently for Tina to continue. "I finally figured out a way to hide most of my money under a floorboard 'til I had enough to hitch a ride with a wagon train. I got myself as far as Grand Island where I saw an ad in a broad sheet saying Lieutenant Capron was looking for a housekeeper. I answered the ad by leaving a message with the dry goods clerk and got me this job."

Elizabeth wonders if she could have been as daring as Tina. She doubts it. "You were very brave." When she blushes, Elizabeth can tell she's unaccustomed to compliments. "What's the dream for your life?"

This time, Tina looks Elizabeth in the eye with her chin raised. "My dream is to meet a nice soldier, get married, and have me a home of my own. As you can see, my dream ain't yet come true but I'm not givin' up on it."

Elizabeth is quiet while she considers Tina's story. "Thank you for telling me about your life. I hope your dreams come true."

Tina's scared-rabbit look returns as if it suddenly occurs to her why she's visiting. "Thanks for listenin', Mrs. Horn. I don't have nobody to talk to but the walls." She reaches down and gives Laddie a pat, then she gets up and walks quickly across the room. "I best be gettin' back. Thanks for the tea."

Elizabeth opens the door. "Come by anytime you can get away, Tina. I'll be sure and get the invitation to the Voogd's."

As promised, the following day, Elizabeth takes the invitation to Vi who greets her with a tired, harried look. She takes the envelope then invites Elizabeth in. "Thanks for bringing this by."

Elizabeth steps just inside the door. "It's an invitation from Mrs. Capron for Christmas dinner." She looks around the disordered room. "How have you been doing?"

Vi moves to the stove to check on her baking. "It's a lot handling everything by myself. Shar's a big help but there's so much to do with Richard away. How about you?"

Elizabeth joins Vi at the stove. "To be honest, it's been an adjustment but, just three more days now and they'll be back."

Vi tucks a stray lock of hair behind her ear. "Let's hope so."

Elizabeth turns to leave. "I won't stay, Vi. I know you're busy. Send Shar over if you need anything."

For the next four days and nights, Elizabeth manages to settle into a routine of living alone and leaving Laddie to sleep in his crate. She certainly doesn't want to have his sleeping on the bed become a habit. Charles would have a fit.

On the fifth day of Charles' absence, she's watchful, expecting to hear his footsteps coming up the path any minute. The day, however, slowly wears on with no Charles in sight. Her anxiety about Charles' delay intensifies. Before dark, she drags her feet along the worn path to the creek. Laddie races ahead. When she reaches the shore, she sees that the flowing water she scooped up yesterday has frozen over. Ice now reaches from shore to shore. *Oh no! Now what do I do? Where is Charles anyway?* Elizabeth has no time to consider the what-ifs. The frigid air is made worse by the unnerving sound of wind whistling through a nearby skeleton of a willow tree. Although it's not yet sunset, the cloud cover gives the end of day a dull, ominous, leaden-blue color. Elizabeth misses the gurgling of the creek and wonders how thick the ice is.

Leaving her buckets on the bank, she goes to the tool box attached to the back of the house and retrieves a shovel. She returns to the creek and tests the ice nearest her with a tentative step. It seems solid so she proceeds further out where she knows the current is swift and the chance of thick ice is diminished. She walks with extreme caution knowing that if she falls, she would be frozen stiff before she's discovered. She ventures out as far as she deems safe, then looks down and sees water running under a wide strip of transparent ice. Swinging the shovel over her head in an arc, she slams it down on the ice, shattering it like a mirror. She quickly scoops the ice off the top, retrieves her buckets, and fills them from the hole.

She leaves the shovel beside the creek and rushes into her house with a filled bucket in each hand. Exhausted from the exertion and tension of the ordeal, she collapses into her rocker and warms herself by the fire. A few minutes later, Elizabeth hoists herself from her rocker, feeds Laddie, then prepares the last of the salt pork and leftover corn bread for her supper. She yearns for fresh meat, which leads her back to thinking of Charles. *What's keeping him? Is he injured, stuck in a snow storm, held up by bandits? What if something happens to him and I'm left a widow, alone in this house?* Elizabeth knows better than to ruminate further. "One day at a time, Elizabeth," she tells herself before preparing for another night alone. Although she can hear wolves howling, she no longer fears their presence and quickly falls asleep.

The following morning, the morning of the sixth day, Elizabeth is determined to keep her mind occupied and her hands busy. She uses the water in the barrel to wash her hands, face, and underwear. She then pours the fresh water from the buckets into the barrel.

After a mid-day meal, she rinses jarred antelope, adds vegetables, and starts a stew to gently simmer over the fire in hopeful anticipation of Charles' arrival. She kneads her bread dough and places it on the hearth to rise.

She busies herself with chores then, shortly before dark, she gives her stew pot a final stir. Thinking she hears noises coming from the road, she stops stirring, the stew bubbles up, and she swivels the pot hook away from the fire. She listens with all her might, Laddie barks and scratches at the door. She whips off her apron, runs to the door and flings it open. She sees Charles taking crates from the back of Richard's wagon. She waves. "Charles!"

She watches as he rushes up the path. He sets the crates down just inside the door, then embraces his wife. "I missed you, Elizabeth."

She hugs her husband with all her might and makes an effort to keep away the tears that are threatening to spill. "I missed you too."

After Charles has hauled in the rest of the supplies, he takes off his coat and throws his satchel on the floor next to his trunk.

Elizabeth returns to her stew pot and swings it over the fire. "Get washed up and we can have supper right away. You must be hungry."

Charles goes to the pitcher and basin and washes his hands and face. "I'm starving. Thanks for having supper ready. How did you know I'd be here?"

Elizabeth dishes up the stew and cuts the bread. "Actually, I thought you'd be here three days ago but, when you didn't show up, I was wishful-thinking that you'd return tonight."

The couple eat in silence for several minutes. The way Charles is scooping up the stew reminds Elizabeth of when they had their first meal at Mrs. Seifert's. When he gets up to pull two bottles of stout from a crate, Elizabeth jumps in. "How was your trip? What kept you so long? Was there a box from my parents?"

Charles returns to the table, sits down and opens the bottles, handing one to Elizabeth. "There was a bad storm about three hours out from Grand Island when we were returning home. We waited it out in an old barn, which we were mighty fortunate to come across." Elizabeth takes Charles' plate, refills it, then sets it in front of him. "When the snow stopped blowing, we were able to make it to Beebee's. But, the next day, we were hit with more wind and snow. That's when we lost another day. Fortunately, we had shelter; unfortunately, we couldn't leave until the following morning. Even then, with the heavy load, it was slow going." Charles wipes his plate with a slice of bread. "What a good meal! Thanks, Darling."

Elizabeth pours her stout into a mug and takes a long drink, glad for the calming affect.

Charles takes a swig from his bottle. "How did you do here alone?"

"To be perfectly honest, Charles, it was more difficult than I thought it would be. You were right about the wolves being in the area and the creek froze over and...oh, Charles..."

Elizabeth comes around the table to hug her husband. "I hope you don't leave again anytime soon!"

Charles sits Elizabeth down on his knee. "I'll do all I can not to but I'm proud of you. There's water in the barrel, wood by the hearth, food in our bellies."

Smiling at the compliment, Elizabeth asks what he brought from Grand Island.

Charles leaves the table and opens one of the crates. He places items on the table. "Everything you asked for and more. Now, don't go rummaging through unopened crates. There are a few surprises."

Elizabeth touches each item, delighted to see all the variety. "Did my parent's package arrive?"

Charles indicates a large, wooden box. "Yes, but let's wait until Christmas Eve to open it."

Elizabeth puts the warming stone near the fire. "Speaking of Christmas Eve, let's invite the Voogd family for supper."

Charles gets up from the table. "That's a great idea, Darling." He reaches for his coat. "Now, I'll take Laddie out and bring in water while you cleanup. Then..." he gives her a wink, "we can snuggle in our bed."

The next morning Elizabeth is up before Charles. While she's fixing breakfast, he takes Laddie with him when he goes for wood and water. By the time they eat, the sun is shining, the wind has calmed to a strong breeze, and Elizabeth is filled with the holiday spirit. After breakfast, she shoos Charles out the door so she can start her puddings. It's a complicated recipe that takes a couple of days to prepare and she wants to get it right. In addition to making one to take to Mrs. Capron's Christmas party, she's also making one for Christmas Eve. *I do hope Vi and her family will come! It will almost be like Christmas back home.*

Elizabeth checks off the ingredients as she assembles them: Suet, apple, orange zest, lemon zest, barley wine, stout, eggs, flour, bread crumbs, spice, brown sugar, currents. She hums the carol "Joy to the World" as she mixes the ingredients. While she's mixing, she remembers her mother saying, "Everyone who does a really good stir gets to make a wish." Since she's the only one in the house, Elizabeth makes many wishes before her arms tire from mixing. When the pudding is finally prepared, she covers the bowls to leave them overnight.

The next morning, after seeing Charles off to work, Elizabeth adds extra flour to the puddings then packs the mixture into lightly greased basins, covers them with parchment, and ties the bundles with string. She places the tied packages into two bowls set over a large pan filled with simmering water. She settles into her rocker with mending in her lap and knitting in the basket on the floor, knowing that her day will be spent carefully watching the water to be sure it doesn't boil away. *It will be worth it to have two glorious puddings for Christmas celebrations. My dear mother would be proud of me!*

CHAPTER TWENTY-TWO

CHRISTMAS ON THE PRAIRIE

On Saturday morning, a week before Christmas, Charles prepares to leave for his shop. "I have a couple of customers picking up Christmas orders today but I should be home early."

With Charles away, her puddings complete, and her Christmas gifts ready to wrap, Elizabeth bundles up for a walk to the Voogd's. Laddie trots at her side. Elizabeth usually allows him to come along because she knows the twins love seeing what they call "an inside dog." Their dog, Buster, is a farm dog relegated to the outdoors and not particularly friendly.

Elizabeth can hear commotion inside the house when she knocks. Shar opens the door.

"Come in, Mrs Horn. Pa's down at the barn, but everyone else is here."

Vi gets up from her spinning wheel, comes to the door, gives Elizabeth a hug, and takes her cape. "So good to see you. What brings you out on a Saturday?"

Elizabeth follows Vi to the fireplace and sits in the offered chair. "Charles had to work today so I thought it was a good time to drop by. Also, I have something to ask all of you."

Vi pours two cups of tea from the pot on the table. "That sounds intriguing."

Elizabeth's flushed with excitement and rushes through the details of her invitation. "Charles and I would like to invite your family to our house for Christmas Eve. We'll have supper, read the Christmas story, and sing carols. We'll start early so as not to keep the twins up too late. Will you come?"

Jan immediately pops up from the corner where she's practicing her addition and rushes up to Elizabeth. "Your house for Christmas Eve? All of us? Will there be presents?"

Vi shakes her finger at her outspoken daughter. "Jan! Mind your manners and stop asking questions."After giving her daughter a final stern look, Vi turns and smiles at Elizabeth. "We'd love to accept your invitation. What can I bring? We'll be a crowd, you know."

Jan stays nearby while the women discuss the particulars. Elizabeth can see that she's hanging on every word and can barely contain herself. Finally, when there is a lull, she uses her polite, inside voice. "Will you be havin' a tree?"

Elizabeth smiles at the little girl, thinking this is just the kind of question she would have asked when she was six-years-old. "Assuming Mr. Horn can find one, we sure will. Do you want to string popcorn chains for decoration?"

Now, Gary and Shar come from the corner. All three children chorus, "Can we?"

Elizabeth's heart warms at their enthusiasm. "I'll ask Mr. Horn to drop off the popping corn on Monday. He brought it back from the trip to Grand Island with your pa. He said it's from Holt County. Apparently, they grow more popping corn than anywhere else in the country." The children beam. "Bring the strings of popped corn with you on Christmas Eve, and we'll decorate the tree together. I have sprigs of bittersweet we can put on for color and some candle stubs for light. How does that sound?"

Jan's jumping up and down with excitement. Gary, on the other hand, remains his quiet, reserved self. He draws a deep breath then looks directly at Elizabeth. "We ain't never had a tree, Mrs. Horn. No room for one. That'll sure be a treat. I'll string lots of corn. Don't you worry 'bout that." He looks down at his stocking feet. "I just learned how to cut paper snowflakes. Want me to bring them too?"

Elizabeth reaches out and ruffles the little boy's thick, brown hair. "Of course, Gary. Bring whatever you'd like."

Vi directs her children to resume their studies. After Elizabeth finishes her tea, she gets up, and takes her cup to Vi's washing-up basin. "I know you're all busy so I'll be getting home now. Please bring blankets to sit on and your table service."

Vi hands Elizabeth her cape. "We will. I'll also bring a side dish big enough for us all."

Before she leaves, Elizabeth looks around the crowded room. The pungent odor of fried onions, wood smoke, and sour milk fill the air but the combination somehow smells sweet. She has a best friend and precious children in her life who will be joining her and Charles for Christmas Eve.

After hugs all around, Elizabeth and Laddie briskly walk home. *What I thought was going to be a sad Christmas away from my family might just become one of my best holidays ever.*

Five days later, on December twenty-third, Charles returns from work with a bundle under his arm and an envelope sticking out of his pocket. Elizabeth rushes over, gives him a kiss, then looks at the bundle. "What's that?"

Charles holds it out. "It's a gift from Ron. Here, open it while I take off my coat."

Elizabeth opens the package and Charles explains. "It's a beef roast. I'm grateful for all the game we get around here but I'm sure hankering for some beef."

She sets the large roast on the table. "How did you get it?"

Charles sits down. "Just as I was locking up to come home, a blonde-haired man of about twenty-five hitched his horse to the post in front of my shop. He asked if I was Charlie Horn. I said I was and asked his name. He said he was Nate Bell, Ron's foreman. I looked down at his boots and, sure enough, I knew he was telling the truth. He gave me the roast and said it was a gift from Ron who asked him to drop it off on his way to Ord."

Elizabeth sits at the table across from Charles. "Did Nate have a message from Ron along with the meat?"

"Yes. He said that Ron wishes us a Merry Christmas and that the roast is for our Christmas supper. Nate also said to tell you that Lucy's doing fine and gave me a letter from her."

Charles pulls the envelope from his pocket and sets it on the table. "Then Nate said, 'Lucy sure is a right nice lady.' When I asked him how he knows her, he said he'd met her a couple of times when she'd come to Ron's in her lady's buggy. Then, he said that he'd paid her a call."

Elizabeth takes the envelope. "Really? Do you think he likes her?"

Charles shrugs his shoulders. "That's exactly what I was wondering so I asked him if he was sweet on Lucy. He said he was. He also said that she's had a heap of troubles and more to come but that it didn't make any difference to him. He said that he'd been through a bit of trouble himself."

Elizabeth gets up to put potatoes in the water that's started to boil. "That's it?"

"He wished me a Merry Christmas and rode away. I didn't open the envelope as it's addressed to you."

Elizabeth returns to the table, tears open the envelope, and removes the letter. It's short and written in a schoolgirl's hand with many misspellings but Elizabeth makes out the meaning. After reading it to herself, she reads it aloud to Charles. "Dear Lizabet, I miss you. Hope you be fine. The lady took me in is real nice. She be Mrs. Mary Becker and is a widow. She has a fine home and I have me a room of my own. Sit down. I have news. I'm having me a baby the end of March. Mrs. Becker takin' good care of me so don't worry none. Merry Christmas. See you in spring. Love, Lucy."

Elizabeth sets the letter down and stares at it in disbelief. After a moment, she mumbles, "A baby! How did I not know she was pregnant when she was here? Did she know and not tell me?"

Charles reaches over and pats his wife's hand. "I'm sure she'll give you all the particulars when we visit."

While Elizabeth dries the dishes after supper, a spark of anger flares up when she considers the injustice of it all. *Lucy's having a baby she doesn't want, by a man she doesn't love, and I'm not even pregnant.* That evening, a feeling of sadness descends on Elizabeth. She sits by the fire in her rocker knitting, grateful for Charles' quiet, unquestioning demeanor.

The next morning dawns clear and cold with only a crust of ice covering the ground. Elizabeth shakes off her melancholy, determined to return to her exuberant self. After breakfast, Charles leaves with Laddie to gather wood, taking longer than usual. Suddenly, he bursts through the door dragging a perfectly formed pine tree behind him. "What do you think, Elizabeth?"

Charles closes the door with his foot just as Laddie scampers in. Elizabeth dries her hands and rushes over.

"As the children say, it's bee-u-ti-ful!" She points. "Let's put it over by Laddie's crate. We'll pull the curtain back from the bed to give us extra space."

Charles sets the tree up in the designated corner. He's already attached two thin pieces of wood to form an X-shaped stand. The couple stand back to check if the tree is standing straight. Laddie runs in circles around them. Charles smiles. "I do believe Laddie approves of our tree." He draws Elizabeth in for a hug. "Merry Christmas Eve!"

Later that morning, while Elizabeth prepares for her guests, she frequently glances over to admire the fragrant tree and the mantle decorated with bittersweet, pine boughs, and her precious birthday angel. She thinks about the presents hidden in the trunks, the special puddings, and her parent's Christmas box still unopened in the corner. Although she misses her family, her heart is full of joy. When Charles comes over to peek in the pot, Elizabeth grabs his hand. "Oh, Darling! I do believe that this is going to be a wonderful first Christmas on the prairie."

"It will indeed, my dear."

After a small noonday meal, Charles lays out long, low boards set on bricks for a make-shift table. The Christmas pudding is ready, the roast is on the spit, and potatoes are nestled in the coals. The gifts for the children are wrapped in old newspapers and laid under the tree. Stubs of candles are attached to tree branches, ready to light.

About four o'clock, Elizabeth is putting the final touches on the covering for the boards when she hears a loud knock. Charles opens the door and the Voogd family tumbles in with Jan and Gary leading the way. Shar is carrying a large bag in her mittened hand followed by Vi who's holding a cooking dish wrapped in tea towels. Richard brings up the rear with an armload of blankets. He kicks the door closed behind them.

Elizabeth directs everyone to lay their coats and capes on the bed. Vi sets her dish near the fire then reaches into the bag that Shar's holding, pulls out dishes, and sets them on the make-shift table. She hands popcorn garlands and snowflakes to the children who are uncharacteristically quiet, seemingly mesmerized by the tree. Gary looks at Elizabeth with wide, serious eyes. "You did it, Mrs. Horn. You got a tree."

Elizabeth comes over, leans down, and puts her arm around Gary's narrow shoulders. "Mr. Horn did. Isn't it beautiful?"

Gary nods, his eyes shining. He points to the popcorn ropes and shows Elizabeth the paper snowflakes. "Gary, you and Jan can put the popcorn ropes on. Shar, will you help them with the taller branches?" While the children eagerly decorate the tree, Elizabeth inserts bittersweet between the branches. After the tree is decorated, she suggests to Gary that he place his snowflakes around the stump to cover the wooden stand.

Jan eyes the gifts. "Are those presents for us?"

"Jan, that's not polite!" scolds her father.

She hangs her head. "I'm sorry for askin', Mrs. Horn."

Elizabeth comes to stand next to the little girl. "Yes, those are for you. Would you like to open them now?" Elizabeth kneels down, reaches beneath the tree, and picks up a small, cloth bag. She pulls out three peppermint sticks, handing one to each child. After they thank her, she picks up three wrapped gifts and sees the children's eyes go wide with surprise that there's another gift for them. She hands one to Shar. "You're first."

Shar looks over the newsprint wrapping before carefully opening the package. Her eyes light up. "A book of poetry! Thank you, Mrs. Horn."

Elizabeth can see genuine delight in the girl's eyes."I thought we could read it together and discuss the meaning over the winter. I'm glad you like it."

She hands a wrapped gift to each of the twins. "You may open your gifts together."

Jan tears open the paper. When she sees the gift, her brows furrow, her eyes narrow. Gary unwraps his gift more carefully but has a similar expression. Trying to understand their apparent disappointment, Elizabeth makes a suggestion. "Look inside your pouch."

Both faces light up when they discover a shiny penny inside. "A penny!" shouts Jan. "I ain't..." when her mother clears her throat, she corrects herself. "I never had a coin before. Thank you."

A man of few words, Gary quietly thanks his hosts.

Elizabeth is glad to see smiles return to their faces. "In Germany, a penny in a new wallet ensures that the owner will never be poor. That's my wish for you."

Jan's pouch is the size of Elizabeth's palm, made of leather with fringe across the bottom, a long cord for putting around the neck, and a beaded flower design across the front. Gary's gift is the same with an arrowhead design. Wondering what's on their minds, Elizabeth points to Jan's pouch. "Do you know what that is, Jan? Is there something about it that's bothering you?"

Jan looks to her mother who nods. "I'm just wonderin' if an Indian made this."

Elizabeth squats down to be eye to eye with the little girl. "I made the pouches."

Jan looks down at the gift then back up at Elizabeth. "But it looks like an Indian thing and we don't much like Indians," she says in a soft voice.

Still in a crouch, Elizabeth looks from Jan to Gary. "I know the Indians did some bad things around here. But some White men and the government in Washington also did bad things to the Indians. There's been good and bad on both sides." When Elizabeth sees the children are listening intently, she continues. "In fact, the beads I used to decorate your medicine bags were given to me by an Indian woman named Winona. She and her son have been kind to Charles and me even though their Pawnee tribe was pushed off their land by the government." The children remain silent, apparently mulling over her words. "The medicine bags are made from the leather Mr. Horn uses to line the boots he makes. They're for treasures you want to save like a special rock, or feather, or a baby tooth." Elizabeth hopes her explanation puts the children's minds at ease though she wonders how it is sitting with Vi and Richard. When Jan puts the pouch string around her neck, her brother does the same.

When Elizabeth stands, Vi goes to the bed, pulls a bundle from under her cape, and hands it to her. Charles stands close while she unwraps the package containing a framed cross-stitched sampler that says "Home Sweet Home". "Thank you, Vi. This is beautiful. As soon as the decorations come down, we'll put it on our mantle."

With the packages opened, the men and twins go outside to walk Laddie making room for the ladies to put the finishing touches on supper. Elizabeth slices the roast, which is perfectly pink in the middle, while Vi pulls potatoes from the coals and heats up the root vegetable casserole. Shar places a blanket on the floor for each person to sit on and Elizabeth lights the lantern and candles just before Laddie and the others return.

After Charles says grace, the group erupts with chatter while dishes are passed down the table. The room smells of roasted meat, pine, and kerosene. Richard sighs. "What a treat to have beef. I occasionally sell grain to ranchers but we seldom have meat like this. Thanks for sharing with us."

Charles responds. "It's all our pleasure, Richard. Elizabeth and I feel fortunate to have your family as friends."

After dinner, Elizabeth heats her pudding, which has a cake-like consistency. Next, she heats a ladle of brandy and carefully pours it over the top of the pudding. She brings it to the table and holds it out in front or her. "Charles, please light our Christmas pudding." He obliges and touches the pudding with the candle flame. A halo of light surrounds the dessert. The children squeal. Elizabeth smiles at her guests. "Merry Christmas!" After the flame goes out, she serves the pudding.

Vi touches her arm. "This pudding is delicious, Elizabeth. Will you show me how to make it?"

"I'd love to." Feeling a sense of pride, she adds, "I'm glad you like it."

After Vi and the children help clear, wash, and dry the dishes, Elizabeth takes Charles' worn Bible from the shelf. "Please get comfortable while I read you the Christmas story from the book of Luke." Jan sits in Shar's lap, Gary's in his mother's. Charles pours Richard and himself small glasses of brandy. The room becomes quiet; the only sounds are the wind and the crackling of the fire. Standing in front of the fireplace, Elizabeth begins. "And it came to pass in those days, that there went out a decree from Caesar Augustus that all the world should be taxed ..."

When she comes to the part, "Suddenly a great company of the heavenly host appeared with the angel praising God and saying, 'Glory to God in the highest heaven, and on earth peace to those on whom his favor rests,'" Elizabeth suggests they all sing "It Came Upon a Midnight Clear." She reads to the end of verse twenty, begins singing "Joy to the World," and everyone joins in. When the song is over, Elizabeth closes the Bible and turns to Charles. "It's time to light the tree."

Charles carefully lights the candle stubs attached to the tree while Elizabeth extinguishes the lantern and other candles. The fireplace glows. The tree sparkles with candlelight, the children are silent and wide-eyed. Elizabeth sees a tear slip down Vi's cheek. Everyone is quiet for several minutes, then, as the candles begin to sputter out, Elizabeth softly begins signing "Silent Night." The others join her. After the song, Elizabeth looks into Charles' eyes and whispers, "Merry Christmas."

After the Voogds leave, she and Charles open the box from Elizabeth's family. The used, primary school books she requested are there along with two tattered books of poetry and *The History of Western Civilization.* There's a roll of thick paper, several tubes of paint, and brushes. A soft bundle is wrapped separately and Elizabeth is delighted to find fabric for a new dress along with thread and buttons. There's a pint of good whiskey for Charles and delicacies too. Chocolate, almonds, a lovely English breakfast tea, and a package of sassafras. "What thoughtful gifts from my family."

Charles draws Elizabeth into his arms. "You're much loved, Darling."

Then, Charles pulls away and begins to unbutton his shirt. "Let's wait until morning to open the gifts we have for each other. I've had all the merriment I can handle for one night." Then, he turns and looks into Elizabeth's eyes, "It's been a wonderful Christmas Eve and you made it so."

Elizabeth smiles as she gets the warming stone ready for their cold bed.

Before sunrise the next morning, Elizabeth hears noises but stays snuggled under the quilt. When she peeks out she sees that Charles has taken Laddie out, brought in water, and added fuel to the banked coals. He sings out, "Merry Christmas, my dear. Rise and shine."

Elizabeth peeks around the curtain. "What are you doing up so early? It's your day to sleep in."

"I don't want to miss a minute of Christmas," Charles says with, what Elizabeth considers, uncharacteristic enthusiasm. She gets up, wraps her shawl around her shoulders, pulls on thick stockings, then walks to the window and peers out. "It snowed! It snowed for Christmas!" She looks at Charles with a mischievous grin. "Does that mean Santa was able to come with his sleigh?"

"Of course. Come see what he left you."

Elizabeth grabs her cape from the peg, puts it over her shawl, then hurries to sit in front of the fire where Charles stands holding a small package wrapped in white butcher paper and tied with string. "Your first gift is something I made just for mornings like this."

She quickly unwraps the soft package and pulls out a beautiful pair of deerskin moccasins lined with gray rabbit fur. She puts them on over her stockings. "Oh Darling, they're perfect! So cozy for wearing around the house. Thank you."

Charles pulls out another small package and waits while she opens it. "I think you deserve new ribbons for your beautiful hair. I hope the colors suit you."

Elizabeth surveys the red, pink, and blue ribbons. "The colors are perfect. Thank you."

It's Elizabeth's turn to pull a package from her trunk. She hands it to Charles. "Merry Christmas." When he tries it on, she thinks the knitted blue sweater is a little large but Charles seems delighted with his gift. He chuckles when she tells him about dying the yarn in berry juice.

"I remember the day you had purple hands. Now I understand why."

At noon, the couple have a small meal of leftover beef, anticipating a big Christmas supper at the Caprons'. The room darkens while Elizabeth washes the dishes. Charles goes to the window. "Looks like another big storm is brewing. I wonder if we'll be able to make it to the party."

Elizabeth is pressing her lavender voile dress when there's a knock on the door. Charles opens it. "Symmons. What brings you out on Christmas Day?"

Private Symmons stamps snow from his boots then steps inside. Charles closes the door to the wind and cold. "I have a message from the Caprons. They're canceling the party for all but those at the fort. They're afraid you might get snowed in and they don't have accommodations for so many guests. They send their apologies."

Elizabeth joins Charles by the door. "Will you be telling the Mitchells and Voogds also?"

"Yes, ma'am. I've spoken with Mr. Mitchell and I'm headed to the Voogds' right now."

Symmons looks back after opening the door to leave. "Merry Christmas."

Charles responds. "Merry Christmas, Joe! Stay safe out there."

Elizabeth puts her dress back in the trunk and stands her iron on the hearth to cool. "You know, Charles. I'm not that disappointed. We had such a lovely time last night and opening our gifts this morning, I feel quite satisfied with our celebrations."

Charles puts his arm around his wife's waist. "I agree."

Elizabeth goes to the shelf and pulls down a bowl. "Besides, now we have this second Christmas pudding all to ourselves." She chuckles. "Let's start supper with dessert!"

CHAPTER TWENTY-THREE

LOST IN SNOW AND ANOTHER LOCUST STORY

Although the first dusting of snow arrived in late October and more at Christmas, there had yet to be the all-out blizzard the Caprons predicted for Christmas Day. The clerk at The Mercantile tells Elizabeth that winters are usually mild in the valley, but she's heard others talk about treacherous storms lasting for several days.

While kneading bread on a Monday morning in mid-January, Elizabeth hears the wind howling louder than usual and her windows rattling. Peeking out through the frosted pane, she sees a dark gray sky. Just after midday, the room turns so dark, she lights a lamp in order to finish her mending. An hour later, snow begins to fall. Elizabeth watches the soft flakes fly by the window and quickly turn the landscape into a sheet of white. Snow cascades down in swirls the likes of which she has never seen, and she worries about Charles finding his way home. Even Laddie seems agitated, pacing back and forth across the room.

By late afternoon, even though the snow continues to fall, Elizabeth decides she must make her way to the privy. The slops are full, and she needs to relieve herself. Dressed in Charles' old canvas hunting jacket, her knitted hat and scarf, but no mittens, she leaves the house and leans into the ferocious wind as she starts her trek to the back of the house. She leaves Laddie behind, knowing that Charles will take him out later. The bucket sloshes over the edge when Elizabeth staggers through the calf-deep snow. Her exposed hands are already red with cold. The privy door is frozen shut, but she manages to yank it open and finds respite from the storm in the tiny space. After accomplishing her chore, she exits the privy only to find the storm has grown stronger. The white world of swirling snow closes in on her like a vise. All traces of her footprints have been erased by the wind or filled in with snow.

At best, Elizabeth has a poor sense of direction. Even if it had been good, with little sun and no view of the horizon or landmarks to guide her, traversing the short distance to the house would have been difficult. She tentatively takes several steps right, then left, then returns to the privy. Trying not to panic, she again paces in one direction then another, talking to herself as she walks. "I refuse to die a few steps from my own front door. Stay calm, Elizabeth, stay calm."

Her teeth are chattering and her frigid hands are becoming numb when Elizabeth faintly hears barking. She hopes it isn't her imagination. Standing perfectly still, she listens. *There it is again! It's coming from my left.* She cautiously moves in that direction, stopping every few steps to listen. Just when she confirms the sound is Laddie barking and thinks she may have found her way back to the front door, she runs smack dab into Charles. "Oh, Charles! I … I heard barking and—" Elizabeth puts her face into Charles' neck and sobs.

"Get inside. You're shaking like a leaf."

Once Elizabeth is safely inside, Charles grabs the basket next to the fireplace and heads back out. He returns shortly with as much firewood as he can uncover. He quickly builds up the fire. Elizabeth continues to sit numbly and Charles removes her wet coat and boots. He places her fur-lined moccasins on her cold feet, then, puts the kettle on. He soon puts a cup of hot, not-for-ladies-only tea into her red, raw hands. "What happened, Elizabeth?"

Feeling a bit foolish, Elizabeth recounts her fateful trip to the privy. They decide that Laddie is the hero of the day. Charles refills Elizabeth cup with hot water. "I'm sorry you had such a scare, Darling. This blizzard's a bad one and it will probably get even worse during the night." While Elizabeth continues to warm up, Charles goes to her ragbag, pulls out rags, then stuffs them along the windows. "These will keep the wind from blowing more snow through the cracks. After the house heats up, I'll keep the fire low for as long as I can. But I'm warning you, we're in for a cold night."

Finally over her scare and warming up, Elizabeth places the sandstone bed warmer near the coals. "At least we'll have warm feet." While the fire is hot, Elizabeth heats leftover antelope stew. They pull the table close to the fireplace and sit down for a late supper. The wind rattles the windows and snow continues to fall. After washing the dishes, Elizabeth passes the sandstone over the bed to heat it before they climb in, spooning to keep warm. Sleep eludes her but she finds comfort in recalling small routines she used to complain about: Setting the dining room table for company, minding her siblings when her mother went shopping, standing still for dress fittings, helping her mother prepare Sunday dinner. Ordinary pleasures like her feather mattress, the warmth of the bedroom she shared with her sister, the smell of pine trees after a rain, gossiping with her school chums, now seem unimaginable. Lulled by the sounds of her husband's steady breathing, Elizabeth finally feels her eyelids grow heavy.

By morning, the storm is over and, although a giant drift completely covers one window, the other yields a shaft of sunlight. Charles stokes the fire then goes out to shovel a path to the privy and get water while Elizabeth melts snow for making coffee. After breakfast, Charles works on new boot designs and finishes reading back copies of the local and regional newspapers while Elizabeth experiments with her new paints and begins reading the history book her parents sent. When she reads of wars and other disasters, her mind spins back to the additional locust story Charles promised to tell. She speaks to him while lighting a lantern. "Remember when you told me something about the locusts last summer? You said you read about the devastation in the newspaper, and that it was even worse than what Richard experienced the year before. Feel like telling me about it?"

He looks up. "Give me a moment to put my work away then I'll recount what I read. The story's hard to believe but the reporting came from reliable sources. Also, I talked with a few people who had firsthand experiences." While he puts away his leather and designs, Elizabeth wipes her brushes and caps her paints. There's nothing she enjoys more than listening to a good story on a cold winter late afternoon. And a true one at that.

The couple settle down companionably in front of the fire with Laddie lying on the floor between them. "First, I'll tell you a bit more about locusts than what Richard had to say." Charles leans back in his chair. "The Rocky Mountain Locust is known to be a stupendous force of nature. It's a dull olive green just an inch and a half long. Working together they can wield an uncanny power. Ordinary grasshoppers never gather in immense clouds. Locusts, on the other hand, have the ability to become gregarious, form massive swarms, and fly astonishing distances." He pauses and cocks his head to the side.

Elizabeth gets up and brings potatoes and a knife to the table. Keeping her hands busy peeling potatoes helps her remain patient with her husband's slow, thoughtful manner.

"It was the immature locusts that marched across the country, devouring foliage as they molted into adulthood. I've heard that they can go for years without swarming. But last year's drought created the perfect conditions. As Richard said, the year before was bad. It was also a summer with little rain. But this summer was worse for much of the midwest and all the way up to Minnesota."

Elizabeth gets up again and sets water to boil for the potatoes. She looks at Charles over her shoulder. "Did people do anything to get rid of them besides what Richard talked about?"

Charles thoughtfully pulls at his beard. "I heard they fired guns, clubbed them, even set fires. Similar to tornadoes, they touched down like funnel clouds in one place, only to leave a neighboring township untouched. It was the largest locust swarm recorded in human history. It's known as Albert's Swarm."

Elizabeth wonders aloud about the name.

"I believe it was named for meteorologist, Albert Child, who is from right here in Nebraska. It's said that he measured the swarm's flight for ten days in June, then he telegraphed for further information from east and west, noting wind speed and carefully calculating the extent of the cloud of insects."

Pausing, Charles gets up and opens his trunk. "Hold on, let me get the paper I saved. I'll read you the details of what Child learned." He pulls out a seven-month-old newspaper and adjusts the lantern to better read the small type. "The swarm was one hundred and ten miles wide, eighteen hundred miles long, and a quarter to a half mile in depth. They covered one-hundred-ninety-eight thousand square miles, an area equal to most of the states along the East Coast."

He looks over at his wife before emphasizing the surprising statistics. "Says here that Child estimated there were three and a half trillion insects, but I heard much higher estimates. The paper goes on to say that they ate the sweat-stained handles of farm implements, chewed the wool off sheep, stripped the trees. They consumed roughly a quarter of the country. The worst and most widespread natural disaster the country has ever seen."

Elizabeth shakes her head from side to side, speechless for the moment. Charles continues to read. "Grasshopper carcasses fouled wells, polluted creeks and rivers, and halted trains laboring up grades, the tracks greasy with crushed bodies." Folding the paper, Charles looks up. "What do you think about that story? Hard to believe it's true, isn't it?"

Still stunned by the details, she thinks about those in the midst of the disaster. "Many thousands must have starved or nearly starved."

Charles slowly nods. "You're right. I heard that soldiers from the fort delivered surplus army clothing to families and found many women and children starving. The men folk had left to find work. Our neighbors were fortunate that it happened south of here."

Elizabeth goes to the mantle, takes down the Bible, and opens it to Exodus. She finds chapter ten and refreshes her memory. "Your story reminds me of when God commanded Moses to raise his hand over the land of Egypt and bring on the locusts." She glances back down to the page. "They covered the surface of the whole country, making the ground look black. Just like in your story, they ate all the crops and not one green thing remained."

The couple have a quiet supper and spend the evening relaxing in front of the fire, contemplating the locust story. After retiring to bed, Elizabeth tosses and turns as she thinks about the starving children and hoards of locusts. She gives a prayer of thanks that the Voogds and other nearby farmers didn't experience a second year of devastation.

CHAPTER TWENTY-FOUR

SAVING THE CHILDREN

The last two weeks in January are uneventful with Charles and Elizabeth returning to their usual routines. Just after supper on Sunday, January thirty-first, there's a knock on the door. Charles looks out and opens it to Peter who holds out a folded piece of paper. "I have a message for Mrs. Horn."

Charles takes the note. "Isn't it late to be delivering messages?"

Peter turns to go. "When Mr. Mitchell brings me a message at the saloon, I take it out for delivery. He pays me well. Best be closing that door. You're letting all the heat out."

Charles thanks Peter, closes the door, and hands the note to Elizabeth who quickly scans the short message. "Mr. Mitchell wants me to substitute teach tomorrow and, possibly, all week. He writes that Miss Harvey has taken to her bed with a fever but left lesson plans on her desk."

She feels a flutter of excitement mixed with dread. "Guess I'm going to get my chance to teach." She takes a deep breath. "I hope I can do a good job."

Putting the bedwarmer near the fire, Charles reassures her. "You'll do fine, Elizabeth, but why don't you bring along your *New York Ledger,* just in case Miss Harvey didn't plan enough to fill the day. You can read the students a tale they've not heard."

Before bed, Elizabeth lays out her best calico work-dress, woolen stockings, and her latest copy of *The Ledger.*

The morning dawns cold and gray with a brisk wind coming out of the north. After bringing in water, Charles hands his canvas jacket to Elizabeth. "Wear this today. You'll need something more than a cape to keep you warm. I have my sweater and my old army jacket."

She sets the jacket by the fire to warm.

With all the cloud cover, the morning is dark as the couple set out on their walk. When they reach town, Charles goes left to his shop; Elizabeth walks right, arriving at the school in plenty of time to start a fire. The door sticks then creaks on it's hinges when she steps out to ring the bell at precisely eight thirty.

Johnny and Greta Henderson; George and Emma Alderman; Fredrick and Franklin, the two small boys she remembers from earlier; and two older children, Stanley and Esther, enter the classroom. Just as Elizabeth's about to close the door, Eli marches in. Elizabeth chooses to ignore the smirk on his face. "Everyone take your seats, please."

When she wraps her desk with a ruler, the children say, "Good morning, Mrs. Horn."

Eli stands. "Where's Miss Harvey—our REAL teacher?"

Once again, Elizabeth ignores Eli's attempt to bait her into a confrontation. "Miss Harvey is ill. She will return as soon as she is able. Now, get out your slates." Although she regularly feeds fuel to the stove, the room remains cold enough that she can see the students' breaths when they recite. The children and Elizabeth keep their coats and mittens on unless they're writing.

After the break at noon, Elizabeth is distracted by the roar of the wind. The children are restless and she knows they're cold. When lunch pails are put away, she decides this is the time to read a story. "I thought you might enjoy an original story from *The New York Ledger*." With the exception of Eli, the children stop their fidgeting and look at her with anticipation in their eyes. She pulls her chair closer to their desks and begins reading. "The streets of London are slick with rain…" She looks up at the class. "Who can tell me where London is?"

Stanley raises his hand. He's small for twelve and swings his feet under the table. "England, Mrs. Horn."

"That's correct, Stanley."

Just as Elizabeth returns to the periodical, there's a great gust of wind. The window panes shake, and smoke billows from the stove. She rushes to the window; the children crowd in behind her. What she sees frightens her more than the roar of the wind. Snow. A great deal of snow! "Return to your desks, children. You've all seen snow before," she says, making an effort to sound matter-of-fact. She tries to disguise the fact that her hands are shaking and her heart is racing. "Stanley, would you like to read the rest of the page?"

Stanley walks to the front of the room. Elizabeth hands him the paper, and he starts to read. "The streets are filled with traffic and…"

Suddenly, the small room reverberates with a loud crash. All heads turn to the door now lying on the floor. Snow and wind rush into the room. Greta, the youngest Henderson, yelps.

Elizabeth tries to control her panic as the children gather near her. Frightened eyes stare up at her, imploring her to give them direction. She sees Eli sauntering along the wall toward the doorway. "Esther, get the long jump rope."

Esther dashes to the corner and retrieves the rope.

"We're going to leave here in an orderly manner and proceed to the house closest to the school. Mrs. Mitchell will welcome us."

The children remain motionless. Esther hands the rope to Elizabeth. Her eyes are wide with fear. "Won't we get lost in the snow, Mrs. Horn?

Elizabeth holds up one end of the rope. "We'll stay together, Esther. No one will be lost. Now, you and Stanley take the other end. The rest of you hold on to the rope between us. Eli, you follow to make sure no one lags behind."

Eli, who's now near the opening, responds. "I ain't being paid to babysit these brats. You are. I'm goin' home." He pulls up his collar. "Good luck finding your way in this storm," he says with a sneer, then walks out the door.

Focusing on the rest of the class, Elizabeth ignores Eli, knowing that she can't physically restrain him. She concentrates on making sure everyone is in place along the rope. "Hold tight to the rope and stay together. Do you understand?" When there's no response, Elizabeth asks again, speaking loudly to be heard over the roar of the wind. "Do you understand?"

Through chattering teeth, the class responds. "Yes, Mrs. Horn."

Elizabeth picks up Greta, the smallest child who is whimpering into her mittens. "It's going to be alright. Hang on to my neck." With the children lined up along the rope, she hollers, "Let's go!"

The storm is as wild as the one in which Elizabeth was lost just weeks earlier. For a moment, she panics as she looks one way then the other in an attempt to get her bearings. She knows the Mitchell's house is just one block over from the school and walks in what, she hopes, is the right direction. Greta puts her face into Elizabeth's neck and she struggles to hold the child with one arm while holding the rope with the other. When she ventures a look back, she sees the children trudging through the deepening snow, heads bent to the wind.

In the dim light, she sees the outline of a house in the distance. A lantern shines in the window. Elizabeth turns and hollers to the children. "We're almost there! Hold on just a little longer." She faintly hears the two in the back encouraging the younger children. Greta gives a sniffle and hugs Elizabeth's neck tighter. "It's alright, Greta. You'll soon be safe and warm."

Using the light as a beacon, Elizabeth shuffles forward. The snow is already above her ankles and pelting her exposed skin. The arm holding Greta is burning with exhaustion. Just as she's about to shift Greta to the other arm, the lantern grows bright and someone shouts into the wind, "Over here!"

It's Mr. Mitchell! He sees us! We made it!

The parade quickly moves forward. Mr. Mitchell holds the door as the children and Elizabeth rush into the warm house. Once inside, she gathers the children around her. "You are all so brave! Your parents will be very proud of you. I certainly am. Now, let's get you warmed up." She then tells the Mitchells about the door.

Mrs. Mitchell brings in an armload of blankets while her husband stokes up the fire. Soon, Elizabeth and the children are sitting near a roaring fire wrapped in blankets and holding mugs of warm milk.

A loud knock on the door startles Elizabeth. Mr. Mitchell opens it to Charles and Peter. They rush in. "Are my wife and the children here?"

Before Mr. Mitchell can answer, Elizabeth calls out. "Charles, I'm here!" Surprised to see her husband, Elizabeth stands and sets Greta, who has not left her side, in Mrs. Mitchell's lap.

Charles rushes over to embrace his wife. She feels her face grow red. "How did you find us?"

Charles moves to the fire. "When the storm kicked up, I started to worry, so I locked up the shop and began walking toward the school to check on you. When I walked by the saloon, Peter saw me and waved me in." Charles pauses to accept a mug of coffee from Mrs. Mitchell. "When I told him where I was going, he asked to come along. When we got to the school and found the door off it's hinges, we started searching for you." Charles warms his hands on the sides of the mug. "Peter spotted a light in the Mitchell's window so we headed this way." He looks around the room at the quiet children. "Thank goodness you're all safe."

Peter comes into the circle. "Hey, Charlie, I think we should go repair that door. I'd hate to see the school house ruined."

Charles gulps down the rest of his coffee then hands his empty mug to Elizabeth. "You're right." He looks over at Mr. Mitchell. "Think we could borrow some tools?"

Mr. Mitchell takes his coat from a peg. "We'll pick up tools on our way out. I'm coming with you."

Word spreads about the whereabouts of the class and, while the men are gone, Mr. Henderson arrives to pick up his children along with George and Emma Alderman. Then, Fredrick's and Franklin's father, who lives in town, comes by. Stanley and Esther, both farm children, remain. Elizabeth can see anxiety on their faces. Just as she's about to reassure them, Mrs. Mitchell speaks. "Don't worry, children. If your parents can't make it to town this afternoon, you're welcome to stay the night."

Stanley, who seemed so confident in the classroom, looks at Elizabeth with a furrowed brow and a mouth clenched tight against possible tears. Then, he turns to Mrs. Mitchell. "But, Mrs. Mitchell, how will they know we're here? What if they can't find us?"

Mrs. Mitchell pats Stanley's shoulder. "When they make it to town, they'll most likely stop at the saloon for information. Don't worry, they'll know where to find you."

Elizabeth comes near and speaks in her confident-teacher-voice. "Mrs. Mitchell is right. Now, let's see if there's something we can read while we wait."

CHAPTER TWENTY-FIVE

FIRE AND NEWS

About a week after the Schoolhouse Blizzard, as the couple refer to the latest storm, Charles returns from work just before sunset, hangs his coat on the peg, and gives Elizabeth a hug.

"You look tired, Darling," Elizabeth remarks.

He walks across the room and slowly eases himself into a chair. "I believe the snow and cold are wearing me down. I'll feel better after I get a hot supper in me."

Laddie starts barking just as Elizabeth pulls the biscuits out of her make-shift oven. Charles gets up to look out the window. He sees Richard drawing up in his wagon. Alarmed, he shoves open the door.

Elizabeth puts her biscuits on the table and rushes over to stand just behind her husband. Richard hollers from the wagon seat and points at the sky. "Grab your buckets, Charlie! I think there's a fire at the fort."

Charles looks up. "I'll be right out."

Elizabeth sees black smoke billowing in the pink and orange sky. The smoke brings back memories of the prairie fire at Dorothy's, causing Elizabeth to shudder. Her husband pulls on his boots, puts on his canvas coat and gloves, then grabs the two water buckets from the corner of the room. Elizabeth puts a biscuit in each of his coat pockets just before he runs out the door to join Richard on the wagon.

While Charles is gone, Elizabeth paces the floor, wondering what's happening at the fort, and worried for the men's safety. When she looks out the window, she can still see smoke in the distant sky although the fort is over a mile away. Laddie paces with her. When he finally settles in his crate, she sits down to eat a plate of over-cooked stew.

The moon is high in the sky, the fire is down to coals in the fireplace when Charles finally returns. Elizabeth rises from her chair when she hears the click of the latch. She opens her mouth in shock at the sight of Charles. His face is dark with ash, his hands red with cold, and icicles cling to his beard. The smell of smoke is pouring off of him. "Are you okay, Charles? Was anyone hurt?"

Charles croaks out, "I'm fine. No one hurt."

Relieved, she helps him out of his coat and puts it near the hearth to dry. After he sits in the rocker, she pulls off his boots. Charles holds his hands to the fire. Although she's dying for more news, Elizabeth remains quiet while he thaws. She can tell from his body language and his persistent quiet that he's shaken. She stokes up the fire and boils water for a hot toddy while reheating the stew. Before the water boils, she pours warm water in a basin so Charles can wash up.

After he's washed the soot from his hands and face, he resumes his seat by the fire. Elizabeth hands him a mug of toddy, pulls up a chair, sits, then speaks in a quiet voice. "Charles, what happened?"

He takes a deep breath and haltingly speaks in a low, serious tone that's barely above a whisper. "It was horrible. The Caprons lost their new home. The concrete shell stands, but the inside is completely gutted from a combination of fire, smoke, and water."

Elizabeth remains silent, shaking her head in disbelief. She gets up, fills a plate with reheated stew, adds a buttered biscuit, then hands it to Charles before sitting back down beside him. "I can't wrap my mind around the fact that their home is destroyed. Do they know how the fire started? Where's the family staying?"

Charles eats a spoonful of stew. "It started in the kitchen. They think the chimney might have been blocked, which sent smoke into the room. Tina warned the family and they were able to get out some of their belongings but, by the time Richard and I arrived, the structure was engulfed in flames." He pauses to take a bite of biscuit. "Many of the soldiers were away on an expedition."

After wiping gravy up with the last of his biscuit, he hands Elizabeth his empty plate. He drops his head into his hands. "We were mighty shorthanded. We did the best we could to put out the fire but there wasn't much we could do to save the house."

Elizabeth asks again about the family.

"As I said, they got out and no one was hurt. However, the young boy, what's his name?"

"Henry."

"Ah, yes, Henry. Someone said that he was coughing from the smoke and they're worried about him since he's sickly anyway. For now, the family will stay in the mostly empty barracks."

Elizabeth gets up and sets Charles' plate in a basin of dishwater. "What about Tina? Did she go with them?"

"Richard and I bundled Tina up in an extra blanket Richard had and got her into the wagon. We dropped her off at the Mitchells after explaining to them what happened. She was so upset that Richard thought she needed the kindness Harriett can give her, plus they have extra bedrooms." Charles looks at his wife and sighs. "Even though Tina had nothing to do with the fire, she feels responsible because it started in the kitchen chimney. She's in a bad way, Elizabeth."

Weary from the drama of the last couple of days, Elizabeth washes the dishes, then she and Charles retire. She's restless most of the night as the vision of the fire comes to her mind again and again.

A few days later, when the snow on the road is mostly packed and the wind has died down, Elizabeth pays a visit to Tina and Harriett. The mile and a half walk into town is cold but Elizabeth is glad for an opportunity to be outside and clear her head. When she approaches the Mitchell's house, the night of the Schoolhouse Blizzard flashes through her mind. It's the first time she's been in town since that day, and she's caught off guard by the fear she still feels in the pit of her stomach. She's also sad that she was only able to teach for a few hours. School was canceled for the rest of the week due to the storm; then Miss Harvey returned to her classroom.

Harriet opens the door and Elizabeth sees a look of surprise on her wrinkled face. "Good afternoon, Harriet. I hope you don't mind my dropping by."

She steps aside and beckons Elizabeth to come in. "Of course not, Elizabeth. Good to see you. I don't get out of the house in the winter so it's lovely to have a visitor. What brings you out on this cold afternoon?"

Elizabeth hands Harriet a basket of freshly made muffins then removes her cape, shawl, hat, mittens, scarf and places them on a chair that Harriett indicates. She follows her into the snug, warm kitchen. "Besides coming to see how you are, I'm also here to see Tina. She's been to my place a couple of times and I'd like to think we're friends. I've been worried about her."

Harriet offers Elizabeth a seat at the table, sits down beside her, then leans in conspiratorially. "She's doing a might better than she was. Still sick with guilt though. Poor thing." Harriet gets up and puts the kettle on to heat. "I told her she can stay with us as long as she needs to. I'm enjoying her help and the company." She returns to the table and whispers near Elizabeth's ear. "She'll be glad to know that she has you for a friend. I believe she thinks everyone blames her for the fire, which, of course, is definitely not true. In fact, she may have saved the family."

When the kettle whistles, Harriett makes a pot of tea and brings it to the table along with two cups, saucers, and a plate for Elizabeth's muffins. Just as she takes her seat, Tina walks into the kitchen and they greet one another. Elizabeth looks up at Tina. "I've heard that you've been through a rough time."

Tina lowers her head. "Yes, ma'am, I have. Mrs. Mitchell's been mighty kind to me though. I don't know what I'd a done without her."

Harriett pats the chair next to her. "Bring your cup over and join us for tea, Tina. Elizabeth didn't come just to see me, she came to visit with you too."

Elizabeth sees Tina's eyes light up at the invitation. She takes a cup from the shelf then joins the ladies. Elizabeth passes her a muffin. "Have you heard anything from the Caprons?"

Tina carefully breaks the muffin in half before she responds. "Private Symmons come by here to tell me the missus and children are going back from where they come from. Camp Ruggles I think it is. They was planning on leavin' as soon as the road got cleared. They ain't comin' back 'til their house is rebuilt." Tina's face crumples. "I feel terrible about the fire, Mrs. Horn. I wish I could have done something to stop it."

Looking concerned, Harriet pats her hand. "Now, now, Dear. We've talked this all out. Catastrophes like this just happen; it was no one's fault. Right, Elizabeth?"

Elizabeth nods. "Exactly right."

Tina's face brightens a little. "There's one tiny, good thing come of all this here tragedy."

Elizabeth sets down her cup. "What's that?"

"Private Symmons asked Mrs. Mitchell if he might come visit me next week on his day off. Now ain't that a silver linin' to the worst possible happenin'?"

Elizabeth smiles at Tina's bit of joy. "It surely is."

"And you know'd what else?"

Elizabeth shakes her head. "What?"

"The Mitchells, they say I can stay here as long as I want. Now ain't that just another silver linin'?"

On her walk home Elizabeth thinks of all that's happened in the last few weeks. Getting the children safely to the Mitchell's during a blizzard, a terrible fire, and Tina's new life with the Mitchells and a beau. "Life is full of surprises, bad and good. Charles and I have to keep preparing for the worst while hoping for the best," Elizabeth mutters to herself as she walks briskly home in the last rays of afternoon sunshine.

When Charles returns from work on a Monday evening in early February, he hangs up his coat then asks, "Do you want the good news or the bad news first?"

Elizabeth wipes her hands on her apron and comes to greet him. "My goodness, you must have had a busy day. Were you at the fort?"

"Yes, and I talked with Lieutenant Heyl who had news. Which do you want?"

Elizabeth returns to her cooking pot. "The good news first."

Charles sits near the fire and pulls off his boots. "There's going to be a Valentine's Dance at the fort in two weeks. We're invited, as are the Voogds, the Mitchells, and a few other folks from town. The men are organizing it themselves. I believe they're hoping to meet some single young ladies. We need to bring a dish to share and wear our dancing shoes."

Elizabeth whirls around. "Oh Charles! That will be such fun. Anything to get us away from this dark, cold house and spend time with other people." She brings a loaf of bread to the table and begins slicing. "And the bad news?"

"The bad news is that there's been unrest to our west. The Sioux have been raiding the Pawnee village and some settlers' homes. They've been warned that if they don't stop, the army will send troops to settle it. Nothing will happen in the next few months since it's nearly impossible to travel any distance." He snags the heel of the loaf and takes a big bite. "Heyl thinks the Sioux are taking advantage of the weather to cause trouble without immediate recourse."

Elizabeth feels her stomach clench with fear. "Does this mean we're in danger?"

"I don't think so. We're too far out of their range at the present time. However, if there continues to be trouble and troops do go in, settlers like myself and Richard may be asked to join them."

Putting down her slicing knife, she looks into Charles' eyes. "You mean you'd go to fight the Indians?"

Charles motions for her to take a seat. "Well, I don't know if it will come to a battle, but Heyl wants to have a show of force to signal the Sioux that we mean business and we have the sheer numbers to overwhelm them." He places his hand over Elizabeth's. "I know it's important to you that I share the details of whatever is happening. I've told you all I know and, at least for now, there's nothing to worry about." When Elizabeth doesn't respond, Charles asks, "What's for supper?"

Even though she has more questions, she can tell that Charles has said all he has to say, so, without comment, she goes to the fire and dishes out plates of savory venison and dumplings.

That night, she awakes to find Charles sitting close to the smoldering fire. He's wrapped in his canvas coat and sitting motionless in the rocker. While she watches, he begins to slowly rock forward and back.

In the morning, Elizabeth asks, "You seem tired this morning. Did you sleep well?"

Charles doesn't look up from his eggs. "Yes, Dear. Did you?"

Heeding Vi's advice about waiting for Charles to talk when he's ready, Elizabeth doesn't press him.

That evening after supper Elizabeth makes an effort to engage Charles in conversation. She keeps her eyes on her mending. "Did you have customers today, Charles?"

"Nope. Just one looker."

Elizabeth gets up to take her cape from its peg by the door. She wraps it firmly around her. She's cold even though she's sitting near the fire. "Any orders from the fort?"

Her husband looks into the fire. "No new recruits expected at the fort this winter so no boots to make, the farmers won't be needing new boots until they return to the fields, and folks in town aren't venturing out much. I'm afraid money will be scarce this winter." The fire sizzles and the room smells of smoke and old grease. Charles mutters just loud enough for Elizabeth to hear. "But, I'll continue to make boots until my supplies run out."

Elizabeth looks at him with alarm building in her chest. She does her best to remain calm. "Good thing we're stocked up on food and fuel." When Charles only nods, she says no more.

A few minutes later, he slowly rises from his chair. "I think we should get to bed early. It's too cold to be comfortable and we need to conserve wood and lantern oil."

Elizabeth watches him walk across the room on his way to the privy. *I've never seen him so slow. It's like he's walking with leaden feet. The combination of the darkness, cold, and lack of work seems to be taking a toll.* Since she isn't tired, she tries to read from the bed by candlelight but finds even her favorite book doesn't hold her interest. *I'm beginning to understand what Vi meant about the challenge of spending the winter in a soddie.*

During the next few days, the air is heavy with the prospect of more snow. The afternoons are cold, dark, and dreary. Even so, Elizabeth feels more upbeat than usual with prospects of the dance only a week away. She's also looking forward to spending time with Vi. Richard will be picking them up in the wagon.

The day before the dance, Elizabeth sits close to the glowing fire for heat and light while she mends Charles' work shirt. Laddie dozes on a blanket close by. *The prospect of going to a dance reminds me of when Charles and I first met.* She sighs with pleasure, recalling the thrill of dancing in Charles' arms. *It seems so long ago.*

CHAPTER TWENTY-SIX

SICKNESS AND DESPERATION

The next day, cold air rushes in when Charles swings open the door while Elizabeth's cleaning up after her midday meal. Her pulse quickens and she rushes to his side. "You're early. Has anything happened?"

Coughing, Charles croaks out a reply. "I'm not feeling well."

Elizabeth feels his forehead. "You're burning up. Get into bed."

Charles undresses and climbs into bed. Elizabeth quickly builds up the fire, brews yarrow tea, and wraps a warm rag around his neck. As the afternoon wears on, his cough subsides but his fever remains high. His face is a fiery red and he's thrashing around in the bed.

Just before sunset, there's a knock at the door. When Elizabeth opens it, she sees Richard with a look of surprise on his face. "Are you and Charles ready for the dance?"

Having lost track of time, she draws Richard into the house to explain. "We're not going." She points to the closed bed curtain. "Charles came home sick with a fever and a cough. He's resting."

Richard looks toward the curtain. "I hope he'll be alright. Let us know if there's anything we can do."

When Richard leaves, Elizabeth sticks her head out the door and waves to Vi who is seated in the wagon.

Evening arrives and Charles has no interest in eating. "Drink this cup of broth at least. You need nourishment, Charles. When you're finished, I'll make you a toddy to help you sleep."

While he sips the broth, Elizabeth returns to the fire. She's mixing the tea, whiskey, and honey, when Charles calls out in a deep, hoarse voice. "You need to get firewood and check the water supply."

She hands him the toddy, with instructions to drink it all, then goes to the corner of the room and checks the level of the water barrel. Seeing that it's not too low, she puts on Charles' coat and her boots, then grabs the sling for the firewood. Laddie, who's usually at her heels when he sees her ready to leave the house, remains close beside the bed. "Laddie, come!"

Snow is beginning to fall. The big flakes cover Elizabeth's knit cap and cling to her lashes. Laddie prances around her ankles. Fortunately, snow has not yet covered the wood pile and she's able to fill the canvas sling with split logs. She hopes one load, added to what's there, is enough to last until morning. When she returns, Charles is sleeping, but Elizabeth can hear his labored breathing. Worry is growing like a weed in her mind. *What if this is more than a cold?*

She eats a supper of corn bread and leftover beans before sitting before the low fire late into the evening. *What if he has pneumonia? How do I get him to Doctor Towar if he gets worse? What if I can't crack a hole in the ice for water?* Covering herself with Charles' heavy coat, she sips hot broth to keep warm. When she's about to climb into bed, she sees that Charles is awake and puts a cool cloth on his forehead. When he finally settles into a restless sleep, she lays beside him for a long, cold, sleepless night.

The next morning, the wind howls like a wounded animal. Elizabeth dresses quickly and, remembering what Charles did prior to the blizzard, stuffs rags around the windows. She rekindles the fire, drinks a cup of tea, and eats a stale muffin.

A coughing spree comes from behind the curtain. When Charles returns to bed after using the chamber pot, Elizabeth offers him broth and a bit of bread and butter. "How are you feeling?"

Charles slowly chews on a crust of bread. "About the same."

When he lays back and slowly closes his eyes, Elizabeth puts his coat on, grabs the shovel and begins to clear a path to the privy. The snow is wet and heavy, but she finally reaches the outhouse door. She then has to dig deep for the strength to pry it open. Remembering the fateful day when she was lost as she carried out a similar mission, Elizabeth is thankful the snow has stopped falling and she can see her way back to the house.

She returns, checks on Charles, then takes the wooden buckets standing next to the water barrel and goes outside with Laddie at her heels. She fills each bucket with the pristine snow then sets the buckets by the fire to melt, thankful she doesn't have to find a way to break through the ice on the creek. At least not yet. She remembers from when she was alone for six days, that the three hundred feet or so walk to the creek isn't the problem. It's breaking through the ice to get the water that's challenging.

Spent, Elizabeth sits in her rocker and sips her tea before she carries on with her chores of baking bread and starting a stew for the mid-day meal. She hopes the smell of food cooking will encourage Charles to eat.

That night, Charles is no better and will only drink a cup of broth. With growing concern, Elizabeth falls asleep in her chair. Late in the night, she awakes and climbs into bed.

The next morning, she knows she must get water from the creek. The water barrel is low and the snow's no longer clean. She puts Charles' coat on along with her hat and mittens. She takes both buckets but leaves one near the wood pile when she picks up the ax. Just as she feared, the creek is frozen over from bank to bank, but the wind has blown away most of the snow and she can see ridges forming a circle. She carefully walks out and taps the ice within the circle with the ax. It cracks but doesn't give away. She hits it harder and water seeps through a hole. She chips away until the hole is large enough for her bucket. She fills the bucket, returns to the wood pile with the ax, picks up the other bucket and treks back to the creek. Never so happy to have two full buckets of water, Elizabeth returns home to find Charles sitting up in bed but still flushed with fever.

The next afternoon, five days after Charles first arrived home with a cough, Elizabeth is wearily stoking the fire with the last of the day's firewood. She hears a knock on the door and looks out the window to see Richard holding a fat, skinned, rabbit by the ears.

She ushers him inside. "It's good to see you, Richard. What brings you over?"

"I was in town this morning and Peter said that Charles hasn't been to his shop since the day of the dance. I came by to check on both of you. Thought you could use some fresh meat."

"Who's here?" Charles croaks from the bed.

Elizabeth pulls back the curtain from around the bed and speaks to him. "It's Richard come to see how you are. Now, lay back down." She leaves the bed and motions for Richard to put the rabbit in a pan near the hearth. "Thanks for the rabbit and for checking on us. As you can see, Charles is still sick. He's not worse or I'd ask you to take him to Dr. Towar, but he's not better either."

Richard nods. "How's your water and wood supply?"

Elizabeth looks over at the depleted wood pile by the hearth. "Charles stacked plenty of wood before the snows came so we have enough for now. I just haven't gotten any yet today. Water is more difficult but I'm managing."

Richard reaches over, takes the sling, and heads toward the door. "I'll bring in wood and enough water to fill your barrel."

Elizabeth follows him to the door. "I didn't realize how much work Charles did to keep things going around here. I have a new appreciation of his contributions, and now yours. You're a good friend to us, Richard."

After he brings in the water and wood, Richard returns home. Elizabeth cuts up the rabbit, puts it into the pot to simmer, then sinks down into her rocker. She puts her head into her hands and lets out a muffled sob as she gives in to her physical and emotional exhaustion. *I don't think I can live another winter in this God forsaken land. When Charles gets better, IF he gets better, I'll admit to my mistake of thinking I was strong enough to be a prairie wife.* Elizabeth blows her nose into her handkerchief. *If he loves me, he'll take me back to Grand Island where he can set up his shop again.*

Feeling a bit better now that she's made a decision about the future, she fleshes out the plan in her mind. *I'll tell him I'll get a job to make up the difference of lost wages from the army.*

The next morning, after another agonizing night of being too tired, too cold, and too worried to sleep well, Elizabeth reaches over and feels Charles' forehead before getting out of bed. It feels cooler and he wakens to her touch. She helps him from the bed so he can relieve himself in the chamber pot. After he returns to the bed, Elizabeth props him up with their two pillows, opens the curtain, then dresses hastily before going to the privy with Laddie racing in front of her. When she returns, she stokes up the fire and pours oatmeal into the boiling water in the pot hanging from the hook. "I'm making you hot porridge. Would you like some coffee with it?"

Charles raises his chin from his chest. "Yes, please." His voice is so soft and low Elizabeth asks again to be sure. "Coffee?" This time he simply nods.

After a lunch of more porridge and a slice of bread, Charles remains sitting. Encouraged that he seems to be improving, Elizabeth smooths his hair. "Would you like me to read to you?"

Charles smiles a tiny smile with eyes half mast and nods. Elizabeth pulls out her *Ledger* and a newspaper then reads for an hour before Charles drifts back to sleep. When he awakens, he eats a small cup of rabbit stew and another slice of bread.

That night, with less worry on her mind, Elizabeth finally sleeps soundly. She awakes to Charles sitting up beside her in bed. "You look better. How do you feel?"

He smiles, his eyes wide open, no longer dark with fever. "Like I could eat a horse."

Elizabeth throws her arms around her husband's neck. "That's a sure sign that you're on the mend. Thank goodness you're better. I was so worried." Tears fill her eyes, and she brushes them away. "I can't imagine what I'd do without you."

Charles tenderly puts a tendril of hair that's escaped her braid behind his wife's ear. "I'm better because you took such good care of me."

Elizabeth chokes back more tears.

"Now, will you do one more thing and fix me breakfast?"

Elizabeth wipes her eyes, blows her nose, gets dressed, goes to the privy, then puts on the kettle.

That afternoon Charles moves from the bed to a chair to read his old newspapers. Elizabeth is sweeping the floor. After a few minutes of reading, Charles calls her over and takes her hand. "Why don't you go visit the Voogds for a spell? It'll do you good to get out of the house. I'll be fine on my own. Besides, you need to hear all about the dance. I'm sorry we had to miss it."

Elizabeth lays her broom aside. "I'll go if you promise to take a nap while I'm gone."

Before she leaves, she tucks blankets around Charles then puts on all of her warmest clothes for the walk to her friend's house. The air is cold but clear; the wind has finally died down to a respectable breeze; the road is mostly cleared; and the sun is doing its best to shine. Elizabeth is happy to be out of the house, and she thinks Laddie smiles back at her as he rushes back for a pat on the head before running ahead. He prances up to the Voogds' front door and barks before Elizabeth has a chance to catch up. When she sees Vi open the door, she feels a smile spread across her face. She rushes forward and is invited inside.

"Elizabeth! It's so good to see you. How's Charles?"

Elizabeth lays her wraps across a nearby chair. "He's much better, thanks, Vi. He's the one who insisted I get out of the house and come for a visit. I hope you don't mind." She looks around the room. "Where is everyone?"

Vi motions for Elizabeth to take a seat by the fire. "They're all out in the barn so we have a few minutes of peace." She eases down into the chair beside Elizabeth and sighs.

Elizabeth notes the weariness in her friend's demeanor and the circles under her eyes. Not wanting to talk about her miserable time at home and Charles' illness, she says, "Charles is better and that's all that matters." She smiles at Vi. "Now, tell me all about the dance and how everyone is doing."

CHAPTER TWENTY-SEVEN

SPRING CLEANING AND QUILT MAKING

On a Wednesday, two full weeks after Charles returned home with a cough and fever, Elizabeth finally flips the page of her wall calendar to March. "Good riddance to February!"

Charles only looks at her as he slowly puts on his coat for his walk to work. Although he tires easily and Elizabeth fears a relapse, he insists on returning to his shop for brief periods. Since he has no customers, Charles spends his time sketching boot designs and making boots to add to his display case.

Elizabeth still awakens at night to see him slumped in the rocker by the fire, but he always returns to bed by morning and she doesn't question him. When their food supplies dwindle, Charles returns to hunting and occasionally brings home a squirrel or rabbit. Beans become a supper staple. One evening when Elizabeth is shaking out the last of the flour to dredge rabbit parts in, Charles comments from his seat at the table. "If you need supplies from The Mercantile, I've arranged for us to buy on credit until business picks up. I'd like to use what little cash we have left to pay Vi for butter and eggs."

Elizabeth adds the rabbit to the hot oil in the spider. "Will we be getting any more supplies from the fort?"

Charles pushes his paper aside. "Likely not since I'm not owed anything. However, Shiriki said if they're able to take down more deer than the soldiers can eat, we'll get some of the surplus. Now that the snow has let up, this might be a possibility. Need to get my strength back so I can go after some real game."

Elizabeth brings corn cakes to the table. "Don't worry, Charles. We'll make do."

By mid-March, Elizabeth's already dreaming of their visit to Ron's ranch. She craves change and variety in her life after being cooped up all winter. She's tired of dust dropping from the ceiling, windows perpetually rattling in the wind, spiders and mice hiding in the corners. The last of the salted meat and jarred vegetables have lost their flavor and Elizabeth yearns for fresh air, fresh food, and fresh conversation. The winter darkness, inside her home and inside her husband, has unnerved her. Less certain about her desire to leave the prairie, Elizabeth decides not to speak to Charles about the desperation she felt while he was sick. She wants to give spring a chance to change her mind.

At supper on Wednesday, Elizabeth moves her too-salty, brined antelope from one side of her plate to the other. "I've been thinking about our trip to Ron's ranch. Have you?"

Charles looks up. "As a matter of fact, my dear, I have. On Monday, I talked to Peter and he's willing to stay in our house and take care of Laddie while we're away." Elizabeth finally takes a small bite of her meat as she waits for Charles to continue. "I thought we'd take the horses rather than hire a wagon. It takes less than a day to get there so all we need is a change of clothes and whatever gifts you've planned. How does that sound?"

Elizabeth jumps up from her chair and throws her arms around her husband's neck. "That sounds wonderful! I can hardly wait. When can we leave?"

Charles kisses her behind the ear. "Easy now. Blizzards occasionally happen in March out here. I'd say another month. By mid-April I believe we'll be out of danger. I spoke to Peter now because I wasn't sure he'd want to give up his room in the back of the saloon for a week, but he said he'd be happy to stay at our place at night and see to Laddie."

Elizabeth clears the table; humming as she washes and dries the dishes. She's grateful for time spent with her neighbors, but she craves conversation with people who don't have the same, dull, day-to-day life she has. She's looking forward to seeing spring color spreading across the landscape, new faces, and riding. She knows their horses have been will cared for at the livery because Charles checks on them regularly but she misses being in the saddle.

When Charles leaves for work the following morning, Elizabeth stays at the open door and breaths in the spring-like air. The sun is shining, the birds are chirping, and she feels a sense of hope that she hasn't felt in months. After her chores are done, she puts on her cape. Laddie happily trots at her side as she briskly walks to Vi's. Entering the house, she feels a hopeful spirit here also. After the children greet her, they return to their studies and Vi takes her wraps. "Good to see you on this spring-like day, Elizabeth. Were your ears ringing?"

Elizabeth takes a seat. "No, what do you mean?"

Vi covers her bread dough and sets it on the hearth. "It means I was thinking about you." She goes to her sewing basket and pulls out a bag. "I've been going through the children's clothes and cut these pieces from articles that were beyond mending. I thought you might like to use them for a project. I remember you saying that your mother taught you to quilt."

Elizabeth takes the bag and looks inside. "These will make a perfect quilt for Lucy's baby! Thank you."

Vi pours hot water into the tea pot. "When do you plan to travel to Ron's?"

"Charles said the middle of April. That gives me time to make the quilt."

Vi brings the pot and two cups to the table. She leans across and speaks in a low voice. "How's Charles?"

Elizabeth blows on her tea then takes a sip. "He's weak from his illness and I still see him sitting by the fire in the middle of the night. I think the trip to Ron's will do him a world of good." Vi remains quiet and Elizabeth ponders whether to share her earlier feelings of desolation with her friend. Just then, the twins come to show her their work pages. When they go back to the bedroom, she gathers her courage. "When Charles was sick, I was ready to give up living here, Vi." Seeing no shocked response from her friend, she continues. "I was at the lowest point of my life. I made up my mind to ask Charles to return to Grand Island. I felt I couldn't bear going through another winter."

Vi quietly nods. "And now?"

Elizabeth leans on her elbows. "I'm not so sure. I haven't mentioned it to him."

Vi pours more tea into Elizabeth's cup. "The first winter is the worst. Plus, Charles was sick. Don't make a hasty decision. Give yourself time."

Knowing that Vi is always busy, Elizabeth doesn't stay long but even the brief visit adds joy to a lovely day. She returns home, eager to start her quilt and feeling relieved that she shared her dark feelings with her friend. *I'll take Vi's advice and not be hasty about my decision to leave. I truly don't want to fail as a prairie wife but I also want to be happy.*

The next morning, when Elizabeth awakes, she decides to springclean the soddie. After Charles leaves, she takes what's left of the jars from the shelves and thoroughly cleans off the soot and dust that have accumulated. Then she airs out the mattress and pillows and washes the sheets. She wipes down the walls, being careful not to disturb the plaster-like coating. She scrubs her black spider, her other cooking utensils, then her table. She puts a bit of oil on a rag and polishes the rocker. Even though the air is cold, she puts her cape on and opens both windows, letting out the smells of winter—smoke, dust, illness, chamber pots, rancid grease, and mice.

Satisfied that she's cleared away bad smells and dark thoughts, Elizabeth brings the mattress and pillows back inside and makes the bed with clean sheets. She starts a pot of soup from yesterday's leftovers before pulling out the quilt scraps Vi gave her. When Charles returns from the shop, Elizabeth is busily choosing fabric and planning a quilt design.

CHAPTER TWENTY-EIGHT

A SURPRISE AT THE RANCH

A light snowfall in early April dampens Elizabeth's spring spirit but she bounces back when she spies an unknown spring flower poking its purple head through the last bit of snow while she and Charles walk along the creek bank on a mild Saturday morning. "Look, Charles!"

Charles stoops to look then stands up. "And listen to that."

"What?"

Charles points to the creek. "The water its flowing again. No more ice."

The following week flies by with Elizabeth busy completing her quilt and Charles beginning to see foot traffic in his shop and orders from the fort. When he returns home early on Friday, Elizabeth sees a bounce in his step that hasn't been there for months. He hangs up his coat then gives his wife a big hug. "Let's leave for Ron's on Monday."

Elizabeth keeps her arms around Charles' neck. "I'll be ready. I can't wait!"

The next day, Peter comes by to talk with Charles about what needs to be done in the house while they're away. While they talk, Elizabeth finishes her laundry, hanging it outside in the breeze.

At supper, she beams when she sees the excitement in her husband's eyes as he makes a suggestion. "Let's pack up tonight so we can get an early start tomorrow. The livery opens at eight."

Elizabeth hurries through her dishes, then she carefully rolls up her new pink and gray dress she made from her Christmas cloth, an extra shift and bloomers, moccasins, and the baby quilt. Along with a change of clothes, Charles' pack includes a gift of moccasins for Ron and the pair of boots he ordered months ago.

The couple are both awake before daylight and Elizabeth puts together a simple breakfast. Taking Laddie with him, Charles replenishes the wood and water supply. The morning is sunny and mild with a cool breeze coming out of the west. Although there's still some mud along the road, the prairie's green with tender new shoots and wildflowers beginning to bloom. Walking hand in hand to town, Elizabeth notices birds singing and crickets chirping. Her heart beats faster from the pure joy of it all.

After saddling their horses, they head northwest. As they trot along, Elizabeth looks over and sees a wide grin on Charles' face. She knows that he's also delighted to be riding across the open prairie, leaving the dark of winter behind. In a couple of hours, they come to where the North Loup River curves toward the road. Tiny stars of light from the sun reflect off the water and there's a clump of soft, welcoming grass nearby. Charles reins in his horse and Elizabeth does the same. "I think this is a good place to rest and water the horses." Charles takes a blanket from his pack and spreads it on the grass. "The ground will be cold, but it will feel good to be out of the saddle. Sure makes a difference when we haven't ridden for a while, doesn't it?"

Elizabeth agrees as she stiffly dismounts. Reaching into the saddlebag, she pulls out buttered bread, the last of her elderberry jam, and two sticks of jerky for their snack while Charles waters and tethers the horses. After Charles settles himself next to her, she takes a bite of bread. "How much farther?"

"About another hour at the most. I've never been to Ron's ranch, but he gave me good directions."

With horses and people watered and fed so they won't arrive hungry, the couple mounts and rides for another hour. Coming over a hill, they spot a spread of buildings nestled along a wide creek. Charles points. "I believe this is it. Yep, there's the sign. Pollack Ranch."

Elizabeth is surprised by the size of the log house, expansive barn, shed, and other outbuildings. After living in one room for seven months, the sprawling home looks like a mansion. Native-stone chimneys flank each end of the house, a split-rail fence encircles the perimeter. A two-person swing hangs from the ceiling with two rustic rocking chairs nearby. When they ride onto the property, a young man approaches them from the barn. Charles looks him over. "Nate?"

"Yes. Thanks for rememberin'. Welcome to Pollack Ranch, Mr. Horn. Ron's bin lookin' forward to yer visit."

Charles helps Elizabeth down from her horse then holds out his hand to Nate. "This is, Nate Bell, the young man I told you about."

"Pleased to meet you, Mrs. Horn. Lucy talks about you all the time."

"I hear she's a friend of yours." Elizabeth can't help but give Nate a big, knowing smile, causing him to blush from his neck to his hairline.

"She surely is, Mrs. Horn. She surely is."

Ron rushes out the door. "Charlie and Elizabeth! So good to see you. Come in, come in." He turns to Nate. "Take care of the horses and bring the Horns' things to the house."

"Yes, sir. Right away."

The interior of the house is nothing like the bachelor quarters Elizabeth imagined. With tall ceilings and wide windows, the great room feels enormous. The raised hearth fireplace takes up one end of the spacious room. A collection of pewter tankards lined up across the mantle give the room a personal touch. A comfortable-looking couch, with a frame made from logs and covered with chocolate-colored cushions and colorful Indian blankets, faces the blazing fire. Matching easy chairs flank the couch. As the men chat, Elizabeth luxuriates in the comfort and warmth of a "real" house. When she sighs with pleasure, Ron looks in her direction. "I'm glad you seem to be feeling comfortable here, Elizabeth. By the way, Lucy and Nate will be joining us for supper."

"Lucy's coming for supper? Tonight?"

Ron smiles. "Yes, tonight. Your room is the one on the right at the end of the hall if you'd like to arrange your things."

Elizabeth leaves the comfort of the couch and rushes down the hall, eager to see their room. There's a wide, high bed that she has to hop up to sit on, a down comforter, a walnut dresser holding a white bowl and pitcher for washing up, and antlers attached to the wall for hanging clothes. A rocker, somewhat like her own, stands in the corner near a small wood stove. The wide plank, hickory floor is covered with an oval, red, black, and yellow wool rug. When she pulls out the quilt for Lucy's baby, she wonders why Ron hasn't mentioned him or her. She decides to tamp down her curiosity and wait until Lucy arrives to give her the news.

After a brief nap in a soft-as-a-cloud-bed, Elizabeth returns to the great room to find the large oak trestle table set for supper. Ron has hired a neighbor lady to cook and enticing smells are coming from the kitchen. "Supper smells wonderful. What are we having?"

Ron nods toward the kitchen. "Go ask Mrs. Greene. I'm sure she'll find something for you to do."

Heading to the kitchen, she glances back to take in Charles and Ron sitting companionably in front of the fire sipping glasses of whiskey. *I'm so glad we're finally here. I can already see a difference in Charles.*

She enters the large, well-equipped kitchen and admires the iron stove with pots bubbling on it's surface. "Hello, Mrs. Greene, I'm Elizabeth." Before Mrs. Greene can respond, there's a knock on the back door. "May I answer it?"

Mrs. Greene pauses her stirring. "Of course."

Lucy walks in and throws her arms around Elizabeth. "It's so good to see you!" Standing behind Lucy, and carrying a wrapped bundle, Nate looks down and shuffles his feet. Lucy takes the bundle from him and steps farther into the kitchen. She carefully opens the blanket, and peers down at the wide-eyed baby nestled inside. "Elizabeth, meet Joy." There's pride in Lucy's eyes.

Elizabeth feels a lump gathering in her throat. "May I hold her?"

Lucy places the bundle into her waiting arms. Elizabeth looks down at the bald baby girl with big brown eyes. "She's beautiful! Why did you name her Joy?"

Looking back at Nate, Lucy explains. "I named her Joy because she brung me so much joy after so much sufferin.' Like it?"

"It's perfect." Elizabeth can't take her eyes off the baby who looks up at her with a broad, toothless grin.

"And guess what?" When she looks up at her friend, Elizabeth notices that Lucy's eyes are sparkling and her cheeks are pink. "Nate and me—we is gittin' married!" Lucy pauses. Elizabeth can tell that she's waiting for the news to sink in, then she continues. "He be willin' to take this here baby as his own and me as his wife. Ain't that somethin'?"

Obviously taken aback by this sudden and unexpected news, Elizabeth takes a deep breath before she responds. She sees four anxious eyes looking at her intently. She assumes Lucy somehow got a divorce from Jake. Thinking that this isn't the time to ask, she simply says, "Congratulations! I'm so happy for you."

When there is a lull, Mrs. Greene herds them out of her kitchen. She has supper to serve.

The group is seated and plates of roast beef and bread are passed from hand to hand along with bowls of baked potatoes, glazed carrots, turnips, and gravy. After everyone's plate is full, Lucy and Nate fill Charles in on news of the wedding while Joy sleeps peacefully in her blankets on the couch.

After coffee and chocolate cake are served, Lucy speaks, directing her words to Charles as she looks toward Ron. "I owe so much to this here friend of yours, Charles. He helped me change my whole life by gitting me a job and a divorce from Jake. And …" Lucy pauses as she takes Nate's hand, "introducin' me to this here wonderful man."

Nate grins.

"It's been all my pleasure," Ron says. "I think you and Nate and that baby over there are going to be a lovely family. I'm glad I was able to play a part in your happiness."

After Nate leaves to take Lucy and the baby back to Mary Becker's house, Ron tells Elizabeth and Charles that he's hosting their wedding in the next few days so the Horns can attend. Elizabeth works to keep her mouth from dropping open. "A wedding? I had no idea there was going to be a wedding. Lucy talked of marriage but the wedding is a surprise. Sure glad I brought my new dress."

Ron smiles at Elizabeth before he continues. "Charlie, you know the special boots you made for me? I'm going to give them to Nate as a wedding gift. We happen to be the same size. Thanks for bringing them. They're beautiful."

Since she'd taken a nap earlier, Elizabeth is still wide awake after Ron retires for the night. The air is chilly, but she's determined to sit on the swing. She grabs Charles' hand. "Come sit with me on the porch." They step outside into the cool night air. Elizabeth looks up at the sliver of a moon and snuggles close to Charles. "Doesn't sitting out here in this swing remind you of sitting on Mrs. Seifert's porch before we were married?"

Charles answers sleepily. "Yes, Dear."

"Isn't Lucy's baby beautiful? I hope we have a bald, big-eyed baby like that someday soon. Don't you?"

Elizabeth senses that Charles, in his slightly inebriated state, is carefully considering his answer before responding.

She waits. "She's a beautiful baby and I do hope we have our own..." Charles pauses. "...all in good time."

Pouting over Charles' apparent lack of enthusiasm about babies, she sits quietly for a few minutes before continuing with chatter about the house. In a few minutes, Charles looks at her. She sees a hopeful look in his eyes. "Tired yet?"

"Yes." She grabs his hand to pull him out of the swing. "You're going to love the bed."

For two lovely days, Elizabeth enjoys Ron's comfortable home. She's a little disappointed that she has only one short visit with Lucy who is busy working, caring for a baby, and preparing for her wedding. With the men frequently away during the day, riding and doing whatever men do, Elizabeth has time to relax on comfortable furniture, stroll around the ranch, and read Ron's leather-bound books. In the evening, they all enjoy Mrs. Greene's cooking.

After breakfast on the third day, Elizabeth carefully dresses for Lucy's wedding. She's glad she packed her new pink and gray frock with its square neckline, white flounces at the wrist, and a ruffle around the bottom. Elizabeth thinks the dress would normally be too casual to wear to a wedding, but it's new and feels appropriate for the ranch. Since she has no hat other than the matching sun bonnet, Elizabeth braids her hair then brings each braid over her head, forming a crown, and carefully pins the braids in place. She looks in the small mirror above the chest, pinches her cheeks; satisfied with her appearance.

Charles helps Ron move the furniture in the great room to the side, making space for the wedding party and guests.

Elizabeth serves as maid of honor, Ron is the best man. Mrs. Becker stands between two freshly scrubbed ranch hands, holding Joy. Ron's neighbor Mrs. Greene and her daughter Rachel, Dr. Smith's daughter, and Charles round out the guests.

Elizabeth asks Ron about the pastor and he responds. "Since he isn't due to rotate back into the area for a few more weeks, Dr. Smith will be officiating the wedding. This is a common practice out here where pastors are few and far between. Doc Smith knows the new family well."

After the short ceremony, Elizabeth helps Mrs. Greene lay out a reception not unlike the reception Mrs. Seiffert had for her. There's cake, lemonade, and punch laced with something that smells strong. Later, the men relax outdoors with cigars while the women tidy up and chat about the wedding. Elizabeth puts her arm around Lucy's shoulders. "You're a beautiful bride."

Lucy blushes. "Thanks. 'Member when I told you I never got me a pretty dress before? Well, I made this one myself. Mrs. Becker give me the fabric as a wedding gift. Ain't that nice?"

Elizabeth smiles at Lucy as she admires the light blue dress featuring mutton sleeves, a gathered waist, and a small white collar. The broach Elizabeth gave Lucy when she left the wagon train is fastened at her neck. Lucy's gleaming, blonde hair is gathered on each side with thin, blue ribbons. She twists hair around her finger as she continues. "Nate's wearin' that there pair of boots Charles made. He said they is the nicest gift he ever got."

When the men return, Elizabeth takes note of Nate's new boots with his straight-legged trousers tucked inside. She realizes that the simple blue cotton shirt he wears was made from the same fabric as Lucy's dress.

By late afternoon, the guests and newlyweds depart. Ron, Charles, and Elizabeth have a late supper, then the couple retire to their room, tired after a busy day. "Wasn't that a lovely wedding?"

Charles sits on the bed. "It was, my dear. I'm so glad we were able to attend."

Elizabeth sighs. "Me too." Elizabeth and Charles are soon cozy in the soft-as-a-cloud bed.

On this last day of her visit, Elizabeth walks up the road to visit Lucy in her new sod house.

As she approaches, with a basket over her arm, she notices that Lucy's house looks much like her own, right down to the bubbling creek out back. After greeting one another, Elizabeth looks down at Joy sleeping in her cradle, covered by the quilt she made. She hands Lucy the basket.

Lucy removes the contents. "Bread and salt?"

"It's a German tradition." Elizabeth smiles. "Brot and salz, the German names, ensure that you will never go hungry in your new home."

Smiling and thanking her friend, Lucy sets her gifts on the table next to a Mason jar filled with an arrangement of colorful wild flowers. An arrowhead sits next to the jar. Elizabeth thinks the group of objects looks like a still life painting and is pleased that Lucy seems to be taking pride in her home. She points. "That arrowhead looks like the one you gave me when we parted on the trail."

"It is like yurs. I picked 'em up at the same time when we was walkin' the trail. One to bring you luck, one to bring me luck. Looks like they is both working."

The women sit at the table and, after a moment, Elizabeth speaks quietly. "I've been wondering about something. Did you know you were pregnant when you were at our house?"

Lucy meets her eyes. "I had me some suspicions. But my courses had stopped before when I weren't gittin' enough to eat so I thought that was it. My stomach was gettin' bigger but I didn't think much of it. I should have told you what I were thinkin' but I was afraid Ron wouldn't take me if he knowed or even suspected."

"When were you certain?"

"Mrs. Becker guessed it right off. As soon as I arrived, she took one look at me and said I was havin' a baby. She was nice about it though. Right motherly, in fact. The worst was tellin' Ron but he just act normal-like."

"Ron's a good man."

Lucy looks down at her folded hands. "Then I had to tell Nate. We started seein' each other right after I got here but we'd only met once or twice. I figured he wouldn't want to see me no more. I wouldn't a blamed him one bit. You coulda knocked me over with a feather when he said he weren't put off by me bein' pregnant. Can you magin' that?"

Elizabeth thinks about all her friend had been though in a few short months. "You're a whole new person from when I first met you. I'm glad you're safe and happy."

When she gets up to leave, Lucy gives her a hug. "I shore is goin' ta miss you. Now that the weather is good, maybe we can visit one 'nother in the summer." Lucy hesitates for a moment before going on. "I want you to be Joy's godmother when we git her baptized. Will you do that?"

"Of course. I'd be honored. I think you've got yourself a good man this time, Lucy, and a beautiful baby. You treat each other well. Okay?"

"Yes, ma'am. I took yer good advice before and I'm takin' it now. You kin count on it."

CHAPTER TWENTY-NINE

BEES AND BIG NEWS

The soddie's windows are open to a cool, late-May breeze. It's still early afternoon when Elizabeth pushes herself out of her rocker. *I'm so tired!* She tidies her hair and struggles into her corset thinking a walk to the Voogd's will do her good. Once she's out the door with Laddie trotting beside her, she feels somewhat renewed. After all, how can she resist spring gracing the prairie with tall grasses spreading to the horizon, multicolored birds returning from their southern homes, brown bunnies chasing one another, and the sun warming her shoulders. Elizabeth hums along with nature's symphony as she walks the familiar path in her worn, brown high-top shoes, blue calico dress, and old, ragged sunbonnet.

Arriving at the Voogd's homestead, she stops to admire Vi's garden and wishes hers looked as lush. The red leaf lettuce is already peeking out of the ground along with spring peas, radish tops, and broccoli.

Looking up, she sees Shar walking toward her on the way to the barn. Her red hair is flying about her face and her long, flour sack dress, covered with a checkered pinafore, is grass stained. She's prodding her two brown and white milk cows, Buelah and Betsy, ahead of her. Elizabeth remembers her saying, "Taking the cows to pasture gives me time to study my history lessons and memorize my poetry in a quiet space."

Shar waves at Elizabeth and shouts over the ringing of the cow bell. "Good to see you, Mrs. Horn. I'll be in after I do the milkin'." Elizabeth waves back.

Before she can knock on the door, she hears Jan shouting to Gary, "Ollie ollie oxen free!" The twins run to give her a hug before returning to their game of hide-n-seek. Vi opens the door and smiles. "Great timing, neighbor. Everyone's out and we can enjoy some rare time alone."

As they sip from cups of steaming mint tea, Elizabeth becomes aware of Vi looking at her. "How are you feeling? You look a bit pale. Have you lost weight?"

She wonders about the odd questions. "This old dress seems to fit fine but I haven't been eating as much as usual. Food seems to have lost its appeal, especially breakfast."

She sees Vi looking at her over the rim of her cup. "Anything else?"

"To be honest, I've been very tired and not quite feeling myself. I've even gotten behind on my gardening. Yours looks beautiful, by the way."

Vi nods with a knowing look. Elizabeth is shocked and a bit embarrassed when she asks her about her courses. She's unaccustomed to speaking about such a personal subject. She rubs her chin as she thinks. "Seems like it's been a while. What with us being away in April, I lost track."

Vi's motherly smile reminds her of the difference in their ages. "I think you're pregnant, Elizabeth. You have all the symptoms. You even have 'the look' about you."

Elizabeth smiles. "I hope you're right." She crosses her arms over her chest. "The notion has crossed my mind, of course, but I've been disappointed before. My cycle isn't always regular." She squirms in her chair, uncomfortable with the silence. She looks down at her hands then up at Vi. "Besides not knowing for sure, I'm frightened that if I'm pregnant, something will happen to the baby. I think I put the possibility of being pregnant out of my mind so it won't cause me worry."

Her friend pats her hand. "You're young and strong, Elizabeth. It's important for you to stay positive."

"I know but, it seems to me that having a baby is especially risky out here." Elizabeth feels a knot of fear in her chest. "Charles suggested I ask you about my lack of appetite. Do you think he suspects?"

Vi gets up to check on her pot of beans. "Probably. He's had nearly twenty more years of life experience than you. Perhaps he wanted you to talk to me first. What will you tell him?"

Elizabeth shrugs her shoulders with uncertainty. "That I'm probably pregnant and I'll be just fine?"

Vi resumes her seat just as the twins rush through the door with a basket of eggs between them. Shar follows, a pail of milk in each hand. In the midst of the commotion, Vi leans across the table and speaks quietly. "I'm here for you, Elizabeth. Ask me anything, anytime."

That evening, as the couple enjoy a dessert of apple hand pies made from the last of the dried fruit, Elizabeth brings up her visit to the Voogds. "I did as you asked and spoke to Vi about my lack of appetite." Feeling warmth spreading across her cheeks, she adds, "She thinks I'm pregnant and she thinks you suspect. Do you?" She's pleased when she sees Charles' eyes light up.

"It crossed my mind. What do you think?"

"I think she might be right. I hope so. I'd love for us to have a baby." Tears well up in her eyes. She retrieves a handkerchief from inside her sleeve.

Charles beckons her to come sit on his lap. "I'd also love for us to have a baby. But you look worried. What else is on your mind?"

Elizabeth keeps her voice and expression neutral, trying to hide the fear she's feeling. "I'm afraid something will happen to our baby. Losing a child seems so common. First, my sister dying, then Baby Louise on the trail. Vi also lost babies. It's all put a fear in me."

Her husband gently cups her face in his hands and looks into her eyes. "Did you talk to Vi about your fears?"

"Yes. She said I was young and strong and need to stay positive."

He gives her a gentle hug. "Sounds like good advice to me. When do you think this baby will arrive?"

"If my calculations are correct, we're likely to have a new baby by the middle of January."

Charles tickles her neck with his whiskers when he whispers in her ear. "Must have been that soft-as-a-cloud bed at Ron's."

A week later, while the couple are eating breakfast, Elizabeth hears pinging sounds. She looks toward the window. "What's that?"

Charles leaves his eggs and toast to look out. "It's hail. Come look. It's starting to cover the ground." The pings grow to plunks as the hail goes from marble size to as big as a hen's egg. "I noticed thunderheads and a drop in temperature when I took Laddie out earlier. I hope it doesn't last. It will ruin your spring vegetables." Charles returns to his eggs. "Thank goodness Richard and most of the other farmers just started planting. A hail storm like this can take out an entire crop once it's sprouted. It would be devastating."

Unable to leave for work because of the hail, Charles begins sketching designs for a cradle. Elizabeth peeks over his shoulder at the drawings. "Seeing those sketches makes having a baby feel more real. All my dreams are coming true, Charles. A wonderful life partner, a home of my own, and now a child. I couldn't be happier!"

Getting up from his seat at the table, he gives his wife a long, loving hug then sits back down. "Do you have any ideas for names?"

"If it's a boy, I think we should call him Charles. Perhaps Anna for a girl. You?"

Charles rests his chin on his knuckles. Elizabeth waits patiently. "I think both are excellent ideas."

She leaves the table to begin her bread making, then turns back. "My, that was easy. I just hope everything else goes as smoothly." Feeling a flutter of anxiety in her chest, Elizabeth says a silent prayer. *Dear God, keep this baby safe as it grows inside of me.*

Later that morning, while punching down her dough, Elizabeth tries to think of something to distract her from worry. She remembers a trip she made to The Mercantile for honey and corn meal a few weeks earlier. She'd depleted her honey supply making toddies for Charles when he was sick. An old, stooped woman carrying a worn, twig basket containing a few jars of honey was slowing making her way down the store steps when Elizabeth approached. She bought two jars from her. *Seems odd that I haven't seen her since.*

The next morning, the sun shines through the windows and, when Elizabeth peeks out, she sees no trace of yesterday's hailstorm. "I do believe it's a perfect day for mushroom hunting. Vi says the best place to find them is under the trees beyond the creek."

Charles puts a vest on over his workshirt. "Are you sure this is the right time of year for mushrooms?"

Elizabeth looks up from washing the breakfast dishes. "Yes, I'm sure. But you're right, Vi told me that timing is everything. Too early and they're hidden, too late and they're dried up or filled with bugs."

Charles hugs his wife good-bye. "Well then, I'll look forward to something made with mushrooms for supper tonight." He picks up his satchel, opens the door, then turns back. "Stay alert. You never know what you might encounter."

Unconcerned about the warning, Elizabeth quickly dries her dishes, sweeps the floor, and wipes down the table; anxious to be on her way. She wants to act like a proper pioneer woman, not some namby-pamby city girl who knows nothing about nature and survival. *I made it through the winter, how hard can mushroom hunting be?*

Finally, she ties the strings of her bonnet under her chin, puts her gathering basket over her arm, gives Laddie a good-bye pat, and leaves the house. Pausing in her walk, she gazes up at the sun and smiles to herself. *It's as yellow as a yolk in my cast-iron skillet.* The air is warm with a hint of summer in the breeze. She walks along the creek; the springy moss cradling each step. Although she's not yet reached a shaded area, she goes over Vi's words. "Morel mushrooms often appear after a nice rain with warm temperatures following." *I think the hailstorm followed by this sunny day is the perfect formula.*

She leaves the creek, enters a shady, wooded area beyond her usual meandering, and is rewarded when she discovers morels popping up under leaves and at the base of small trees. Because they uniquely resemble sponges, she's confident that she's not picking a poisonous variety of mushroom. When her basket is nearly filled, she stops to admire purple violets blanketing a nearby slope. Stooped over, she hears rustling behind a bush to her left. A prickling sensation goes through her. *Is that an animal? An Indian?* Her hands tremble and her heart races. The rustling stops and there's a moment of complete silence. Even the hum of insects and birdsong seems to ebb.

The Bee Lady, who Elizabeth recognizes from meeting her on the steps of The Mercantile, slowly appears from behind the bush with a basket similar to Elizabeth's resting on the crook of her arm. "Good afternoon, Child. I see you've found the morels."

Elizabeth stares at her, relieved to be looking into a friendly face.

"I hope you're enjoying the honey. The bees are quite busy with the clover beginning to bloom."

Still recovering from her fear, she simply nods.

"Would you like to see my hives? Bees are quite something you know. Perhaps you'd like more honey?"

Elizabeth finally responds, aware that her words are spilling out in a rush. "I'm so relieved to see that it's you! Yes, I'd love to see your bees and yes, I'd like more honey. It's a favorite of my husband's."

The woman bends down and picks a mushroom. Flicking away the loamy, black soil, she straightens with joints cracking like dry twigs, and puts it in her basket. She motions with a gnarled hand. "Come along then."

Elizabeth follows the old woman along a narrow, barely visible trail that leads to a mossy log crossing a shallow, sandy creek. The trail widens after the women pass through a small grove of chartreuse willows. Now that the path is wider, Elizabeth draws alongside her companion. Stooped, she's even smaller than Lucy. With a face as brown and wrinkled as old parchment, she resembles something out of Elizabeth's fairy tales. She's wearing worn work boots, a pair of men's trousers covered by a brown, homespun dress, a dirty apron, and a threadbare, black shawl. She has a man's black felt hat pulled tight over her head. A wisp of white hair feathers across her wrinkled forehead. She uses a long, curved walking stick to propel herself along at an amazing clip. Elizabeth's eyes are drawn to her broken nails and weathered hands, deeply lined with blue veins.

As they slow to a more moderate walk, Elizabeth looks around, wondering where her house could possibly be. She understands the mystery when she spots a stovepipe coming out of the top of a small hill with a worn, wooden door across the front. Elizabeth can make out primitive bee boxes, or hives, in a distant field surrounded by white and lavender clover blossoms. Even from a distance, she takes in their sweet scent.

After Angie slips her basket into the dugout, she takes Elizabeth's and also places it just inside the door. Then, she slowly and quietly walks toward her hives. Elizabeth follows close behind. The old woman motions with an arm covered in crepe-like skin. "Come, Elizabeth, don't be afraid. My bees are very gentle if you remain calm."

"You know my name?"

The woman looks up into her eyes. "It is Elizabeth, isn't it?"

"Yes. What's your name?"

"I'm commonly known in these parts as the Bee Lady but my given name is Angie."

When they reach the apiary, Elizabeth sees the pride on the woman's wizened face when she pulls a honey frame from a nearby hive. "Here are my beauties." Her smile reveals black and broken teeth.

Elizabeth tries to be brave but feels herself shying away. She watches in wonder as the bees gently alight on Angie's outstretched hands and arms.

"Don't you need protection from their stings?"

Angie doesn't respond to her question. Instead, she begins to softly hum. Elizabeth stands stock still and listens intently. She recognizes the tune to be the lullaby she hummed in Gretchen's ear the morning Baby Louise died. It's also the song she sang to Dorothy's children as they huddled in the creek the day of the prairie fire. When she begins to hum along, a few bees float down and sit on her shoulder. She sees Angie's mouth turn up at the corners. "Ain't they a wonder?"

Afraid to stop her humming, she nods imperceptibly as she marvels at the experience. Replacing the frame, Angie motions for Elizabeth to follow her back to the dugout, where she retrieves her basket of mushrooms and sets it down beside her along with a jar of honey. A small leather pouch remains in her hand.

Elizabeth picks up the basket and the jar. "Thank you, Angie. I'll bring you something for the honey on another day if that's alright."

"Of course, Missy. That there honey belongs to the bees, I just share it with others." Patting her arm, the woman gives Elizabeth a type of benediction. "You'll be blessed with children someday. All will be well."

Elizabeth pulls her brows together. "But how can you know that? You barely know me."

Angie continues. "When I tell you all will be well, I don't mean life won't bring you heartache from time to time." She reaches into the small bag she's holding and pulls out a bracelet with rows of tiny white and black glass beads, alternating with gray. She hands it to Elizabeth. "This bracelet will remind you that sometimes there's great joy, sometimes darkness, but mostly life is just life—neither black or white."

Delighted with her gift, Elizabeth immediately slips it on her wrist, pats her heart and thanks Angie who dismisses her. "Go now and may God's grace be with you."

Angie's words and gift give Elizabeth a sense of calm. It's like having her dear grandmother speak to her across time and space. Not wanting to break the feeling of reverence, she asks no more questions although many dance in her head. Only a few words were spoken between them, yet she feels a strong kinship with this old woman.

She watches as Angie turns, enters her dugout, pulling the scarred and dented door closed behind her. Elizabeth stares at the entrance for a long moment, fingers her new bracelet, then calmly and peacefully threads her way home.

CHAPTER THIRTY

ROBBERY AND LOST CHILDREN

July brings sweltering temperatures, high humidity, and more wind. It also produces blooming wildflowers including clumps of yellow, orange, and lavender coreopsis, which host a profusion of butterflies. Red and white clover carpet the ground in the sunniest spaces attracting honeybees. Queen Anne's Lace, or what the homesteaders call Cow Parsnip, give the landscape a feminine touch with their white, lacy blooms reaching as high as Elizabeth's head. Meadowlarks, red-winged blackbirds, and goldfinch soar from ground to sky and back again.

Elizabeth is carrying buckets of water from the creek to irrigate her garden when she sees Charles marching up the path hours before his usual return home. She's pouring water over her bean and squash plants when he approaches. Without a word, he takes her empty buckets and walks to the creek for a refill. He waters the next two rows of vegetables then repeats the process. When he returns, she stands waiting for him with her hands on her hips. "What's going on, Charles?"

Passing her on his way to the house, he looks back. "Let's talk inside." When they reach the house, they remove their muddy boots, and pour themselves cool cups of water.

Annoyed with Charles' silence, Elizabeth sits on the edge of a kitchen chair. "Well?"

Charles slumps into the rocker. "I was robbed."

Elizabeth sits up straighter. "Are you okay? Who robbed you? What did they take?" She can see the anger in her husband's flashing, black eyes. His face is red. Then, unaccountably, she sees his lips lift in a tiny smile. He pauses and takes a breath. Elizabeth fidgets with her apron while she waits for him to respond.

"I was robbed at gunpoint this afternoon by Jesse James who left an IOU note for all the boots in my shop."

Elizabeth sucks in her breath. "THE Jesse James? The leader of the James Brothers Gang?"

"The same. He walked into my shop and asked for all the boots on my shelves. When I hesitated, he pulled a pistol from his holster. Holding the gun in one hand, and a gunny sack in the other, he repeated his demand. After I filled the sack, he holstered his gun and asked me what the boots were worth." Charles takes a sip of water. "After I told him the amount, he grabbed a slip of paper from the counter, wrote it down, then signed it, *IOU Jesse James.* After that, he threw the sack of boots over his shoulder, walked out, got on his horse, and rode away."

Speechless, Elizabeth stares at Charles for a moment. "Thank goodness you weren't hurt, but you must have been frightened."

Charles' forehead wrinkles as he considers the question. "To be honest, I was more angry than frightened. The James Brothers aren't known for physical violence. I never felt my life was in danger as long as I did as he asked. But I'm mad as hell that he stole all my boots—about eight pair in all. Those boots represented several months of hard work, say nothing of the cost of materials. Losing them means no sales to townspeople and settlers for the time being." He puts his head into his hands. "Just as I was recovering from the winter."

Elizabeth feels the familiar anxiety return to her stomach. "Will we be okay?"

Charles glances at her, then looks away. "I recently delivered a boot order to the fort so we have a bit of cash and credit but, it's a good thing your garden is doing well and game is plentiful. Without boots to sell, we may find our summer to be as difficult as our winter."

The couple are quiet during supper; each contemplating the sacrifices they'll need to make in the next few months.

One week later, Charles returns from work with *The Valley County Herald.* He holds it up for Elizabeth to see, then sits down at the table. "Listen to this, Elizabeth." He opens the paper and reads. "The Union Pacific Railroad was robbed on July twelfth when it stopped for mail just south of Wood River, Nebraska." He sets the paper down and looks at Elizabeth. "That's two days after I was robbed!"

Elizabeth draws up a chair next to his and watches closely as he runs his finger down the newspaper column. "The reporter goes on to quote the local sheriff who speculates that the train was robbed by The James Gang."

The next evening, Charles rushes through the door after work. Elizabeth turns from the pot she's stirring and watches as he drops a wrapped package on the bed then walks to the fireplace. "Guess what happened today?"

Elizabeth angles the pot away from the fire. "I can't imagine. I hope it isn't more bad news."

He sits down at the table. "About one o'clock today, Jesse James walked boldly into my shop. With a tip of his hat, he slapped the money he owed me for the stolen boots on the counter, turned on his heel, mounted his horse, and swiftly rode out of town."

Speechless, Elizabeth puts her spoon aside and sits in the chair opposite Charles.

"Even though he paid me in full for the boots, he left me with the IOU." Charles holds up the slip of paper then gets up and walks to the bed. "I have another surprise." He picks up the package and hands it to Elizabeth.

She tosses the paper aside. "New riding boots! They're beautiful. Thank you, darling!"

"I know the winter was hard for you and, for a while, you thought we'd also have a difficult summer. Being ladies boots, they're currently the only pair left in my shop and I want you to have them. I want you to know I appreciate how brave you've been and how hard you've worked these last six months."

Three days later, the couple sit talking over breakfast when they hear a knock. Charles gets up and opens the door. "What brings you out so early, Peter?"

Elizabeth gets up from the table and goes to the coffee pot. "Would you like some coffee?"

Peter removes his cap. "No thank you, Mrs. Horn. I'm here to ask for Charlie's help."

Charles beckons him to sit down. "What do you need, Peter?"

He sits on the edge of the chair. "Mr. and Mrs. Alderman's children, George and Emma, are missing. They're only five and seven years old. Apparently, they wandered off three days ago with the family dog."

Elizabeth puts her hand on her chest. "Oh dear!"

Peter looks at her then continues. "The Aldermans and their neighbor spent the first day looking for them. The second day, they came to the fort for help. Sergeant Myers and Corporal Schreck joined in the search. Last night, I heard someone in the bar talking about a larger search party forming this morning. That's why I'm here."

Elizabeth's heart beats faster. *Another tragic story involving children!* Out loud, she says, "So many terrible things can happen to children alone on the prairie. The poor parents must be desperate."

Peter nods. "Indeed, I believe they are. I'm going to join in on the search and wondered if you'd like to come with me."

Charles gets up from the table. "Of course! Let's go back to town and fetch my horses from the stable. We can cover more ground on horseback." He strides toward the door; Peter follows.

Elizabeth rushes forward. "I'll search along the creek and beyond..." She turns to Charles. "...where I found the mushrooms. I'll meet you at the fort this afternoon."

Charles gives his wife a brief hug. "Let's pray we find those children in time."

Turning toward the fireplace, Elizabeth calls back. "Good luck." She puts up her hair, pulls on her old boots, and uses the outhouse. When she returns, she beckons Laddie to come with her, thinking he might be helpful in the search. She walks briskly to the creek, looks in all directions then calls out. "Emma. George. Are you there?" She continues to walk and call, stopping frequently to look behind logs and bushes. On and on she walks and calls until she gets as far as Angie's dugout. She knocks on the door. When there's no response, she goes to the apiary where she sees her tending the bees.

"I heard you calling, Child. What's happening?"

"The Alderman children are lost. They've been gone for three days. Have you seen them?"

Angie retrieves her nearby walking stick and leans on it. "I know who you speak of but I haven't seen them. I hope it's not too late."

Discouraged and on the verge of tears, Elizabeth replies, "Me too. I must go now. Take care of yourself, Angie."

Retracing her steps, Elizabeth continues to call for the children. When she looks into the sky, she sees buzzards over head. *Oh no! What if they're circling two dead children?* She does a careful search of the area below the birds but only finds the remains of a possum carcass. Her voice grows hoarse as she gives a final, desperate, shout. "Emma. George. Where are you?"

After more than four hours of searching, she returns home and looks down at her dog. "Laddie, why can't we find those children?" He looks up at her with sad, brown, puppy dog eyes and licks her hand. Dejected and thirsty, she enters the house, has a stick of jerky, a slice of bread with jam, and a ladle of water. Renewed, she walks toward the fort, leaving Laddie behind.

Just as she reaches the edge of fort property, she sees Charles and Peter on horseback trotting near the parade grounds. Shielding her eyes from the sun, she notices people gathering at the far end and prays it means good news. She picks up her pace, walking in their direction.

Charles and Peter are dismounting just as Elizabeth reaches the grounds. She waves to them and cups her hands in front of her mouth. "Wait for me!" After she joins them, the three walk over to Lieutenant Capron to see if there's news about the children.

Charles addresses him. "What's happened, Lieutenant?"

"Dern near a miracle—that's what happened. Sergeant Myers and Corporal Schreck found the children in the shelter of a washout not more than two miles from here." Capron points. "See that big Newfoundland dog over there?"

Elizabeth follows his finger. She sees an enormous black and white dog with a shaggy, mud-caked coat full of burrs. His tongue lolls to the side of his mouth as he accepts a hug from a man who looks to be his master.

Capron continues. "That dog stayed with the children and protected them for three days. Three whole days! The children are getting checked out by Dr. Towar in the infirmary but their father said they're hungry and dirty but seemed to be otherwise unharmed."

Elizabeth bows her head. "Thank you, God!" She takes Charles' hand as she watches the family tearfully gathering before leaving the parade grounds. She turns to Charles. "Thank goodness they were found!" Physically and emotionally exhausted from the day, the couple return home, eat a meager, cold supper, then retire early.

The next day starts as usual with Elizabeth having morning sickness. After vomiting in the outhouse, she returns to the hearth to prepare Charles' breakfast. When he leaves for work, she takes a rest in her rocker. *I'm so tired! Vi says it's normal but I hope I get my energy back soon.*

Two days later, just after Charles leaves for work, Elizabeth notices drops of blood on her bloomers when she uses the privy. Tears immediately well up in her eyes. She returns to the house, puts rags in her underwear, then rests quietly in her rocker, hoping the bleeding will stop. "Dear God, please don't let anything bad happen. You know how much we want this baby, Lord."

The morning crawls by. In the early afternoon, Elizabeth experiences extreme cramping. She uses the chamber pot and notices clots along with heavy bleeding. *What if the bleeding doesn't stop? What if I bleed to death alone in this house?*

By late afternoon, the bleeding lessens but Elizabeth instinctively knows her pregnancy is over. Sobbing, with her face in her hands, she offers up another prayer. "Lord, please give me the strength to accept this loss. Amen." Cried out and exhausted, she crawls into bed. She jerks awake when she hears Charles open the door.

She sits up and Charles rushes to the edge of the bed. "What's wrong, Elizabeth?"

"Oh, Charles, I had a miscarriage! Our baby is gone." Charles sits on the bed and holds his wife close while she sobs into his chest. "I'm so sorry."

"Sorry? You have nothing to be sorry for, Darling. These things happen. It's no one's fault."

"I know that's true but I still feel like I've failed you. I've worked so hard to be the kind of wife you need and now I let you down on the most important part."

Charles strokes her long, thick hair that she earlier freed from the confines of braids. "You haven't let me down at all. You're a wonderful wife. You've turned a square room made of dirt and grass into a home; you cook amazing meals over an open fire; you've cultivated friendships and served your community." Charles points to his chest. "Best of all, you keep loving this old bird. We're a family as long as we have each other. I hope we have children someday but, if we don't, I'm content with our family of two."

When Elizabeth begins to protest, he puts his finger to her lips. "I'm not a farmer who needs children to help with the work in order to succeed. We'll get through this together."

Elizabeth snuffles and her husband hands her a clean handkerchief from his vest pocket. After she blows her nose and dries her face, a faint smile spreads across her lips. "You're right. We are a family. I'll be alright but it will take time. Losing a baby was my worst fear and now it's happened. I need to be sad for a while."

Charles continues to look at his wife with tears filling his eyes. He wipes them away, gets off the bed, and reaches for her hand, helping her out of bed and into her rocker. He brings her a cup of water, then stokes the fire, heats up left-over beans, and brings them to the table along with bread and jam. Elizabeth joins him. "Thank you for fixing supper."

"Do you need anything else?"

Elizabeth spoons beans into her mouth, finding she's surprisingly hungry. "Just a good night's rest."

The next morning she doesn't get up when Charles takes Laddie out. When he returns with the water, he encourages her to stay in bed and rest. "Would you mind if I ask Vi to drop in to see you later?" he asks as he grabs a stale corn muffin and prepares to leave for work.

"That's fine." Elizabeth feels nothing; not happy, not sad, not mad. Just nothing. After her husband leaves, she dozes off and on.

Late morning, there's a knock on the door and she slowly leaves the bed, puts on her shawl, and opens it to Vi who throws her arms around her friend. "I'm so sorry. Charles told me the sad news."

"Oh, Vi. I'm so brokenhearted. We wanted this baby so badly," she sobs into Vi's shoulder. When she finally pulls away, Elizabeth sees the caring in Vi's eyes.

"How are you feeling today?"

Elizabeth offers Vi a seat and a cup of tea before she answers. "Physically, I feel tired but fine. The bleeding has mostly stopped and there's no more cramping. There's no sign of infection." When Vi remains silent, she continues with tears running down her cheeks. "But I'm so sad. I feel like I let Charles down."

Vi gets up from her seat, kneels beside Elizabeth's chair, and looks into her eyes. "Charles loves you very much. You know in your heart that he will love you whether you have a child or not, right?"

Elizabeth reluctantly nods.

"I believe you'll have a child someday. This one just wasn't meant to be." When Elizabeth nods again, Vi continues. "A miscarriage this early in a first pregnancy isn't unusual. Out here, about one in four pregnancies end in the first trimester." Vi returns to her chair and sips her tea. "You didn't do anything to cause this, Elizabeth. It may have happened because the fetus didn't form as it should, in which case a miscarriage is a blessing in disguise. You're also very young."

Elizabeth mumbles. "A few weeks ago, Angie, the Bee Lady, said I would have children someday. I thought it was strange how she put it—not 'a baby in January' but 'children someday'. Maybe her intuition is as strong as it seems."

"You spoke with the Bee Lady? I've seen her once or twice at The Mercantile."

"I'll tell you about her sometime, Vi. Right now, I think I need a nap. Thanks so much for stopping by. I'm feeling better after our talk."

CHAPTER THIRTY-ONE

FRIENDS TO THE RESCUE

It's a Thursday morning in early September. The sky is still dark when Elizabeth is awakened by Charles suddenly sitting up in bed. "What is it, Charles?"

"Laddie's growling. I think we have an intruder. Stay here."

Suddenly, a loud banging on the door causes Laddie to bark at full volume. Charles looks out the window. He calls to Elizabeth. "It's Shar."

She gets out of bed and wraps her shawl around her shoulders. Charles pulls on his pants then opens the door. Shar flies in, her red hair swirling wildly about her flushed face. Tears are in her eyes. She kicks off her muddy boots just inside the door then bends over to catch her breath before she tries to speak. "My pa's … been injured. Ma's with him. She needs help to get the doctor … he can't walk. Please come as fast as you can."

Charles doesn't hesitate. "I'll get my boots."

Elizabeth ladles out a cup of water and hands it to the girl. "What happened?"

Shar snuffles and chokes back a sob. Elizabeth gets her a hanky. "Ma said he stepped in a gopher hole on his way to the barn in the dark this morning. She thinks he broke his ankle. She told me to come get help." Shar finishes drinking her water then she and Charles run out the door.

"I'll be right behind you," Elizabeth shouts after them. She runs to the privy, with Laddie trailing behind, returns, dresses, piles her hair under a bonnet, grabs Charles' whiskey bottle, clean rags, a basket of leftover biscuits, and heads out the door, leaving Laddie behind.

When she arrives at the house, Shar answers the door with the twins huddled behind her. "Ma is out back with Pa. Mr. Horn hitched up the wagon and is on his way to the fort to fetch the doctor."

Elizabeth hands Shar the basket. "Here are biscuits for you kids. I'll go out back and see what I can do to help your folks." She hurries to the barn just as the sunrise spreads a red glow across a lavender-flowered field of ready-to-harvest alfalfa. Suddenly, the barnyard comes to life with the rooster cock-a-doodling, the cows mooing, the dog barking, and the chickens clucking. She finds Vi kneeling beside Richard who's propped against a tree stump. Vi's still in her shift, with an old shirt of Richard's over the top and her hair in a plait. Her eyes are dark with worry.

"Thanks for coming, Elizabeth." Richard nods then Vi continues. "I don't think there's much we can do until Doctor Towar gets here. We're pretty sure his ankle's broken. Charles and I propped him up against this stump."

Richard looks in Elizabeth's direction, his eyes dark and his complexion grey. Elizabeth walks to his side. "How about a little whiskey to ease the pain, Richard?"

"I'd be much obliged." He reaches for the bottle.

"Easy there, Cowboy, don't want you passing out on me," Vi says.

The cows continue bawling in the barn and Elizabeth offers to prepare breakfast for the children while Shar does the milking. She retraces her steps to the house and walks in. Jan is sitting in the corner with her knees drawn up to her chin. She jumps up when she sees Elizabeth. "Is Pa going to be alright?" she asks tearfully.

"Yes, he'll be fine, but it's going to take a while for him to mend. You and your brother will have to take on extra chores for a while. Can you do that?"

Gary solemnly nods.

"Yes, ma'am," Jan says, her voice serious. "We can be good helpers. Just tell us what we need to do."

Elizabeth pulls out Vi's black spider pan and places it near the fire. "Right now, you need to eat a good breakfast. Will you do that?" Two heads nod in unison. While she's making corn cakes, Shar goes to milk the cows.

The hour it takes for Charles to return with the doctor feels like days to Elizabeth. The children have dutifully eaten their breakfasts by the time the Voogd's buckboard pulls into the farmyard. Elizabeth finds a blanket, leaves Shar with the children, and returns to Vi and Richard.

After checking him over, Doctor Towar puts a temporary splint on Richard's ankle so he can be moved. He points toward the blanket still in Elizabeth's hands. "Glad you brought a blanket, Mrs. Horn. We'll use it as a stretcher to get our patient into the house."

Elizabeth lays the blanket on the ground next to Richard who carefully moves onto it with Charles' help. The doctor continues. "Charles, you and your wife take these corners; Mrs. Voogd and I will take the two at his feet." After they carefully bring Richard to the house and lie him on the bed, Elizabeth watches the doctor survey the room. "Take the youngsters outside," he says to Shar. "I'm going to set your pa's ankle right here on the bed. Stay out of the house until I send word."

"Yes, Doctor." Shar motions for the twins to follow her. When they pass by, Elizabeth sees the fear on their faces.

The doctor address the adults. "I don't want to take the chance of transporting our patient to the fort's infirmary as the bone might break through the skin." Towar then joins Vi at the head of the bed. "Mrs. Horn, please hand me the bottle of chloroform from my bag. I also need a clean rag."

Elizabeth goes to the table where she left her rags then retrieves the chloroform from the doctor's bag and hands both to him. The doctor sprinkles chloroform on the rag and speaks to Richard. "Breathe deeply. You'll be out before you know it." Once he's unconscious, the doctor issues further instructions. "Charles, you and Mrs. Horn stand on either side of Richard and be ready to hold his shoulders steady while I pull the foot down and realign the bones."

Before he moves to the head of the bed, Charles pulls a chair over for Vi. She sits with her head in her hands.

Charles joins Elizabeth and the doctor continues his instructions. "The chloroform will cause Richard to become excited and restless, but he'll be unconscious and feeling no pain. He's a strong man. Don't be afraid to use force. I'll work quickly to be done before he wakes."

When the doctor pulls on Richard's leg, he thrashes from side to side as predicted. Elizabeth uses all her strength to help Charles hold his shoulders steady, keeping his upper body still. When Towar realigns the bones, Richard cries out. Vi moans. Elizabeth gasps.

After the bones are properly realigned and the splint is put back in place, Towar looks at Charles. "Bring Richard to the infirmary when he's up to it so I can put a proper cast on his leg."

Charles nods. "Of course."

Elizabeth looks at Vi who's white as a sheet. She sees her get up from her chair, let out a shaky breath, then say, in a squeaky voice, "Thank you, Doctor."

Towar turns to her. "It's a blessing the bones didn't break through, Mrs. Voogd. He should have little or no infection. Swelling and pain; yes, but I believe we saved his foot. If all goes well, he won't need an amputation." The doctor puts the chloroform back in his bag. "He'll be on crutches for quite some time, Mrs. Voogd. At least six weeks. Don't let him put any weight on that foot. Tell him it's doctor's orders."

"Yes, sir."

The doctor closes his bag and issues final instructions. "He needs to elevate that leg all day today and as much as possible for the next several days. I have a set of crutches in the buckboard. Charles, please retrieve them and let Shar know she can bring the children back in."

Just after Charles leaves the house, Richard's eyes flicker open; Vi strokes his forehead. "The doctor says you're going to be alright, Richard, but you're going to have to take it easy for a while."

Still dazed from the chloroform and pain, Richard doesn't respond.

The children enter the house as quiet as mice. Vi motions them to the bed and they gaze down at their pa. "I'll be okay," he mumbles. "Nothin' can keep this old sodbuster down. Don't you worry none 'bout your pa."

Charles returns with the crutches, puts them in the corner, stands next to Elizabeth, and whispers in her ear. "Richard may not be worried about himself, but I know he's worried about his livelihood. His alfalfa crop is ready to harvest."

Elizabeth has no response. The adrenalin that sustained her since before sunrise has dissipated and she feels drained. She knows, however, that just as Richard helped Charles when he didn't have the skill, time, or tools to build their sod house, they must find a way to help him harvest his crops and prepare for winter.

Charles takes the doctor back to the fort then returns the buckboard to the homestead. While he's gone, Elizabeth makes sure Vi eats breakfast and has what she needs for the day. Richard, with his leg propped up, falls into a fretful sleep. Shar has the children doing their schoolwork in the barn.

Elizabeth refills Vi's tea cup. "Don't worry, Vi, he'll be fine."

"But, what about the harvest and all the other work Richard does from before sunrise to dark? I can't do it all, not even with Shar's help."

"Charles and I will help you and so will your other neighbors. Trust me. We'll find a way to get the harvest in."

Vi hugs her friend, checks on her husband, then returns to the kitchen and her morning chores.

That evening Charles returns home later than usual.

"Supper's ready. I was beginning to worry."

He kisses his wife on the cheek. "I'm late because I stopped at the school and spoke with the Henderson children, along with Stanley and Esther. They live on the homesteads closest to the Voogds. I asked them to tell their parents about Richard's accident and to meet us here tomorrow evening to come up with a plan to harvest the alfalfa. I also spoke to Peter, Mr. Mitchell, and Towar. The doctor will ask around to see if any soldiers can help when they're off-duty."

The next evening, the Horn's house is full of willing helpers including: Joe Henderson, George Alderman senior, Peter, Stanley's pa, and Private Symmons. Charles address the group. "Thank you for coming. As you know, Richard's laid up and his alfalfa field is in need of harvesting. I know it's a busy time for most of you but with all of us working together, it should only take a few days. Are you all available to start work on Monday morning?"

Elizabeth, standing near the fireplace, sees heads nod all around. After chatting amongst themselves for a few minutes, the men disperse and the Horns bring their chairs outside to sit in the cool evening air. Elizabeth turns to Charles. "That went well."

"We have a good team and Henderson said he'll instruct us non-farmers on what to do."

"Vi and I will get a head start cooking food over the weekend. There are a dozen mouths to feed if you count the three children. I'm sure some of the wives will send food."

Charles whistles for Laddie to come closer. He doesn't want him to venture too far away in the dark. "I'll get out first thing in the morning and hunt for game."

Satisfied that they're ready for the mission of harvesting Richard's crops, the couple call Laddie and return inside as the mosquitos begin to swarm.

Charles, Elizabeth, and Vi join their neighbors in Richard's field just before sunrise on Monday. The Voogd's nearest neighbor, Joe Henderson, with his sunburned, stubble-covered baby face, dark uncut hair, and dirty dungarees explains the process of harvesting alfalfa to the inexperienced men. "We'll cut the alfalfa then put it in windrows, or long lines to dry out in the wind. After it's dry, we'll put as much as we can in the barn and cover the rest. Let's bring in this alfalfa first. We can harvest the turkey red wheat later."

The men organize into groups and begin the backbreaking work of cutting the alfalfa hay by hand with scythes. Richard can't afford a horse drawn hay machine, nor can his neighbors. Without enough equipment to go around, the men send Elizabeth and Vi to the house to prepare the noon meal. Walking back, they pass Richard hobbling out to the field on crutches while trying to keep his new plaster cast clean and dry. Elizabeth notices that his face is drawn and he's fidgeting uneasily with a stock of wheat in his mouth. Vi admonishes him for coming out but he's determined to stay.

The women work steadily all morning preparing the noon meal. Vi supervises the preparation. "It looks like Mrs. Mitchell sent two loaves of bread, someone dropped off a corn casserole, and Henderson brought venison." She turns to her daughter. "Shar, you get busy with the pudding and, if you'll chop those vegetables, Elizabeth, I'll sear venison for stew."

As she chops, Elizabeth smiles at the twins who are busy shelling peas.

Vi moves closer to Elizabeth and speaks in hushed tones. "Richard's having a hard time with this. Although he's grateful for the help, he feels disgraced. Lately, he's even doubted he did the right thing in bringing us out here."

Feeling a flutter in her chest, Elizabeth responds. "I hope he's not considering giving up."

"I don't think so, but he feels like we've had to experience hardship with little to show for it. Last night he rehashed the year the locusts destroyed our crops, his inability to afford school for Shar, and bemoaned the hard work I endure."

Elizabeth puts her arm around Vi's shoulders. "I can't imagine what you're going through. You work so hard even when Richard is well." She puts her cut up vegetables into the pot. "Don't you think Richard will feel more positive once he can get back to work?"

Vi stirs the venison. "I hope so. I'm definitely not ready to give up. I'm confident that our life will eventually get easier."

The weather continues to be hot and dry allowing the hay to be raked and stored. On Wednesday, Elizabeth overhears Henderson speaking to Richard as she brings out the final meal. "After we get work done in our own fields, Richard, we'll return to harvest your wheat."

Richard pushes back from the tree he's leaning against. "I can't thank you all enough for what you done for us. You tell the others for me, will you Henderson? I'm not much for makin' speeches."

The dawn to dusk flurry of activity on behalf of their neighbors brings healing to the Horns. "It's been good for me to see to the needs of others rather than sitting around feeling sorry for myself," Elizabeth confesses as she and Charles return home after the final day of harvest. "I know you still see me crying sometimes, but I am moving forward."

Charles kicks a clod of dirt. "All the physical activity did me good too. I'm thankful that Richard is healing." He shakes his head. "I can't tell you how many legs I saw amputated when I was in the war. Amputation was the first consideration when there was a bullet to the leg because it prevented gangrene from setting in. Richard is fortunate there wasn't a wound and has a doc who knows what he's doing. A less experienced man could have bungled the job."

Elizabeth takes his arm. "We have to keep counting our blessings no matter what happens. Right, Charles?"

"Absolutely."

CHAPTER THIRTY-TWO

UNEXPECTED DIAGNOSIS

While the mid-September morning is still cool, Elizabeth carries water from the creek, then irrigates and weeds her garden. Her beans, beets, winter squash, and watermelon are flourishing. After a quick noonday meal, she walks the mile to Vi's to help her with her garden or other chores that need doing. Vi's workload has multiplied considerably and Elizabeth wants to do what she can to help. The road is dry and dusty but clouds overhead bring the promise of a shower. Before reaching the farmstead, she sees Vi and the twins kneeling in the dirt beside the garden. In the distance, she sees Shar wielding a pitchfork into a stack of hay. When the not-so-friendly farm dog barks at her, Gary gets up and shoos him toward the barn. "Thanks Gary, I don't think Buster likes me much."

Vi wipes the sweat from her forehead with her sleeve. "Good to see you, Elizabeth." To the twins she says, "You can go see to the eggs."

When she begins to rise, Elizabeth steps forward. "Don't get up. I'm here to help."

"Thanks. I can use another pair of hands."

Elizabeth kneels and begins pulling weeds. The loamy scent of rich, black soil mixed with the aroma of hay, cow manure, and sweat fill her nostrils. *Ahh, the sweet smells of my world.* Without pausing her weeding, she asks, "How's everyone doing?"

"Richard seems to be healing nicely. He's impatient with the inactivity but he seems to be coping." Vi pauses as she uses all her strength to pull up a hunk of buffalo grass. "I think Shar was greatly impacted by his accident. She's become an adult overnight. She's taking her responsibilities very seriously and doing all the barn chores by herself. She doesn't have as much time to spend with the twins, but they too have risen to the occasion and are more independent with their studies. All in all, things are going better than I expected."

Elizabeth pulls weeds that are about to choke out the last of Vi's tomato plants. "I hope you're taking care of yourself too."

Vi shrugs. Elizabeth changes the subject sensing that Vi wants to move on from talking about her predicament. "I've been thinking a lot about my first year on the prairie. A year ago, I thought that sleeping with a man and drinking a glass of wine turned me into a real woman, but I was mistaken." Elizabeth knows her words sound a bit high-minded, but she continues to share her thoughts with her friend. "Although those experiences were part of the journey, my becoming a woman has been day by day as I've experienced the joys and sorrows of life on the prairie." She turns to look at her friend. "Your family continues to be one of our greatest blessings. I can't imagine my life here without you, Vi."

Both women are quiet as they concentrate on the task at hand. Vi breaks the silence. "I think it's all about cooperation and friendship. People out here take pride in what they claim is the rugged individualism of the frontier, but I think it's most difficult for those who choose to go it alone. Helping each other is what it's really all about."

After their serious discussion, the women talk of a new recipe they want to try and some rumors about the Caprons' return. When they finish weeding, Elizabeth hollers greetings to the kids, then returns home to start supper and fold her laundry.

A few hours later, Elizabeth thinks Charles looks tired when he walks through the door after work. After he's settled in the rocker, she pauses from ladling beans into bowls. "What do you think about having a party to celebrate my birthday, our anniversary, and our first year in the soddie?" She sets the bowls on the table. Charles says the blessing and chews a mouthful of beans before responding.

"If we have this party, what would you think about inviting Ron, Lucy, Nate, and baby Joy?"

"Oh, Charles, could we?"

"The difficulty is finding them a place to stay." Charles leans back in his chair. "Perhaps Lucy and her family could stay with the Mitchells and Ron can stay with us. I've heard that Harriett loves babies."

Elizabeth places a bowl of fresh, wild raspberries and a pitcher of cream on the table. "She does! That's a great solution. I'll ask her about it tomorrow. Does this mean we're having a party?"

Charles pours thick cream over the berries. "Of course."

After supper they take a walk with Laddie. "Are you feeling alright, Charles?"

"Yes, Darling, why do you ask?"

"You seem tired lately and you look a bit pale. Frankly, I'm surprised you so readily agreed to the party—but I'm glad you did. It will be such fun!"

The next morning, Elizabeth gets up at dawn, fixes breakfast, then works in her garden, harvesting tomatoes with plans to bottle them for winter. She also harvests and lays aside acorn and butternut squash thinking they will last many months.

After a quick meal of leftover beans, she washes up, brushes off her dress, and puts her corset on to walk to town and pay a visit to Harriet. She's delighted when her friend readily agrees to house Lucy and her family. Later that week, Elizabeth drops by the Voogds' to issue them an invitation, leaving only one person left to invite.

Although it seems unlikely that she'll attend, Elizabeth wants to include Angie. Their time together was brief, but Elizabeth feels like they made an uncanny connection, and she wants her to be part of the celebration.

However, her visit is delayed when, a few days before the party, Charles makes an announcement after breakfast. "I'm going to drop by and see Doc Towar today."

Elizabeth sets down the dish she's washing and turns. "Why? What's wrong? Are you feeling ill?"

"I'm not feeling ill exactly, just not myself. I've been very tired lately and, no matter how much sleep I get, I can't shake this listlessness. Maybe he has some tonic that will perk me up."

Elizabeth shrugs off the notion she might be overstepping and asks, "Do you mind if I come with you? Sometimes it helps when more than one person hears what the doctor's saying. Are you going first thing?"

Charles takes his canvas bag from the corner. "I thought I'd go midday. You're welcome to join me."

After Charles leaves for work, Elizabeth hurries through her morning chores with an anxious heart wondering what might be wrong with her husband. She leaves the house early so she can meet Charles at the edge of the parade grounds. She waves when she sees him approach.

Charles smiles when he sees her and takes his wife's hand as they walk to the infirmary. "Remember, you're there to hear what doc says. Right?"

"Right."

The infirmary door is open and Doctor Towar smiles when he sees the couple enter. "Good afternoon. What brings you two to see me?"

Charles motions for Elizabeth to proceed him through the door then shakes the doctor's hand. "It's me that needs to talk to you, Doc. Elizabeth's here because she says four ears are better than two when it comes to listening to doctors."

"Have a seat on the table, Charles. You may sit in that chair, Mrs. Horn." The doctor points. "Now tell me what's going on."

After Charles describes his symptoms, the doctor looks down his throat, feels each side of his neck, and thumps his knees. He gets out his stethoscope and listens to his heart. He listens from the backside, then returns to the front and pauses. "Do you recall having scarlet fever as a child?"

"Yes, I did."

Towar places the stethoscope over Charles' heart again. "How old were you?"

"It was a few years before I left for America. I was probably fifteen or a bit younger. I was quite ill. So ill, in fact, that my mother used it as an excuse to try to keep me home. She wasn't happy about me moving abroad."

The doctor takes his stethoscope out of his ears and lets it hang around his neck. "I'm hearing a murmur in your heart. I'm also detecting a rapid and small pulse. I believe the scarlet fever left you with permanent valvular lesions."

Elizabeth can't help but ask, "Will you explain that, Sir?"

The doctor looks from Elizabeth to Charles. "The body's reaction to the scarlet fever may have left scars on Charles' heart leading to the symptoms he's experiencing; the listlessness, pallor, shadowed eyes. All are common."

Elizabeth sees a resigned look cross Charles' brow. "What's the cure?"

"I'm sorry to say that there isn't a cure—at least not now. The main thing is to spare your heart unnecessary labor. You're very fortunate that you're not a farmer or a builder of some sort. If you were, you might not enjoy a long life. Your trade will, hopefully, enable you to live many productive years. You need to take it easy and get plenty of rest. Go about your normal chores but don't do things that will put unnecessary stress on your heart…" The doctor pauses then resumes. "… like harvesting alfalfa. This recent exertion didn't cause additional injury, but it may have exasperated your symptoms."

Charles gets down from the table. "Anything else I need to know?"

"I know this is a lot to take in, but I have confidence that you'll adjust your life accordingly. You seem quite healthy in every other way. I'd like to check on you at least every six months to see if there's a change."

Charles shakes the doctor's hand. "Thanks, Doc."

Elizabeth's heart pounds as she lets out a breath. Respecting Charles' wishes, she thanks the doctor and leaves without asking further questions.

"I'm going back to work," Charles says as they cross the parade grounds. "We can talk about this when I get home." Elizabeth gives him an uncustomary kiss in public then walks home.

When they discuss the visit over supper, Elizabeth thinks her husband is taking the diagnosis in stride and she makes an effort to do the same. She doesn't want to worry Charles unnecessarily by overreacting. She also decides to keep the news to herself, thinking that it's Charles' story to tell.

The next morning, after Charles leaves for work, Elizabeth decides to visit Angie. She thinks that locating the Bee Lady will be a tonic for her own troubled heart. Remembering that she never paid for her last jar of honey, she puts a small bag of cornmeal and a jar of coffee grounds in a basket and sets out to locate Angie's dugout. As she crosses the creek and walks along the nearly hidden trail, Elizabeth barely notices the red sumac and chartreuse hedge apples. *What if something happens to Charles? How will I manage? He's such a good man, he shouldn't have to live with this burden.*

"Are you looking for something, Child?"

Elizabeth jumps when she hears Angie's low, gravelly voice just behind her. "Angie! I didn't see you. How long have you been there?"

Angle looks up at her. "Awhile. Your mind was occupied."

"I was looking for you. And you're right, my mind is quite occupied today."

Angie motions to Elizabeth. "Come. We'll go to my place and have a bite of bread and honey."

Elizabeth again follows the gnomelike figure through the undergrowth. When they reach the dugout, Angie points to a stump, inviting her to sit while she goes inside. As she waits, Elizabeth notices distant bird calls. She breathes in the slightly moldy smell of fallen leaves, unclenches her jaw, and relaxes her shoulders. In a few minutes, Angie returns with two slices of black bread smothered in thick, golden honey. Elizabeth feels soothed just being in Angie's presence. Instead of the usual questions flooding her mind, she has nothing to say and soaks in the tranquility of the moment.

Bees are alighting here and there, but they're of no concern to Elizabeth or Angie as they sit in companionable silence. The only sound, besides the bees, is the rustling of leaves and the licking of honey-covered fingers. Elizabeth looks over and sees sympathy in her friend's old, rummy eyes.

"I'm sorry you lost your baby. Life can be hard at times."

Looking at her hands, Elizabeth pops the final bite of bread into her mouth, takes her time to chew, then swallows. "Thank you. I won't even ask how you know. You just know, right?"

Angie blinks.

Elizabeth brushes the crumbs from her stained housedress. "Yes, life can be very hard. It seems like if it isn't one thing, it's another."

"And now it's Charles."

Elizabeth draws a circle in the dirt with the toe of her new boot. "Yes, how did you know?"

Angie quietly laces her gnarled fingers. "I see concern in your eyes and it's not only for yourself."

"The doctor told us yesterday that he has a heart condition." Elizabeth looks down. "I wasn't planning on saying anything and that's not why I'm here, but it does have me preoccupied and I appreciate your concern."

Angie speaks in a stern voice. "See that he takes care of himself."

Elizabeth feels the strength of Angie's declaration. "Yes, ma'am." For once, Elizabeth takes her time to speak. Finally, she issues her invitation to the party.

"Thank you for the invitation. I may be there, or I may not. Every day tells me what it wants from me. I cannot predict. I'm glad you're celebrating even though you have had two challenging life events recently. You have proven to be strong in body, mind, and spirit. You have become a true woman of the prairie. I am proud of you, Elizabeth."

Thinking this is the most sincere and meaningful compliment she's ever received, tears gather in the corners of Elizabeth's eyes as she looks at Angie who simply nods. Wiping away the tears with her thumbs, Elizabeth takes the items from her basket and hands them to Angie. "I almost forgot. I brought these in exchange for the jar of honey you gave me in the spring."

Angie gets up and puts the items inside her primitive door. She turns back to Elizabeth and stands before her. "Heed the meaning of the bracelet you wear, Child, and it will bring you peace of mind."

When Angie ambles past her toward the hives, Elizabeth knows the visit is over. She picks up her basket and returns home feeling renewed. As she walks, she fingers the beads of her bracelet. Light, dark, gray. This surely is the lesson of life.

CHAPTER THIRTY-THREE

A CELEBRATION OF LIFE

On a late September afternoon, the day before the party, Elizabeth is busy with preparations when she hears a wagon in the road. She dries her hands and rushes down the path. Ron pulls the wagon to a stop and secures the horses. "It's so good to see you all. Come in, come in." Joy is squirming in Lucy's arms as Nate helps her down from the wagon.

Ron remains on the wagon seat and Nate returns to the back of the wagon. Charles leaves the house and joins Ron, explaining himself to Elizabeth. "I'm going to go to town with Ron and Nate and get Ron's wagon and horses settled at the livery stable. After supper we'll all walk back to town and introduce Nate and his family to the Mitchells."

Elizabeth waves the men off then she and Lucy walk to the house. "I'm glad we have some time alone." Lucy settles into a chair, Elizabeth stands nearby gazing down at Joy. "She's grown so much. May I hold her?"

Lucy places the squirmy little girl in Elizabeth's arms. "She's a handful. She's gettin' to the stage where she wants to move around and explore everythin'. Just startin' to crawl."

Elizabeth can't help but feel a pang of jealously as she sits down and bounces the baby on her knee. Joy's hair has started to come in and brown ringlets frame her chubby, pink, baby face. When Elizabeth pulls out a cloth doll she's hidden in her pocket, Joy grabs it, stuffs the doll's feet in her mouth, then grins up at her. After a few minutes, Elizabeth looks over at Lucy. "You look wonderful. Being a wife and mother certainly agrees with you."

Laddie comes to investigate this new being in his domain. Joy responds to a lick on the hand with a gurgle.

"I's really happy and countin' my blessings every day. How've you been?"

Elizabeth takes a breath and hands the squirming baby back to Lucy. "To be honest, we've had a rough few months."

Lucy begins nursing the baby to keep her still. Elizabeth can see concern on her face. "Not long after we left Ron's ranch, I discovered I was pregnant. We were so happy, Lucy." Elizabeth pulls a hanky from her dress pocket and wipes her nose. "But, at not quite three months, I lost the baby."

Lucy reaches across and takes Elizabeth's hand. "Oh, Lisabeth! I'm so sorry."

"I was really sad, Lucy. It was the thing I dreaded most. But now I'm doing better. I still have bad days, but Charles and I are both on the mend."

"I know you're a strong woman. Remember me tellin' you that?"

"I do." Elizabeth stands. "Now, let's talk about where you'll be staying." Elizabeth starts supper while telling Lucy about the Mitchell's and their love of children.

When the men return, everyone has supper. Charles and Elizabeth sit on the bed to eat, the others sit around the table. After supper, the group walks to the Mitchells to make introductions and get the family settled. Elizabeth, Charles, and Ron return home and Laddie welcomes them.

"I'm going to bed early, Charles," Elizabeth says. "Big day tomorrow. You and Ron chat. You won't keep me up. Good night."

Elizabeth hopes that her early bedtime will give Charles the opportunity to talk with Ron about his heart condition. She's worried that he might be in denial about the severity of the diagnosis and what it can mean for their future. As she drifts off, Elizabeth is relieved to hear snippets of conversation where Charles is explaining his condition to his friend and Ron responding in a supportive manner.

At breakfast, before the others arrive, Ron clears his throat and looks from Elizabeth to Charles. "I saved this bit of news until now so I can tell you both at the same time."

Charles and Elizabeth look at one another.

"I'm getting married." Ron pauses. "She's new to Burwell, started teaching school last fall, and I met her at a school board meeting just after you came for a visit. I started courting her right away and we set a date for Christmastime."

"Congratulations, Ron," Charles says. "That's great news, isn't it, Elizabeth?"

"Yes, of course. Why didn't you bring her with you? What's her name? Where's she from?"

Ron looks from one friend to the other and grins. "It's the beginning of the school year so she couldn't get away. Otherwise, she would have come. She's anxious to meet you and I'd love to have us get together before the wedding. Maybe you can make a trip to the ranch before snow falls."

Elizabeth cocks her head. "And....?"

Ron takes a sip of coffee. "Her name is Clarise and she's from New York. Came out here by way of wagon train like you and Lucy. She's twenty-one years old, very independent, and speaks her mind." Ron looks directly at Elizabeth. "You'll like her."

Elizabeth removes the breakfast dishes. "You know, I wanted to be a teacher at one time. I can understand Clarise's love of teaching children."

Laddie starts to bark, and Charles opens the door. "Richard's here with the table. I'll give him a hand."

Ron rushes to the door. "Let me, Charlie. You help Elizabeth."

When the serving tables are in place, Elizabeth and Vi cover them with cakes, platters of bread, and meat. The guests are bringing their own plates and utensils. Harriett arrives with a large, clay pitcher filled with gold and amber fall mums from her garden to use as decoration. Charles brings out chairs for the Mitchells. Joe and Nate are having a friendly chat as are Tina and Lucy. Harriett plays patty-cake with Joy while Mr. Mitchell plays peek-a-boo over her shoulder.

The guests assemble around the tables. Elizabeth senses birds overhead. She looks up. Buzzards. Refusing to let their presence spoil her day, she takes a deep breath to calm her racing heart. She's quickly distracted when Ron quiets the guests, bows his head, then speaks. "Dear God, we ask that you continue to bless Charlie and Elizabeth. We thank you for sending them our way and for what they mean to us and this community. Thank you for this fine, fall day and bless this food and the hands that made it. Amen." He raises his glass. "To the Horns and all of us who love them!"

"To the Horns!" The loud response frightens Joy for a moment, and she puckers up to cry.

"Don't cry, baby." Private Joe comes to the rescue with his harmonica and begins playing "Mary Had a Little Lamb" which settles her down immediately.

The guests fill their plates and stand in companionable groups or sit on blankets. Elizabeth takes a moment to look around. *How would I have gotten through this year without these wonderful people? Along with Charles, they are the heart and soul of my life.*

Elizabeth leaves to use the privy. When she reaches the side of the house, she sees Angie quietly surveying the gathering. She rushes over and takes her elbow. "I'm so glad you could come, Angie. Please join us."

Without taking a step, Angie continues to watch the party. "I'm heading to town with my honey. Just stopped by to wish you a happy birthday." Angie hands Elizabeth a jar of amber honey, then looks up into her eyes. "Friends are the essence of life, Child. Except for Boy, I've never been good at making them. It's my biggest regret. But you … you're rich in friendships."

"Boy? Tell me about him."

"Another day, perhaps…." Angie suddenly clutches her chest and drops her basket. Glass jars break when they hit the ground and honey oozes out onto the dirt strip around the house.

Elizabeth grabs her arm. "What's wrong? Come, sit down." Before Elizabeth can guide her to a chair, Angie falls forward. Elizabeth catches her. "Help! My friend is ill." As Charles and the others run toward them, Elizabeth eases

Angie to the ground. She loosens the scarf around her neck and takes off the old, felt hat. Angie's lips move, and Elizabeth puts her ear close in order to hear her faint whisper.

"Take care of my bees, Elizabeth, and they will take care of you. Tell them that I've gone or they'll be angry." Then, her arm goes limp, her mouth slack, and her eyes glassy.

Charles leans over, puts his ear to Angie's chest, then a finger to the artery in her neck. "She's gone, Darling. Probably a heart attack. I'm so sorry. I know she was your friend."

With tears streaming down her face, Elizabeth looks into Charles' eyes. "More like my fairy godmother."

Mr. Mitchell scratches his head as the others stand nearby in stunned silence. The only sound is Joy making gurgling sounds. Mitchell asks, "Who was she? She looks familiar."

Elizabeth, still crouching next to Angie's body, swipes at the tears with her sleeve. "She was Angie, the Bee Lady. A few times a year she sold honey at The Mercantile." Elizabeth looks around at her friends. "She was a very special lady. A very special lady, indeed."

As she smooths the greasy strands of hair from Angie's forehead, a ray of sunshine bounces off the surface of glass beads, drawing Elizabeth's attention to her bracelet. *Black for the sadness of losing a friend and the end of life; white for the love of my precious husband and dear friends; and gray for the lowering sun, the fluffy white clouds, and the sweet smell of honey.*

AUTHOR INTERVIEW

The goal of the novelist is not only to hold up a mirror to the world, but to imagine what's possible. I hope you felt a connection to Elizabeth as you read her story. In my view, she was the sort of woman who was willing to take the risk of moving into the unknown to pave the way for her future and women of future generations. May we do the same in whatever way we can, wherever we find ourselves.

QUESTION: Why did you write this particular story, set in this time?
AUTHOR: I wrote this story to convey the importance of friends, the strength of women, the value of cooperation, and what life was like in the Sand Hills of Nebraska in 1875/76.

The two main characters, Charles and Elizabeth Horn, were my great grandparents and I wanted to share what I knew of their early life. I learned some facts about them from my dad who was the son of Charles' and Elizabeth's first born, Charles Junior, who was the first baby born in Wood River, Nebraska where the Horns moved after living two years in a sod house near Fort Hartsuff. The Horns eventually had five children.

My late dad told me about his grandmother handling a mule team, the robbery by Jesse James (we had the IOU for many years until it was destroyed in a flood), the story about the Horn name, and information about them living near

Fort Hartsuff. My dad lived much of his adult life in Grand Island, Nebraska, where I grew up.

I learned additional facts from Charles' and Elizabeth's granddaughter, Audrey Horn Linderkamp, who generously sent me photos and newspaper clippings about her grandparents with whom she lived much of her childhood after of death of her parents.

QUESTION: So this is a true story?
ANSWER: It's historical fiction. I incorporated stories from family lore, then I researched and included the historical, cultural, and political backdrop of the times. To round out the story, I added my own interpretation of what it was like traveling with a wagon train, the Horn's relationship, and life in a sod house on the prairie. Without minimizing the hardship of living during that era, I wanted to demonstrate the positive times in the lives of pioneers; especially those of Elizabeth, Lucy, Vi, and Tina.

The devastating stories and statistics about the buffalo are true. The good news is that the National Bison Legacy Act, signed on May 9, 2016, officially made the bison our national mammal. This historic event represents a true comeback story. The grasshopper accounts, the story about the children and their dog being lost, the visit from the Knight, and the Caprons home burning (although it wasn't in 1876), are also factual.

QUESTION: Since you grew up in Nebraska, did you draw on your personal experiences?
ANSWER: Yes. As a free-range kid (my mother died when I was eight and I'm an only child), I picnicked and practiced

target shooting with my dad near the North Loop and Platte rivers. My dad and I hunted morel mushrooms. The constant Nebraska wind was my playmate as I rode my bike down country roads or clung to my sled as it flew behind my dad's car on snowy days.

Summer 2021, I spent a week in the Sand Hills living at a guest farm and a dude ranch near where the Horn's sod house once stood. Fort Hartsuff is now a state historical park and has been restored to how it was during the time the Horns lived nearby. I spent a day at the fort, walked along Bean Creek, and stood where Calamus once flourished. I also explored Happy Jack's Chalk Mine and enjoyed lunch in Burwell, a town not far from Ron's fictional ranch. After leaving the Sand Hills, I visited Pioneer Village in Minden, Nebraska and toured a real sod house.

QUESTION: The stories of Jesse James' robbery, the lost children and their dog, Elizabeth being only fifteen, and the Horn name seem implausible and yet, you used them anyway. Why?
ANSWER: Rita Weiman, playwright and author, wrote, "Truth is too strange for fiction. The adventures of human experience are almost invariably too amazing, too shocking, too horrible, and too apparently exaggerated to be transcribed exactly as they meet us. In sharp black type on any printed page but that of a newspaper, they would appear absurd, the wildest stretch of imagination."

Although I totally agree with Ms Weiman, I wanted to be true to my ancestors' experience and the history of the times.

QUESTION: Did you ever meet your great-grandparents?

ANSWER: I vaguely remember Elizabeth. She was bedridden for the last ten years of her life following a severe stroke. She died when I was five. I didn't know Charles. He retired early from bootmaking due to poor health and died years before his wife of an unknown cause.

QUESTION: Do you still live in Nebraska?
ANSWER: No. I wrote this book with a view of palm trees and afternoon storm clouds as a Florida transplant. I will, however, always sigh with a sense of belonging when I see the horizon across the corn fields of Nebraska. No matter that I've lived away for well over fifty years, Nebraska's beautiful sparse and windy landscape will always signal home to me.

QUESTION: What's next for you?
AUTHOR: My next book is another historical fiction inspired by the fictional character, Angie, the Bee Lady. As I was writing *The Bootmaker's Wife*, I wondered about Angie's background and how she became an elderly gnome-like person living alone in a dugout raising bees. The manuscript of "The Bee Lady," begins in 1820 when Angie is ten years old.

DISCUSSION QUESTIONS

1. What do you think your greatest challenges would have been traveling west with a wagon train?

2. In what ways did the prairie life as described in the book differ from your expectations?

3. Abuse of children and women was common on the prairie. What were some of the environmental, psychological, cultural circumstances that contributed to this fact? How were these portrayed in the story?

4. Charles' ability to earn a living wasn't directly predicated on the weather or other natural phenomena. What risks did he encounter? How did his profession influence their life?

5. Children grew up much faster in the 1800's than they do today. Were you surprised by Elizabeth's skills and insights at such a young age? How would you have handled the challenges she faced at fifteen?

6. Childbirth and raising a child to adulthood were very dangerous and anxiety-ridden events for parents. In what ways can you identify with the many child loss experiences portrayed in this book?

7. Why do you think friends meant so much to Elizabeth—or was it the author's bias? Do you think this desire for friendship was true for most pioneer women? Is it still true today?

8. How did you relate to and understand the significance of Angie, the Bee Lady? Was her character too fantasy-like for you or did you appreciate the mystery and other-worldliness of her role in the book? Why do you think the author included her?

9. Were you able to picture what life was like in a dugout or a sod house? Could you have lived in that environment? How did Charles' improvements make a difference? What did these special touches say about Charles and his relationship with Elizabeth?

10. If you had to move across the country in a covered wagon and take only a few items, what would they be?

11. Elizabeth and Charles were troubled by the destruction of the buffalo, the forests, and the displacement of the Indians. What would your opinion have been or that of your ancestors?

12. Elizabeth and Charles enjoyed good food. How did descriptions of food resonate with you?

13. Why do you think having a baby was so important to Elizabeth?

ACKNOWLEDGEMENTS

Every book must start with an interesting story idea. Growing up about eighty miles south of where Charles and Elizabeth established their first home near Fort Hartsuff, cemented my love for Nebraska. But it was my beloved dad, Leon Horn, the son of Charles' and Elizabeth's first child, who told me the stories of his grandparents, which sparked my interest in the pioneer era and their particular story. Thanks, Dad.

Many holes existed between the tales my dad told and additional family facts. Thanks to Elizabeth and Charles' granddaughter, Audrey Horn Linderkamp, for sharing diary entries, photos, and clippings about her grandparents and their family.

In addition to family members, I want to thank James Domeier, superintendent of Fort Hartsuff State Historical Park, for providing me with historical records as well as an extensive tour of the grounds and buildings of the restored fort. Jim also suggested I read *The Trail of the Loup,* a documentary written by H.W. Foght and originally published in 1906. Many of the true stories (some told to Foght first-hand) and personalities I used came from this public domain book. Thank you, Mr. Foght and Mr. Domeier!

Just as every book needs a good story idea, every manuscript needs a great editor. Elena Hartwell is the best! Even with an excellent editor, a meticulous proofreader is always necessary. Thank you to my new friend, Rosalie Krusemark, for your professional expertise.

When a manuscript is in it's infancy, an honest and knowledgeable critique group is invaluable. Thanks to the Marco Island Writers' Critique Group for giving me honest feedback.

Before a manuscript is formatted, published and offered to the world, BETA or first-readers, read the manuscript and offer their opinions. Thank you Bob Alston, Lois Colaprete, Mary Hughes, and Martha Bordwell for being my BETA readers.

No one wants to read an unattractive book. That's why I enlisted Lance Buckley and his team to design the book cover and interior of both the e-book and print version. Thanks for your patience and expertise.

Without these sixteen people and their invaluable input, *The Bootmaker's Wife* would only be a pipe dream of an old lady.

Made in United States
Orlando, FL
26 December 2022

27734147R00192